My Husband's Murder

KATIE LOWE

HarperCollins*Publishers*

HarperCollins*Publishers*
1 London Bridge Street
London SE1 9GF

www.harpercollins.co.uk

HarperCollins*Publishers*
1st Floor, Watermarque Building, Ringsend Road
Dublin 4, Ireland

First published by HarperCollins*Publishers* 2021
as *The Murder of Graham Catton*
This paperback edition 2022
1

A catalogue record for this book is available from the British Library

ISBN: 978-0-00-828906-5

This novel is entirely a work of fiction.
The names, characters and incidents portrayed in it are
the work of the author's imagination. Any resemblance to
actual persons, living or dead, events or localities is
entirely coincidental.

Set in Sabon LT Std by Palimpsest Book Production Limited,
Falkirk, Stirlingshire

Printed and bound in the UK using 100% Renewable Electricity
by CPI Group (UK) Ltd

MIX
Paper from
responsible sources
FSC
www.fsc.org
FSC™ C007454

For my family,
for whom I'll never have the words.

'I will take this opportunity of cautioning you against all imprudent curiosity; let no incentive from it ever tempt you to seek an explanation of former occurrences; be assured your happiness depends entirely on your ignorance of them'

Regina Maria Roche, *Clermont*

BEFORE

1

London, 2008

It's the sound of my husband's blood on the floorboards that wakes me.

Like a dripping faucet.

Tap. Tap. Tap.

Soft little splashes on the bedroom floor.

I stand over our bed, and I look at him, looking at me, and I think of the day we moved in.

I don't know why it comes to me, then, but it does: the two of us aching and dripping with sweat.

We christened this bed. We made it ours. And when I peeled my body from his, he stared at me, dazed and gasping – stunned by the force of my love.

He's looking at me in the same way, now.

Later, I will be asked about this moment: if I saw the body, if I looked. I'll tell them I couldn't, of course. That I shielded my eyes, and ran to find help.

But I don't. I stand over him, watching. The only sound is the tapping, and my – only my – breath.

He's quite clearly dead: perfectly still, his lips cracked and grey. And in his throat, the knife – *my* knife, a wedding gift – is angled sharply, like a conquering flag.

I stand over him, and try to piece together a story that makes sense. An explanation.

I remember words exchanged in the kitchen. A woman's perfume on his skin. The bloody slick of wine around a glass, sediment clinging to the base. His footsteps, leaving me behind.

And after that: nothing.

Only an absence, a blur.

Now, I look at the face of the man I once loved, his pale body cooling in the pre-dawn light.

And I do not feel a thing.

2

'I don't remember,' I say, in a voice that's hoarse from screaming – another thing I can't recall.

'I heard a tapping noise. Like this.' I tap-tap-tap on the metal desk. The strip light flickers overhead. 'More of . . . More of a drip. And then I opened my eyes.'

The officers questioning me – a man and a woman, both fresh-faced and focused – nod.

They don't believe me. And I can't say I blame them. I'm not sure I'd believe me, if our roles were reversed.

'I was on the floor,' I go on. Evie, our daughter – my daughter – shivers in her sleep, her head resting on my lap, body stretched across the bed I've built with empty chairs. I run a finger through her curls, the way he used to do with mine. 'I must've hit my head. I was dizzy. But I got up, and . . .' I close my eyes, hoping they'll take the hint.

He was dead, I want to say. *You know that part.*

But I can't. Not in front of Evie. I need to protect her from that, for the moment at least.

When I'm asked to sign my statement, they've typed it in, on my behalf. *I found the victim to be clearly deceased, via a single stab wound to his carotid artery.* There's something soothing about the medical wording – the bare facts of it. Still, I correct it. 'I didn't know it was . . . the artery. Won't that be for the coroner to . . . You know?'

The male officer smiles. 'My fault. I thought you were a doctor, so . . .' I know what he's saying. *So you'd know where to stick the knife.*

'I'm a psychiatrist,' I say. Not that it makes a difference: I still went to medical school; still know the basics of anatomy. But I'm not sure he knows that.

He nods, eyebrow raised. 'Noted. Sign here.'

After eleven hours, they let me go. They don't say it, but I know: this is conditional. A one-way flight to Barbados, right now, would all but confirm my guilt.

I check us into a nearby hotel, where I see myself for the first time in the greenish bathroom light.

I'm surprised at my own expression – the blankness of it. As though I'm expecting to find myself mid-scream, rigid as a Halloween mask. But aside from the faint sheen of filth on my skin, the clot of dried blood at the back of my head, I'm still very much myself. This is not something I expect to work in my favour.

I imagine conversations taking place at the police station. *Not exactly a looker,* I think they'll say. *A bit mismatched, weren't they?*

Or: *She's not very friendly. Closed-off. Like she's hiding something.*

I can't dispute any of this. They'll think it, because it's true.

Still, I shower off the day, and crawl into bed with Evie. I smell home on her skin, and pull her close.

People say motherhood brings it out in you: a need to protect your child that verges on madness.

Only now do I realize it's true.

3

The Friday eleven days later is my daughter's sixth birthday. And for the first time since the murder, I don't turn on the news.

It's a day off for us both – from Graham's face, and the home we shared, flashing across the screen. From the lurid details of the scene, referred to euphemistically – though I realize (in a way I hadn't before) that there's no such thing as an acceptable euphemism when the victim – or suspect – is you.

Instead, we order ice cream on room service, and use a lighter to make her wish. She's so focused when she blows it out that I flinch at the knock that follows. I unlock the door, and open it slowly, almost expecting him.

But it's the officers who questioned me before: Stevens, tall and bulky, clean-shaven; and O'Hare, slight, with a TV smile.

It's over, I realize. *They know.*

'Come in,' I say. Too brightly. I hear myself, sounding unhinged.

Stevens is poker-faced. 'This won't take long.'

I glance at O'Hare, who smiles. It seems automatic; the good cop by default, because she's a *girl*.

I sense movement in the corridor beyond, and I wonder who's watching. Who'll be there when they lead me away.

But then, O'Hare begins to speak.

The words themselves escape me, but their meaning is perfectly clear.

'A burglary gone wrong,' she says. 'Suspect in custody. Yes, we're absolutely sure.'

Stevens doesn't take his eyes off me throughout. I can feel it in his stare: he doesn't believe it – doesn't believe me. He has doubts, but the evidence is clear. His instinct, in this case, is outweighed by the facts.

I understand his surprise.

But I keep this to myself. I say nothing.

I nod. I close the door, and lock it shut.

For a week, I turn housekeeping away. I stack room-service trays in teetering piles by our door. I settle Evie in front of cartoons for hours on end, much to her delight (never allowed, when Graham was alive). I don't shower. I can't eat. I watch myself from above, circling the room like a caged animal.

Like a woman going mad.

I see my husband, there, on the bed, newspaper slung over his lap. He taps his pen on the page and fixes me with a smile. *Five-letter word, starting with 'g', an 'i' in the middle,* he says. *Appropriate response to the death of a loved one.*

I blink, and he disappears.

So like him to make a joke at a time like this.

So like him to always have the last word.

9

EPISODE ONE

4

Derbyshire, 2018

'For God's sake, Hannah. You can't spend your whole life obsessing over the past. Eventually, you're going to have to move on.' Sarah leans back in her black leather throne and smiles. 'Sorry, but it's true. You and Dan have been together for – how many years now?'

I clear my throat. The dregs of a tasteless herbal tea cling to my tongue. 'Seven.'

'And Evie *adores* him, doesn't she?'

'Yeah. I think she prefers him to me, which is—'

'*And* he's sweet, in a *Bear in the Big Blue House* kind of way.' She downs the last of her tea, and grimaces. 'No, I'm sorry. I can't do it. This is like warmed-up pond water. I need coffee.'

I stand and click the kettle on again. 'At least we can say we tried.'

It's a luxury not to have to sit in the bleak staff room, on the edge of the unit, constantly interrupted by nurses with urgent questions, or patients requesting a 'quick' chat.

Unlike the rest of us, in the age of 'austerity', Sarah has her own office, filled with beaming photos of her husband and children (two boys, both gap-toothed and luminous), expensive-looking sculptures and paintings – and her own working kettle and cafetière.

Our weekly catch-ups are supposed to be essential meetings about what's happening 'on the ground' in the department she runs. More often than not, however, they turn out more like this.

'I used to think about fucking him when the kids were little, you know. Like, extremely detailed fantasies?'

I blink. The kettle hits the boil. 'Dan?'

'Oh, God, no. The bear.' A pause. 'Just me then?'

'. . . Yeah.'

Her laugh is an open-mouthed cackle – the same one I'd been stunned by when we'd first met. Sarah, at eighteen: smudged eyeliner and white-blonde, unbrushed hair, making cadavers mime to Madonna, while coming first in the class in everything. For all her gestures towards professionalism, a terrifying twenty-something years later, she's still the same. Still outrageous. And still the one to beat.

'I'm surprised,' she says. 'I thought you and I always shared a type.'

'Do I need to remind you about the string of moony Jon Bon Jovi types that passed through your sheets, way back when? *Not* my type, at all.'

'In my defence, that just proves consistency in *mine*. Jon Bon Jovi and that bear had the same hair for most of the nineties, didn't they?'

'My God.' I stir the muddy coffee and put the cafetière on the desk between us. 'Did someone just have a breakthrough?'

'I *knew* I was paying you for something.'

A barb, there – though I barely feel it. I'm used to it by now. She was always top of the class, and I was – always – right beneath her, in second place. That hasn't changed, no matter what else may have, since.

'Seriously, though.' She reaches for a sachet of sweetener, and shakes it out with a flick of her wrist. 'What *is* stopping you? Dan's clearly not going anywhere – and neither are you.' Another jab, delivered with the ruthless whip-speed of a rattlesnake. She moves on before I can respond – though not so quickly that it doesn't land. 'So why wouldn't you make it official?'

'Ugh. I don't know.' I twist Graham's ring around my finger, and squeeze the diamond in my palm. 'I just wish he hadn't bought that ring. He knows I don't want to get married again.'

'Are you sure it's for you?' She grins. 'I mean, just because you found it in your house doesn't mean it's yours.'

'That would almost be a relief.'

'And you say *I'm* a cold-hearted old cow.'

'*You* are.'

She looks at me with a kind of tenderness, and I bristle. I know what's coming next. 'Hannah, I know you think I'm a broken record with this, but . . . wouldn't a fresh start do you good? You drive, what? An hour and a half every day to get here – and Evie's about to move to sixth form, so it's as good a time as any. And I can't imagine there's much news for Dan to report on in the middle of nowhere. Why *not* change things up a bit?'

'Because I *like* it there.'

She runs her tongue along her teeth. She's waiting for me to go on. For Sarah – a resolute city-dweller – the idea of living in a remote, rural village seems like the worst of all punishments. I see the same look in the eyes of our inpatients when we ask them to hand over their phones: as though we've asked them to sever their connection with life itself.

What Sarah doesn't see, though, is that Hawkwood, for me, *is* a kind of connection. I put myself back together there. It's where I found security, made new memories; it's where I watched Evie grow up. The idea of losing that – again – is destabilizing. I can't do it. And I don't *want* to.

'Anyway, I don't see what moving has to do with it,' I say, after a pause. 'We don't have to *move* to get married.'

'I know. But if you moved, I wouldn't have to drive so far to do the whole Matron of Honour bit. We could use it as an excuse to get drunk *all the time*.'

'*You* could, you mean.'

'Exactly. My boring sober friend, finally useful for *something*.' She winks. 'The thing is, I'm really not saying you should settle for Dan, if that's what you feel like you're doing. You're smart, and you're pretty, and you're a catch, and if you want to get back on the market, I'm more than happy to live vicariously through you while you do so. I hear Tinder is a hoot.'

I brace myself for what's coming next. Compliments from Sarah are almost always followed by some suggestion or advice that would otherwise be too callous to say outright. The 'shit sandwich', one of the nurses called it, once – a description that's horribly apt.

She leans back in her chair, brow arched, eyes fixed on me over the rim of her cup. 'I don't think that's it, though – is it? You actually *do* want to be with him.'

'Yeah. I do.'

'There you go, look. All you have to do is say that to him. In those exact words. At the end of an aisle. While wearing a big white dress.'

I sigh. 'You're going to think I'm ridiculous.'

'Oh, sweetie. I already do.' Her smile is wicked, and knowing. She'd looked at me in the same way when she offered me the job – though not before calling me a 'daft cow' for doubting myself, and her. At that point, though, we hadn't spoken in years. My personnel file, sent over by my former employer – no doubt detailing my negative outcomes in forensic detail – sat on the desk between us. I suppose she must've looked at it. But she didn't bring it up that day, and she hasn't mentioned it since. 'Go on,' she says, now. 'Spit it out.'

'I guess I just thought there'd be . . . I don't know. More of a . . .'

'Oh, no. Don't say it. Please don't say it.'

'What?'

She grimaces. 'A *spark*.'

'. . . Yeah.'

She places her coffee on the file in front of her, and leans forward, her hands folded under her chin. 'Hannah,' she says, gently. 'I need you to listen to me carefully when I say this.'

'What?'

'And I need you to *not* be offended by it.'

'Oh, God.'

'. . . You're old now.'

17

'You're older.'

'By two months. And the difference between you and me is, I'm at peace with it. I buy three different creams for my face. I use them in a specific order, on the advice of some ten-year-old self-proclaimed beauty expert on YouTube. And—' She cuts off my interruption with a raised palm – '*I'm* not deluding myself by thinking that love at our age is going to feel the same as love at eighteen.'

I lean back in my chair. I know she's right – not that I plan to concede. 'We're not *that* old, you know. Fifty's still a fair way off.'

'I know. But what I'm trying to say is . . . he's a nice guy. He loves you. And maybe comparing falling in love with him to whatever you felt when you were falling for Graham at eighteen isn't all that healthy. Or fair. On any of you.'

'Wow, Sarah – why don't you tell me how you really feel?'

'I'm sorry,' she says, after a rare pause. 'You know I'm not trying to make you feel bad, don't you? I just want you to—'

'Yeah, I know. And you're right.' I glance at the clock. 'I'd better get going. You know Amy Barker's being readmitted this week, don't you?'

'I saw. I'm already dreading our inevitable call from her *lovely* mother. I still hear those awful nails of hers clicking in my sleep.'

'Well, when you do speak to her – ask her where she gets her Botox done, will you? Since I'm so *old*, and all. I could do with a referral.'

'You know,' she says, 'I'll still love you when you're *really* old. Colostomy bag and all.'

'I can see it. The two of us, being wheeled over to the nursing home TV, just in time for *Bear in the Big Blue House*.'

She winks, and lays a sheaf of papers across her desk. 'The boys are out camping all weekend if you want to start sooner.'

'You're disgusting,' I call as the door closes with a muffled click behind.

5

Dan leans over the arm of the sofa, book spread-eagled on the floor. 'There she is.' He makes a face as I kick off my shoes. 'Oh dear. Long day?'

It's like he sees straight through me, the moment I walk through the door. After a long drive home, replaying my conversation with Sarah in my mind, I'm exhausted, and he knows it.

But I can't tell him why. Not this time. He still doesn't know I found the ring.

I hang up my jacket and bag, and smile. 'The longest. Where's Evie?'

'Upstairs. Revising. Or sleeping. Possibly both.' He rolls up to standing. 'Have you heard about this thing they're doing now? Listening to revision tapes when they're sleeping?'

'I doubt it's tapes, somehow,' I say. 'And I'm pretty sure that method was doing the rounds in the eighties. Didn't work then, either.'

He wraps his arms around me. The smell of him is, as

always, a balm. 'All right, doc. Don't tell her that, though. She's convinced it's going to change her life. And anyway, it can't hurt, can it?'

It could, I think, *if it replaces 'real' revision.* But then, I know Evie. Her grades are impeccable. She's almost too conscientious, approaching her schoolwork with a focus that manages to skirt outright anxiety – most of the time.

'No,' I say. 'You're probably right.'

He laughs, and lets go. 'Even broken clocks are right twice a day. Dinner's in the oven, so if you want to . . .'

My phone vibrates in my palm, and I glance at it.

I turn cold.

The distinctive logo: white handcuffs, a 'C' on a blood-red square.

The words, pixel-sharp: *Conviction, Season Four: Trailer – The Murder of Graham Catton.*

I've known, for months, that this might be coming. But denial's a powerful thing, and I thought – ridiculously, I know – that if I refused to talk, they might not have enough to go on.

I look up at Dan, who's still talking, though I can't make sense of the words.

I follow him into the kitchen, and cut him off mid-sentence. 'I need to talk to you about something.'

He looks over his shoulder, searches my face – and smiles. 'All right. Sit. I'll put the kettle on.'

As he pours the tea, I sit at the table. I don't know quite how to position myself. Hands resting on the surface: too formal. On my lap, it looks as though I have something to hide. When he turns around, I'm somewhere in between.

'OK.' He takes a seat beside me, fumbling with a packet of biscuits. 'What's up?'

I hold out an open palm. 'Give me those.'

'You hate these. They're junk food.'

'I need junk food, right now.'

'Wow. This *must* be bad.'

'Not funny.' I tear open the packet, and take a bite. The sugar dissolves on my tongue. I feel something light up in my brain, a synapse twitching in response. It's one of the many things I've given up, over the years, along with alcohol, smoking (of course), red meat, bread . . . Dan, thanks to some (admittedly helpful) cultural conditioning, seems to think all women go through this: the gradual removal of pleasures from their lives, a slow self-sacrifice; a futile battle against ageing. All I know is this: I crave clarity more than I crave those pleasures.

Most of the time.

He reaches for a biscuit. 'Is this about *Conviction*?'

I freeze. 'How did you know?'

'They called me. A couple of months ago. I told them where to stick it, but—'

'They called *here*?'

'No, no – they caught me at work. Tried the whole "one hack to another" spiel, though it didn't get them far. Obviously.' He shifts heavily in his seat. 'I was going to bring it up at the time, but I thought . . . well, since you hadn't said anything, I figured they'd decided against it. Plumped for another story instead.'

A shadow brushes the window outside, crossing the table between us. A bird, I suppose, or a bat. 'Apparently not.'

'Did you talk to them?'

'No. I . . . I thought the same as you, I guess. That if they couldn't talk to me, they'd let it drop. I didn't expect them to go ahead anyhow.'

'I could've told you all journalists are untrustworthy bastards. Not that these guys *are*. Journalists, I mean.' There's an itch of scorn in his voice. Professional jealousy, perhaps. He's spent his life reporting news, and had some success, until the financial crisis and the internet pulled the floor out of the market. He moved back to Hawkwood – his home town – the year before I did, to edit the county *Gazette*.

Conviction, on the other hand – real journalists or otherwise – boasts a following in the millions. I know the numbers almost by heart. I've been refreshing their website every day since they called.

'Look,' he says, finally. He leans forward – tentatively, like he's expecting me to recoil. He winds his fingers through mine. 'Hey. I mean it. Look at me.' I meet his eyes, briefly; then look away. 'I know you don't like talking about what happened to him. And I get that. You want to move on. But . . .'

'Dan—'

'I'm just saying . . . Would it be worth thinking about it? Talking about it, I mean?'

'I don't *need* to talk about it.' I stare into my cup, watching the lazy curl of steam rising. 'The thing is . . . I went to the trial. I heard all the evidence. And that gave me closure. Because they *proved* it was him.' There's confidence in my voice as I say this, though it feels empty. Like a lie. Still, I go on. 'Going back over it all, now . . . It's been too long. I don't know that I'd be able to do it without—'

I'm silenced by movement overhead. Evie's footsteps creak on the beams above, and she emerges at the top of the stairs. More than ever, she's her father's ghost, her head tilted, an eyebrow raised in confusion. 'Is something burning?'

Dan's chair screeches on the tile. 'Shit. I forgot to . . .'

23

'How did you not *smell* it?' She laughs. 'You want to know what he said to me earlier? That *I* needed to concentrate on "the task at hand". Good advice, huh?'

'Very.' As she sits, I resist the urge to reach for her hair, or to make one of the comments I know she'll parrot back, mockingly. Still, I miss being able to run a comb through her curls. To squeeze them between finger and thumb, and watch them spring back. 'How's the studying going?'

'Fine. All on track.' She glances at Dan. Then at me. 'What was so interesting that you nearly set the house on fire talking about it?'

My perceptive little girl. I could throttle her sometimes.

Dan doesn't acknowledge the comment. *Over to you,* he's saying. *Play this however you think is best.*

I sigh. 'We were . . . We were talking about what happened to your dad.'

If there's a reaction I'm expecting, it doesn't show. Her face is blank, detached. Calm.

'I don't know if you've heard of a podcast called *Conviction*—'

A blink. 'The one about Barry Gibbons?'

I nod. Gibbons, the subject of *Conviction*'s second season, was exonerated after serving twenty years in prison for the rape and murder of a teenage girl. The podcast's army of fans – every one of them, it seemed, a kind of armchair detective – went on to uncover evidence that not only proved that he hadn't committed the crime, but that the real killer had gone on to repeat his attacks for almost a decade after Gibbons had been locked away, seemingly without the authorities making the link. It was enough to turn *Conviction* from a poor imitation of better-known true-crime podcasts to a global sensation in its own right.

Evie gnaws at the cuff of her hoodie. It's a habit I've warned her against, but today I let it go. She puts the pieces together with awful quickness. 'They're doing a series on him – on the guy who killed Dad?'

'Yeah.' I glance at Dan, who offers an encouraging smile. 'I don't know why—' I begin. 'I mean . . . I don't know what they've found to make them think there's something wrong there, but—'

'Wow.' She's thinking. Processing. 'Do you think . . .' She pauses, choosing her words. 'Do you think it's possible? That it wasn't him?'

I feel Dan's attention sharpen at the question. He couldn't ask it outright. But she can.

'Honestly, Evie, I don't know. I didn't, until this happened. I thought the case against him was pretty clear-cut, but it was a long time ago, and I was . . . I was a bit of a mess. And I have to think, rationally, that if they've decided to devote a season to looking into the case, then . . . they must think there's something there to find.'

She glances at the blank face of her phone. She isn't reading anything. She's just buying time to think.

When she puts it down, she's resolute. 'I guess that's good, then. If he's innocent. If he's been in prison all this time and he didn't do it, then it's a good thing someone's looking into it.'

Her faith takes me aback – both in vague notions of innocence and justice, and in me. The possibility that *I* might have something to do with it – that I might have anything to hide, at all – doesn't appear to have occurred to either of them.

She sees something in my face, and her expression changes. The look in her eyes breaks my heart. 'Mum. It'll be fine. Don't worry.'

'I know.' Another lie. 'I'm just . . . I'm nervous about what they're going to dig up.'

Dan laughs. 'Come on, Hannah. What do you think they're going to find? That you got a B in one of your GCSEs? That it took you three attempts to pass your driving test?' He gasps. 'I just remembered that time when you called in sick with the "flu". You're screwed if that comes out.'

Evie groans. 'Oh my God, Dan. Never talk about that stuff in front of me. Ever.'

I laugh, in spite of everything. Being with them – watching them joke together, cosy and familiar – warms me.

'Seriously, Hannah. I get why you'd be concerned. It's going to dredge up a lot of stuff from the past – and you won't be able to stay out of it. You were *married* to the guy. But you're as strait-laced as they come. Aside from the fact you leave wet towels on the bed, and you never use a coaster, you're almost perfect.'

Evie rolls her eyes. 'Look at him, trying to be romantic.'

He grins. 'A for effort, right?'

I do my best to force a smile. 'You're probably right.' It's another lie. Once the series begins, I know there'll be no escaping the past. The things I might have done. The things I *know* I've done. This story I've spent ten years wrangling, in my own mind: now, it's someone else's to tell.

'Thank you,' I add. 'Really. For being so . . .'

He waves a hand, batting the thought away, before I have to say it.

Thank you for believing in me, I want to say, though I can't. *Thank you for thinking the best of me. I'm sorry it isn't true.*

'You're all right,' he says. 'And trust me. Whatever happens, with all this . . . we'll get through it. You, me, and Evie. As long as we're together, we'll be OK.' There's a brief pause, just long enough for the words to settle. And then, he does me another kindness. He moves on. 'So . . . what are we going to do about dinner?'

Evie peers at the blackened tray. 'What even *is* that?'

'It's what the French call *flambé*,' Dan says, pointedly. 'But I think we might have to write it off. Not sure you two are developed enough in the palate.'

'How about pizza?' My tone is too bright, too sharp. Both stare at me blankly.

Evie's the first to react. '*You* want pizza?'

'Well, it's my fault dinner's ruined. The least I can do is suggest something hideously unhealthy to make up for it.' I wince. I'm a psychiatrist at an eating disorders clinic. I know better than to demonize food in front of a teenage girl. 'It's not so bad once in a while, anyway.'

Evie brings up the menu on her phone. 'It says they can deliver in an hour.'

I see my opportunity, and grab it. 'Order it for collection. You guys order whatever you want and I'll go fetch it.'

Dan mimes an expression of shock, one hand clutching his chest.

'Not a word, mister. Or *you're* going to get it. On foot.'

I leave them on the sofa, some laugh-tracked American sitcom blaring on the TV. Evie seems thrilled at the way the night's unfolded, our usual rules relaxed to accommodate my 'news'. Dan, too, appears to be enjoying himself – though I'm sure later he'll want to 'check in' and 'make sure everything's OK'.

I love him for it. I do. But right now, I need to be alone. Just for a minute.

Just while I work this out.

I pull off the main road, down an old dirt track, gravel crackling under the wheels. I drive on through the trees until they part, and I stop. The old limestone quarry opens up beyond, the water still an eerie blue in the darkness. Either side of me are warning signs: *Think! Would you swim in ammonia or bleach?* And, *This water is known to contain: Car wrecks. Dead animals. Excrement. Rubbish. Swimming may result in death.*

In the distance, I see the shadow of Hawkwood House, moonlight illuminating the broken windows, the gaping holes in the roofs and walls. Looking out at it soothes me, as it always does: it's an anchor, a tether to the past. Coming here feels like coming home.

With the engine off, I can hear the rustle of the wind in the leaves, the faint scratch and call of creatures overhead. I think I see something moving, there, between the trees. My pulse quickens in response, though I know it's silly. I've lived here long enough by now to know that the woods have a life of their own. There's *always* something moving in there.

I glance at my screen, and click play.

'In our next season of *Conviction* . . .' the host, Anna Byers says, her voice roused with theatrical flourish. The music swells, staccato strings straight out of a Hitchcock noir.

I recognize the first voice instantly. He's older now – the tell-tale smoker's rattle in his throat. But it's him. Stevens. The officer who questioned me for hours on that first night, and watched me, every day, in court. 'There was something about the crime scene that just wasn't right. It was like something out of a film. I've seen a lot of homicides in the years since, but . . . That's the one that keeps me up at night.'

A click. A whirr of rolling tape. I hear my own voice, playing back. 'I told you. I don't remember anything. I don't know.' I feel, bone-deep, the exhaustion; the frustration I'd felt, after hours of answering the same questions, of repeating my answers again and again. I feel the press of Evie's head on my lap. The steel desk under my bare, cold arms.

But none of that comes through in these words. All I hear is callousness. The voice of a woman who doesn't care that her husband is dead.

Another voice. Another spark of recognition. 'They went to incredible lengths to make themselves *look* like the perfect couple.' I can see him now: those small, sunken eyes in ashen skin, always a little slick with sweat. Darren. The best man at our wedding. My husband's closest friend. 'But I always knew something was off. After they charged that kid . . . It never seemed right to me. I just thought she had everybody fooled.'

And another. A woman. Someone I don't know. 'I thought my son would get a fair trial. That's what they tell you: trust the process, the system works, and all that . . . But the system *doesn't* work. My son isn't a murderer. He's a victim.'

I close my eyes. Grip my hands tight around the steering wheel, the ridges carving knots into my palms.

'That's all to come,' Anna Byers says now. 'This season, on *Conviction*.'

6

There are worse things to be haunted by than ghosts.

My husband wrote that, I'm sure of it. It was one of those lines he was a little too proud of. The kind he'd say out loud, proudly, for me to groan at.

I'd smile, pretending to be teasing – but we both knew I wasn't.

Now, though, as I run through the woods, the wet earth sucking at my feet . . . I think he might be right.

Today, the first episode of *Conviction* goes live. The past seems to catch at my ankles and tug at my hair; the voices of strangers and people I used to know whip through my mind, pulling the breath from my throat.

Dan told me not to google it. 'Trust me,' he'd said, meeting my eye in the bathroom mirror. 'You won't find anything on there that makes you feel *any* better. About anything.'

So I didn't.

Until last night.

Late last night.

Now, I run faster, the branches reaching for me as I pass.

She had everybody fooled, Darren had said, in the trailer. And he's right. It's a skill of mine, to be able to make everyone think I'm something that I'm not.

Everyone. Including myself. But I can't outrun the things I read. The rabid delight of strangers, all calling for justice – for my husband's death, and for the boy convicted of his murder – without knowing either man at all.

The thought makes me run faster still, though my lungs, my calves, all ache in protest. But still, I run – towards my destination. Towards the place that never fails to soothe me. The place I *need* to be.

I've never told anyone why I really moved here. As far as Sarah, Dan, and Evie are concerned, it was a pin-in-a-map decision. I saw a patch of green earth, a mass of water I thought was a lake, a few rolling hills – and after all that had happened in the city, it was enough. As soon as Graham's life insurance paid out, I bought a cottage plucked straight from a picture book, and I started over again. A clean break – this, as good a place as any.

It's not that I *told* anyone that was the reason. It's a story they wrote themselves, built out of clues accidentally dropped – reading meaning where there was none. I simply didn't correct them.

Because psychiatrists, as a rule, avoid words like 'crazy', or 'nuts'. Our job is to remove the stigma around mental health.

But it's these words I hear, in my mind, when I think about the *real* reason; when I see it, looming up ahead, turrets and chimneys spiralling up behind the wall around the grounds. Hawkwood House – or rather, its ruins – seems almost to glow against the grey sky and loamy green hills, the black woods and cliffs behind.

It *is* nuts. It *is* crazy. But it's a place that's fascinated me since before Evie was born. And when Graham died – in that strange and eerie after – it seemed like the only place I could go.

I like to imagine it alive, still a working hospital – a home – for women who needed respite from their lives. It had music rooms, chapels, an aviary – even a spa, of sorts, a pool set under a coloured glass dome – all of which, its founders seemed to think, would help its patients to find joy in their lives again. That intention spoke to me. It still does now, when I'd do anything for a break from this life that I've built, and from the one I lived before.

It gives me something like peace, even though it's derelict, long abandoned. If anything, I'm grateful for that. Because with no one else around, it feels like mine.

My heart pounds faster as I reach the gate – and stop. A clumsy stop that's almost slapstick, like a cartoon character hitting a pane of glass.

In the shadow of the open door, I see her. A woman dressed all in white, long black hair spilling down her back in loose curls. In the early-morning light, she's a blink away from a ghost. As she walks the building's perimeter, I see the car parked behind the moss-covered fountain: a black Mercedes, low-slung and glossy as a beetle.

The realization makes my cheeks burn hot. From the way she looks at the building, the frank, businesslike assessment of its flaws and scale; the way she chatters into her phone, hands gesturing, as though giving instructions, I know: she's a property developer. A vulture, come to pick over the bones of Hawkwood House. In a year, more than likely, it'll be no more than another block of soulless luxury flats.

She turns towards the gate, squints at me, and smiles. She waves and takes a step in my direction.

I turn around, and I run.

'You can't spend the rest of your life obsessing over the past,' Sarah said. *Has* said, over and over again, in the ten years since I moved here. Now, for the first time, I start to think she might be right.

7

I swipe my card through the scanner. The unit doors heave open with a pneumatic whoosh.

My favourite nurse, Joanna – *everyone's* favourite nurse, beloved by patients and staff alike – emerges from behind the reception desk and beckons me over. 'Borrow you a sec?'

My stomach drops. She disappears again, before I can read anything in her face.

'What's up?'

She hands me the department's tattered iPad. 'I thought you should probably see this.'

The screen blinks, threateningly, as it always does when unplugged. She reattaches the charging cable, and the words *The Ten Commandments* glow at the top of the screen.

I glance at Joanna. 'What am I looking at?'

She blushes. 'I know I probably shouldn't, but . . . I've been keeping an eye on Amy online since she left, last time. Now she's back . . . I thought you should know what she's been writing. On her blog.'

I'm not entirely sure how to react, as far as my professional obligations go. Monitoring patient activity online – especially after they've been discharged – has always been a bit of a grey area. Officially, it isn't something we do. And most of our patients have private accounts – with aliases neither we, nor their parents, could ever reasonably be expected to guess.

Still, that doesn't stop us trying, sometimes.

Call it curiosity. Call it an invasion of privacy. Or call it extended patient care.

I look down at the screen. *Number 1: You will do whatever it takes to achieve your goals. Number 2: Willpower is EVERYTHING – do not lose it.*

I wince. Warning signs, for a patient like Amy, whose anorexia turns supposed self-control into slow death, self-destruction. 'Oh dear.'

Joanna nods. 'I just thought you should know. Because she's saying she's fine. I'm not sure if she's in denial, or what, but . . .'

'I'll let you know. We've got her phone, right?'

'Yeah. She's checked in and ready for you.'

'Great.' My own phone vibrates in my pocket. I hand the tablet back. 'Let me know if anything else comes up.'

I glance at the notification as I walk towards the day-room, calves still aching from my morning run.

@ConvictionPod tweeted: Four hours to go. Episode One goes live at 1 p.m. GMT. Get ready for our most twisted season yet.

The floor seems to give way beneath me.

I regain my balance and walk on, as though everything's fine. But it isn't. And I'm not sure it ever will be again.

* * *

'Amy.'

She tips her head back over the rim of the tattered day-room sofa. 'Doc.'

It's an affectation that reminds me of another patient, on another ward. A girl I couldn't save. The thought of Amy ending up the same way sends a chill through me. I force a smile. 'Come on. Let's have a chat.'

She rolls up and shuffles towards me. As she passes, I touch her shoulder lightly with my palm. Through the layers, I feel the nub of her shoulder, all sinew and bone. She'd been doing so well, before. Automatically, I wonder what's caused her to relapse – although deep down, I know better. Illnesses like hers fight with claws and teeth. Sometimes, they just come back.

This is her fourth admission under section, though she's been a patient, on and off, for almost nine years. As I follow her to the consulting room, I pause to let her make cheery conversation with one of the cleaning staff. I smile and nod along, realizing uneasily that she – a patient – is on first-name terms with a staff member I couldn't pick out of a line-up.

I wonder if this is the sort of thing that will be held up as evidence of my bad character, once people realize this season of *Conviction* is about me.

I commit his name to memory.

Just in case.

Finally, we're alone. 'So. Ames.' She sits, instantly picking at the fraying threads of the old armchair. I take a seat opposite, my elbows on my knees, eyes level with hers. 'I'd say it's good to see you, but . . . well, you know we were all hoping this time it'd stick.'

'I'd say I'm glad to be back, but . . . yeah.'

I smile. She smiles back, a toothy grin. I wonder, sometimes, whether we're *supposed* to like our patients. During my training, it seemed as though clinical detachment was the goal – the defining characteristic of the good doctor. But I can't help but feel a kind of attachment to Amy, and the other girls who pass through the unit.

I want them to get better – of course I do. But I also understand what makes them the way they are. It's not the desire to die that makes them choose hunger; compulsive, relentless exercise; or both. It's a need to control the way they live.

'So, tell me. What's been going on since we last caught up?' Her eyes flit to my hands. I show my palms. She won't talk as freely if I'm taking notes, so – today, at least – I don't. 'No pen. The floor is yours.'

She laughs. It's brittle, a snicker at the gallows. 'I thought I was doing OK. Which, I know it doesn't look like it, but . . . I was, for a while. You can look at my weight chart. I maintained for seven weeks.'

'I saw. That was really, really good. The longest stretch you've had as an outpatient – right?'

She nods. 'Yeah.'

'Did anything happen, that week, that made things start to take a turn? Anything that you can pinpoint as a trigger, perhaps?'

She purses her lips. One of the advantages of having worked with her for so long: I know whatever's coming next will be a lie. 'No. I kept wondering what it was, even when it was happening. I just . . . I couldn't control it. It just came back.'

'Well, you've done the right thing. And you'll be thrilled to hear you've made it back just in time to catch movie night tomorrow.'

'Oh, yay.' She clicks her tongue. No one rails against the

department's poor choice of films with quite as much heart as Amy. I'm glad to see she's still as ferocious as ever. 'What classic 1980s B-movie do we have to look forward to, this time? Tell me it's *Back to the Future* again, please.'

'*Back to the Future* isn't a B-movie. It's a classic. And you're always welcome to suggest alternatives.'

'Pfft. Remember how much trouble I got into when I asked for *The Hunger Games*?' She raises her palms. 'A *genuine* mistake. It's not my fault if they're going to give these things triggering names.'

I laugh. I can't help myself. 'You know I can't condone that kind of thing.'

'Yeah, well . . . I watched it while I was out, and it was fine. You'd like it.'

I wonder what I've done, or said, that's given her this impression; what hint of personal information I've given, accidentally, over the years we've worked together. 'Would I?'

'Yeah.' She doesn't elaborate, and a silence falls. Already, I know this will bother me for the rest of the day. It's almost certainly nothing, but it feels like a slip: evidence of a mistake I've made, some vital piece of personal information I've handed over without thinking.

It wouldn't be the first time it's happened. But I promised myself I'd be better. I promised I wouldn't let it happen again.

I reach for my notebook and pen, and change the subject. 'How's your mum?'

She rolls her neck around, the bones a sharp 'V' in the centre. I feel my own throat tighten in response. When she looks back at me, her expression has cooled. I'm not the only one, it turns out, who can pull up the barriers. 'She's fine. I mean, given her only daughter's mental, she's doing OK.'

'You're not "mental", Amy. You know that. You have an illness. That's all.'

'That's not how she sees it.'

I say nothing for a moment. I wait for her to go on. But she doesn't.

'Do you think it'd be helpful to share some of these feelings with her in our next review?' I say, finally. She looks at me doubtfully, as though she's waiting for the punchline to the joke. 'If we can open up the lines of communication a little, you might find she's able to take a step back. It's possible that she's just saying all these things because she just doesn't know what else to do. She might just be trying to express her concern.'

'Concern, yeah. She's expressing plenty of that. But trust me, it's not about my health.' She looks down at her hands, the bitten-down nails bluish underneath. 'I'll talk to her, if that's what you want. But I don't think it's going to help.'

With her face covered by her hair, for a moment she's the echo of Evie: the same unbrushed tangle of curls, the same angular pose. It makes something ache in me. An instinct for protection.

'She loves you, Amy. She's your mum.'

Don't be so hard on her, I want to say. But I don't.

She looks up. For a split second, I think I've managed to get through.

And then it's gone.

'Are we done?' she says flatly.

'Amy—'

'Can I go now? Please?'

I sigh. 'If you want to.'

She stands and leaves. The door slams, heavily, behind.

8

I click, swipe, and refresh. Still nothing.

Foam clings to the sides of my cup. I wrap my hands around what's left of the warmth, and look once again at my phone. The screen is still blank. Since the notification, forty minutes ago – *Slight delay with uploads, here – not a ploy for suspense, we promise. AB.* – nothing.

A watched pot never boils, they say.

I click the screen on, and off again.

'Spare any change?'

There's a startling blankness in the eyes of the woman in front of me, her hair a matted, filthy mess, hands thick with dirt. I feel a pang of sympathy, a there-but-for-the-grace-of-God sting. 'Let me . . . Hang on.' I root around in my pockets, but come up short. I bend down and search through my bag. I find a few coins, nothing that counts for much, really – but I hand them over, and she turns and shambles away.

The stare of the woman behind her – her eyes fixed on me – makes my cheeks flush with the sudden recognition.

'I *thought* it was you!' she says, her tone far friendlier than it ought to be, given the circumstances – the fact I'd turned and run when we'd made eye contact on the grounds of Hawkwood House. She strides towards me, beaming brightly.

'Sorry, I . . .' I trail off. I have no idea what to say. 'You must think I'm completely mad.'

She looks at me, blankly. 'Why?'

I'm thrown off. 'Didn't you . . . ?' I trail off.

'You *are* Hannah Catton . . . aren't you?'

My old name. It reverberates through me.

'McLelland. Catton was . . .' I blink. 'I'm sorry – I'm confused. I thought you recognized me from . . . running. I'm probably having a moment, but—'

'Oh dear.' She laughs. 'This is awkward. You don't recognize me, do you?'

I stare at her. 'No.'

'Darcy?' She scans my eyes for some sign of recognition. 'From the Buyon Clinic? Two thousand and . . . something?'

An image begins to form in my mind, the vague outlines of an intern, the year the cracks began to show at Buyon, my former hospital. 'Darcy . . . Burke – right?'

'Yes!' She beams. 'Quite glad you didn't recognize me, really. Braces and extra-strength conditioner: two things my twenty-three-year-old self should've learned about *much* sooner.'

The image of her settles in my mind. A shy girl, a little buck-toothed, dark eyes. A wild, frizzy mass of hair, constantly escaping from a bun. A good enough intern, but . . . not all that memorable.

Still, I return her smile. I click back into my professional mode, my default. 'Well, it's nice to see you again. What have you been doing with yourself since?'

41

'Well, once I'd qualified, I actually went back there – to Buyon?' Her eyes scan my face, hopefully. Again, my stomach drops. I wonder what she knows. 'Just on a fixed-term contract. But it must've been after you'd left. Which . . .' She pauses. 'Sorry, you're trying to enjoy a quiet coffee, and here I am, telling you my life story. You're busy, aren't you?'

'No, not at all.' A lie; politeness, nothing more. 'I've got to head back to work soon, but – sit, sit.'

'You're sure?'

'Of course. Tell me everything you can in—' I reach for my phone. But it isn't there. 'Oh . . .' I pat my pockets, handbag. I scan the table again, uselessly lifting the napkin, my empty cup. 'My phone is . . .'

Her eyes widen. 'Have you lost it?'

I think of Dan, warning Evie about a spate of mobile phone thefts in the area, weeks earlier. *Don't leave your phone out on the table,* he'd said. *You might as well be asking someone to steal it.* I think of the woman I handed my change to. She'd disappeared, right away – without stopping to ask anyone else for theirs.

Frustration coils, hot, in my chest. 'Yeah, I . . . Yeah.'

'Oh, no. Do you want to use mine?'

'It's fine,' I say. It isn't. 'Just . . . Let me know when it's quarter to, would you?'

'Will do.' She pauses. She's nervous. 'Are you sure you're OK?'

'I'm fine.'

A silence falls for a moment. I realize I'm being cold. None of this is her fault. It's mine. 'So you went back to Buyon, and . . .'

She smiles, apologetically. 'Yeah. In . . . 2006, I think? Something like that. I was hoping you'd still be there, but they said you'd not long left. Apparently I'd only just missed you.'

I feel a chill spread over my skin. I've always wondered what the 'official' story was, after I left. I wonder if she knows; if she's choosing not to say it, to sidestep my shame. Closed doors, endless, blank-faced questions: the words 'competence' and 'fitness to practice' echo in my mind. 'Of course, that meant I had to work under that *awful* Dr Andrews – do you remember him?'

I do: not a man I'd easily forget. I feel his unwelcome hands on the small of my back, a sharp swell of disgust and shame. '*Very* well. He was my husband's best friend.'

She presses her hands to her mouth. 'I've put my foot in it, haven't I?'

'Not at all.' I picture him, arm slung around my husband's shoulders – the two of them drunk, stupid with it. 'If he hasn't been done for sexual harassment by now, I'll eat my hat.'

'Thank *God*.' She laughs – a laugh that feels familiar. I warm to her a little more. 'Men, eh?' Her tone is light, half-joking, though there's the barest hint of a bite in it. She's been through something, perhaps recently, that makes her mean it.

'So why *did* you leave?' She asks this like it's the most natural question in the world.

And maybe it is. But it's something I've worked so hard to forget. I have no intention of dredging it up for an intern I barely remember. Especially not now.

'Oh, you know. My little girl was a toddler at that point, and . . . they grow up so fast. I didn't want to miss it.' A phrase from my old script, vague and meaningless.

'And now, you're here.'

There's a question there. I volley it back. 'And so are you.'

'Yes!' She beams. I wonder if she's been waiting for me to ask; whether she *did*, in fact, see me running from the Hawkwood gates this morning. I do my best to suppress another blush at the thought. 'It's kind of top-secret at this point, but . . .' She taps her nose with two fingers, twice. 'I'm setting up a clinic of my own. Well . . . trying to, anyway. Very early stages.'

I feel a hard, tight knot in my throat I can't explain. More accurately: would prefer not to explain. I know exactly what it is. It's envy.

'Wow.'

'Yeah. I've bought this *beautiful* old property, about an hour away from here. Hawkwood House. I don't know if you'd know it – it's an old—'

'I live there.' The words fall out, unwelcome. I laugh, weakly. 'Not *there,* I mean. But in Hawkwood. The village. So, yeah. I know it pretty well.'

'You're not serious.'

'I am.' I pause. I know she's looking for approval. But the cold, jealous part of me won't let her have it. 'I didn't even realize it was for sale.'

'Well . . . It wasn't. Not actively, but . . .' She grimaces. 'You're going to think I'm tacky.'

'Try me.'

'Well, it started when my dad passed away.' She raises a hand to stop the platitude before I can say it. 'It was a few years ago, so it's fine. But he left behind quite a bit of money, and I haven't been sure what to do with it. It's only me, because my mum and sister both died when we were kids, so . . .' A cloud of red crosses the base of her neck. I feel ashamed, suddenly, for being so mean-spirited, so petty.

I reinforce my smile a little. She goes on.

'So, I've spent the last few years hopping from place to place: out to Europe, to the States, what have you – a *disaster* for my CV, I have no doubt – looking at properties. I wanted to open a residential centre of sorts – do something good with Dad's money, you know? But I couldn't find anywhere that felt right. Which, I know, sounds extremely woo-woo and new-agey. But . . . well, it's true. Most of these old places have these *awful* stories of abuse and God-knows-what attached to them. I wanted to find somewhere that had . . .' She trails off.

'Good intentions?' I offer, after a pause.

'*Exactly.*'

All at once, I know where this is going. The realization gnaws at me, viciously.

'So, I'd pretty much decided to sack the whole thing off and come home. Go back to work, spend the cash on a big house and do a charity run once in a while to offset the guilt . . . But then, I was googling something – I don't even know what, honestly – and I found this post about Hawkwood House on some message board. Literally from 2002. Some random person, asking about the history of the place. They were looking for the archives, or something, trying to find . . .'

I lose myself, for a moment.

Just a split second, but I'm back there, in the kitchen of our London home. Typing searches into Google, eight months pregnant. A distraction.

The root of all that's happened since.

That was me, I almost say out loud. *I was asking about the archives. I wrote that.*

'But – again, this sounds *completely* irrational, out loud, but – I thought it might be a sign. So I decided to take a look at the place. My last one, and then I'd give up. And it was *perfect*.'

I say nothing. I smile, and I wait for her to go on. Still, it feels almost as though she's stolen something from me. And with this, a sharp, distinctive tug: the urge to take it back.

'And so, eventually, I managed to get hold of the current owners. They could tell I wanted it, so they came back with this *ludicrous* price, but . . . Well, I'm hoping it'll be worth it when it's done.' She laughs. 'Otherwise, quite frankly, I'm screwed. Daddy's ghost will haunt me to the grave.'

'It'll be fine,' I say, with as much brightness as I can bear. Still, I hear it: the lukewarm distance in my tone. 'It sounds like a lovely idea, and I'm sure—'

'Is there any chance you'd—' She seems to catch herself, mid-interruption, and winces. When she goes on, she's shy; a little anxious. 'Would you like to come and have a look around? I'd love to get your thoughts on the plans, and I'd be *more* than happy to pay for your time.'

I search around for the right response; for some reason to decline. But there's nothing. No good reason to say no. And, deep down, the fact is: I don't want to.

She seems to sense my hesitation. 'Sorry – is that a really weird thing to ask?' she says. 'It's just . . . I don't know anyone in the area, and—'

I stand. 'I'd better get back to work, but . . . sure. I've always wanted to see what's inside the old place, so . . . that sounds nice.'

'Amazing. Oh, I'm so thrilled. *So* thrilled.' In an instant, she hands me her phone. 'Put your number in there, and I'll call you so you've got mine. We can co-ordinate something when you're not too busy.'

I feel an itch of frustration, again. 'I've lost my phone, so—'

'Oh, shit – of course. Email, then?'

I glance at the glossy screen in my hand; the wallpaper a snapshot of a hallway that must be Hawkwood's, moss creeping through the black-and-white chequered tiles. My stomach flips at the sight of them, the vivid flash of something that feels like coming home.

'Here,' I say, attempting to disguise the tremble in my voice. I press the phone into her palm, and smile. 'I'd better get going. But – thank you for the invitation. Really. I can't wait to look around.'

Before I leave, I go back inside the café.

The waitress looks me up and down as I approach the bar. I dislike her instantly. 'Has anyone handed in a phone?'

'No. Did you leave it here?'

I gesture towards the window. 'I was sitting outside, with the lady in the white suit.'

She looks out. Squints. 'Where?'

I don't have the patience for this right now. There are four tables outside. She can't be that hard to spot.

'There,' I say, turning to where I'd left Darcy, playing with her phone.

'I'll probably camp out here for a bit', she'd said, moving my cup to an empty table. 'This weather is gorgeous, and I've got a stack of admin to do, so . . .'

My cheeks flush, hot. 'Oh. She's . . . She's gone.'

The waitress eyes me, doubtfully. 'Well, I'll keep an eye out.'

I stutter my thanks, and step out into the warm afternoon air.

A bus roars past, a hot, metallic gust rushing through my hair. From the thrown-open door of a shop, I hear a song I know by heart, but haven't sung in years.

I feel a memory join me – another day, in another street, in another life. It steps into my skin, and stalks me, all the way back.

9

London, 1998

I feel the sun on my skin, sweat clinging to the back of my neck; the unmistakable pulse of movement underground, the slap and click of footsteps on the pavement.

I am blind, steered by his hands at my shoulders. One of my curls pulls, caught under his thumb.

'I don't know why we have to do this. People are going to think you're trying to kidnap me. Or we're into some kind of kinky sex games or something.'

He scoffs, his breath hot at my ear. 'Haven't you ever heard of romance?'

'Is that what this is?'

He doesn't reply. But I can feel him smiling.

As we shuffle along, I imagine strangers staring at us. I wonder if they're jealous of me, of my perfect life. And then I remember. This is London. More likely no one's noticed us at all.

We stop. He spins me around to face him, and the kiss he gives me is one I know I'll remember. Better, almost, on reflection, than right now, when I'm doing the work of feeling: of committing every detail to memory.

I know where we are, even before he loosens the scarf. I knew where we were going, in fact, before we even left the flat. Still, for his benefit, I gasp as I look up, and admire our soon-to-be home. Our first without housemates or lodgers. The first place we can be together, all manner of suggestion, there, in the word: *alone*.

His parents have paid the deposit, though I offered – *wanted* – to contribute. It was misplaced pride, on my part, he told me. *Totally* unnecessary. Because it's a gift. A beautiful, generous gift. But in a way I can't quite explain – and certainly can't justify – it feels spoiled, this way. The house that we'll share has been paid for by him, and chosen by him, without needing my input at all. Some part of me chafes against that.

Because I want to choose my life for myself.

And then there's the way he talks about it: as 'a little starter home'. He doesn't know what this means to me, because I haven't told him – but it's bigger than anywhere I've ever lived. (Maybe he's right. Maybe I *do* have a problem with pride.)

But the sky is pink and gold, and his smile is electric. I know how badly he wants this to be perfect. So, for him, I smile back.

'This is it.' The keys in his hand dig into my palm as he speaks. 'Are you ready?'

'I'm ready.'

'I love you,' he says, pulling me into him. 'God, I love you. I'm so glad I finally get you all to myself.' Another long, slow kiss. As though all we have is time.

A cyclist shouts something as he passes, a jab. I feel Graham tense, his grip squeezing my fingers as he turns. I pull a hand free, and turn his face back to me; his cheeks burn hot against my palm.

'I think he was probably telling us to get a room. Which I'd quite like to do,' I say, between kisses. 'Come on.'

His eyes search mine. He's trying to guess what I'm thinking. To pre-empt it. To make it right.

Because our new life, at last, begins here. But in the face of all that expectation, every slip, no matter how small, feels like an omen. So I smile, and he smiles back.

He leads me through the back doorway, black-and-white tiles marking the way. It's old-fashioned, with something imperious about it. The squeak of my tattered trainers on the gleaming floor seems completely out of place.

You'll settle in, I tell myself. *It'll feel like home, eventually.*

For now, though, I feel like an unwelcome guest. Less a guest, in fact, than an intruder. In the stairwell, my hand still in his, he stops. I know what he's thinking.

'No,' I say. 'Inside.'

He pouts, and it ripples through me, like a stone thrown in a pond. He whispers something in my ear – it doesn't matter what. His lips press to my neck, and the hairs there rise to the touch.

I'm so easily swayed when he's like this.

I imagine the next few minutes in my mind, as though played on a screen: my skirt hitched high by hungry hands, back pressed against the wall with a force that's both too much, and just right. The illicit pang of it, of his skin touching mine in the stairwell, where our soon-to-be neighbours might see. Where they will, almost certainly, hear. But then, a thing I don't expect.

He rocks me back and forth in his arms. Slowly. Tenderly.

He hums a song in my ear, and I know it, instantly. I'd made it our song, months before – privately. At the time, I'd been too embarrassed to tell him. I thought he'd laugh.

Now, I realize, he'd done the same. One hand pressed to my shoulder; the other, the small of my back. We rock from side to side, a secret dance to a song that only we can hear.

And for a little while, all our slights and little sadnesses slip away, until there's only us. Two people, held in perfect time, blazing with a love so intense that the rest of the world shields its eyes, and turns away.

10

Derbyshire, 2018

The afternoon that follows is the longest of my life.

I find myself glancing furtively at nursing staff and consultants, as though any of them have had the time to not only listen to *Conviction*, but to trace the woman in their story back to me. I do the same with the patients, even though none of them have phones or tablets and couldn't listen if they tried. It is ridiculous, paranoid behaviour, made worse by the loss of my phone. I think – jealously, bitterly – of all the people who *have* heard it, now; wonder how many more, with every minute that inches by.

When I pull the car into the drive, I see Dan and Evie, through the window. They look out, at me, but neither of them smile.

I can tell, right away, that something's wrong.

I stand, ludicrously, outside the door, fumbling with my keys, though I know it won't be locked. I'm buying myself time with this. I need to set my mask.

But when I walk inside, my tone is all wrong. It's too cheerful. Too much. 'Everything OK?'

Dan stares at me with unbridled concern. 'We were worried about you. You weren't answering your phone.'

'Oh my God. I – I lost it. Sorry. I should've found another way to—'

'Jesus, Mum.' Evie leans back in her chair, her weariness oddly adult. I almost laugh, a combination of love and relief. 'We thought something awful had happened.'

'I'm so sorry. I went out for a coffee, and . . . Well, I should've listened to Dan's advice. I was giving some change to a homeless lady, and . . .' I shrug. 'I'm an idiot. Sorry.'

Dan reaches out, squeezing my palm. 'That's what you get for being nice. Don't make *that* mistake again.' I wonder if I'm being optimistic, finding a comfort in his touch.

Surely if *Conviction* had come up with something terrible, he'd be icy with me now.

Then again, this is Dan: a man who'll go to the ends of the earth to avoid confrontation. I've always loved that about him. But now, it seems like a fault. I need to know how he really feels. If he's going to walk away.

I squeeze back. 'I won't.'

'Evie's football team are through to the regional semi-finals,' he says, before I can burrow deeper. It's a hint: a reminder of the thing I should've asked as soon as I walked through the door.

'Wow.' As though her excellent grades weren't enough, she's captain of her school's netball and football teams. The result: a hallway filled with jerseys and football boots; a complex schedule of tournaments, practice games, and prize-givings to which Dan drives her, cheerfully and without complaint.

'It's not that big a deal,' Evie says, though the blush on her cheek says otherwise.

'It's brilliant, Evie. Really.' I glance at Dan. 'I'm proud of you. We both are.'

She colours a little more. 'Thanks.'

Dan stands, and pats his empty chair. 'Sit. Dinner won't be long.'

All the day's exhaustion hits me, the adrenaline draining away. 'You're amazing.'

'I know.' There's a pause. I see Evie meet his eye, and look away. 'So . . . I'm guessing you haven't listened to . . .' He trails off. There's no need to say it.

'No. Have you?'

They look at each other again. 'Yeah.' Evie gives me an apologetic smile.

'People are saying Anna Byers has lost her touch,' Dan says, a hint of satisfaction in his tone. He slides the tablet across the table, the news app open to a shot of Byers in a dim-lit studio, eyes lowered in a familiar pose. I see what she's doing, with this: positioning herself like the many media stars who've come before, with the same brooding, pensive stare.

The words glow, vividly, below.

After a record-breaking second season — resulting in the release of accused murderer Barry Gibbons — it was inevitable that Conviction's third could never quite live up to the hype. But with their fourth, on the murder of literature professor Graham Catton in 2008, the pressure is on for Anna Byers and her team to stage something of a return to form.

Their much-promoted trailer and publicity campaign — a slicker operation than previous seasons, showing something of Conviction's ambitions to be taken seriously as real media players — teased intrigue, sex, and, of course, murder. One episode in, though, we've had forty-five minutes of gloomy introspection, most of which has been pulled from the victim's (frankly, parchment-dry) lectures, read by the victim himself.

Nausea settles in my throat. The very idea of hearing his voice is enough to chill me; it's like a visitation from a ghost. I stare at the screen, and force myself to read on.

Far be it from us to demand more scandal, and more drama — in fact, much of the water-cooler conversation among media types is divided on whether Byers's choice to tell something of a slower, less tabloidesque tale is a positive thing for audio storytelling, in a world that demands plot twists and instant gratification. But there's a difference between narratives that are purposefully careful and slow, and those that are self-indulgent and dull. And at this early stage in the season, the consensus is that Conviction seems to be leaning a little too much towards the latter.

I look up, my face set in a grimace: another mask. The truth is, I don't know how to react. 'Wow.'

Evie's careful, when she speaks. 'I think they're being kind of unfair. Not that I'm exactly *for* them doing it, but . . . I actually didn't think it was as bad as everyone's saying. Although I guess . . .' She pokes her thumb through her sleeve and bites it. 'I guess I'm probably biased.'

I feel a sharp stab of guilt. My daughter wants to hear her father's voice. Of *course* she does.

'Well, that's fair enough. I mean, even *I* found it weird hearing him talk,' Dan says. 'It's going to be a whole different experience for you two, but . . . I don't know. Some of the inflections he had reminded me of you, Evie.'

He's right. I've noticed it, little fragments of her father in her voice, things that make no sense given he's been dead since she was nearly six years old. I can't help but bristle at the comparison. At the idea of her finding a connection with him, after all this time.

'Do you remember much about him?'

I look at Dan, surprised that he's asked the question outright. It's one I've wanted to ask Evie myself, several times, over the years. But I've always lost my nerve. I'm afraid of hearing something I'd rather I didn't know.

'Not really. Random stuff, like . . . I had a playhouse, right?'

The room lurches around me, and resettles. 'Yeah. It was . . . It was a Christmas present.'

She beams. 'I wasn't sure if I'd imagined that. But I do remember it. He used to do puppet shows at the windows, didn't he?'

'He did.'

'And I remember him coming home from work. Not, like, one specific memory. I just remember it was always part of our day. He used to pick me up and throw me in the air, as soon as he got in.'

57

It's amazing, how vividly she remembers these details. But it makes sense. He loved her. That, at least, was true.

'I used to tell him off for it,' I say, faintly. 'When he got back late. I'd have finally managed to get you to sleep, and . . . he couldn't help himself. He had to wake you up.'

A brief, unmistakable sadness crosses her face. She blinks it away. 'What an asshole.'

'*Total* asshole.'

Evie's phone lights up, and she reaches for it. 'Do you mind if I . . . ?'

Dan nods. 'Dinner's nearly ready. Be quick.'

She slips out of the door with impressive speed.

Dan places a mug of tea on the table beside me. 'We're going to need to get in touch with the insurance about your phone. I'll dig out the details in a bit.'

I reach up for a kiss. 'Thank you.'

'It's really not as bad as you think, you know. *Conviction*, I mean. It's fine.'

'I know. I'm just . . . nervous, I guess.'

He bends to pull a tray from the oven, hot air filling the tiny kitchen. 'Would it help if we listened to it together?'

'No, it's fine. I *will* listen to it. I just . . .'

'No pressure.' He smiles, the same smile that I know, so well, after all these years together. The one I fell in love with when he brought Evie to my door, after she'd slipped through a gap in the dry-stone wall at nine years old. I assumed he'd think I was a bad mother, for failing to notice my little girl had run away.

But he didn't. He thought the best of me from the start.

'Change of subject.' He bites into a stray pepper, escaped from the tray, and smiles. He chews, open-mouthed, a thing he knows I hate, but loves to tease me with. 'A little birdie told me someone here is in *love*.'

'Dan!' Evie's voice rings through the house. 'I am *not*.' She reappears at the top of the stairs. 'He's a liar. Don't believe a word he says.'

'Pffft.' He grins. I know how much he loves these moments, these play-fights.

'Evie's got a boyfriend,' he sings, nasally. 'K-I-S-S-I—'

'Oh my God,' she groans. 'I hate you.'

He makes kissing noises as she sits at the table, a pleading look in her eyes. 'It is like having two kids here sometimes, you know that?' I say, gently.

He lays down the plates between us, delivering mine with a kiss. 'That's why you love me. I keep you on your toes.'

'Ah – I *knew* there was a reason I kept you around.' I look over at Evie, her eyes fixed on her food. She knows what's coming next. 'So . . . Who's this secret fella?'

'No one. I don't know what he's talking about.'

Poor Evie. She's never lied to me before – or at least not about anything important. Even the little white lies she'd tell as a child – the ones every child tells to test boundaries, the ones necessary for their development – she'd quickly admit, before I could turn them into a teachable moment.

What this means, though, now, is that she's *terrible* at it. The lie is written all over her face.

I glance at Dan. He winks. *Drop it*, he seems to say. *I'll fill you in later.*

I don't want to, of course. The therapist in me wants to dig deeper. To keep questioning her until I find out what I want to know.

But she isn't a patient. She's my daughter.

I can't make her do anything – or at least, not in quite the same way I can with the girls on the unit. For them, giving me what I want is part of the game they have to play in order to be signed out – to return to their homes, their families, and friends.

Whereas in real life – no matter how much I might want things to be otherwise – people can walk away at any time.

'All right,' I say, after a pause. 'Never mind, then. Let's move on.'

I leave them in front of the TV. They know where I'm going, without my having to say it. I take my laptop up to the bedroom, and untangle the headphones from my bag. My heart thumps as I click to the *Conviction* page, the new banner a photo I haven't seen in years, though the memory surges back with it, instantly.

I see the Polaroid flash in my eyes. I feel the cold press of Graham's hand, his lips on my face. I'm laughing, open-mouthed – both of us soaked to the skin. For years after, he'd say he was saving my life that day. I'd insist it was the other way around. Either way, we were drunk – students, dressed in our graduation-ball finest – and while we'd intended a romantic, photo-opportunity kiss at the edge of the lake, we'd failed to account for the slippery mud on its banks.

I feel a laugh in my throat. We'd been so happy back then. An email alert bubbles up in the corner of the screen. I stare at the subject line for a moment. *You have 455 connections awaiting your response!* My stomach churns as it disappears.

I draw breath. Before I can lose my nerve, I press play.

60

There's a shuffle of papers, somewhere close to the mic. A distant cough, further away.

I can see him, in my mind. His hands gripping the lectern, glancing down at his notes. Dressed the part – clean-cut, pushing his hair back from his face each time he made a point he wasn't quite sure of.

The only person who saw that tic for what it was, of course, was me. To everyone else, he was all confidence. All knowledge. All smiles.

'"She had left the last blood of her husband / Staining a pillow. Their whole story / Hung – a miasma – round that stain." We can hear the detachment in Hughes's narrative voice throughout the poem, in which he and his wife take "possession" of a house which is contaminated by the ghosts of its previous inhabitants.' He draws breath. A draught flutters the curtains. 'There's an inevitability to it, as though, by finding the omens, their "sour odour", he might have sensed even then that only one of them would make it out alive, though they would be haunted by their memories; their guilt, their complicity, their shame.'

'It's hard to tell,' Anna Byers begins, 'what exactly drew Graham Catton to talk about this particular poem during his inaugural lecture: a departure from his usual research which, according to his colleagues, resolutely avoided "biographical" readings of his authors' works.

'And yet,' she goes on, 'on the night of his inaugural lecture – a defining moment in any academic career, where family, friends, and colleagues would have been invited along to hear the newly minted professor's work – Graham Catton took a wholly new tack: a long, impassioned talk on communication and intimacy in which the poet Ted Hughes deals almost exclusively with his relationship with his wife, the troubled poet Sylvia Plath, and her impact on his life.'

I remember him writing that piece. I can see the papers spread across the countertop; can hear him whispering the words to himself, rehearsing. I see him looking up at Evie with a smile. I see her, eyes fixed on his lips, opening and closing hers in imitation.

The music shifts to a minor key. I feel the change in the air; see him reaching for his jacket, slung over a chair. Not meeting my eye, as he turns to leave. 'In this, his final lecture, he spoke of the pain of a failing marriage, to an audience which did not include his wife.' She says the word 'wife' with a kind of disdain: a blade in it. 'He couldn't have known, then, that he was foreshadowing his own death: describing the scene of the crime in which he would be the victim, the pillow stained with his own blood.'

The familiar violins return, *Conviction*'s twitching theme. Another email bubbles up. *Darcy Burke. Subject: Come visit?* But I'm paralysed. I watch it disappear.

'Police concluded it was an intruder – a burglary gone wrong. A random attack, terrible and senseless – like a bolt from the blue. And, sure, that's possible. Terrible things do happen to ordinary people. Some horrors you just can't predict.

'But Professor Catton *did* predict his own murder. In the months – years – leading up to his death, the people who loved him, and the students and colleagues who admired his work, all saw changes in him. They describe a man doing his best to keep his life together, all the while aware of the heavy sword of fate hanging, terribly, over his head.'

Graham coughs, lightly, clearing his throat. 'And yet, no matter how in love we may be; however intimate our relationships, our ways of seeing into the other's soul – as Hughes does, almost by accident, in "Visit" – we are trapped with only our own stories, and the hope that others may hear them. As he writes of Plath's journal: '"You are ten years dead. It is only a story. / Your story. My story."'

11

The next morning, I shower in water so scalding, my skin burns, hot to the touch. I haven't slept; only watched Dan's sleeping form, playing Graham's words over and over in my mind.

I dress in my work clothes, rolling tights on to dried-out legs, only pausing to examine a glossy blue vein that seems new. 'You're old now,' Sarah said. And today, I feel it. As though I've aged ten years overnight.

Still, I shuffle into a pencil skirt, and adjust the collar of a crisp, white blouse. I straighten my hair, with a little more attention than usual. I wear foundation and mascara. I feel like a child playing dress-up. Like an actress, playing a part.

At the kitchen table, I reopen my laptop, the screen just as it was last night, after the episode, when I'd clicked – or rather, slammed – it shut. Now, in the pre-dawn darkness, my screen and the blinking coffee machine LED are the only sources of light.

I click on my email. The red dot reads a helpless 999+. I'd known it wouldn't be long before the pieces fell into place –

before someone attached my married name to the person I am now. But I hadn't expected it to happen quite so fast.

Joseph Kent and 861 others are awaiting your response! the first message says. I click.

Among the faces that stare back at me as I scroll – *The world's largest professional network*, the banner declares, in rippling blue and white – there's not a single name I know.

They're rubberneckers, professional or otherwise: journalists, bloggers, 'personalities', mixed among people with no link, whatsoever, to me. A data analyst from Cairo. A Melbourne-based chemical engineer. A 'tech pirate-slash-innovateur' from California.

I wonder what it is they're expecting to find, among the bones of the LinkedIn profile I never use; that hasn't been updated since I first set it up, years ago.

I close the window. I delete one email, and the next, and the next.

And then, I stop.

I stare at the subject line. Come visit?

The text beneath is short, to the point – sent from a phone. Am sure you're not free tomorrow, but I'm away for a week or so after that, so . . . Would love to show you around. Come any time – on my own there all day, company v welcome! I glance at the timestamp. It was sent last night.

I click on the attachment. It takes me a moment to work out what, exactly, I'm looking at: darkness, broken by shafts of light so thick they look like paintbrush strokes. I zoom in, and the details begin to turn real. It's one of the hallways in Hawkwood House, the light sweeping in from the dorm rooms, heavy with dust. The floor is littered with chipped plaster and curled wallpaper. Glossy green ivy creeps into the ornate mouldings, appearing through the cracks in the walls.

It's eerie. And it's gorgeous. I'm lost in it, desperate to walk through its halls.

'You're up early.'

I jump, and snap the laptop shut. 'I couldn't sleep. Thought I'd order a new phone, rather than just lying there thinking about it.'

'Fair enough.' Dan shuffles to the coffee machine. It growls, coming furiously to life.

I know he's going to ask me about *Conviction*. I can feel it. I felt it last night, when he crawled into bed beside me, while I pretended to sleep.

But I can't talk about it.

Not yet. Not to him. So, I change the subject. 'Tell me about this boyfriend situation.'

He turns, leaning against the sink. 'You *know* about us? He's just a fling, Hannah, I swear. You're the one I want to be with.'

I roll my eyes. Normally, I'd play along.

But today I'm exhausted. I don't have the energy for it. 'Come on. Before she wakes up.'

He looks chastened, and instantly, I feel guilty. He doesn't deserve to be snapped at.

'I don't actually know that much. She's texting someone. I asked her who it was. Put my investigative hat on, asked the right questions . . .' He taps his nose. 'I can spot a telling blush a mile away. It's why they pay me the big bucks. Or why they used to, anyway.'

I smile. It's an apology, of sorts. 'What's the saying? "You can't kid a kidder"?'

'Hmmm. Nope, never heard that one.'

Overhead, an alarm rattles on. Evie's bed creaks, and her

footsteps pace across the floor into the bathroom. Dan sits beside me, his face still craggy with sleep.

'I'm worried about her lying about it,' I whisper. 'It's not like her.'

'Oh, come on, Hannah. You know as well as I do, as far as teenage girls go, she's an angel.'

'That's exactly why I'm worried.'

'Didn't you have a secret boyfriend when you were her age? It's a rite of passage.' He rolls a crick from his neck. 'Mine was Lauren Abbott. We skipped school and made out instead of going to Chemistry. That's about all I remember, but at the time, I thought she was the love of my life.'

I laugh. Somehow, it sounds cold. 'Good to know.'

'Are you jealous? Because you needn't be. Last I heard, she was on her fourth husband. All of whom are *far* richer and better-looking than me.'

'I guess I should be grateful for that.'

'Oh, definitely.' He grins, playfully. 'I *am* a catch in other ways, after all. Like . . .' He leans in towards me, a suggestion on his lips.

'Mum?' Evie's voice rings through the cottage.

Dan pulls a face, and leans back. I look up. 'Yeah?'

'Where's my netball kit?'

He stands. 'Get that phone ordered. I've got this one.'

As he leaves, I reopen my laptop and look again at the picture of Hawkwood House. The pieces seem to shift with each viewing, like one of those Magic Eye pictures I could never quite make out.

The photo just isn't enough. I need to stand there, to touch it; to breathe it in.

I send one email, then another. When Dan and Evie come

downstairs, I'm in the final phase of ordering my replacement phone.

'Have a good day at work,' Dan says, a kiss planted – as usual – on my head.

'Thanks. You too,' I say in reply.

It's been just a day since the first episode aired.

And already, I'm spinning a lie.

12

I look up at the iron gates, their black paint now furred with rust. My car purrs, behind, as I stand frozen, palms curled around the bars. It's the only sound; even the birds have gone quiet.

I've wanted this for years: to step into the grounds of Hawkwood House and walk there, taking it in. Making it mine. But now, on the verge of doing so, my chest feels tight, the urge to turn and drive away hot in my blood.

I know what this is, of course. It's guilt. For calling in sick – not calling, in fact, but firing off a single-line email. I blamed my missing phone, but the truth was, I didn't want to hear Sarah's voice; didn't want to speak to anyone at all.

I've worked so hard – since Graham died, and Sarah took me on – to be the picture of professionalism. And for the most part, I've succeeded. I've gone about my job with jaw-clenching determination, like a woman making up for something: focused, punctual, reliable.

It was *my* idea to change our rotas to include the full team at weekends, rather than a reduced staff, so our patients would get something close to round-the-clock care. And yet, here I am, playing hooky on a Saturday; lying to everyone close to me, again.

I lock the car. I push the gates open, just a little, and walk the avenue of tangled trees that leads towards the house.

I've seen it from a distance, so many times – but up close, there's a magic to it. I feel like a child falling into a picture book.

The house itself is further away than I'd imagined, set what must be a full half-mile from the main gates. Still, with every step, I see new details: the creamy facade blackening, riddled with ivy, the cracked windows refracting the light. Over the door, an inscription in Latin, chiselled into the stone: *vincit qui se vincit*. 'She conquers who conquers herself'. The history of it seems fresh in the air, the house's ghosts passing through and around me, almost alive.

I think of the women who've stood here before, every one of them called insane. I think of my grandmother; I wonder whether she stood where I am now. I imagine women in white; patients gathered in a cluster under the knotted elm, one reading aloud from a book. A visiting boy runs headlong over the grass, mown in smooth and sweeping lines. Another girl, her dress spilling around her as she lies, sticks out a curious tongue, tasting the honey on the air.

I blink, and they all disappear. I continue my walk alone.

'Hello?' I call into the empty hallway, through the half-open door. I nudge it open and step inside. 'Darcy? It's Hannah.'

Silence.

A swirl of leaves scrapes across the floor, caught in the breeze. The wet, green odour of mould is inescapable. I hold my breath as I look around, my eyes slowly adjusting to the gloom.

It's almost too much to take in at once: the destruction, the wildness that's spread over everything. The wallpaper is black and green with decay, peeling in strips that slump on the floor; there's graffiti everywhere, bright, chalky colours that seem to glow in the dark. And those chequered tiles, cracked and shattered.

It feels like a dead place. 'Darcy?' I call again. But she can't be here. Because I've never felt more alone.

There's a faint knocking sound in the distance, like a door brushing, soft, against the wind. Not a knocking, in fact, but a tapping. I see my husband's blue-white hand, hanging limp by the side of the bed.

I shake the memory off.

A tile gives way beneath my feet, and I clutch hold of a railing, furry with moss. As I steady myself, I follow it up: a vast, wooden staircase, hugging the sides of the hall. There are animals carved into the wood, bared teeth dripping with entrails, luscious as fruit: corroded, but still unmistakably there.

'*Gorgeous*, isn't it?'

I spin around. My heart thuds violently in my chest.

'That's one word for it,' I say at last, restraining a laugh at the sight of her, so out of place here, among the dirt and the mess. The soft black of her suit is too tailored, the knees and cuffs smeared with dust, a powdery grey that clings in patches to her elbows, her hair.

'I'm *so* glad you came,' she says, beaming. 'And that you haven't run away screaming at the sight of me. I feel like an extra from a horror movie.'

'I wasn't going to say anything, but . . .'

71

'I thought I'd try and dress the part of the lady of the house . . .' She gestures to her suit and laughs, the sudden bark of it sparking a flutter of wings overhead. I look up to see what I suppose must once have been the circular cage of a glass dome, boarded over with rotting wood. Between the gaps, birds peer down, eyeing us with frank curiosity.

Darcy's hand flits to her chest. 'This is why I'm such a mess. Because I keep getting spooked by the resident wildlife. I almost fell headfirst down the stairs when I heard something scuttling around behind me. I still don't know what it was.' She seems to catch herself, mid-thought. '*Not* that I'm trying to scare you off. Please don't leave now I've said that.'

'Never,' I say, with more enthusiasm than I mean. I'd only been here for five minutes before I started imagining things. I fix on a smile. 'I've wanted to look around this place for years. It's . . . It's stunning.'

She laughs, seeing straight through the lie. 'Come on. Let me walk you around. Show you what we've got planned.'

Broken glass, dead leaves, and fallen plaster crackle underfoot as we walk. Darcy talks, brightly, about her plans, though I zone out. I can't help it – I'm lost in my own vision of the house as it used to be, the wallpaper pulled back to reveal the bright, candied colours beneath; the fireplaces and window-seats restored, their marble and gold designs glowing once again; the thick, full curtains, no longer black with rot, but gleaming elegantly in the morning light. For a moment, I almost manage to forget all that's happening in the world beyond – all the worry and horror and fear. I let myself disappear into it; let the house pull me further inside.

I think of the 1950s brochure I'd found, mixed in with other scraps of local history in the nearby library. *The principle at Hawkwood House is to provide comfortable and happy surroundings for both voluntary and committed patients, with the aim of allowing them to rest and recover in a state of peace and tranquility*. I compare the ruins all around me with the photographs I've seen, in black and white; the stories I've imagined of the house, my mind reaching to fill the gaps.

I feel Darcy's eyes on me. I've been quiet for too long, lost in thought.

'Wow,' I say, stiffly. Apparently it's the right response.

She goes on. 'And it's got fifty-five individual rooms, across three different wings. I'm thinking short-term, long-term, and young people.'

We pass an open door. Something moves inside, among the brush, the broken glass. 'Mixed?'

'Female only. I want to keep as much of it as possible in line with the history of the place – or at least, the intentions behind it.'

I feel another pull of envy as she scans my face.

Still, I say nothing. I smile, and we go on.

And, as we walk, it occurs to me that it might in fact be more of a kindness to say nothing. To *not* encourage her.

Because this renovation seems like a doomed project. The further we go into the house, the more overwhelming the destruction seems. It's devastating: the old music room, its roof entirely fallen through, a tree spiralling up through the absent floors above. A corridor of patient rooms, lit in shafts through the joists, holding up nothing at all, the rooms spilling into each other through crumbling walls. An enormous bathroom, floor, walls, and ceiling all covered with moss, a single cracked bathtub standing, bow-legged, in the centre.

It's impossible, without enormous investments of time and money, and even then, I wonder if it isn't only a dream. A lovely fantasy.

You're just jealous, Graham whispers.

It's a memory, I'm sure of it.

But something about it feels real. Like he's beside me, his lips pressed to my ear.

I shiver, involuntarily, and pretend to bat a spiderweb from my hair.

'I think we can do it,' Darcy says. Her eyes are unfixed, looking past me. For a moment, I feel as though she's responding to someone else. To him. 'Obviously it's going to take a huge amount of work – don't think I don't know that. But still . . . I think it's possible.'

She scans my face again, and I smile. 'It's really something.' It's a platitude, and she knows it. The brightness fades a little from her eyes.

'Let me show you the *pièce de résistance*. I've been saving it for last, anyway. And if you're not convinced then, I'll let you go home.' I follow, in silence. I'm a little surprised by the admission, though she's right: I'm not convinced. Still, I'm not used to being caught in a lie – even one of omission.

Better get used to it, Graham says.

This time, I know it's real. I feel the cold rush of breath on my cheek.

Darcy looks at me, warily. 'Are you OK?'

'I'm fine,' I say, a little too quickly. My throat clenches tight around the words. 'Just . . . caught a draught.'

'Probably a ghost passing through. My mum used to say that. Not that it was much of a comfort to a five-year-old.'

I laugh, brushing the gooseflesh from my arms. *It's freezing in here*, I realize. *It's just a draught. Just the overreaction of an overexcited mind.*

She pushes a door, a rush of dust sweeping out in front. After the darkness of the bathroom, the light inside seems, for a moment, blinding. As my eyes adjust, I take it in. Enormous stained-glass windows, shot through with holes, turning the sunbeams green, and gold, and blue. A shallow empty pool, its tiles turned black with mould, fills the space, the air fat with the stink of damp, of old rot, seeping through.

'It's the sun room,' she says, voice church-hushed. 'It gets light all day long. The sun rises over there, and' – I follow her hand, the sunlight blinking through the broken glass – 'sets here. With the right heating, and the right lights . . . a new pool, obviously, and maybe some treatment rooms in the orangery outside . . . Imagine it. It'll be luxurious. I want it to have all the features of a spa, so when the patients aren't working with their doctors, they can work on themselves. On *healing*.'

'Wow.' I walk around to the edge of the pool, the pattern on the cracked mosaic floor too filthy to make out. 'It's . . . It sounds amazing.' The air is clotted with dust, and heady; I feel a cold slick of sweat spread over my skin, like a wave.

You're just tired, I tell myself, mouth suddenly parched and gasping. *It's fine.* But the words have the ring of a lie, a self-delusion. *He was here. I felt him. I know it.*

'Hannah?' There's a chill in Darcy's voice now. 'What's wrong?'

I take a long, low breath, and close my eyes. 'I'm – I'm sorry. I just . . .' I shake my head and try to blink the shiver of memory away. 'It's fine.'

'You don't *look* fine. Come on.' Arm around my shoulder, she steers me towards an ancient lounger covered in a filthy white sheet. 'Come and have a seat for a minute. You've gone a bit pale.'

'I'm fine, honestly, I—' As I speak, though, a new wave of sickness passes through me. She makes some attempt to sweep the filth from the chair, and I sit, gratefully. I press my eyes to the balls of my hands, my pulse shuddering in my wrists.

She crouches in front of me. 'Take a deep breath. In. Now, out. That's it. You're OK.'

I gather myself, shame creeping in, though I'm still cold, bone-deep, with fear. 'I'm so sorry – I don't know what just happened. I . . .' The words fall away. I close my eyes again.

'Was it . . . I mean, if you don't mind me asking: do you suffer from panic attacks?'

There's a soft professionalism in her tone. I know it well – I've used it myself – but still, it grates. Because she's right. It must've been a panic attack: the racing heart, the dizziness, the horror.

That's all it was, I tell myself. *A panic attack. That's all.*

'I don't, but . . . you're probably right.' I take another steadying breath. 'I'm so sorry. You must think I'm completely mad.'

She opens her mouth, as though about to speak, and pauses. Her bottom teeth are a little yellowed, nicotined. The imperfection comes as a surprise.

'I don't want to sound like some kind of stalker, but . . .' She glances away. 'I read about this *Conviction* thing. I googled you. Last night,' she adds, quickly. 'Just to see if you were working anywhere at the moment. After I'd sent that email, I realized I hadn't taken into account the fact you probably had a job to go to, so . . .'

I stare at her. I don't know what to say.

'I'm probably overstepping the mark, but . . . I think it's disgusting.' A shiver runs through her. She reminds me of a little bird shaking its feathers out after the rain. 'How they can do that to people . . . I really have no idea. It's obscene.'

I smile. I'm grateful for her, for reflecting back the anger that's been lodged inside my chest since the first trailer went live – though I've swallowed it.

It's not fair, I told myself, when it first appeared, feeling the knot of it tighten, clenching like a fist. *You can't be angry about this. You don't have the right.*

She looks at me expectantly, waiting for my response. I think of the things I imagine I'm supposed to say in this situation: that I only want justice done. That I'm fine with it all, so long as they catch my husband's killer. But that's all bullshit, all lies. I wish they'd leave well alone.

'Thank you,' I say, finally. 'You're probably right. It's . . . It's just been a lot. I guess it's getting to me more than I realized.'

'Is there any – I don't know – legal action you can take?' She screws up her face, her nose crinkled, like a child catching a bad smell. 'I suppose it probably counts as "free speech" or what have you.'

I laugh, grimly. 'I suppose it does.'

'Look,' she says, squeezing my knee. Her hand is cold, like Graham's breath – or rather, what I *thought* was Graham's breath. But it wasn't. It couldn't have been. 'For what it's worth – we didn't know each other well, back then. But I *know* you didn't kill your husband. No matter what some sleazy podcast wants to imply. I'm absolutely sure of it.'

How? I think, grimly. *How could you possibly know that?* But I keep this to myself. 'Thank you. That means a lot.'

In the silence that follows, I feel a pinch of guilt. An urge, suddenly, to tell the truth.

I look up at the cracked glass overhead, the sun gleaming through in tinted shafts, and I stand.

'I'm sorry, Darcy,' I say, meeting her eye. 'I haven't been completely honest.' She blanches, and I realize the conclusion she's jumped to. 'No – oh, God, not about . . .' I laugh. 'I mean about Hawkwood House. I don't really know *why* I didn't mention it before, but . . . my grandmother was a patient here. In the fifties.'

The realization spreads, slowly, across her face. 'You wrote that post – on the message board. That was you.'

I pause, trying to read her expression. 'Yeah. I'd . . . I'd forgotten about it, honestly. Until you mentioned it, I'd . . . Well, it sort of blindsided me. Which is why I didn't say anything at the time.'

'Wow.' There's a pause. 'What was her name?'

'Margot.' I feel a chill. There's something uncanny about saying her name out loud. Especially here. I leave her second name unsaid, though it's the same as mine. Darcy seems to intuit it, anyway.

'Wow,' she says, again. 'Well, if I find anything with her name on, I'll absolutely let you know.' She shoots a glance at her phone and winces. 'I'm sorry to boot you out, but the contractor's coming in half an hour – do you mind?'

'Oh – no, of course not,' I say, though the sudden change of pace is disorienting. All through the morning, spent wandering leisurely through the mess, it's felt as though we've had all the time in the world. I reach for my bag, and stand, the words in her email appearing, with lightning clarity, in my mind: *On my own there all day, company v welcome.*

She's throwing me out, I realize, my gut giving an awful lurch. *She doesn't want me here.*

Possessive, Graham says. I can hear the smile on his lips.

'OK, then,' she says, brightly, as we reach the main doors. There's no suggestion of anything wrong in her expression. 'Well, thank you for coming. Really. It's been such a pleasure.'

'Thank you for showing me around. And if there's anything I can help with—'

'Thanks,' she says, coolly.

She closes the door before I turn away. I walk back to the car, eyes fixed on the gravel underfoot. I can feel a storm on the air, the bright, sharp glimmer in everything. And as I pull the car door open, I think I feel him on the icy breeze.

Goodbye, Hannah, his memory says. *Goodnight, sweetheart.*

13

When I pull up at home, hours later, I feel like a child caught in a lie. I climb out of my car, and squeeze past Sarah's, an inch-wide gap between it and the swaying hedge. Through the crack in the curtains, I see candlelight flicker; the two of them leaning in, heads lowered in quiet discussion.

By the time I open the front door, I'm drowned, soaked through by the hammering rain. They stop talking when they hear me come in.

'I didn't know we had plans,' I say, casually.

Sarah laughs. 'Very cool, for someone skiving off work.'

I glance at Dan, his expression a combination of sympathy and concern. I can't stand it. I look away.

'I'm joking,' Sarah adds. 'Jesus. Don't look so panicked. It's fine.'

I drop my bag and peer into the darkness upstairs. 'Where's Evie?'

'Lissa's,' Dan says. 'They've got some kind of . . . project.'

I shoot him a look. I know he knows more than that. He's

fanatical – endearingly so, though I'm not sure either she or I really appreciate it – about helping Evie with her schoolwork. So this shrug is, for Dan, the silent treatment. But if Sarah notices the tension, she chooses to ignore it. 'Ideal circumstances for you and me to watch a shitty movie and get quietly pissed, then. Well – for *me* to get pissed, anyway.'

Dan reaches into the fridge; the light inside stays off. 'There's been a power cut, so there's pizza coming. I'll get out of your way once it's here, so you pair can have a girls' night.'

I know what he's saying. They've planned this together, the two of them.

I don't know what's going on with her, he'll have said.

I'll talk to her, she'll have replied. *Don't worry. She's just like that, sometimes.*

The thought of them, here, comparing notes, makes me itch. It sparks a memory.

Sarah's silhouette in the door of my student bedroom; Graham's voice in the hallway outside. Words I can't quite make out, the two of them whispering. I roll up on my bed and tell him to leave. She squeezes his arm as he goes, and tells him all I need is space.

The doorbell rings. 'Saved by the bell,' the two of them say, in unison.

I say nothing. Just smile, blankly, as the memory fades away.

'So . . .' Sarah curls on the sofa beside me, her bare foot cold on mine. We're in the same positions we'd taken on the half-collapsed sofa in our student house, cosily intertwined. We've formed habits now, playing out the same roles over and over. 'Are you going to tell me why you decided to leave me one doctor short today?'

The wind rattles the windows, a hollow whisper. 'I'm sorry,' I say, meaning it. 'I just . . .' I toy with the idea of telling her everything. About the house; about Darcy; about the fact I heard Graham's voice in a way that seemed more tangible than memory alone.

It'd be a relief, I think, to tell her – to tell anyone, really – the absolute truth. To just start talking, and see where I ended up. After all these years of refusing help – professional help, of the kind on which I've built my career – it might finally be time to reach out. In the end, though, she speaks first. The thought curls back up, and slinks into hiding again.

'I get it, Hannah. Really. I do. All this *Conviction* stuff . . .' She reaches for another slice of pizza, pulling apart a string of cheese between finger and thumb. 'Why didn't you mention it? I only found out because the nurses were gossiping about it.'

'Oh, God.' I feel my cheeks flare, hot. 'Really?'

'No, not really. Of *course* I bloody knew before. I was just waiting for you to bring it up.'

Somehow, this feels worse. 'I'm sorry,' I say, automatically, again.

She waves the apology away, and reaches for the wine. 'I know you don't, but . . .' She refills her glass and hovers the bottle over mine. 'I feel like it'd be rude not to offer, given the circumstances.'

It's been so long since I last had a drink that, these days, I decline almost without thinking. And yet, the thought of it now – the cosy, soothing warmth of it, spreading through my chest – brings an itch of temptation I'd all but forgotten.

I scan her face. 'Is this some sort of trap?'

'Oh, no. *No*, no. You know I don't *like* sharing booze. But you *are* my best friend, so . . . I'm happy to make an exception. If you're desperate.'

I say nothing.

'I'll take silence as assent,' she says, pouring a splash into my empty tumbler. 'No pressure.'

'Thanks.' I look at the half-empty cup. For now, I leave it where it is.

'Hannah,' she says, gently. 'Can I be honest with you? About this whole . . . thing?'

'You always are.'

I wait for her to volley back some cutting remark. But she's silent. My stomach turns over as she peers into her glass, steeling herself.

I know, I imagine her saying. *I know everything. All of it. You evil bitch.*

She draws breath, and looks up. 'It's just . . . Well, even *I* felt kind of traumatized by the stuff on the trailer. I had no *idea* it was like that. I mean . . . I always thought he'd put up a fight, at least. The fact he was just lying in bed, sleeping . . .' She sighs through her teeth. 'I just want you to know I feel like I kind of . . . understand, now. Or understand a little better, at least.'

I try to muster a reply. 'Sarah . . .'

She reaches for a napkin and dabs it to her eyes, now ringed with red. 'I'm really trying not to get all weird on you,' she says. 'Honestly, this is fucking mortifying.'

I offer a smile and reach for her hand. 'It really is. And that's a poor word choice, given the circumstances.'

'Oh, shut it, you soulless . . .' She bats me away. 'This is me trying to have a feeling. To express an *emotion.*'

'Yeah, well . . . I get enough of that at work.'

'When you *go* to work, sure. You've got no excuse, today.'

'Touché.'

A silence settles between us. In over twenty years of friendship, I'm not sure I've ever seen her cry. It's one of the things I like about her – one of the ways in which we've always been so similar.

I'm not sure I can bear it.

I reach for the wine and take a sip. Almost immediately, I feel something loosening inside me. 'I really *am* sorry about that, you know.'

'Forget it. It's fine. I'm used to covering for you, you dippy cow. But . . .' She glances at the doorway behind and lowers her voice. 'Do you mind if I give you some completely unsolicited advice?'

She's going to, whether I say yes or not. I take another sip, and smile.

'You need to be honest with *him*.' She points a finger to the ceiling; I imagine him listening above. 'I'm not about to start analysing the pair of you, but I can't imagine it's easy for him hearing how talented and brilliant your ex-husband was, before he was "cut down in the prime of his life", or what have you. If you start pushing him away, lying to him – even if you *do* just need some time to yourself, which *is* understandable, given the circumstances . . . he's going to struggle with that.'

I know her well enough to catch her meaning.

He is *struggling with that,* she's saying.

Whether he told her that outright, or she simply intuited it, is immaterial. She's right.

'I know. I know. I don't know what I was thinking. I just . . .' I close my eyes. Sip the wine again. 'Something happened today.'

There's a pause before she speaks. 'What?'

It's easier to say it, I realize, without looking at her; without meeting her eye. I reach for a slice of pizza, and stare at it, uselessly. 'I heard his voice. Graham's voice. Like he was there.'

She says nothing for a moment. Only reaches for her wine and takes a slow, thoughtful sip. 'Is there any chance . . .' I feel a sharp slice of fear in my chest. 'God, I feel awful even bringing this up.'

'Go on.'

'It's just . . . well, when you gave me your disclosure file – before. Obviously it had the details around you being signed off, and, God knows, with Darren having written it, I barely took any notice – not of *that* prick. But I'd be being a shitty friend to you, right now, if I didn't ask.'

My mouth is dry; the words are sandpaper in my throat. It occurs to me that he could've written anything in my personnel files. I'd never know. They're transferred from clinic to clinic, on request. 'Ask what?'

'It said something in there about . . . about delusions. But it also said you were seeking treatment, and I know you've got this *thing* about not talking to me about this stuff, so I didn't want to ask – and I figured you must have it all . . . under control. Or maybe it'd never happened in the first place, and Darren was making it up, like the sneaky, sabotaging little shit that he is.'

There's a hopefulness in her voice as she says this. I toy with the idea of telling her that she's right: Darren lied. But the space in which I might have spoken closes, and I say nothing.

She goes on, the effort of hiding her disappointment rippling in her voice. 'It was probably the wrong call, on my part, not to ask, but . . . you'd been through such a lot. I didn't want to make things worse. And I figured – well, I *know* you. Better than anyone else, probably. So, if you ever *did* seem to . . . well, wobble a bit – I'd notice.

'Which is why I kind of *have* to ask you, now, if everything's OK. Up here.' She taps her head with two fingers, gently. It's a sweet, naive gesture. It's all wrong, and yet, I appreciate it.

'That was . . . different,' I say, finally. 'It was . . .' I think about all that I'd have to explain, to make sense of that time. Lucie Wexworth's death, her blood on my hands. The court case. My husband's affair. The weight of it pins me in place; holds the words back inside my throat. 'Really, Sarah. I'm fine. Honestly.'

'Look, Hannah, I'm really not trying to grill you on any of this. I've got your back, either way. Even if you told me you were hallucinating Barney the fucking Dinosaur dressed as a cocktail waitress in the corner over there . . . we'd work it out.'

'What is it with you and giant Muppets at the moment? First Bear in the Big Blue House, now Barney . . . Should I read something into this?'

'Whoa, whoa. Barney the Dinosaur is definitely not a Muppet.'

'Oh, come *on*—'

'No, really. I'm sure of it.' She reaches for her phone and types something in, fingers hovering just above the glass.

'You know that's not my point, right? That this is about the Muppety features, rather than the—'

'Ha! Listen to this. "Executives at PBS thought Barney had appeal because he was *not as neurotic* as Big Bird." Maybe that's why he's springing to mind for me, now. Some kind of weird projection thing . . .' She scrolls a little further, and clicks around for a moment, distracted by something on her phone.

'I'm not under the illusion he's really there,' I say, returning – forcefully – to the point. I need her to believe me, now, when I say this. Even if I don't quite believe it myself. I need her to trust me. To see that I'm still capable, still every inch the doctor she took on. 'Graham, I mean. I just . . . It's just a feeling, that's all.'

She looks at me, squarely. 'Your birthday's December, right?'

'Why?'

'Just checking. Want to make sure I've got plenty of time to dig out my Righteous Brothers records to go with the pottery wheel I'm going to buy you.'

'You are *such* a bitch. I'm trying to grieve, you know.'

I reach for the bottle. As I top up our drinks, she slides a palm over her glass. 'No, no. I won't be able to drive at this rate.' She lays her phone on the coffee table and shuffles forward in her seat.

'You could always stay,' I say, knowing exactly how this sounds. It's childish of me to ask, just so I don't have to be alone with Dan. So I don't have to talk to him, while he looks at me with sympathetic eyes. 'I can make you up a bed.'

'No, no. Nige will kill me. He doesn't cope well in the mornings even *with* me around. If I'm not there, the kids will end up going to the wrong school, dressed in superhero costumes and glued together with jam. Which I know isn't very feminist of me. I'd train him up better, but . . .'

But you love it, I don't say. *I know.*

87

She'd told me about it on another night like this – admitting, then, that she'd known about Evie's birth; had heard about it from a mutual friend, joking about our perfect lives. She'd bought a card. She'd dialled my number, over and over and again – but never made the call.

'I was dying of envy,' she'd said, that night. 'It sounds nuts, but I'd just found out I'd probably never have kids myself. And so hearing about yours – *especially* yours, when I was always your bloody third wheel with Graham . . . I'm really sorry. I just couldn't do it.'

The guilt I'd felt then – a sharp skewer of it, straight through me – returns, with full force.

It was my fault we hadn't been speaking then. I'd left her behind, too absorbed in my marriage. My own problems. That she'd need *me* to call *her* hadn't even crossed my mind.

'Hannah,' she says, now. 'I love you to death. You know that, don't you?' It's bracing, this level of outright affection from Sarah. I don't quite know what to do with it. 'Jesus, don't look at me like that. I'm trying to be nice.'

'Sorry. You just . . . You took me by surprise there. With that . . . whatever that was.'

'I just . . . I need you to know you can always talk to me. About anything.'

I don't quite know what to say. I try to break the mood with a joke. 'Even the fact I stabbed my husband in the throat with a kitchen knife?'

I expect her to laugh. But she doesn't. For a moment, there's a silence between us. I feel swallowed up by it. Eaten alive.

'I'm joking,' I say, finally. 'Obviously.'

She laughs. It's barely convincing. 'Duh. Of course.' She pinches her forehead between finger and thumb. 'I'm knackered.

Sorry. Not quite keeping up. I'd better head out.' She grabs her phone and glances at something. Pockets it, and smiles.

'You *know* I was joking, there – right?'

'Jesus, Hannah. As if you even have to ask.'

I'm not sure I believe her. But I can't ask again.

She pulls her coat over her shoulders, and leans down to kiss me on the head. 'I'll see you Monday, right?'

'Yeah. Sorry again about today.'

She bats the apology away. 'Just go apologize to *him*,' she says, the last two words mouthed, finger pointed at the ceiling. 'OK?'

As the front door closes, I drag myself off the sofa. I realize, as I stand, that I'm drunk. Only a little, mind: just enough for the world around me to seem vaguely liquid, my movements slowed, slicing the air.

I remember this feeling, all too well.

Not again, I tell myself. *Never again.*

The dregs of the bottle cling, like blood, to the porcelain sink as I pour them away, and go to bed.

I press the steaming flannel to my skin, the sting electric. Two black smears on the damp white cloth; the smudge of foundation in a flesh tone not quite mine. I look into the mirror, and I don't see myself at all.

I see the woman under the greenish blinking light, in a dank hotel. I'm the wife who, hours before, watched a swirl of blood – real blood, this time – wind down her own bathroom drain.

A shadow moves in the darkness behind, and I wonder, briefly, if it's him. But it's only Dan. He steps into the bathroom, eyes fixed on mine in the mirror. We flicker in the light of the ancient candle I've placed on the counter's edge. The tap hisses; the flannel drips a steady beat. Tap. Tap. Tap.

'Where'd you go today?'

I rinse my face again. He stands, waiting for an answer.

An answer, that is, to a question he has every right to ask.

But I can't help it. Right now, I'm the woman I was before. I don't want him to know.

'I just needed some space,' I say. 'You know.' A shrug; a smile. I wring the flannel, tight.

I reach for the toothbrush, and see the doubt in his eyes as he watches, reflected behind. The conversation we should've had plays out in front of me. He should've made some kind of joke – about my disappearing, again. About pizza for dinner, again. About how Sarah no doubt analysed him, in the way I know he can't stand, before I finally arrived: his saviour.

I should've laughed. A little stiffly, perhaps, but still – enough to break the ice between us. He should've looked me in the eye, the way he does, sometimes, when he knows I'm telling a lie.

And I should've pulled him into me, my arms resting on his shoulders as he lifted me on to the countertop, and made it all OK.

The fog of the past that's hung over me since I left Hawkwood House dissipates. I slip back into myself, the real me, and I realize: *I want that. I want him.* I spit a foamy glut of toothpaste into the sink and watch it disappear.

'I'm sorry.' I meet his eyes through the mirror. 'Really, I am. I shouldn't have lied to you. I just . . .'

I see something in him uncoiling. I know he hates confrontation; he'll do anything to avoid it. His relief is visible in the way his lip falls slightly, his jaw no longer clenched.

'I get it,' he says. 'I know.'

'Do you?'

'I mean, as much as I can.' He shoulders the doorframe, heavily. 'For what it's worth, though, I'd understand it even better, if you'd let me.'

Trust me, I think. *You wouldn't.*

I turn around and lean against the sink. It's an invitation. A distraction. He smiles, and takes it. He turns the shower on with a gentle nudge of the tap. I love the sour end-of-day tang that lingers in his sweat; the sound of his stubble scratching the back of my neck. It's so familiar, such a comfort, that for a moment we are all there is. I want to drown in him. I let myself slacken; let his fingers pluck apart buttons and creep underneath.

'I love you,' he whispers, with a tenderness that melts me.

I don't get my chance to reply.

The crack echoes, and the darkness swallows us whole.

My skin turns to gooseflesh. I am frozen, all the way through.

'What the hell?' Dan peels away from me and crouches in the darkness. 'The candle . . . It fell.' He hisses, his fingertips caught in the wax. 'It must've been a draught.'

'I'm sorry,' I say, automatically.

Dan thinks I'm talking to him.

'It's fine,' he says. 'No harm done.'

But he doesn't see it. Either because he can't, or because he's choosing not to: he's missing the point. Neither of us were close enough to the candle to touch it. It was heavy, the size of a saucer, three wicks in a thick pool of wax. And no draught, even in our ancient cottage, would be enough to make something that heavy move.

Dan steps outside to fetch something to clear the mess. As

my eyes begin to adjust to the darkness, I reach for my thrown-off shirt. I misstep, and a shard of glass claws into the arch of my foot, an agony that comes in nauseating waves. I gasp and cling to the sink, bent double with pain.

When I catch my breath, I look in the mirror again. And I recognize, all too well, the face of the woman staring back.

EPISODE TWO

14

London, 2002

My feet are bare: ice cold on the black-and-white tiles.

Graham left me in bed this morning, his palm on the curve of my belly. 'Make sure you rest up,' he said. 'Watch TV, if you have to do something. If not . . . just sleep. OK?' He kissed me, his lips still tasting of toothpaste. 'I'll be back as soon as I can,' he told me, and left. And I tried. For an hour, I lay there, staring up at the ceiling, trying to sleep.

But between the heartburn, the insatiable thumps and kicks, the sense – I swear – of my baby curling her tiny thumbs around my ribs, I couldn't do it. I couldn't lie still. So I sat up. I threw on a dressing gown that smelled of him. I made a vain attempt at pulling on socks. After a monumental struggle, I gave up.

Now, I curl my toes around the edge of the stool. I warm my palms on a steaming mug, and stare at it: the laptop. Our laptop.

I've been thinking about my mother a lot lately. Which I guess makes sense.

It's hard not to miss her, going through this alone – not that she'd have been much help. Half the reason I'm the way I am now is thanks to the ambition she had for me: a relentless perfectionism that meant, whatever I did, it wasn't enough.

I slide the laptop across the counter. I open it up and log in. I open a browser window, and look at nothing in particular.

'Don't end up a single mum,' she used to say. 'Trust me. You're a good girl, and this is still the hardest thing I've ever done.' She'd say it with a smile, but I knew, even as a child, that she meant it.

'Don't end up like I did, or I'll come back and haunt you,' she said, another time, just before she died. Her voice was barely above a whisper, but the look in her eyes possessed the same force it always had. 'I'll kill you if you don't end up happy. Not after all I've sacrificed. No way.'

If she'd been around, now, she'd have been a nightmare: my whole pregnancy, rife with issues, would've been a source of constant panic. It would've been my fault, somehow. As if I'd chosen to do it on purpose. To act up.

Still, there's something about carrying my own little girl that makes me miss her – more than I have in years. I want to see her face. To hear her voice. More than anything, I just want to ask her what to do. I type her name into the search bar. *Evelyn McLelland*, Google says. *About 139,000 results.*

I scroll past the obituaries of women I don't know, who aren't her. The first page, the second and third, all bring up nothing.

Not that I really expected them to. She certainly wasn't ever online herself – she died long before that would've been a possibility – and she never really mentioned any family who might've posted an obituary online. It was only Graham and I, and a few of her work colleagues, at her funeral – not least because I hadn't known whom she'd want me to invite.

The only time she'd mentioned anyone at all, in fact, was right at the very end, delirious and glass-eyed on pain medication, her teeth spackled with blood. She looked at me, that day, and told me I was 'just like her'.

'Who?' I'd asked, trying to ground her, to bring her back to the moment.

'My mother,' she'd replied, before choking again.

It had been the first time she'd ever spoken about her to me. It would also be the last.

I continue to scroll. I find nothing. Until page fifteen.

I don't suppose I'd have clicked it, if it weren't for a half-memory, a thing I might have imagined. She'd said, once, that she'd grown up in the Peak District. Or maybe it was the Lake District. I can't quite be sure. *Archive Clipping: Peaks Gazette*, the title reads. *15 July 1953*. I click.

Black Widow pleads diminished responsibility at trial for murder of husband, daughter; attempted murder of youngest child.

My baby kicks in my stomach, like a warning. I steady myself on the barstool and read on.

Margot McLelland appeared at Derbyshire Crown Court on Tuesday, dressed entirely in black, charged with two counts of first-degree murder and one of attempted murder. Mrs McLelland was silent throughout the hearing, her solicitor claiming that the accused had no recollection of the events which led her to attempt to murder her family, who – according to neighbours – appeared to be as happy as any other.

A ripple of nausea spreads through me. I sip my still-too-hot tea, attempting to push it back down.

Police claim that Mrs McLelland waited for her husband and daughters to fall asleep, before rising from her bed and slipping into the family kitchen. There, she opened the oven and turned on the gas, before placing towels and clothes under all windows and doors.

McLelland then left through the family's front door, using her coat to block the air from escaping under the door behind her. She sat on a park bench close to the family's home for what is believed to be several hours, seemingly watching for signs of movement inside the house.

Her husband, Mr Alan McLelland – a bank manager, well respected by his colleagues and peers – and her eldest daughter, Samantha, were found in their beds, seemingly having passed away peacefully as they slept. The couple's youngest daughter, Evelyn McLelland, survived only after neighbours broke into the house, finding the child, aged five, unconscious, but pressed up against a window. Police believe the girl had been attempting to get her mother's attention, having seen her in the street outside, though it seems Mrs McLelland chose to ignore her daughter's increasingly desperate cries for help.

I think of my mother, the oxygen mask covering her face. I hear her, telling the doctors she'd been treated for carbon monoxide poisoning, years before – the result of a faulty boiler in her childhood home.

It was, they said, why she suffered such dramatic mood swings; why words were always on the tip of her tongue. And it was, they said, the root of the lung disease that killed her, at thirty-nine.

My daughter kicks again. Grief washes over me in a way it hasn't in years. *It wasn't an accident,* I realize. *My mum was murdered. A slow, agonizing death – caused by her own mother.*

I rub my belly, trying to calm my own kicking child.

In the wake of her plea, the article goes on, *Mrs McLelland was sent to the Hawkwood House psychiatric facility for further assessment and monitoring. The trial is expected to continue later this year.*

The kick in my stomach becomes an ache. I close my eyes and try to catch my breath. I think of my mother's feverish words, spilling out of her, at the end: 'My mother. You're just like her.'

The next few hours pass in a kind of mania. I bounce from one search to another, without any logic or plan – only a raw and gnawing need to know what happened, and why. But I find nothing. No more newspaper clippings; no more notes from the trial. Nothing at all.

Eventually, I begin searching for the institution itself: Hawkwood House. I've never heard of it, though that's hardly surprising – most of the old asylums disappeared in the eighties, when 'care in the community' was introduced. Still, I remember poring through the archives of one, years earlier, after they'd been handed over to my university in the name of research. I wonder whether Hawkwood's have survived in the same way.

I find a few photos of the house on Google; another click leads me to a land registry listing, which describes it as *an early private psychiatric hospital, opened in 1792,* with a few details about the history of the building – but not much else.

Finally, I land on a local history forum. I scroll up and down for a while, uselessly. And then, I sign up. I type and retype my post, a knot of foreboding in my throat. Something tells me I shouldn't. That I should leave it be. But I can't.

I'm trying to find out more about an asylum known as Hawkwood House, I write. *My grandmother was a patient there, and I'm curious about the kind of treatments provided. Can anyone shed any light on what happened to their archives after they closed?*

I think of my ideal reader: the caretaker and guardian of Hawkwood's past. I add in a line – manipulatively, I know – designed to make them trust me. To make them *want* to let me in. *I'm told the centre was fantastic. It had really good intentions behind it – very modern, above and beyond anywhere else operating at the time.*

I stare at the words. I reread them, three times, and wonder if I ought to tell the truth. *My grandmother was sent there after she murdered her family. I need to know why she did it, so I can make sure I never do the same.* My imaginary reader grimaces, and clicks away; I think better of it. I click post. An error message flashes back. *Your post will not appear on this board until you have activated your account. Please click the link in the verification email sent to the account with which you registered.*

'Shit,' I mutter, aloud.

I open another window. Type in the address of my email provider. The screen loads, and I stare at it, blankly. I don't recognize any of these messages.

Subject: Re: Re: Re: Tomorrow . . . x
Subject: Thinking about you
Subject: Always

I click the first. It loads, agonizingly slowly. Or so it feels. Maybe it's simply that time slows around me to cushion the blow.

I can't wait to see you. I can't stop thinking about what I'm going to do to you, when I get you to myself.

The sender's email is one I don't recognize. A throwaway account, I suppose, a random pattern of numbers.

I glance at the icon in the corner. My husband's face smiles, brightly, back.

I am logged into his account.

Tell her you have a meeting, and then come see me. I hear the words he'd said, in bed, last night. 'I have a meeting tomorrow. I'll be back by lunchtime, but . . . I can't get out of it.'

'It's your day off,' I'd said, all too aware of the scratch of neediness in my voice. 'I thought we could spend it in bed. Together.' He'd wrapped his arms around me and squeezed me tight.

'Don't be like that, sweetheart. You know if I could get out of it, I would.'

I want you to teach me a lesson. Because I've been a very, very bad girl.

A fissure crack in my heart splits open, and tears in two. My baby – *his* baby – shivers, once, and stops.

I feel a dampness spreading, a warmth beneath me; I hear a steady tapping on the tile. I look down at the blood. There's so much of it, it seems impossible that it could've come from me.

But it has. The stain spreads through my robe and slips hot between my legs. Where she'd been kicking, now, an awful, eerie stillness.

I knock the mug from the counter as I try to stand, and as it shatters, hear the hiss of torn skin on the sole of my foot. I slip on the already blood-slicked floor, and my throat aches with the force of my scream.

Hours later, I wake in a hospital bed, split in two. I turn my head, slowly, the room chasing a little behind. My husband has his back to me, shoulder blades like clipped wings through his shirt. He hasn't noticed I'm awake.

Still, I suppose he feels me looking. He turns, a bundle of blankets in his arms; a tiny pink fist reaching for his collar. 'Sweetheart,' he says, a crack in his voice. 'You're OK. You're both OK.'

My mouth is too dry, my tongue too thick to speak.

'She's beautiful,' he says. 'She's perfect.' *Give her to me,* I want to say. *Give her to me, right now.*

He's three feet away, and he doesn't move. 'We could've lost her,' he says. 'What were you doing? I told you to stay in bed.'

She's mine, I want to say, but I can't.

'You were supposed to be resting. For her, as much as you.'

Give her to me, I plead with him, voicelessly. I know he sees it. He steps back, and sits in the armchair, shoulders slumped with exhaustion.

'I thought I was going to lose you both. I . . .' He leans into the bundle in his arms, and presses his lips to my baby's head. I try to speak. What emerges is an awful croak.

He looks at me. At the water on the table beside me, just out of reach. Hate winds through me, lighting up my veins. But I keep this to myself.

'It was an accident,' I say, in a voice that's not my own. 'I'm sorry.'

15

Derbyshire, 2018

The cursor blinks, and I scan the words again.

Thanks for showing me round last week – great to hear your plans for HH. If you need anything else, I now have a working phone – number in signature below. Call me any time.

I've rewritten it what feels like hundreds of times in the days since, trying to find the right balance. Between friendly and professional. Between envy and curiosity. Outside the staff-room door, I hear the lilting patter of gossip. I wonder if it's about me.

I take a breath, and press send. I lean back in my chair and try to ignore the fear gnawing at my bones like a dog.

Countdown to Episode Two, Conviction tweeted earlier. *Get your popcorn ready. It's on.*

When my phone vibrates, I flinch. I glance down at the screen. It's a number I don't know. My stomach flips as I answer.

'Too soon?' Darcy's voice echoes, bell-like. I can hear her heels clacking on Hawkwood's hallway floors. Something about it soothes me.

'That was *very* fast.'

'Sorry. I just . . . I've been drafting an apology for days, but I haven't quite managed to send it. I thought if I didn't call you right away, I'd end up doing the same thing again. I felt like you thought maybe I was trying to get rid of you, last time . . .' She trails off. 'Anyway, I'm *so* sorry. It wasn't even worth it. The contractors were a whole two hours late, if you can believe that.'

'Oh dear,' I say, stiffly. I'm not sure I *do* believe it. I think she and I are more alike than she realizes. Or perhaps she does – realize it, I mean – and this is a way of drawing me in. 'Friends close, enemies closer,' as the saying goes. 'Well, don't worry. I didn't think anything of it. How's it all going?'

'Terribly. *Obviously* it's all going to be much more difficult and expensive than I'd planned. I'm totally out of my depth. Which is why I plan to take *complete* advantage of your offer of help.'

I laugh. 'Oh, really?' I shiver, feeling myself watched, and look up. Sarah storms in, a bad mood clouding her face. I'm suddenly protective of Darcy, of my attachment to the house – a thing I know Sarah will discourage me from pursuing, the moment I explain. Or worse, she'll wade in and offer to help herself.

She's better placed to do so, after all, knowing far more about managing a unit than I do. She's the better woman for the job. She always has been. Darcy seems to catch the pause. 'I mean – only if you don't mind, that is. I wouldn't want to—'

'It's fine. I'd be happy to.'

Sarah flops down on the sofa opposite. *Wrap it up,* she mouths, twirling her fingers around in the air.

'Oh, I'm *so* grateful. Do you think you could come back? One day this week, maybe, or—'

'Great,' I say, finally, cutting her off mid-sentence. 'I'm at work, so . . . Text me when's good, and I'll let you know.'

'You're amazing. Thank—'

'Looking forward to it. Mmm-hmm. OK then. Bye.'

I click the screen to black, and turn my attention to Sarah, who's sliding ancient magazines around the coffee table. 'What?'

'Hmm?'

'What's so important that it's brought you down here to slum it with the rest of us? I know it's not the coffee, or the reading material.'

'Oh, nothing – I just wanted to see how you were doing. But I've got five minutes, tops – so if you're going mental, tell me quick.'

'I don't even know where to begin explaining why that's inappropriate.'

'Then don't. Who was that?'

'A friend of Dan's.' I'm surprised how easily the lie slips out. 'An aspiring novelist, apparently. She wants to "pick my brains" on what we do.'

She examines a hangnail, and tugs at it with her teeth. 'Do you really think that's wise?'

'What do you mean?'

'I mean, given the circumstances, with all this attention on you, from. . . Do you think it's a good idea to let a stranger – *anyone*, really – get too close right now?'

I laugh, though I know she has a point. 'What are you saying – that she's some kind of plant?'

'Jesus, no. You're not that interesting. I'm just saying . . . there are people looking to buy stories about you, just to trade on *Conviction*'s popularity. You don't want—'

'Wait – wait. Has someone approached you about that?'

'Come *on*, Hannah. You can't be surprised, surely. You're married-not-married to a journalist, for God's sake.'

'What do you mean?'

She sighs and goes on, as though explaining a complex concept to a child. 'It's the bloody circle of life. Something dramatic happens on the internet, where people can access it for free. The media have to make money somehow, so they wade in and exploit every other ludicrous angle to sell papers, based on people's interest in the original, freely available thing. The people creating the free stuff benefit from the increased attention, so they make more. And so on, forever.'

She stops, seeming to consider, for a split second, whether to go on. 'So, yes, I've been approached about giving "my perspective on the Graham Catton case". I've been offered a lot of money to do it. But I'm your best friend, and even if I wasn't, I'm your boss. I think HR would have a fucking *fit* if I started leaking employee files, don't you?'

I think of our conversation, days earlier: the 'delusions' in my file, among other horrors: things that would, without a doubt, go against me in the court of public opinion. In criminal court, too, I suppose.

I wonder if she's trying to tell me something, in telling me this: if it's a reminder of the secrets she's keeping. Of how good she is – has always been – to me. Something in me prickles, sensing the undercurrent: the threat.

But then I remember Graham. 'You're being paranoid,' he'd told me, so many times. 'There's nothing to worry about. It's all in your head.'

Sarah's eyes flit to the clock. 'Fuck. Fucking board meeting. Got to go.' She stands, wiping invisible dust from her skirt with both hands. 'Are you ready for tonight?'

'Nope.' I stand, too, though my next meeting isn't for another twenty minutes. But I need to step outside. I'm too hot; the air around me seems to have turned thick, arid. 'It's happening, though, isn't it? I don't have much choice either way.'

'And you're listening to it with Dan?'

'Yeah. It feels . . . sensible. Like if we listen to it together, I can . . . I don't know. Reassure him, I suppose. Correct whatever it is they're going to say about me. Or whoever.'

'That makes sense. Look – if you want me to . . . come over, afterwards, or whatever, you know to give me a call, don't you?'

'Yeah. Thanks.'

At the door, she turns. 'And remember what I said, about these . . . friends of friends. Just be careful, won't you?'

She doesn't wait for an answer. My phone buzzes again in my hand: Tomorrow?

I stare at it for a moment. And then, I reply.

No problem. See you there.

I watch the smokers outside the hospital doors. For the first time in years, I feel the itch of it: the old craving. A habit I'd given up as a teenager, not long after my mum's first hospitalization. I haven't touched one, since. The air outside is bracing, compared with the stuffy heat inside, the dust from powdered shakes and ancient radiators adding to the effect. I walk around the unit, slowly, letting the fresh air fill my lungs.

I glance at my phone to check the time. Ten minutes until my next appointment. I sit on an empty bench and open a browser window. *Hawkwood House,* I type, slowly, into the search bar. *What happened to archives.*

I recognize my post – the top result – instantly. I'd clicked the verification link, weeks after I returned home with Evie. I was sleep-deprived, and exhausted, and I couldn't quite remember what it had been for. It was just an automatic click. As the window slid into view, Evie began snuffling, growing to a scream. I'd closed the window, and forgotten all about it.

I click. There's one reply. Last updated: 12 April 2008. @ hmcll, have you read this? Might help with your search. My pulse rises a little in anticipation. I tap the link with my thumb. Nothing. Tap it again. The screen turns white and reloads. 404 error. Page could not be found. I squeeze the phone tight in my palm. I stand and return to the unit.

'Tell me about this blog of yours.'

Amy's eyes widen, the whites like half-moons. She pulls her sweatshirt around her, and says nothing.

'I know you've been asking the nurses to give you the iPad. And I think it's only fair that you understand why they're going to continue to say no.'

I'm playing a part today. Sometimes, it's necessary to be more authoritative with these girls, though it's never come naturally to me. It's a professional flaw of mine. Deep down, whether it's good for my patients or not, I want to be liked.

But I've made this mistake before. It's a mark on my ledger, a cross against my name. A death, for which I was – beyond all reasonable doubt – responsible.

It's a mistake I don't intend to make again.

'Amy, I'm not trying to pick on you, or be mean, by bringing this up.' She rolls her eyes. I choose to ignore it. 'I just need to understand what's going on. Because it's clearly a destructive behaviour for you. And the impulse still seems to be there to do it.'

She says nothing. Only looks down at her hands, fingers tapping on her knees.

'Do you want to know what I think?' I raise a hand. 'Don't answer that. I know you don't.' These words, and this action, feel hackneyed, old hat. I've delivered this speech more times than I can count, with more patients than I care to remember. 'But I'm going to tell you anyway.'

She sighs. 'Of course you are.'

I let the words linger, a beat longer than polite. I watch the blush creep into her cheeks. She's not a bad girl. This bravado doesn't suit her, and she knows it.

'I think you know, better than anyone else, that recovery is much, much harder than staying where you are. Moving forward takes work and, at the moment, I think you're choosing to take the easy option instead.'

She looks down at her palms.

'You *know* these things you've written, they're . . .' I adjust my tone. I soften. 'I think you write them down to convince yourself they're true. But they're not.'

She looks up, her eyes fierce. 'Well, you'd know all about that.'

'Excuse me?' My tone is icy.

I feel a thud of guilt. *Teenagers,* I remind myself. *Push them, and they push back, three times as hard.*

I'm gentler when I speak. 'Tell me what you mean.'

'I heard the nurses talking about it. About your husband.'

I say nothing. I wait for her to go on.

'They were talking about it in the staff room, but . . . the door was open. I could hear them. We all could.'

'And what did they say?'

'Just that . . .' She looks away, all her ferocity evaporating. 'I don't want to get them into trouble.'

'You won't. But I *do* need to know, Amy. Because if there are other patients thinking I can't help them, because of some rumour going around about me . . .' I know, as I say this, that I'm overstepping my bounds; I know I ought to gloss over it. To address it with the nurses directly.

But I know they won't tell me the truth.

'You'll be doing me a favour by telling me. Because if I need to reassure you – and the rest of the patients, here – then I will. But I can't do that if I don't know what exactly I'm reassuring you about.'

She shrugs. 'It was just that . . . They said they didn't believe you when you said you couldn't remember what happened. Not that they thought you'd *killed* him or anything – they weren't saying that. But they just thought maybe you didn't want to say what had really happened because it was . . . risky. Like maybe you were threatened into keeping quiet, or something.'

I nod. 'OK. That's helpful, Amy. Thank you.'

She says nothing. Only looks at me, curiously.

She's waiting for me to deny it.

To tell her the nurses are wrong. And I could, without – technically – lying. Because the theory the nurses are spreading, according to Amy, at least, is the only one I *know* for a fact isn't true.

'It's probably not appropriate for me to go into too much detail about my personal life. Therapeutically . . . it's inadvisable. But . . .' I try for a carefree laugh. It falls flat. 'Well, it's hardly my private business any more, is it?'

'I guess not.'

'The thing is, I really *don't* remember what happened. It's not all that uncommon. Every mind copes with trauma in a different way. And there's no way to predict how any given person is *going* to react, until they're in that situation. Some people remember the event so clearly that it's almost like watching a movie. A lot of the time, with people like that, they're part *of* the memory, but they're also disconnected from it. It's why people talk about having an "out of body" experience. The memory's there, but – to help them cope with it – their mind puts them at a kind of remove.'

There's a flicker of something in her face here; almost, I think, an identification.

She knows this feeling; knows it well. With this look, I've learned more than she's ever shared with me, in almost a decade of therapy.

'But then, you have other people who, for whatever reason, block the whole thing out. Maybe they'll remember fragments: smells, sounds, certain words, which will trigger a sense of recognition, or . . . something like that. But their minds, to protect them from experiencing the trauma itself, will just . . . go elsewhere. They'll dissociate from it, in theory because committing it to memory is worse than remembering . . . nothing at all.'

She's silent for a moment. 'Well, they're both shitty options.'

I smile, and tap my pen against the page. 'The thing is, if I could remember what happened – I'm speaking only from my *own* experience here, but . . . I think if I could remember, I'd probably want to work through it. Because I *do* believe – from working with other patients, with other traumas – that it's better to process things like this than to let them fester. Which is why I'm always pushing you to talk. I know you hate it, and I know it's an uncomfortable feeling – it's scary, trying to face something you've kept inside for so long. But it's *got* to be better than the alternative.'

I scan her face. I want to see if she believes me. Because I've never felt like more of a hypocrite. I see her uncoiling in the silence. I say nothing. I wait for her to speak.

'OK,' she says, finally. 'Yeah.'

'Yeah?'

'Yeah. OK. Let's talk.'

By the time we finish our session, I'm elated. It's a rare thing, to really get through to a patient. And for it to be Amy – whom I've watched grow up, the living shadow of Lucie, the girl I lost – feels like a personal victory. It almost makes the horror of *Conviction* worthwhile, for giving me an excuse to open up; to break down the therapeutic boundaries between us.

But, of course, it can't last. As soon as I step outside, I scroll through the hundreds of notifications on my phone: the influx of emails from strangers, texts from half-forgotten friends.

Episode Two has gone live.

I throw my phone into my locker and walk away.

The insistent buzz of it gnaws at me each time I pass for the rest of the day.

16

'Are you ready?' Dan's eyes glimmer in the dim light, the phone upturned on the table between us. 'Because really – if you don't want to do this, you don't have to.' And he's right. I don't have to. *I* suggested this. There's no arguing that fact.

But it feels like my hand has been forced. Because it's not a choice. I can't disappear from him, each week, when the episode airs. I have to sit with him, to remind him who I really am. Or at least, who I've made him believe I am.

'No,' I say, with a reassuring smile. 'I want to. I think . . . I think it'll help.'

He picks up his phone. 'Battery's at twenty-four per cent. Should be enough.' He presses play, and I hold my breath. It feels like we're attending a séance, waiting for a ghost.

'A good story,' Graham says, all echoes and reverberations, the ancient tape wavering. 'A good story has a life of its own. It's a thing that lives and breathes. A thing that comes to life in a kind of agreement between the teller and the listener – a shared fantasy that makes even the wildest illusions real. They make us complicit, when we believe in them. They make us say, "Yes, I agree – I accept it. It exists for me."'

The screen turns black, and the music begins.

'Graham Catton loved stories,' Anna Byers says, gently. 'They were his great passion. He built his life around them, because he believed stories had *power*. He knew that they had the power to change things – to bring worlds to life, and to alter the course of history.

'But the team prosecuting his murder knew that, too. They knew how to use that grain of truth to construct a story – one that led the jury to find guilt, where there was only bad luck, and coincidence.'

The music picks up the pace. My pulse rises in response.

'They were led by a Mr Alastair Guildford, QC, a well-respected criminal barrister, with an impressive track record in prosecuting similar cases. Even the people who *liked* him called him "the bulldog", thanks to his approach to questioning witnesses. He'd find their weaknesses, and refuse to let them go. It's a skill that made him exceptionally good at his job.'

I remember him, in hushed conversation with Graham's mother and the rest of his family. He seemed to make a point of never speaking to me. I wondered if that was a tactical decision: if he could only argue his case so long as I didn't disprove it. If the stink of guilt on me – to him, so attuned to it – might throw him off his game.

'I'm going to read his closing statement in its entirety, so that you can get a sense of what the prosecution wanted the jury to believe. Imagine yourself one of them – the twelve strangers listening, at the end of a nine-week-long trial. Put yourself in their shoes as you listen – and try to work out what *you* would believe.'

She takes a breath. The music changes, and she begins to play her part.

'"The fact is, ladies and gentlemen, that for all the obfuscation on the part of the defence, we *know* what happened, on that awful night. The chain of events can be read in the bruises Mrs Catton wore"' – *Doctor,* I thought then, and think again, now, *Dr Catton* – '"in the blood that covered the walls of the Catton home, which soaked into their sheets and made a mockery of the life that they'd made. We can follow the defendant, Mike Philips, in our minds, as he slips into their home through an unlocked door – the sign of a sense of security and peace, if ever there was one."'

In the memory, he turns to me, with a split-second glance. The jury's eyes follow and settle there. There's a woman among them who looks like me. I wonder if this will work in my favour; if our similarity will make her more inclined to take my side, or if she'll recognize in me her own worst impulses – the version of herself she'd prefer not to see.

'"We can see him, surprised to find Mrs Catton in the hallway, having left her husband sleeping as she went to check on her daughter, in bed. He hides, for a moment, in the bathroom. When Mrs Catton turns to face him, he takes his opportunity. He grabs her throat, like this."' I see his hand, stubby fingers forming a half-moon in the air.

The audience – jury, gallery, all of them – are rapt. They can see me, held there. They've seen women like me, like this, a thousand times, on screen; they've read this story in a thousand books. They can picture it without blinking. Without feeling it at all.

'"He grabs her, and slams her into the wall, with incredible – ruthless – violence. She is knocked unconscious, instantly."'

It may not feel real to them. But this – *this* is a moment that feels real to me. The memory of the impact aches in my teeth.

Dan's fingers wind through mine and squeeze. His skin is deathly white, eyes hollow as bruises. I squeeze back. I remember the time Graham fractured a bone in his foot in a weekend rugby match. *His* foot. Not mine. But still, I felt it. I felt myself walk unsteadily on stairs, my ankle aping his roll to the right for weeks. I wonder if Dan feels the same.

As the thought rises, he rubs his free hand on his throat. Guilt threatens to swallow me whole.

'"This is a vicious assault. But, at this point, the defendant could have left. We might then have viewed the attack on Mrs Catton as a mere moment of panic, of lashing out – of self-preservation, even. Philips was, after all, an inexperienced burglar – he didn't know any better.

'"And even if, after the assault, he'd taken what he came for – the couples' mobile phones, jewellery, cash – and then run . . . His might have been a crime we could, as onlookers, have found a way to understand. Poverty, after all, makes people do reckless things. And for the Cattons, losing a few material possessions would, yes, have been a violation – but one that they could no doubt live with.

'"But the facts of the case – the *facts* of what happened, in the Catton home, that night – tell a different story. Because Mike Philips looks down at the unconscious woman lying at his feet. And he feels something in him change. He becomes aware of the power he has, in this situation. And he *likes* it."'

Anna Byers goes on, right away, though I remember it differently. I remember the silence. I remember the pitying eyes of the jury on me, while I tried to look impassively on. I remember the sour, sickly taste in my mouth. The sense that something had been missed; that some part of this story was wrong.

'"He feels the weight of the knife in his hand – the one he'd pulled, minutes earlier, from the kitchen, intending to use it only as a threat. But now, he's excited. He's alive. Now, it feels full of a dark – an evil – potential. He leaves Mrs Catton unconscious on the floor, and walks on.

'"Through the half-open bedroom door, he sees Graham Catton, asleep in his bed. He closes the door behind him. Graham Catton doesn't hear a thing."'

The music swells and recedes. Across the table, Dan shivers, and then smiles, apologetically. I smile, weakly, back.

'"He's a deep sleeper. He doesn't hear his wife being knocked unconscious two rooms away – and he doesn't hear Mike Philips's footsteps on the hardwood floor. It's only at the last moment – while the defendant stands over him, watching him sleep – that he opens his eyes. Just in time to see the face of the man who will take his life.

'"Mike Philips – the man in front of you today – plunges the knife into his throat, once. Decisively. Like a man who knows exactly what he means to do."'

There, for a moment, and gone: Graham's body, in front of my eyes. The wound in the neck, the teeth terribly bared, skin already turning slack and chalky white. Dan clears his throat, nervously – and the memory disappears.

'"*This* is what the evidence shows. *This* is what Mike Philips did to this innocent husband and father. Maybe he waited to watch him die; it certainly wouldn't have taken long. And he wouldn't have been afraid of Catton fighting back. A wound like the one he inflicted would have his victim unconscious in no time at all.

'"What we know is that, after, he walked away, leaving almost no trace of himself behind. He walked by the still-unconscious body of Mrs Catton, and closed the door behind him, disappearing into the night.

'"When he got home, at last, he threw his gloves into the bins outside his flat. He climbed the stairs and went to sleep. And the next morning – after leaving a wife without a husband, and a five-year-old girl without a father – he went out to play football, as though he didn't have a care in the world."'

The music cuts in again. A swell, a grand fermata. I wait. Hold my breath. Dan shakes his head, almost imperceptibly, and looks at me. 'I'm so sorry,' he mouths, aged by it. Stricken.

I want to mouth something back, to offer some comfort. But I can't.

'The thing is, though . . .' Byers draws breath. I feel her lean into the mic. Gone is the soothing voice adopted as she'd played the barrister's part. Now she's all herself; all teeth, cheerfully bared. I wonder if she imagines me among her listeners. I wonder if it's my face she pictures in the darkness beyond.

'For all Guildford's fabulous speeches, and all his admittedly convincing storytelling . . . the evidence *doesn't* really show that. These things we *know happened*. The chain of events *we can follow* – so many of these are founded in what on one hand might be a reasonable assessment of the case as provided by police, but on the other might be described as barely more than a fantasy. A story. Something spun, frankly, out of thin air, by a detective so determined to get a conviction that she would ignore clear gaps in the evidence in front of her, just to put someone away.

'We'll look at what that evidence is, right after this.'

I take the phone, and press stop. The silence engulfs us. I stand and flick on a light. I pretend to see something outside as I pull the curtains closed. The truth is, I don't want to have to meet Dan's eye.

'I'm going to check on Evie,' I say, stiffly. 'I'll just be a sec.' I climb the stairs without looking back.

Three knocks, and silence. I'm so close to her door, I can see the curve of the grain in the wood.

'Evie?' I knock again. 'Can I come in?'

There's no answer. I toy with the idea of opening the door anyway. Of pushing it open, just a crack, and peering inside. But it's something I've never done. I know, from the girls on the unit, that teenagers need privacy. That the overbearing mothers are more damaging than the uninterested ones, in nine cases out of ten.

I press my forehead to the door, and knock, gently, again. 'I'd like to talk to you, Evie. Please.'

I hear the soft hiss of music, quickly hushed. Headphones. I feel his hand on my shoulder, a comfort.

I turn, grateful for it. But there's nobody there.

'Are you OK?' Dan says, when I return.

I slump into my chair. 'She won't talk to me.'

He reaches for my hand. The warmth of it comes as a surprise. 'She'll be fine. Give her some time. She's probably just working it out.'

That's what I'm afraid of, I think. 'Are *you* OK?' It's a deflection. He nods, and swallows. The knot in his throat bobs, a grim reminder. 'I just . . . I feel terrible. I don't know what to say. I wish . . .'

My stomach flips. I imagine the things he might be about to say. *I wish you'd been honest with me. I wish I'd known all this before we met. I wish I wasn't so attached to your daughter. Because, then, it'd be easy to walk away.*

'I'm just really sorry, Hannah. Really.'

I point at the phone, sitting between us like an unexploded bomb. 'Shall we . . . ?'

He opens his mouth to say something, but closes it again.

He picks up the phone and presses play, skipping quickly past the ads.

'. . . a compelling story. And one the jurors would, no doubt, have been grateful for. Because – however they might look on TV, or sound on podcasts like this one – criminal trials are, as a rule, kind of dull. After weeks of waiting around, hearing witnesses grilled on details that seem insignificant, being shuttled back and forth from the jury room, it's easy to lose sight of the narrative – to get lost in the specifics.

'Which is what makes these closing statements so important. It's an opportunity for the legal teams, on both sides, to tie up their arguments in a story that's easy for the jurors to follow and – more importantly – to remember. So, when they're locked in that stuffy little room with eleven other people they're sick of looking at, they're all at least in agreement about the facts of the case.

'Except, the thing is: Guildford's closing statement was a masterclass of smoke and mirrors. "We know this," he said. "The evidence shows this to be true."

'But evidence is open to interpretation. And it's possible to interpret this case's evidence in a totally different way.'

Dan frowns. I know what he's thinking. *You can't 'interpret' proof.*

I can almost hear him scoffing at the words, in another situation; listening to some other case. One that's not quite so close to home.

The music picks up. It feels like a tease and a threat. Like a cat toying with a caged bird.

'Let's start with the eyewitness testimony from someone we'll call Miss B. At trial, she told jurors that she saw Philips running from the scene, at about the time of the attack. She looked across the courtroom, and pointed at him. "Yes," she said. "It was him I saw."'

I remember this moment: the swell of gratitude I felt for this girl who was so clear in her recollection, so confident in what she'd seen. I'd wanted to believe her, when I'd been told there was a witness – and she made it so blissfully easy to do.

'Hard to argue with – right?' Byers goes on. 'But the thing is, Miss B. wasn't always so sure.

'In her initial statement, she says that she saw the man from behind. She says it was dark. She can't describe him with any more specificity than this: a male, of average build, and average height. She says he might've been wearing trainers, from the sound they made on the pavement. But then, she says, it could've been a jogger, out for a late-night run. An insomniac, trying to burn off some energy. She is – put simply – a terrible witness.

'And in any other case, her statement would've been filed away, unlikely to be used, unless it happened to corroborate something else that turned up later on.

'But the officers in this case took a different approach.

'The psychologist Elizabeth Loftus, an expert on witness

121

testimony, says "people believe that memory works like a recording device. You just record the information, then you call it up and play it back when you want to answer questions or identify images. But memory works a little bit more like a Wikipedia page. You can go in there and change it. But so can other people."'

Dan glances at me, looking for confirmation. I nod without meeting his eye.

'There's no way the detectives don't know this. Even if they're not aware of the theory behind it, they're experienced officers. They know *exactly* how to handle a witness.

'Or rather – how *not* to. Let's listen to a clip from their second interview with Miss B., three weeks after her first statement. After they'd decided Mike Philips was their suspect. We'll come back to *how* they decided that, shortly.'

A tape crackles on, an airy hiss.

I recognize the voice as it speaks. I see the female officer who'd questioned me that first night – her skin pale, sallow in the flickering light.

'And you said it was a black sports coat he was wearing – is that right?' She sounds much older, more assured, on the tape.

The girl's voice is barely audible, the hiss rising as Byers increases the volume. 'I . . . Yeah. Yeah.'

'"*You* said",' Byers says, her voice venomous. 'That's what Detective O'Hare tells Miss B. "*You* said it was a black sports coat he was wearing."

'Now, that's quite the statement. Because throughout the whole of their conversation prior, there's actually no mention of a jacket at all. Not once do they talk about what the man Miss B. saw was wearing – until now.

'Miss B. *did*, however, have a conversation with the very *first* officer that she spoke to when she contacted the police to say she thought she'd seen something, the night of the attack. He scribbled down a few notes, which are largely illegible – except for two words.

"Grey hoodie". It's an item of clothing that will never be mentioned again.'

I see Dan give a silent sigh. He seems to know where this is going before I do. He reaches for a pen, and a receipt. I think of all the times I've found these scribbled notes on scraps of paper around the house, the occasional word that, for him, sums up a whole train of thought. The beginnings of a story. A clue.

'That black sports coat, though? That's important to the officers. Because they needed a witness to say they'd seen a man wearing one at the scene, that night, to make their case. But they couldn't find one, no matter how hard they looked. So they brought Miss B. back in. And with that clever trick – that swift little manipulation – they made *her* that witness. It was the last piece of the puzzle. Right after they spoke to Miss B., they went to Mike Philips's home, and made their arrest.'

Dan shuffles in his seat, his eyes fixed on the phone. I think about reaching for his hand. But I can't.

'So – how did they get to Mike? How did they decide they needed their witness – their extremely *unreliable* witness – to ID him, of all people? I mean, this is the Met. They've probably got plenty of other evidence that's watertight. Maybe the CPS were putting the brakes on, and the Met needed one final thing to persuade CPS to let them pull Mike in. Right?'

I feel unsteadied, as though I've missed a step. I am falling, in slow motion.

'According to the charging documents, police first became aware of Mike Philips after they received an "anonymous tip", three days after Graham Catton's murder, from a woman claiming to be a friend of Mike's. She allegedly told them he'd confessed to a murder while drunk – saying that he thought he'd killed two people, but the local news said it was just one. There was only one murder reported on the local news that week that fit the bill: Graham Catton's. But before the call handler could ask for more details, the anonymous caller hung up.'

Dan looks up, and I shrug. This is new to me. No anonymous call was ever mentioned at trial.

'Pretty compelling, you might think,' Anna Byers goes on. 'But we've seen this before, in plenty of other cases. There's no such thing as an anonymous tip without a motive behind it. It's possible that the caller wants justice to be done, sure – but it's also possible that they've got their own reasons for putting someone else in the crosshairs. And in this case – when the Met's own record of this "anonymous call" lists two different times, several hours apart – it's worth bearing in mind that there is a legitimate question around whether it ever happened at all. Because *one* of these officers – PC Rachel O'Hare – was, in fact, already aware of Mike Philips. His was a name she knew well.'

The music picks up, building to something. I hear the threat in Anna Byers's voice as she speaks.

'Nine months *before* his arrest for the murder of Graham Catton, Mike Philips was arrested on a possession charge. A misdemeanour, really – officers found a small bag of cannabis in his pocket during a routine stop-and-search and took him into custody. So far, so normal. But a week later, Mike made a complaint to the Independent Office for Police Conduct – the IOPC – claiming he'd sustained injuries during his arrest, thanks to the officers' use of unnecessary force. He provided photos, taken by his mother when he finally arrived home, showing cuts and bruising to his face and wrists. I've seen these photos, myself, and . . . they're not easy to look at. It's hard to believe they were the result of anything but a brutal assault. And apparently the IOPC agreed. Following an internal investigation by the Met, one of the officers involved – PC David Paulson – was suspended for eight weeks. His suspension began a week before Graham Catton's murder. Ten days before the anonymous call. And two weeks before PC O'Hare – who, coincidentally, had been partnered with Paulson throughout her training, before she moved over to the homicide team – made Mike Philips an official suspect in the case.'

'Now, it's *possible* that this is a coincidence. But for me . . . it raises doubts. Oh – and the fact that Rachel O'Hare's sister was, by this point, PC Dave Paulson's wife? Bingo. We have ourselves one *suspicious*-looking arrest.'

Dan sighs through his teeth. 'Jesus.' There's something in his expression that hurts. And it's only when he speaks again that I realize: it's relief.

'This isn't your fault, Hannah,' he says. 'This wasn't . . . You couldn't have known any of this.'

And he's right. I couldn't. I didn't. In this respect, at least, I have nothing to hide. But it's the first time Dan's suggested he thinks that I might.

There is more, of course. Piece by piece, Anna Byers dismantles the case against Mike Philips; the case I'd found so compelling – so easy to believe – at trial.

The composite sketch drawn from 'Miss B.'s' description, drawn *after* she'd crossed paths with Philips in the police station that day – according to Byers, a slip that happened entirely by design.

The mobile-phone data – cell-tower evidence that supposedly placed Philips in our home at the time of the murder – actually covering almost a square kilometre of London, including the bar he'd told police he was drinking in that night.

Even the gloves, glossy with my husband's blood – even these, Byers shows, weren't as damning as they'd seemed at the trial. Because, as Byers says, 'Mike doesn't dispute that he, at one time, owned these, or similar, gloves. He accepts that there's a strong likelihood – *almost* a guarantee – that they're his.

'The thing is, they're the only thing linking this supposed murderer to the victim. The crime scene – the Catton home – was swept for DNA. Not a *trace* of Mike's was found there. He didn't leave so much as a fingerprint, or a single hair. In terms of this aspect of the forensic evidence, Mike simply *was not there*. It is only the gloves that connect them.

'But Graham Catton's murder took place in September. Philips had no recollection of having seen, or worn, these gloves since the previous winter. Around the time he was arrested for possession of a class C drug and made a complaint against the officer who beat him during his arrest. He doesn't recall seeing them again until they were held up in front of him, when he was questioned by the officer who wanted him locked away.'

I see Dan's mouth open at this. He catches himself before he speaks, but I know – of course – what he was going to say.

No recollection? Isn't that what people say when they don't want to incriminate themselves?

By the time Byers reaches the end of her case, I feel like I'm drowning. I look at Dan, his eyes fixed on his phone. Throughout, he's scoffed and groaned at the appropriate points, in what felt like a kindness – like charity. But he's pale now. He looks exhausted. *Look at me*, I will him, silently.

But he doesn't. There's a change in the music: a steady, persistent beat. A slap of footsteps on pavement.

'Let me tell you an alternative story – one I think makes *much* more sense,' Anna Byers says, at last. 'It's a story about corruption and vengeance. After Mike's complaint, it was only a matter of time. He had no way of knowing it, but a countdown started, the second he contacted the IOPC. They already *had* the evidence – a pair of gloves that belonged to him, and a sports coat that didn't – so for Paulson and O'Hare, it was just a matter of finding the crime. They *knew* Mike wasn't in the Catton house that night. But they also knew he was close enough to the scene for them to use cell-tower evidence to place him there. They *knew* he wasn't wearing a black sports coat – nor, for the record, was he wearing the grey hoodie Miss B. apparently originally mentioned – but they also knew that they could manipulate their witness into saying he was, and then into describing him for the sketch artist by tampering with the line-up procedure. And they knew they wouldn't find *his* DNA at the scene.

'But they didn't need to. They had access to the house, and to Graham Catton's blood. They had Mike's gloves, with his DNA inside them, and they had *a* black sports coat, almost identical to the one Mike was photographed in, at the time of his previous arrest. They had the pieces. All they needed to do was arrange them into the kind of story a jury would believe. And it worked. It's been a decade. Mike's still in prison. And all the while, all the evidence pointing towards an alternative suspect – a much more *convincing* suspect, who we *know* was there the night of Graham Catton's murder – remains undisclosed.

'But not for much longer. That's next time, on *Conviction*.'

17

Dan presses thumbs to temples; shakes his head. 'This is ridiculous. It's a conspiracy theory, dressed up as journalistic integrity. They're making a case, rather than reporting the facts.' He looks at me with a smile that doesn't reach his eyes. 'It's fake news.'

I force a laugh, though it's hollow.

He thumbs my palm, a little harder than usual. As though he's trying to make a point.

'Hannah,' he says, gently. 'If they're right about any of this, all it proves is that the police didn't do their jobs.'

This isn't a statement that makes me feel any better.

'You can't hold yourself responsible for that,' he goes on.

I feel a knot of frustration growing. Over the years, I've come to accept the fact he can't stand silence; it's impossible to sit in a room with him and just be. Now, though, it seems like an assault.

'You were a *victim* in all this.'

I close my eyes. He's expecting a response; I can feel it. 'I'm sorry,' I say, finally.

I'm not entirely sure what, exactly, I'm apologizing for. It doesn't matter. The words do nothing to alleviate the guilt I feel creeping over my skin. Because, deep down, I knew it wasn't him. But I wanted to believe it, so I could move on.

'Hannah,' Dan says. 'Look at me.'

I look up. 'Please, Dan. I need a minute to process all this, so . . . could you please just shut up? Just this one time. *Please.*'

His face crumples, hurt. He lets go of my hand.

'I'm sorry,' I say. 'I didn't mean that. I'm just . . .'

'It's fine,' he says. A lie, of course. It isn't.

'Dan—'

'Don't worry about it.' He stands, his chair groaning as it scrapes across the tiles. 'I need to take a shower, so . . .'

'Oh, come on – don't—'

'Seriously, it's fine.' He plants a kiss on my head. It's a way of avoiding my eye. 'I love you.'

'I love you, too,' I say, as he walks away.

I close my eyes, forehead pressed to the table. Now he's gone, I've never felt more alone.

Well what the fuck do you expect????

I begin typing back, but Sarah is faster.

You can't do that, H. Not to him. Not now. I know it's hard, but you need to contain your inner bitch.

I laugh, softly, in the silence. *When you work out how, can you let me know?*

'What are you laughing at?'

I turn, an old trapped nerve in my neck sparking at the sudden motion. Evie stands behind me, in ancient pyjamas, an empty glass in her hand.

'Hi,' I say, clumsily. 'It's just Sarah.' I pause. 'She says I'm being a bitch to Dan.'

Evie gives me a sardonic smile. 'You probably are.'

I shoot her a look. A warning. But I don't correct her. Instead, I tap the chair beside me. I can't bear to ask her to join me, outright. I don't think I can take the rejection.

She pauses, for a moment, considering. And then, she sits.

And I am useless. I don't know what to do next. A decade of training, the best part of two more spent working with troubled kids. And yet, now, with my own daughter, I draw a blank. I take her glass and fill it. I wince at my reflection in the black window, and whip the curtain shut.

'I listened to *Conviction*,' she says, finally.

'Yeah?' I try my best to sound relaxed. To adopt the same tranquil tone I use at work, with my other girls. I turn back and gently place the glass beside her. 'What did you think?'

She looks into the glass. 'I don't know. I mean . . . I don't think it was him. Do you?'

My heart gives an awful lurch. 'No. I don't think so. I did, before, but . . . it seems unlikely, if everything they're saying is true.'

She nods. The silence falls between us, again.

'Anna Byers, though . . .'

My stomach drops.

'She's really annoying, isn't she?'

The laugh that escapes me seems to take her aback. It takes *me* aback. 'That is definitely one word for her, yes.' Evie grins, proudly. I'm reminded, for a split second, of her as a child – three or four years old, maybe – purposely misbehaving in ways she knew I'd find too adorable to punish. I'd be too flushed with love to insist that she stop.

'You know,' I say, carefully. 'I think – based on what she said at the end of the last episode . . . I think we probably have to be prepared for her to consider the possibility that . . .'

'That it was you?' she says, filling the space.

'Yeah.'

She seems to consider this; I see it in the tell-tale press of her fist to her lips, through her sleeve. 'You didn't, though,' she says. Like it's an indisputable fact.

Because it is, I realize. *Even considering the possibility that her mother could have murdered her father would shatter her world into pieces.*

'So it'll be fine,' she goes on, without seeming to notice my silence. 'We just need to ride it out.'

I smile and open my arms, and she rushes into them. 'Just apologize to Dan. He'll be OK,' Evie mumbles through our hug. I breathe in her hair – her strawberry shampoo, the same one I've been buying since she was a child, dreading the day she decides it's no longer cool – and I squeeze her, tight.

I crawl into bed beside Dan. He's lying in the same position Graham had, that night, the cords of his throat exposed. I curl into him, grateful for his warmth.

'I'm sorry,' I say, softly. 'About earlier. You didn't deserve that.'

He turns to face me. In the darkness, the lines of his face seem deeper, more clearly marked. I smooth them with my thumb, and he smiles.

'I know this is hard on you,' he says. 'I know that. But . . . I'm here *with* you. I will be, through all of it. You need to trust me on that.'

I look for the lie in his eyes; the doubt.

But there's nothing. Only trust and kindness: a love I know I don't deserve.

18

The dead weight of Dan's arm pins me down when I wake.

After my weak apology, I'd climbed on top of him, and tried to make him forget.

But Graham's face stared up at me, gasping, the entire time.

I shrug him off and step into the bathroom. I turn the shower on, and disappear into the steam.

19

London, 2002

My calves prickle in the scorching water. A rash of gooseflesh rises on my exposed skin. Slowly – carefully – I lower myself into the too-hot bath. I close my eyes, dry with exhaustion. Evie is sleeping in the next room. And my husband is not home. Three months have passed, and I still haven't told him what I know.

I'm not sure I have to. When I came home from the hospital, the house was in ruins; the same scattered mess I'd left when I'd fallen. The same teardrops of blood on the tiles.

But the laptop was gone. I haven't seen it since. For a little while, I convinced myself I'd imagined it. No – that's not true. I *told* myself I'd imagined it, not believing it at all. But I had a newborn child who needed me. I'd been torn apart by the surgery, which – in saving my baby and me – meant she'd be the last child I'd ever have.

Now, though, he's late. Again. His old patterns, resumed

after a twelve-week break. So, now, I have to face it. My husband – the man I loved – was having an affair. He was fucking another woman while I stayed home, fat with his child.

He's probably doing the same thing, now.

I pinch my new folds between finger and thumb. Healed to a glossy blue, the scar on my belly dissects me in two, stretch marks patterning the sides. None of this has stopped him fucking me, of course. He's a man who deserves to have it all.

The loyal wife and baby girl at home. The nineteen-year-old, bent over, hairless little cunt dripping for him at his desk. Another frisson of goosebumps passes through me, imagining them. I wonder if they ever think of me.

I slip a little deeper underwater. I let it drown me. And when he comes home, hours later, I smile as though there's nothing wrong with us at all.

20

Derbyshire, 2018

The hand at my shoulder makes me flinch. I drop the shampoo bottle, the rattle deafening.

'Whoa, whoa,' Dan says, stepping back. 'I was just coming to say good morning.'

'Well, I'm awake now – so thanks.'

He reaches for a toothbrush. 'I'm taking Evie to football this morning, if you want to come.'

I glance at him in the mirror. Neither he nor Evie ever invite me to her sports events – it's their time together, the way they bond. I've always been glad of it, not due to any lack of interest on my part – I'm just grateful that the two of them *want* to spend time alone, without my having to force them to.

They're worried about me, I realize with a thud.

'I'd love to, but . . .' I wince. 'I'm *really* tired. I kind of had my heart set on spending some quality time on the sofa.'

Another lie. I think of the text I sent, late last night, to Darcy. I'd told her I'd be at Hawkwood House for ten. I'd planned to leave just after Dan and Evie left for the match.

'Is it awful of me to say no?'

Dan smiles. I think I see relief in it. 'Of course it isn't. If anything, I'd be more concerned if you said yes.'

'You know me so well.'

He spits into the sink. 'All right. Well, enjoy your day off. I'll see you later.'

I lean out of the shower and kiss him goodbye. When I hear the front door close, half an hour later, I slip into my trainers. I watch Dan's car pull away, Evie chattering in the front seat. I pull on my jacket and leave.

I see Darcy in the distance as I walk towards the house. She doesn't notice me approaching, her back to me as she shifts boxes – with surprising strength, given her size – one by one, through the main entrance doors.

When I reach the courtyard, she's still inside. I grab a box – unlabelled, ominously groaning, as though the bottom is about to give – and head through the doors.

'Hello?'

She turns so abruptly it's clear I've startled her. Her hand flutters briefly to her throat.

'Oh, God,' she says, running towards me, ponytail bobbing in the dusty light. 'Sorry – let me take that, it's heavy.'

'It's fine,' I smile, though the box pulls the skin taut in my hands. 'What's in here, anyway?'

She laughs, steering me towards the staircase. 'It's a toolkit. A proper one. It's actually embarrassing that I've never owned one before now, but . . . well, I figured if I had one of my

137

own, I could do a few bits here and there. Hang photos, put up shelves, that kind of thing.'

I glance around the hall, still in the same bleak state of disrepair. If anything, today's bright sunshine makes the destruction seem worse: a shaft of dusty light points to a pile of rubble in one corner. The moss and leaves are all the greener, as though nature is proving a point, staking its claim on the house, both inside and out.

You're delusional, I think. Except the words in my mind aren't in my voice. They're in his.

She looks over her shoulder, as though she's heard something, and I follow her gaze. There's nothing there.

'Pop that box there,' she says, the cheer in her voice ringing hollow, just as mine had moments before. 'Leave the rest for now. I want to show you something.'

I slide the box through a gaping hole in the bannister and shake off the weight. A flash of pain – weeks of tension whipping through me – tears through my neck. I pinch it, uselessly, with finger and thumb, and I follow her into the belly of the house.

She's quiet as we walk, though the roar of birdsong deafens from the eaves above, and the mouldering beams seem to groan as we pass.

'So,' I say, my voice a little too loud. 'How did it go with the contractors?' I'm not sure I care; she might, in fact, have already told me. It certainly *feels* like something I already know. But I want to hear a human voice. To bring some normality to the chill.

'Ugh.' She rolls her eyes. 'I think they're trying to rinse me for every penny I'm worth, honestly. You'd think when you're trying to build a *hospital*, people would go a little easier on

you, but I could all but see the pound signs in their eyes. So
. . . I'm negotiating. Trying to play hardball,' she adds with a
wink.

I offer a sympathetic smile, though deep down I'm aching
to ask for details; to know what, exactly, she's prepared to
spend to bring Hawkwood House back from a ruin.

'Still,' she goes on. 'We'll get there. Even if I have to lay
every brick myself.'

We? I think, with a pang of something I think might be
hope: a counterpoint to the envy I've felt since meeting Darcy.
I'll admit, it's part of the reason I'm here, a fantasy that sustains
me at the moment: of working with her here, at Hawkwood
House. Of staking my claim to this place, and making it my
own.

She stops at an empty doorway, the panel angled jauntily
beside it. 'On that post you made, you mentioned the archives
– right?'

My heart lurches at the memory. She smiles, and gestures
towards the door. 'Go on. Have a look.'

I step inside, my pulse feverish. The room is pitch black,
windowless. I can't see a thing. There's a click, behind, and I
flinch. A thin beam of light cuts the space in two. Darcy hands
me a pocket torch, and clicks on another.

Slowly, things begin to settle into view: a broad oak desk,
its leather scratched and peeling under brittle, yellow pages.
Around the walls: bookcases, filing cabinets, cardboard boxes
spilling over with papers. The labels on each box are faded,
the handwriting unmistakably ancient: a black, liquid scrawl.

'Oh, wow.' I run two fingers through the dirt on the desk.
They press deeper than I expect, the dust a half-inch thick.
'This is . . . Wow.'

As Darcy examines the shelves, opening boxes seemingly at random, I reach for a thick, cloth-bound book open on the desk. *The Medical Case Book,* it reads, *as prescribed by the Commissioners in Lunacy, 1917–1919.* I flip the pages, the handwriting greyed by time.

Miss York, one reads, *remains convinced that the nurses are actresses, employed by her husband to taunt her. When staff attempt to explain to Miss York that this is not the case, she winds her hair tightly about her neck and feigns strangulation.*

Another: *Mrs Keane feels that everyone is against her. She claims that other patients visit her room in the night, tapping on her door incessantly and pulling the pillow from beneath her head as she sleeps. Staff have attempted to explain to Mrs Keane that all patient rooms, including hers, are locked at night, making this impossible.*

And another still: *Miss Levy believes she is being spoken to by unseen visitors to the house. As a result of these supposed visitors, Miss Levy experiences days of uncontrollable weeping, which are not helped by sedation, and are largely disruptive to other patients.*

I feel Darcy's eyes on me, and look up.

'This is amazing,' I say. And I mean it. I could spend days in here – weeks, months, even – working my way through these ancient files. Finding my way to my grandmother. Solving, at last, her case; identifying whatever similarity my mother saw between us.

'That's one way of putting it.' Darcy slides a box across the desk, the dust rising up in a cloud. 'Look at these.'

I reach inside, and feel the distinctive gloss of photographs, the ridges of ancient prints. I hold a handful to the light.

'They're like the Charcot ones – did you have to study

those at uni?' Her words come quickly, as though she's unnerved by the silence. I recognize her tone from my own, minutes before – though now, I feel a euphoric kind of calm. 'I hated them. So these . . .' She shivers. 'I hate these even more.'

I see, instantly, what she means. I remember the prints from the *Iconographie*, glossy pages in ragged textbooks: the women treated for hysteria at the Salpêtrière in the 1870s. There's an eerie similarity in the faces of these women, sepia-toned and faded with age, their expressions turned liquid, movement captured by the camera's slow glare.

One, in particular, draws me in.

A dark-haired woman – a girl really, an adolescent swell in the curve of her cheeks – stares up at the ceiling above as she lies in bed, hair fanned across the pillow.

Another photo is of this girl, too: upright, open-mouthed, eyes fixed directly down the camera's lens. I feel a kind of recognition in the look. There's a movie-star quality to her, the sharp defiance of her pose, her arms folded, chin lowered, a sharply raised brow.

Each picture is almost perfect, but for the absolute blankness in her eyes. It's almost as though the pose itself is a thing of habit: but the emptiness there makes her as uncanny as a doll.

'Aren't they horrible?'

'They're fascinating.'

She laughs, and I pick through the others. The girl whose face blurs, though her body appears perfectly still. The ancient woman whose craggy features take on a lit-from-below shadow, like a Halloween mask.

And then, the one whose eyes I recognize, first. The one

who looks like me. Not me, not now. But the woman I see, sometimes, in the mirror: whose eyes, devoid of emotion, look back with a coldness which feels like possession.

Sweetheart, Graham says.

I feel his hand at my waist. I flinch and spin around, but there's nothing – no one – there.

The house groans, and a crash ricochets through the corridor beyond. I feel Darcy's cold hand around mine, and he's gone. Now, there's only silence, and the terrible, black stink of death.

I glance at Darcy, half-lit, her torch blinking out from beneath the desk. Her expression is one of pure terror.

I'm not imagining things, I realize. *She heard that, too.* I reach for my phone, relieved to see three bars of signal. 'Come on,' I say. 'Let's go.'

I am playing a part, now, by taking control. My heart is thudding, violently, in my chest; an ice-cold sweat dapples my skin. The phone in my palm seems inept protection against the terrors running through my mind, the ghosts returned from the dead.

As we walk through the corridor, silence seems to blanket everything. The birds have stopped singing. They've gone. Now, there's only our footsteps; Darcy's shuddering breath. In the corner of my eye, I see her: deathly pale, the greenish light heightening the terror in her expression.

We reach the door to the main hall, and she steps forward, both hands around the door's carved handle. She presses her ear to the wood, and looks again at me.

My breath catches in my throat as she pushes the door ajar.

Her laugh breaks the silence like a gunshot. 'Oh my God.'

In the mess, it takes me a moment to make it out: the jagged crack in the staircase, the cavernous space where I'd placed the box before.

I follow her, and see the black split in the stairs, ripped like a seam. 'Oh, Darcy, I'm so sorry, I . . .'

She turns to me, wide-eyed. There's a split-second pause before she laughs. 'Are you kidding? I've been going up and down those bloody things – I could've died here, on my own, and . . .' She pales, noticeably, at the thought. 'You did me a favour,' she adds, seeming to shake it off. 'God, imagine.'

I feel a sudden pang of pity for her, here, alone. Recall her mention of her mother, father, and sister – all dead. Her half-joking invitation, before, because she knew no one in the area; had, as far as I can tell, no friends.

'You know,' I say, feeling oddly nervous, like a teenager asking a date to prom. 'If you ever want company, or help . . . I'm happy to come here. Or if you need a break from the place, you could come to mine. I'm only up the road, and . . . we have electricity, about sixty per cent of the time.'

She laughs – more of a snort, really – without meeting my eye. 'You can tell I'm losing it here, can't you?'

I feel my cheeks flush, rebuffed. 'No, no – it's not—'

'Honestly, you're not wrong to think it. I read this . . . this *thing*. I didn't think anything of it, at the time, but it really got under my skin.'

My stomach turns cold. I wonder if it's something she's read about me.

'It was in that thread of yours – do you remember it? That reply?'

I force a non-committal shrug. 'Sorry, I—'

'It was about why they closed down. More of an urban

myth, really, but . . . basically, the patients started saying they were hearing voices.'

I stare at her, a terrible sickness creeping through me.

Sweetheart, please, Graham says, again. *Please don't do this.*

'I know that's par for the course, in a psychiatric institution, but the way it was written . . . I don't know. It was like a ghost story. It really creeped me out. So now, every time I hear a rustle of wings, or a creaky beam, I near enough have a heart attack.'

My heart thuds, horribly, in response. I turn my eyes to the fallen-through stairs, so I don't have to meet her stare. 'I think that's fair enough, given the circumstances.'

'I know it sounds completely mad,' she goes on. She's back-tracking, I realize. I wonder whether to tell her that it doesn't. That I think there might be something in it. But I don't get the chance.

'Anyway,' she says, 'it's getting dark. I'd better pack up and head out.'

I look out of the empty window, the sky shot through with streaks of pink.

How did it get so late? I think, with a thump of guilt. *Dan's going to think I've disappeared. Again.*

'But come back any time. *Please* come back,' she adds, ushering me towards the door. '*Mi* haunted mansion *es tu* haunted mansion.' A pause. She sees something in my face, and smiles – though there's a flicker of doubt in it. 'I'm joking. It's a joke.'

'You too. Come to me, I mean,' I say, stiffly. 'Any time.'

She wraps her arms around me, a hug that throws me off balance.

'Thank you. Really. You make me feel so much more *sane*.'

21

As I reach the car, my phone buzzes, three times in quick succession. Three messages, hours apart, from Dan.

Have got dinner in if you've gone to shops. Abort mission! ☺

Hello? Are you with S?

Where are you? S says you're not with her. Please let me know you're OK.

I know I had signal, inside. I'm sure of it.

I look back at the house, at the top of the hill.

That's it, I think, with a resolution that feels final: like the closing of a door. *I'm done. I'm not coming back.*

I begin typing a reply, before thinking better of it. What would I say? 'I'm a rational person, Dan – but I've been secretly visiting a house that I'm increasingly convinced contains my murdered husband's ghost. And today, I think that very house blocked your innocuous texts about dinner from getting through.'

It sounds so utterly absurd – more so with every passing minute, now I'm outside, in the sharp, fresh air – I almost

145

laugh. I slip the phone back in my pocket, my hand brushing against the photograph of Margot. Of me.

I pull it out and examine it again.

I wasn't imagining the similarity between us: the sharp, cold arch of our brows, the high cheekbones, the wild mass of curls. My mother was right. Margot and I were one and the same.

I stuff the photo back into my pocket, and I drive. I see her face in the rear-view mirror all the way home.

I let myself in, the smallness and simplicity of the cottage a relief, a ward against the darkness and gloom of the house.

All the little things I've come, over time, to bristle against – the imperfections: the ugly, pocked carpets we've never found time to replace; the wallpaper in the hallway tattered, a hideous green; the scattered mess for which both Evie and I are to blame, Dan constantly making jokes about his 'whirlwind' girls – seem, now, like delicious little comforts.

It's superstitious, perhaps. But here, at least, I feel safe.

Here, those things I'd felt – imagined – at the house seem like nothing more than errant draughts; nothing more than tricks of the light.

'Dan?' I call out as I kick off my shoes. I flick the switch, and curse under my breath as the bulb remains determinedly out.

I hang up my coat and call again. 'Hello? Anybody home?'

I see a shadow move in the kitchen, flickering in a candle's light. I follow it.

'There you are,' I say as Dan turns to face me, and I see his expression. 'I'm sorry – I . . .' I wave my phone in the air. 'I think this is a dud. I just got all of your messages at once.'

'Where were you?'

I slip into a cold stream of memory. Graham and I, in our kitchen, hundreds of miles and a decade from here. The words are different, but their tone is the same: that familiar mix of disappointment and despair.

'You can't keep doing this, Hannah,' he says – *they* say, both of them, each wearing the other's skin. 'Not to me. It's not fair. I love you, and—'

Evie's bedroom door creaks overhead, her footsteps padding softly to the bathroom.

She's enough to break the spell.

I'm alone, with Dan, in our cottage, and Graham is ten years gone.

'I'm so sorry,' I say again. I mean it, though I'm not sure he believes me. 'I didn't mean to . . .'

My eyes catch on the table behind. Two candles; the bottle of champagne we've kept in the cupboard for years, waiting for the 'right' celebration. And the blue velvet box I'd found, weeks before, in the pocket of Dan's coat – the perfect sapphire gleaming within. I'd forgotten all about it.

'Oh,' I say, stiffly. 'I . . .'

The buzz seems to ring through my teeth.

The lights turn on, one by one, as the power returns. Devices flash on in sequence: oven, coffee machine, laptop charger, clock.

And then, out of the corner of my eye, I see him again.

This time, he's real.

This time, he's absolutely there.

'The investigation into the 2008 murder of Graham Catton has today been reopened,' the voiceover says, as my husband smiles at me from the TV screen.

Instinctively – with the same magnetic pull I'd felt the night we met, and on so many nights that followed – I find myself pulled to him.

I kneel in front of the screen, static nipping at my fingers, while Dan watches, forgotten, behind.

22

It's a photograph I took that they're using.

He's outside our old house, some stranger's initials carved into the brick wall behind, his hands tight around the handles of the bike he'd bought, and was so endearingly proud of.

I remember the way the air was that day, humid and stewing, the smell of melting tarmac and rotting meat, the fruit-fly hum from the bins just out of shot. The noise of London basking in a heatwave: chatter and music and laughter, glasses clinking, filled with ice.

The baby monitor in my hand. A sweet little snuffle, enough to pull me back inside.

'I need to talk to Evie,' I say now.

Dan opens his mouth to say something, but doesn't. I leave him standing there, face to face with my husband's ghost.

The newsreader's voice stalks me up the stairs. 'Seemingly looking to pre-empt another overturned conviction by the popular podcast *Conviction* – whose fourth season has already raised numerous concerns about flaws in the police investigation

– a spokesperson from the Met today said that "in light of new public concerns", they would welcome any information with regards to Professor Catton's murder,' she says, her tone flat, coolly professional. 'As yet, there has been no comment on whether Michael Philips – whose family have campaigned for his innocence since he was charged with the murder over a decade ago – will be released, or whether further appeals will take place.'

I knock at Evie's door. Gently, at first. There's no answer. I knock again.

'Evie?'

I hear a shuffling inside. But still, no answer. I knock again. And then, I break my rule. I push the door open. Just a crack. 'Evie, sweetheart—'

I stop. *Sweetheart*. That's his word. Not mine.

'I'm OK, Mum,' she says. 'I'm just tired.' There's a current of something in her tone I don't recognize. Not, at least, in her.

I push the door a little more and step inside.

'Mum,' she says. 'Please. I just want to go to sleep.'

A lie. She's suppressing tears. I can hear it, her throat clenched around the words. I close the door behind, and sit beside her on the bed. I'm invading her space; forcing her to let me in. I know this, and I do it anyway. 'I won't stay. I just . . . I need to talk to you.'

She pulls the covers up around her, like a shield. 'If it's about Dad, I already know.'

Fear slips through my veins, ice-cold. *You can't*, I think, automatically.

'I saw it on Twitter. They're reopening the case. I get it.'

'Oh.' I try to disguise the relief in my voice. 'It's . . . I'm sorry you had to find out like that.'

'It's fine.' She doesn't meet my eye. She's hiding something. I can feel it.

'Evie . . . What's wrong?' She shakes her head. I wonder if she's willing me not to ask again, or willing herself not to crack.

I open my arms. 'Come here.'

And she does. She curls into me, like a child. I wonder if I'm imagining the fact she seems smaller, now. She's always been slight, but athletically so. She's never felt quite this delicate.

I scan the room for signs, for clues, for something that might explain what's happening to her. I see her laptop on the desk behind, the screen pitch black. I wonder what she does on there, at night; what she's been reading. Whether she searches for news about me.

She says something, muffled between sobs. I squeeze tighter, as though I might hold her together through sheer will alone. 'Shhh,' I say, gently. 'Deep breaths. It's OK. It's all right.' Finally – after another swell of tears, rising and falling like a wave – she pulls away.

'I've done something stupid.' She doesn't look at me; keeps her gaze fixed on the empty space between us. My stomach flips. Still, I set my face to a sympathetic blankness, and reach for her hand.

'I'm sure whatever it is, it isn't as bad as you think,' I say, though I don't believe it. 'If you tell me what it is, we can fix it.'

She shakes her head again. I let her sit, for a moment, in the silence. To gather herself. She reaches for her phone. She taps once, then again, and hands it to me. I stare at the screen, the words smudging into view. It's a screenshot, from an app I don't recognize, with a countdown in the corner.

Evie's name and photo have been blurred out, though I see both, there, in the replies beneath – a conversation I already know will dissolve into arguments about privacy, truth, and free speech. Her words, though, are clear.

> All my family and I want is justice. My dad was murdered, and the only thing we've ever wanted is for the person who killed him to pay for the life that they took. That's literally all we ask. If that's not Mike Philips, then I stand behind the campaign to free him – and behind the call for a new investigation into who really DID murder my dad, Graham Catton.

And above the screenshot, the *Conviction* logo, handcuffs open and swinging, their response in a single, icy tweet: *Wonder if this'll still stand after Episode Three?*

'Oh, Evie,' I say, my voice barely more than a croak. 'What . . . What were you thinking?'

I know this is the wrong thing to say. It's too accusatory. Too cold. I know this, but the bright blue flame of anger in the pit of me makes me do it. I can't help myself. I've always had a temper.

Her cheeks flush, two red blotches mottled with tears. 'I didn't think anyone would . . .' She shakes her head. 'My profile is private. It's only my friends on there, so . . .'

I draw breath, slowly. *How could you be so stupid?* I want to say. But I don't. I scroll down through the replies.

> Sorry, I know she's only 16 but how dumb IS she?

> Maybe she ISN'T – maybe she's scared of her mum – cry for help???

> I would be scared if I lived in that house lol . . . hide the knives at bedtime haha

Inappropriate but she is CUTE, look!

Beneath the last, a photo of Evie and her friends, all clutching enormous iced drinks and posing. The faces of the other girls have been covered with heart-eyed emojis. Only Evie beams, brightly, back.

She's a child, I think, a tremor of rage rattling through me. *How dare you?*

I hear the creak of the stairs behind, Dan's footsteps heavy on the carpet. He peers through the door. 'Everything OK?'

I place the phone face down on the bed. '*Conviction* has somehow got hold of something Evie posted on . . .'

'Snapchat,' Evie whispers.

'Snapchat,' I echo. 'It's all over Twitter.'

Dan leans against the doorframe. 'Oh dear.' I wonder if I'm imagining the stiffness in his tone. Not that I can begrudge him that. Not after how I've behaved this evening.

'I just thought . . .' Evie begins. 'I wanted to do something. It's not fair that they get to say whatever they want, while we have to . . .' She trails off. 'It isn't *fair.*'

'What does Callum think of all this?' Dan says. I look at him; he looks determinedly past me, refusing to meet my eye. I turn to Evie, who looks away from us both.

'Who's Callum?' I say, finally. She doesn't answer.

I look back at Dan. He sighs. 'Evie's boyfriend.' This time, there's no mistaking it: he's being purposely cold.

I shake my head. 'Evie, I don't know if it's wise to be—'

'Don't, Mum. I knew you'd say that, so . . . don't.'

I'm used to this flash of indignation from the girls on the unit. I'm hardened to it: usually, it's my job to let it go. But coming from her – my sweet little girl – it hits me like a blow to the chest. The anger in my voice ripples through, electric. 'What's that supposed to mean?'

'You have to control *everything*. It's like . . . pathological, or something. You force everyone to do what you want them to do, or else you play the victim.'

I stare at her. I know what this is.

The part of me that deals with teenagers, day in, day out, knows she's lashing out; knows that her anger is likely to dissipate as quickly as it's appeared. I know I ought to walk away. To let her think about it and calm down; to wait for the inevitable apology, the retraction. As a professional, I *know* this. But as her mother . . . I can't.

'You don't know what you're talking about,' I hear myself say, in a voice that seems to come from someone else. 'You have no *idea* what you're—'

Evie's face turns a deathly white. She looks away, her eyes brimming with tears.

'You have *no* idea—' I say, again, stumbling over the words. I feel as though I'm watching the scene from above. As though I'm not myself.

Dan's hand touches my shoulder, and I flinch. 'Get *off* me.'

'Whoa, whoa.' He raises his palms in submission. 'It's OK. Let's just take a timeout, shall we?'

I stare at him for a moment. And then, I stand and leave, slamming the door behind.

At the foot of the stairs, all my anger dissipates. It's replaced by something that feels like grief; has the same sharp, needling itch. The news has moved on to some puff-piece, a feel-good local-interest story. I flick it off and step into the kitchen. I blow out the candles, useless in the bright overhead light, and

I uncork the champagne, the bottle slick with condensation. I pour one glass. And another. I stare into the empty seat opposite. The open box. The ring. Graham has disappeared again. And all I have is the mess he's left behind.

'Are you going to tell me what that was about?'

I look up from my empty glass. Dan is at the sink, watching me.

'I'm sorry. I . . . I honestly don't know. I need to apologize to her.'

I rise to stand, but he shakes his head. 'I'd leave it. I think you could both do with time to cool off.'

I search his face, looking for some sign of cruelty; some reason not to trust him when he says this.

But there's nothing. Only concern. Only – somehow – love.

'I'm so sorry,' I say. 'For everything. This is all my fault.'

He drags the empty chair close to me and sits, his knees touching mine. He presses his forehead to mine, his hand at my neck. 'Hannah. I love you.'

I wait for him to go on. To tell me it isn't my fault; to tell me he *knows* I didn't ask for any of this. To tell me I'm the victim. That he believes me, no matter what. But he doesn't. I feel a new piece of me break open, a hairline crack that splits apart. I pull away. 'When were you going to tell me about this Callum boy?'

His shoulders slump. 'She told me his name this morning. I'd have told you this afternoon, if you hadn't disappeared.' His eyes flit back and forth, reading my expression. 'You know, Hannah, it's not *me* that's keeping secrets here.'

'I told you – I didn't get your texts.'

'You told me *that*. But you also told me you were going to stay home, and then you just . . . disappeared.'

There's an accusation in his voice. He sounds like Graham. I can't help but harden; turn cold.

'Oh, for God's sake, Dan. I went for a drive. I needed some air. That's all.'

A lie. But I don't want to tell him about Hawkwood House. Because I'm not going back. There's no point trying to explain it. Not now.

The memory swells again. I see Graham there, in his eyes. I feel my hand twitch, the urge to push him away. The urge to hurt him. I reach for the champagne and pour another slug into the glass. It's warm now, a little sour.

'Dan,' I say, my tone as calm as I can make it. 'I don't know what you want from me. My whole life is being picked over by these . . . these strangers. Sometimes I just need some space. Some *privacy*. That's all.'

He nods. It's reluctant, I can see. But he doesn't want to argue. He never does.

'OK,' he says. 'I'm sorry.'

'I'm sorry, too. I really . . . I do appreciate you. For everything.'

It's a weak reply, non-committal; made more so by the ring, still gleaming in its box between us. Neither of us seems quite prepared to acknowledge it, knowing that the moment we do, the night we might have had will be made solid, all too horribly real.

He takes the glass from my hand, and sips. 'She hasn't *met* him yet,' he says, finally. My stomach drops, the floor slipping briefly out from under me. 'I don't think it's anything to be too concerned about,' he goes on. 'Apparently they have mutual friends, or what have you – but that's why she's been cagey about it. She figured as soon as we found *that* out, she'd be banned from talking to him.'

As soon as you *found out,* I think he's saying.

And he's right.

Because that *is* my gut response. I've seen too many girls broken in two by predatory online relationships – catfishing, they call it – on the part of much older men, hiding behind clean-cut teenage profiles. I know the worst that can happen in these situations. I've seen it first-hand, multiple times.

'So you're saying we *can't* ban her from talking to him?'

He laughs, faintly. 'I don't think so.'

'I just . . . Don't you think it's dangerous? With everything going on . . . He could be anyone.'

'From what she's told me, they've been talking for a while now. At least six months. She showed me a few photos, and . . . I don't know. I think we should keep an eye on it, but . . . he's making her happy. And they don't seem to want to take it any further at the moment, so . . .'

I sigh. 'Fine. But I don't want her meeting him unaccompanied, when they do.'

'Yes, boss.' He smiles, his brow crinkling. I feel myself begin to thaw.

'Give me that.' I take the glass back. 'I needed this tonight. So . . . thanks.'

'It hasn't gone *quite* how I intended it to, I'll be honest.'

A pang of guilt rings through me. 'I'm sorry. Really.' This time, I mean it. I wonder if he can tell. He reaches for the ring and slides it into his pocket. 'It's just . . . the timing's off. That's all.'

He stands, placing a kiss on my head. 'I'm going to have a shower.'

It's an invitation, though I choose not to hear it. I smile, and watch him leave. He climbs the stairs as though he's weighted; like a man dragged down into the earth.

I rest my forehead on the table, exhausted. I close my eyes.

You're meant to be looking after her, Graham mutters, his voice rabid with disgust.

And he's right. Of course he is. But when I sit up – a retort vicious on my lips – he isn't there.

EPISODE THREE

23

London, 2004

The crackle of keys in the lock wakes me. I sit upright, hands gripping the edge of the sofa. My heart flutters like a caged bird.

'Hannah?' he calls, his voice echoing through the hall. I scan the living room. The toys scattered across the floor; the empty plate, a half-eaten banana browning in the air. The crust of wine at the base of my mug.

I'm unsteady on my feet as I stand, grabbing the cup and plate. 'In the kitchen,' I call back, my voice sharp.

When he enters, the mug is submerged, the bubbles scalding. I tip the banana into the bin and smile. 'Hi.'

'Hello.' His eyes skim over me, looking for the lie. He knows me well enough to sense it. This is something that works both ways.

'You're back early,' I say, brightly. 'I've just put her down for her nap.'

He looks over his shoulder into the living room. 'It's a mess in here.'

'She's a toddler. They're messy.'

He murmurs something non-committal in response, and drops his bag down on the counter.

I feel him step towards me. My back is to him; the hairs on my neck prickle, a shiver that ripples down my spine. I wonder if he sees it.

He places both hands around my hips, snaking around my waist. 'I missed you today,' he whispers. 'I kept thinking about it. Coming home to my wife.' He says the word with a bite, with relish. I hate myself for responding to it; for feeling a warmth thread through me, making me weak.

'Did you?' *That makes a change,* I keep to myself.

'Mmm-hmm.' I hear the ribboning click of his zip, his knuckles nudging my spine as he paws at my waistband. 'I was hoping I'd get you to myself, for a change. Looks like I got lucky.'

For a moment, I think it's a trap. But it isn't. He only wants what he wants, right now. And so, I bend for him. I let him have just that.

When he's done, he wraps his palm around my chin, and turns me towards him for a kiss. I watch the inevitable disgust creep over his face as he pulls away.

He wipes his lips. 'Have you been drinking?'

I wonder, briefly, whether to lie. But I know he'll catch me out, somehow. He always does.

'I'm tired.' The excuse curdles the air between us. 'I haven't had a good night's sleep in days, and . . .'

'So you decided to get drunk while our daughter's—' He catches himself, his tone rising. He lowers his voice to a whisper.

'While she's sleeping?' He steps back from me, as though burned. 'I just . . .' He zips up his trousers, a thing that's almost comic, so wholly at odds with the fury in his expression. 'I can't believe you. You're meant to be looking after her.'

'It was one glass of wine. I wasn't *drunk*. Don't act like—'

'Oh.' He laughs. 'Oh! Well, in that case, it's *fine*. You weren't *drunk*. Just lightly incapacitated. That's OK then.'

A silence falls, and I stare at him. I say the words I've been rehearsing for weeks. The ones I didn't think I'd have the nerve to say.

'I don't want to do this any more.'

'You don't want to do *what*?'

The venom in his tone makes my resolve buckle.

I grip the sides of the counter, and steady myself. 'I want to go back to work.' He raises an eyebrow, but says nothing. I go on. 'We could easily afford childcare with my salary, and . . . I think it'd be good for me. To get out again. To do something . . .'

'Something . . . what? Fulfilling? Worthwhile?'

'Don't twist this, Graham. You have *no* idea what it's like, being here all day. I love her to death, but . . . I need some adult company. I'm starting to feel like I'm losing it.'

I see some piece of him crack, at this. I wonder if I'm getting through. He leans against the counter, arms folded. 'What about those mother-and-baby groups? Don't you go to those?'

I try to steady my tone. He's being reasonable. 'I tried, but . . .' I think of the crime shows I watch, in the early hours: the ones he says make me stupid. 'Cheap thrills for fat housewives,' he calls them. But I find them riveting.

'Anything you say can and will be used against you,' they say. I feel that, keenly, now.

163

'They're not really my kind of people.'

'Hmmm.'

I watch him turn this over in his mind. He reaches into the fridge for a beer; removes the cap with his teeth in the way he knows I hate. 'Not your kind of people how?'

They're obsessed with their babies, I want to say. *They're better mothers than me, because somehow they never get bored. They don't want to do anything but compare designer buggies, and brag about sleep routines. I love my daughter to death – but I need other things in my life, too.*

I don't say this, of course. Instead, I lie. 'They're just . . . All they do is bitch about their husbands and gossip about each other.' The reality is the opposite – a kind of warfare, a competition around whose husband is the most *involved*, the most loving. The next part, though, is entirely true. 'I can't take it. They drive me nuts.'

He nods, though there's something in his expression that makes me wonder if he really believes me. I feel braced, waiting for him to trip me up. But he doesn't.

'Darren's at a clinic in Notting Hill at the moment. I'll give him a call. He might be able to find you something part-time.'

I bristle at this: at the idea of him talking to Darren on my behalf. Of finding me an *appropriate* job. But I know better than to argue the details. This is the best outcome I could have hoped for. Better than I'd *dared* to hope for, really; in the weeks and months in which I've toyed with asking the question, the only answer I imagined him giving was 'no'. I wonder, briefly, if I've been too hard on him; if I've let my anger get the better of me. If I've projected too much, turning my husband into a monster he's not.

'Thank you,' I say. 'I love you.'

'Mmm.' He scoops up his bag, and walks away.

Moments later, I hear Evie's giggle through the baby monitor. 'We'll find someone who can look after you properly,' he says, his voice sing-song, teasing.

It's a jab I know he wants me to hear.

24

Derbyshire, 2018

'Don't be so melodramatic. You're not a bad mother,' Sarah's voice crackles through the phone. 'You never met mine, did you? *She* was a bad mother. We're talking full *Mommie Dearest*.'

I look out of the window at our ancient apple tree, whipping in the wind. 'From what you've told me, that's a low bar.'

'Well, yes. But it's true. You're overthinking it. You're hardly Vicky Barker, are you?'

'*Also* a low bar.' I pause. 'I've arranged for her to come in, by the way. I want to talk her through Amy's treatment plan.'

Sarah gives a derisive snort. 'Ever the optimist. It isn't going to help, and you know it.'

'It's worth a try, surely.' The hurt – the wounded pride – in my voice shows through. I brush it off. 'We at least need to say we've tried. Remember the complaint she made, last time?'

'Ugh, yes. "I find it incredible that I am not more involved

166

in my daughter's recovery." As though she isn't the reason the poor girl's sick.'

I think of the way Evie stared at me, when I screamed at her; the wary way she's eyed me, in the days since. The hollows under her eyes, the exhaustion in her posture at the dinner table. The awful comments she's no doubt read in response to her post; the replies to *Conviction*'s announcement that their third episode would be called *Another Version of the Truth*.

Hannah Catton was the only other person in that house except for a five-year-old girl. She did it. It's obvious. This series sucks.

Just spill what you have on the wife so @MetPolice can FINALLY arrest the right person!!!

Lock her UP. Lock her UP.

I wonder what's going through my daughter's head when she reads these things. I wonder if she blames me for all this.

'Maybe she's just not great at communicating how she feels,' I say. 'If she's—'

I'm cut short by Sarah's bark of a laugh. 'She isn't *you*, Hannah. Stop trying to relate to her. It's my professional opinion that she's a sociopath with no soul, and . . . you're not.'

The hot swell of a sob rises in my throat, unwelcome. I'm embarrassed at being so transparent; at being caught. But then, Sarah is my oldest friend – and a talented doctor. If anyone was going to catch that, and pull me up on it, it'd be her. 'That's the nicest thing you've ever said to me.'

She lets this slide. 'Look – all I'm saying is, don't go in there trying to build some kind of identification with her. She'll use it against you, I guarantee it. Just give her the facts, but . . . don't expect too much. OK?'

My phone vibrates against my ear. 'Hold on a sec,' I say, glancing at the screen.

Conviction: Episode Three is now available to download.

'—looking at,' Sarah says as I put the phone back to my ear.

'What?'

'I know what you're looking at. I got the notification too.'

I think of all the other people – the millions of them, as Anna Byers so proudly reminds me, at the start of every episode – all glancing at their phones at the same time. Every one of them feeling the same fleeting prickle of excitement. Some of them already listening; already typing their thoughts in real time online.

I pull out a chair and sit. 'I don't think I can do it.'

She's silent for a moment. I wait for her to tell me, once again, that I'm being melodramatic; that I'm overreacting. But she doesn't. 'I don't see any way you get around it, honestly. It's going to be traumatic – there's no avoiding that. But I think *not* knowing what's on there is probably going to be worse.'

I nod. Then, remember I'm alone. 'I know. I just . . . I'm going to wait for Dan. I promised him I would. But if you listen to it first, will you . . . will you let me know how bad it is?'

She sighs. 'Sure. But don't kid yourself, Han. She's gunning for you. She all but said that at the end of the last one. I can't exactly sugar the pill.'

In spite of everything, I laugh. It sounds bitter, hateful. 'You've never once done that, anyway. I wouldn't expect anything else.'

'All right, all right. I'll text you later then.'

'Thank you. Really. For everything.'

I practically hear her wince. 'Whatever. I'm hanging up now.'

And she does. I'm alone, in the cottage, once again. Alone, but for the eyes I feel watching me, all the time. I close my own, and tell myself again: he is not there.

25

'Let's go back to the scene of the crime, shall we?' Anna Byers says. I can hear her relishing this. Can practically see her licking her lips in delight.

Dan gnaws at his thumb, a habit I've never seen before, though it's one I'm getting increasingly used to. I unclench my fists under the table and reach for his hand. He gives me an unfixed smile, one that doesn't reach his eyes.

Since our argument – since I felt Graham in our home (though he isn't – I know that, but this doesn't make the feeling go away) – I've been trying to make things right. I've been forcing a closeness between us, something that feels futile, but compulsive.

Every night, I press my body against his. In the mornings, I kiss him until he wakes. I settle myself over him, and make him hold me.

And yet, I can't seem to traverse it: the distance that's settled between us. The way he looks at me a little differently. Like he's trying to blink someone else away. Just as I've been doing, to him.

'If you know how to do a cached search on Google, you can find the original advert for the Catton house: a "luxury home" with "three bedrooms, two bathrooms, and a large open-plan living space". And it *was* luxurious. A perfect balance between the townhouse's own original features – a gorgeous moulded fireplace, hardwood floors, and tall, ornate windows – and those quintessentially modern requirements. Granite countertops; steel *everything* in the kitchen. White *everything* in the bathroom, bedrooms, and . . . well, pretty much everywhere else.'

I smell the fresh paint, the day we moved in. I feel the tread of my trainers on the tile.

'In fact, that's one of the things that struck police, when they arrived on the scene. The resolute perfection of it all. It reads almost like a children's story. In the neat, white sheets, in the neat, white bedroom of the neat, white house on the neat, white street . . . the body, the violent spurt of blood from the single wound to Graham's carotid artery seemed like some kind of aberration – a thing so awful, it couldn't possibly be real.'

I see it, in my mind.

I'd never seen death, face to face, before then.

When my mother died, I'd looked away. I couldn't face it, being confronted with her loss.

But I *looked* at him. I looked until I was absolutely sure he was dead.

'But here's the thing,' Byers goes on. 'I don't know if you've been in any homes that have five-year-olds in them lately, but they don't exactly lend themselves to pristine white furnishings. No parent I know goes to bed with an immaculate house – let alone one scrubbed from top to bottom. It's just not possible

171

with kids that age. They're mess-making machines. You either accept that, or you go insane.'

'There was definitely something a little off about it,' a new voice says, with more authority than he'd had, before, when we met; with an arrogance, now, that chills me. 'It was too clean – you could smell the bleach in the air.'

'This is DCI Mark Stevens,' Byers says coolly. 'He was one of the first on the scene, and one of the lead officers on the Catton investigation, working alongside Rachel O'Hare.'

'She said she was a "clean freak" . . .'

Dan's expression changes. He catches himself, almost – but not quite – before I can see it. All at once, I hear every joke he's made about the mess that seems to trail Evie and me everywhere we go; the way he could use it, if he ever lost sight of us, to track us down.

My claim to be a 'clean freak' was a lie – and he knows it.

'. . . but we performed a thorough search of the house, and the bins outside, and found only the usual waste – nothing to suggest there'd been an attempt to clean up, beyond what we could already see. So we chose to focus on what we had – lots of blood, and a murder weapon.'

Byers chips in again. 'That weapon: a knife. A very *good* knife, in fact: a top-of-the-range eight-inch Messermeister Meridian Elite Stealth Chef's Knife. Light, and low-resistance, with a razor-sharp blade. To quote their website: "You can chop, slice, dice, and mince your way through extended cutting tasks without fatigue."

'That knife had Hannah Catton's prints all over it.'

I hear a hiss, a slice. I feel it stop in my hand as it meets something hard.

My breath catches in my throat.

I hear the discomfort in Stevens's voice as he speaks. 'We were reasonably certain she *had* used the knife, earlier that evening – again, we'd searched the bins, and found evidence that she'd prepared food, so it wasn't outside the realms of possibility for there to be prints on the handle. I would say, though . . .' He pauses, choosing his words carefully. 'I don't want to get into a game of professional mudslinging, but . . . there were some flaws in the report we received from forensics, of which I, personally, was unaware until they were recently brought to my attention.'

I wonder what he's doing here. If he's been pushed into talking to *Conviction* as a kind of damage control, on behalf of the Met; or if he's here willingly.

If I, for him, am the one that got away.

I think of the way he looked at me the day they gave me the news, and every subsequent day at trial.

There's no way it isn't the latter.

'What *we* found,' Byers says, 'is a set of Graham Catton's prints on the knife. You can view the pictures on the website, but there's one important thing to note about the way those two sets of prints intersect. They're going in *opposite directions*.'

I feel his warm, living hand against mine. The press of it.

'As though Hannah held the knife in the right direction, and Graham held it back, his fingers intertwined in hers.'

I feel the knife's weighted handle, slick with my sweat.

'Forensics *did*, however, note the absence of prints belonging to Mike Philips. "However," the report says, "this does not rule out the possibility of the perpetrator wearing gloves – leading to smudging of existing prints from victim's wife."'

A door creaks overhead, and I tap the stop button, instinctively.

I look at Dan. He doesn't look at me.

Evie pads down the stairs, her slippered feet appearing first. 'Hi, darling,' I say. I sound like a parody of myself. Like someone feigning innocence, in spite of overwhelming evidence to the contrary. 'How's your day?'

She clicks the kettle on without speaking. The silence between us is awful.

Since our argument, we've found an uneasy truce – our conversations mediated by Dan, largely consisting of small talk.

Now, though, something has changed.

She turns to face me. 'Are you listening to *Conviction*?' There's a fierceness to her, her shoulders squared and eyes bright.

I nod. I look again at Dan, who still hasn't met my eye. She drags a chair along the tiles, and sits. 'Go on, then.'

'Evie . . .' Dan says, softly.

'It's fine. I just want to listen to it with you.' The silence falls again. She's defiant, daring me to say no. I reach for the phone, and I press play.

'And then, there's the blood. Remember, at trial, the prosecution said that Graham Catton opened his eyes – just for a moment – to see the man who would take his life. It's a vivid image – that split second of absolute terror.

'But . . . Graham Catton was six foot four. He played rugby at university. He was, by all accounts, a pretty strong, athletic guy. Mike Philips, on the other hand, is five eight, and – at eighteen – pretty scrawny. Sure, he's got a knife – but does it *really* make sense for Catton to just lie there, and take it, with absolutely no struggle at all? Because he's a family man. He doesn't know where his wife and daughter are, at this point. He's got *everything* to lose.

'And no one who knew Graham Catton – *no one* who's spoken to us for this series – has given one *ounce* of credibility to the idea he'd give that up without a fight.'

'No way,' a new voice says. I recognize it immediately: I can smell the sour odour on his breath, feel him leering a little too close. 'What you have to understand about Graham was that he *loved* his family. More than anything.'

Byers interjects: 'This is Darren Andrews – Graham Catton's best friend, and Hannah Catton's sometime Clinical Director at the clinic where they both worked.'

'He and I would argue about it, sometimes. Because their marriage wasn't perfect, and a lot of the time, he'd try to keep things to himself – when they were having problems, or whatever – because he wanted to protect them. Especially that little girl. He was mad about her. Absolutely lovestruck.

'But that meant if any of us said anything about Hannah – not that we were necessarily out of line, just giving friendly advice, or whatever – he'd . . . well, he'd get pretty angry about it. You'd see him resisting the urge to tell you where to stick it, at the very best of times.

'So the suggestion, for me, that he just lay there and slept through this guy knocking his wife out – which, also, by the way, doesn't ring true, because he was one of the lightest sleepers I ever met – and then, when he finally woke up, just lay there and took it, knowing his daughter was in the next room?

'Absolutely not. It just isn't possible. I'm sorry, but someone is lying here.'

There's no music, now. No sound, but for a thick and chilling silence between words, like the air between snow.

I glance at Evie, her expression impassive, though the two

clouds of red on her cheeks give her away. She's mourning him, now, in a way that she hasn't before. Because while I've always told her the truth – that he loved her more than anything else in the world – it's different, hearing it from a stranger. More believable, somehow.

'So,' Anna Byers resumes. 'Let's go ahead and say there are flaws in the way the evidence was read, back in 2008. Maybe that means there's an alternative reading – a different way of approaching the facts.'

Stevens clears his throat. 'We did consider an alternative theory – for longer than you might think. But . . .' Again, he pauses. 'I'm totally prepared to accept that I'm at fault here, as much as anyone. Rachel O'Hare left the Met in 2010, and has been following a different career path since.'

There's that damage control, I think. A clever move. One bad apple. That's all.

'But at the time we were working on this case, she and I were equals – in every respect. So I didn't have the authority to contradict her, or she, me. In the end, we had to go on what we had, and her case for charging Mr Philips was – I thought – convincing. There was more evidence to support her hunch than mine. So the case went her way.'

'DCI Stevens wouldn't tell us what, exactly, his alternative theory was,' Byers says. 'Which is fair enough. In his position, I wouldn't either. But I'd like to walk you through mine.'

She takes a breath. 'Let's say you're a sleeping Graham Catton.' A slow, eerie music rises behind. 'You're peacefully in bed. In your sleep, you feel the presence of footsteps you recognize. A pattern you know intimately well: familiar soles on familiar floorboards. You don't move, as your wife climbs, naked, on top of you, though you welcome her presence. Her legs around you are a comfort. You're half-asleep. It's been a long day.'

I can't look at Dan, though I feel the air sharpen between us. I know what he's thinking. I did that, this morning. To him.

I was trying to make things right.

'It's only when you feel the cold, sharp point of the blade against your neck that you realize something's wrong. You open your eyes, and in hers, there's anger. A black, seething hate. You'd argued earlier, sure – but all couples do. You try to say that to her. You beg her not to do the thing she's threatening to do. It's a conversation that takes place in whispers, so you don't wake your child. God knows this is a thing you don't want your little girl to see. You wind your fingers between hers, gently. The two of you, now, hold the blade.

'But while you're stronger, she's in the position of power. The angles, the way she's holding you there – and, yes, the fact you've just woken up – all combine to put her at a distinct advantage. All she's got to do is push down, once, and hard. You know you'll bleed out in minutes. It might be less than that. You talk, and you talk. It's amazing how long you rationalize it. How long you try to talk her out of it, not only to preserve your own life, but that of your family's, as a whole.

'After all, it's not the first time you've had to deal with a situation like this. You love her, but you accept that she's . . . well, fiery. You've picked up the scattered shards of plates thrown at the wall. You've apologized to neighbours for the screaming. You've always thought of it as something that, together, you would overcome. But it's hard to believe that, now. Not any more. You can't go on like this.'

A shiver of recognition passes through me. Something about this rings true.

'Because now, it's life or death. The fact that she's calm shows she means it. This isn't just another blind rage. And no matter what you say, when words are all you have – when you really are paralysed with the knowledge that, to avoid getting hurt yourself, you have to hurt the woman you love – it doesn't work. She simply doesn't hear you. She doesn't want to.

'And so, you do the thing *you* don't want to do, in order to save yourself. It's all you can do not to shake as you do it – to remain, as far as you can, still – until the moment you reach up, and grab her throat with the hand that was, moments before, around the knife she's pressing at yours. You need to push her away. To free your other arm; to restrain her. Surprise is the only weapon you have.

'But it doesn't work. The second you move, she sticks in the knife. You're done for. It hurts to die like this – in the moments you're conscious. And when you're not, she waits, and watches as you slip away. And she doesn't feel a thing.'

These final words cut through me. I stand, and turn on the lights; as they flicker on, a shadow – his shadow – slips past the glass. There, in a blink, and then gone. Neither Evie nor Dan seem to notice. They're both perfectly still, staring at the black screen of my phone.

'So many tiny mistakes; so many questions,' Byers says now. The closing music begins, a familiar, steady beat. 'It's like the old Swiss-cheese theory. For those of you who weren't forced to read pop-psych business books in the nineties, let me recap. You've got one slice of cheese, with one set of holes. On top, you lay another, and another, and another. Keep on going, until you've got yourself a little stack.

178

'Chances are, it'll hold up OK. The holes are random. There's only a small chance one hole will overlap another, and so only a small chance of these individual holes causing a problem. But still . . . a small chance is more than no chance at all. And when those holes line up exactly – well, that's when you've got a problem. That's when innocent people end up in prison, while real killers get away with murder.

'An obsessively cleaned house. An off day in forensics. A suspect with nothing to tie him to the crime but an anonymous call; a speck of DNA on a glove he'd lost, and a police force with a grudge. A litany of questions all answered one way, when another is just as – if not more – plausible. And so, the real killer slips through that hole and escapes. While Mike Philips, unsuspecting – unaware the hole is even there, like a character in a Looney Tunes cartoon – puts a foot wrong, and falls straight through. And spends the next ten years of his life behind bars.'

The credits roll. Dan reaches for the phone, and clicks it off. The silence between us is interminable. I sit. I will one of them to meet my eye. Finally, Evie looks up. She scans my face, as though searching for something. 'I just don't get it.'

'It's *very* flimsy.' Dan's tone is measured, careful. 'It isn't much of a case. All very circumstantial.'

I feel a flicker of hope, the spark of a match. And then it goes out.

'Not that,' Evie says. 'I don't get why you'd—'

She stops, mid-sentence. Her phone vibrates, as does Dan's. They look at each other. I feel an icy foreboding, a chill that seeps through me. In her phone's bright light, I see every flash of emotion on Evie's face: confusion, turning to horror, to an awful, wrenching grief. She gives a low, animal moan – a sound

179

I've never heard from her before. A sound I never want to hear again.

'What the . . .' Dan says. He's pale, too. A sweat ripples over his skin, and I wonder if he's going to be sick.

'Evie, what – what is it?'

She hands me her phone without looking at me. Without saying a word. I see my face in the messenger bubble; my name.

Look what Mummy did, it says. And beneath, the photo of Graham held up in court. The violent flash of red at his throat, an incongruous brightness exposed. The eyes, half-rolled-back and half-closed, the expression a mask of pain. The blackening blood, all around him, turned crisp on the stained white sheets. I look at Dan, who hands me his phone, wordlessly. The image on his screen is the same. The message to him: *You're next.*

26

'No, Dan – they can't *do* this.'

I hear the fury in my voice, misdirected. The white-hot force of my rage.

He doesn't deserve it, of course. He's right to tell me not to do what I *want* to do, now: to call the number Anna Byers left, months ago, and tell her just what I think of her listeners.

The account – a copy of my own, my name and face attached to an otherwise empty Facebook profile – has been deleted. Which means, according to Dan, there's no hope of tracking down whoever created it. It's probably for the best. I don't know what I'd do if I could.

'I know,' he says soothingly. 'It's not right. But if you call her now, she's going to use it against you. You'll be portrayed as some madwoman who can't control her temper. You *know* that.'

'I don't care. To send that to Evie – to you—'

'It's one person, Hannah. Not even a person – a *troll*. Anna

181

Byers can't be responsible for the behaviour of people like that.'

'She's pretty fucking happy to encourage them, though, isn't she?'

His shoulders slump. He squeezes his forehead between finger and thumb; moves them down to his eyes, as though trying to erase the image of my husband's corpse. All at once, I feel the exhaustion hit me. I sit, elbows resting on the table. 'I'm sorry.'

'It's not your fault,' he says. It's automatic, this response, unthinking. He doesn't open his eyes.

But it is, I think. *If I'd only told the truth at the time, none of this would be happening now.*

I reach for my phone and start typing. I need to talk to Sarah. I need her to take my side; to join me in my righteous fury. But then I remember – she'd said she'd text me after the show. And she hasn't.

She believes them, I realize. *She thinks it was me.*

Dan opens his eyes. 'Do you want me to talk to Evie?' I feel my cheeks burn, hot. I think I know what he's saying: *Talk to her. Smooth it over.* And he's right. After the messages, she'd disappeared upstairs. I'd called after her, but she'd told me to leave her alone. I'll admit: in that moment, I was relieved. Because I didn't know what to say. I still don't.

'It'll be OK,' he says as I stand. 'We'll be fine. We'll get through this.'

I smile, a weak assent. But I'm not sure I believe that, now. I'm not sure he believes it, either.

She doesn't look at me when I enter. She's cross-legged on the bed, looking out at the cool, black sky.

I close the door behind, and sit at the desk, a nervous tang in my throat. I want to touch her, but I'm afraid she'll pull away. I'm not sure I'll survive it if she does.

'Evie. Look at me. Please.'

She turns to face me. Her eyes are dewy, red against the pale white of her skin. Her lip trembles, just as it did when she was a child – when I'd take away sugary sweets, or toys I thought she ought to grow out of. It was all for her own good. Everything I did, I thought I was doing for the best.

'You have every right to be upset.' I swallow the knot in my throat. I try to find the words I'd say to a girl who wasn't my own: to be rational, balanced. 'That message – you didn't deserve that. Whoever sent it to you . . . they're clearly someone very cruel, and very selfish.'

I am grasping for something: a sticking plaster, some way to make things right. In the end, there's only one thing I can say.

'I'm so sorry, Evie. For all of this. I really am.'

She looks up, a false boldness in her eyes. I see through it immediately. 'What happened?' she says slowly. Cautiously. 'To Dad. What happened?'

I look down at my hands, the veins rivering through them, raised up against the skin. I wonder if it would be easier to tell her that I did it: that we fought, because we'd come to hate each other. That I wanted him to die.

If I did that, I suppose, it would all be over. Evie would cry, maybe scream; Dan's footsteps would follow on the stairs. He'd call the police, and they'd take me away. I'd be charged with my husband's murder, and my daughter's heart would break – but it'd be a clean break, this way. She'd have facts she could hold on to: closure of sorts. It would be better than this – the torture of not knowing, of doubting me more, every day. Of being told by the whole world that I did it, while trying desperately to believe otherwise.

I could end it all, so easily.

Anna Byers could have her conviction, and her listeners could move on to someone else. These strangers sending Evie and Dan their pathetic, cruel messages – they could bask in it: the satisfaction of being proven right.

It's this last thought that sways me: that helps me decide.

I look at Evie. 'I wish I could tell you.'

'You really don't remember anything?'

'It's not that I don't remember,' I say, reaching for her hand. She lets me take it – a kindness. 'I *do* have flashes of . . . well, moments. But . . .' I pause. 'Anna Byers actually made the point pretty well in the first episode. Memory isn't reliable, and over time . . . it can be changed. So sometimes, I'll think I remember something about the night . . . the night your dad died. But I honestly don't know if those are *real* memories, or just my brain trying to fill the gaps.'

'So what *do* you remember?' She's pushing me, now.

For once, I don't push back. 'I remember putting you to bed. He got home late, so it was right before he got home. And . . . I'm pretty sure I had a bath. My hair was damp when I woke up, and I remember being in the bathroom at one point.'

I see the blood swirl down the sink. Red lines in the cracks of my palm. I blink them away.

'And I know he and I . . . I know we *did* have a disagreement, that night.' I see her eyes widen at this. 'Not a big one. It wasn't even an argument, really. I just know we were annoyed at each other about something stupid. Or at least, it seemed stupid, when I . . . when I found him. If I'd known what would happen to him, later, I . . .'

I trail off. Because I hear his breath, close to my ear; catch the sour taste of the day on his skin.

'*Put the knife down, Hannah,*' Graham says.

It's a memory, not an imagining. I know he said these words.

Evie looks at me, a hurt spreading across her face. I wonder what she's seen in my expression.

'I'm so sorry, Mum. Please don't cry. I'm sorry.'

She throws her arms around me. I press my face into her sweatshirt. I smell the strawberry scent in her hair.

'I love you,' I say, squeezing her tight.

'I love you, too, Mum,' she says, squeezing back. 'I'm so sorry I didn't believe you. I know you didn't kill him. You wouldn't.'

She goes on, trying to convince herself that I couldn't have done it. That it wasn't me.

But Graham's words still ring in my mind. *Put the knife down, Hannah. Please.*

27

LOVE LESSONS: CONVICTION PROF CATTON'S EXTRA-CURRICULAR ACTIVITIES WITH BOMBSHELL BABE.

I stare at the headline, and the picture beside it: the long-legged bottle-blonde in a roll-neck sweatshirt and heels, her face a combination of pride and false grief. She's front-page news and thrilled about it, *dying* to tell her story: how my husband took advantage of her, how he saw her for the innocent young girl that she was, and persuaded her to do things she'd never normally do.

I can't stop thinking about what I'm going to do to you, when I get you to myself.

That's what she'd said to him.

Teach me a lesson. Because I've been a very, very bad girl.

I grab one copy of every paper. I slam a ten-pound note on the counter and I leave, throwing the papers on the back seat. The shop assistant watches as I drive away. I wonder if she realizes who I am. If she's seen me – my home, my car, my dead husband and his slut of a mistress – online, or in the news.

I pull over at the edge of the woods, the old quarry glinting below. Just beyond, Hawkwood House gleams, impossibly bright, against the grey sky, no signs of life for miles around.

I check the dashboard clock. Fifteen minutes, max, until I have to be back on my way to work. I wonder if that's time enough to read the whole, repulsive story. To digest it, and pull myself back together again.

Probably not.

But I can't help myself. It's a compulsion, thumbing a wound that's never quite healed.

I glance at my phone. *Eagle has landed,* a text from Dan reads. He's dropped Evie at school; will continue to do so for as long as the podcast continues, thanks to the risk of some sleazy reporter – or, worse still, a stranger, of the kind who sent photos of Graham's body to my little girl – approaching her as she walks to the gates.

Thank you, I reply. I think about it, for a moment. *Love you,* I add, with a kiss.

And then, I steel myself. I reach into the back seat for the papers, and rest the stack on the wheel.

The subject of true crime sensation Conviction's *latest series, Professor Graham Catton, was extremely KINKY in the bedroom – and beyond – up for ANYTHING, ANYTIME, ANYWHERE. That's according to his former pupil, Megan Wallace, who claims that her ex-Prof was 'the best sex I've ever had. Without a doubt.'*

Hatred – for this woman, and for him – snakes through my veins, a livid sting. A clot of vomit lodges in the back of my throat. I swallow it down, and read on, my fingertip leaving a smudge on the page.

The lecturing Lothario – murdered in his marital bed in 2008 – was OBSESSED with Ms Wallace, passing her FILTHY poetry in class, and insisting when they met that she ROLE PLAY kinky characters from fiction.

'I didn't know he was married, when we met,' Ms Wallace says. 'But over time he opened up about it. He couldn't not. She was quite controlling – always checking up on him. Once, she called while we were – well, you know. And he answered. Because he said she'd "literally kill him", if he didn't.

'It's bothered me, ever since he died. Because I think SHE KNEW about us. And I'm almost certain that SHE KILLED HIM for it.'

I feel the anger rising now. It's almost freeing, the intensity of it: I understand what it would mean to be blind with rage. To see red.

I punch the car window with the full force of it.

The window shakes, violently; my fingers crumple with a gluey crack.

I let the pain seep through me.

And I scream, and scream, and scream.

'Are you OK?' Joanna looks up at me from the nurses' station as I pass. I hadn't realized she was there.

The pain in my fist now feels like a low buzz, occasionally interrupted by a blistering current: a nerve firing off. There's something soothing about it, this pain – so absolutely tangible, so viciously real. It's a kind of tether: a connection to something I can't quite explain.

I raise my hand, and she gasps. 'I trapped it in the car door.' I give an affected shrug. 'Can you . . . Do you have a minute to help me strap it up?'

She opens her mouth, and closes it again. 'Sure. Come on.'

I follow her into an office, the ward seeming more homely today, somehow; more of a comfort. I pass the signs pasted there, entreaties to live in letters clipped from sugar paper. I catch the saccharine smell of powdered shakes: a reminder of simpler times, the childhood pleasures of penny sweets and Angel Delight.

She pulls two chairs close together, and sits. She pats her lap, and I join her, resting my hand across it. It's swollen, the knuckles barely visible beneath the stark red skin, the first smoky curl of a bruise appearing at the base of my hand.

'You must've been really mad at your car.' She meets my eye as she says it: it's an invitation. An opportunity to tell the truth.

I wince as she unrolls a bandage beneath my hand. 'Just not paying attention.'

She looks up. 'I think it's broken, Hannah. You need to go down to A & E and get an X-ray. Strapping it up isn't going to do you any good.'

'It's fine.' Frustration ripples through my voice. I smile, attempting to offset my tone. 'I've got a meeting this morning. I can't miss it. I'll go and get it looked at after that.'

'Amy's mum?'

I nod.

'That's going to be fun.'

I think of my conversation with Sarah the night before; the way she'd taken the same tone.

Sarah, who still hadn't texted me, last time I checked.

I pull my hand away, instinctively, to reach for my phone. Joanna takes it, gently, back.

'Would you mind if I . . .' She fixes her eyes on tying the bandage, light fingers careful around the bruise. 'If I sat in? I really want to get more experience, and . . .'

'Of course,' I say, after a pause. I realize what I've been brought to now, trying to imagine an ulterior motive for our best nurse sitting in on a patient review. *You're being paranoid,* I think, in his voice. 'You're more than welcome.'

She lifts my hand up, tenderly. 'There you go. But please, *please* get it looked at in a bit. And keep it elevated. It'll set wrong if you don't get it sorted.'

I examine the dressing, and smile. 'You're a star. Thanks, Joanna.'

When she turns away, I let the hand drop to my side. The pulse of pain, the throb of it, sharpens me: makes the pain of a memory I can't quite catch hold of seem real.

'So sorry,' I say as I close the door behind me. 'One of those days.'

I smile at Amy and her mother first; then at the other members of Amy's care team. Only the doctors smile back, with professional blankness. Amy's eyes are fixed on her hands, her knuckles baring through skin, sharp as teeth.

Her mother eyes me with unbridled suspicion. I have the measure of her – both through my conversations with Amy and our previous meetings. All her life, she's been protected by her looks, which have brought her love and unearned admiration, despite (if not encouraging) an absence of compassion or understanding for – as far as I can tell – anyone or anything beyond herself: the living face of narcissism, old skin too taut over dermal fillers, lips perversely pursed.

That said, she'd no doubt tell me (if I could only pin her down and burrow into that psyche of hers) that she has it all: a husband who's never around, but who happily pays for the lifestyle she thinks she deserves.

This way of thinking – valuing beauty as an asset, with thinness as one of many essential components of this – has grown thorns in her daughter. Neither, though, seems to quite see the link.

'So,' I say, flipping open my notepad with my working hand. 'Have I missed anything?'

I glance at Joanna, who smiles, thrilled to be asked.

'We haven't started yet, no. Mrs Barker was just telling us about her holiday. Tanzania. It sounds gorgeous.' There's a barb in the comment, all but imperceptible, though those of us working with Amy catch it: the disregard her mother feels, to holiday – and brag about it – here, in front of the daughter she's left in our care.

'Lovely.' My tone is one of professional sweetness. Already, I feel my dislike for this woman rising to the surface of my skin. I contain it. 'OK, so let's crack on. Amy, is there anything you'd particularly like to chat through today?'

She looks up. Today, more than ever, she reminds me of Lucie. The patient I lost; the one whose bones I feel aching, alongside my own. She turns to Joanna, as though for moral support. 'Not really.'

'All right,' I say. 'Well, I'll start things off. Obviously this is Amy's fourth stay with us, which suggests that the treatments we've been through so far haven't quite managed to stick – but that doesn't mean they won't. I've told Amy this before, but it bears repeating – many of the patients we'd consider to have had what's termed a "successful recovery" have had to go through the programme multiple times before they see a marked improvement. But that doesn't mean they don't get there, over—'

A phone buzzes, abruptly. Mrs Barker reaches for it and snaps it off with a blood-red nail. 'Sorry. Go on.'

I try to pick up my thread. 'One of the things we're keen to work on, this time around . . .' Her expression changes a little: a strange flash of a look I can't place spreads across her face. I look back at Amy. 'One of the most important—'

'Hold on,' Mrs Barker says. 'Stop.'

The silence seems endless. I see her revelling in it: in having wrested control of the meeting before it's begun.

'Yes?' I say, finally.

'When you say "*we're* keen to work on" things, you don't mean *you*, surely.'

It isn't a question. I feel the eyes of the clinical staff on me. Amy, too, looks up now, brought into sudden focus from her daze. 'I don't think—'

'I mean, really, I assumed I'd been called in to speak to the Clinical Director. To find out why, exactly, this hospital – this taxpayer-funded NHS hospital, for God's sake – seems to consider an accused murderer an appropriate guardian for my child.'

I feel the words like a slap. I look down at my hands, their position the echo of Amy's moments before. I press one into the other, the hot swell of pain a tether to the moment. She's lying. *I* invited her in. She knew she'd find me here. She just wanted to take the chance to tear me down, face to face.

'Mrs Barker,' Joanna says. 'I don't think that's—'

'Don't try to cover for her.' Her tone is unflinching. 'I know who she is. She killed her husband. And I *thought* you were bringing me here to apologize for letting her treat my daughter, and to explain to me how such an obscene oversight could have happened.'

Hate kindles and sparks in my chest. 'Amy,' I say, my voice ice-cold. 'Would you like to wait in the lounge for a little bit? We'll come and fetch you when we're done here.'

She nods and stands, pacing silently to the door. It closes behind her with a click.

'Mrs Barker.' She looks at me, a cruel smile on her lips. 'If you would prefer that I find another doctor to work with your daughter, I'm sure we can arrange for that to happen. But Amy and I have been working together for quite some time, and she *has* made progress, compared to her first stay with us. To interrupt the relationship now—'

'As opposed to what? When you go to prison?' She laughs. 'I'd rather take my chances.'

'OK then.' I snap my notebook shut; Joanna flinches beside me. 'I'll start making arrangements.' I stand, my legs unsteady, no longer my own. 'I'll leave you to it.'

In the corridor outside, I walk until I'm out of sight; then break into a run.

I push the toilet doors and slip into a cubicle, my heartbeat thunderous.

'Fucking *bitch*,' I scream, pressing my bruised hand against the metal toilet-roll holder. 'Fucking *cow*.'

I hear a laugh from the next cubicle, and I freeze.

One of Amy's bright pink trainers peeks out from beneath the gap. 'She has that effect on everyone, trust me.'

'Oh my God. Amy – I'm so sorry. I didn't—'

193

'Seriously, don't worry about it. It's literally my internal monologue whenever I'm home, so . . .'

I laugh, grimly. I can't help it. I try to adopt my usual professional tone. 'Well, it was inappropriate of me. I shouldn't have said that, whether I thought it or not.'

There's no answer. I unlock the cubicle door, and I wait.

Finally, Amy emerges. In the mirror's reflection, she's Lucie: her ghost made bones and flesh.

'I'm really sorry, Amy,' I say, finally. 'I wish I could've carried on working with you, but . . . your mum wants you to see another doctor.'

She looks down at the floor, her expression wounded. She's been let down so many times. And now I'm walking away – without a fight. 'You shouldn't let them. My mum doesn't know what she's talking about.'

'If I can get back on board with your treatment, I will.' I reach for her shoulder and squeeze. 'I promise, Amy. I'll do whatever I can. And if I can't work with you directly, I'll still work with whoever's taking over to make sure they're . . . doing right by you.'

She says nothing. Her silence is devastating.

'Amy . . .'

'I'd better get back to the lounge,' she says, flatly. 'They're probably looking for me.'

I nod, my throat clenched tight. 'Right. I'll see you around – OK?'

'Yeah. Whatever. Bye.'

28

London, 2005

I feel him before I see him: leering over me as he so often does, while I'm trying to work. I wait, for a beat, and I look up.

'Dr Andrews.'

'I think you and I are on a first-name basis at this point, surely?'

The nurses' eyes flit back and forth, watching the tension ricochet between us. I wonder what conclusion they've jumped to. Likely the most obvious, from the tone he takes only with me: that we've had, at some point in the past, a torrid affair, or a drunken fuck at a networking event. That I'm lying to myself, having come to Buyon on his invitation – that he isn't expecting it to continue.

Favours for favours, after all.

He rests his hand on the back of my chair; I feel his knuckles brush the nape of my neck. 'Can we have a quick chat?'

I shift in my seat, as far from his hand as I can get. 'Sure.'

'In my office, please.' My stomach flips. I've done something wrong. He gives an icy laugh. 'Jesus, Hannah. Don't look like such a deer in headlights. I'm not *quite* the bastard you think I am.'

Oh, but you are, I think as I fix on my most accommodating smile and follow him through the gardens. I resent it, but it's true: the Buyon is an exceptional clinic. Private, of course – luxury bathrooms and Egyptian cotton bedding don't come as standard on the NHS. But their 'treatment philosophy', too, is stunningly perceptive. I can imagine it working for the patients – *clients*, I self-correct, still stuck in my old habits – far better than anything I've ever used before.

And yet, I wonder what it was, exactly, that made the board at Buyon select Darren Andrews, of all people, as their Clinical Director. I wonder what quality he has that I can't see, my image of him tied up with the memory of a red-eyed, drunken student, imposing in the same rugby-built way as Graham, but with none of my husband's charm.

I remember him, regally perched on a tattered couch one night in student halls, pressing faces together between ape-like hands. 'I'm a matchmaker,' he'd said as the girl squealed, half-playful, though I saw the tight fist around her ponytail. 'Just go with it. Trust me. You'll enjoy it.'

And she had, in the end, though she hadn't had much choice. The boy she'd been paired with leered forwards, their skulls knocking together with a meaty thud – Darren grinning between them, all chapped lips and tombstone teeth.

I remember, too, the 'Who, me?' shrug he'd given, on another occasion, tipping a pot of steaming coffee over Sarah's hand-written essay, an hour before deadline, resenting her for being so much better – so much more capable of the work – than him. 'Misogynistic fuck,' she'd called him in response. And in the decade or so since then, he's done nothing to prove her wrong. If she and I were still in touch, I'd tell her everything about him, every day: all the tiny, awful ways he's still the bullish boy we used to know.

He opens the door, and I step quickly through, avoiding his inevitable touch. A voice calls after him. 'Dr Andrews – can I talk to you a minute?'

The girl striding towards us clearly isn't a patient: she has the flushed cheeks and build of a girl who spends her time outside, blonde hair tied up in the tight bun of an athlete or a dancer.

'Ms Wexworth. How can I help?' His tone is snidely obsequious, as it always is, with our patients' families and friends: the kind of charm that burns.

She turns to me, enormous designer sunglasses blinding in the sunlight. Still, I can see, in her appraising scan, swift and brutally efficient, that she's already determined my worth, and found me wanting. She turns back to Darren. 'I was hoping to talk to you about Lucie. She says she's making progress, but . . . well, look at her.'

I almost laugh. This girl – 'Sophie Wexworth', her visitor's badge reads – addressing Darren with such open dislike . . . I can't help it. I'm already rooting for her in this fight.

'I assure you,' Darren says, with a toady smile, 'your sister is getting the very best clinical care. But if your family has concerns, I'm sure you understand that this is a conversation it would be more appropriate for me to have with your parents.'

'My family don't.' Her voice is clipped, sharp. 'But *I* do. She's been here for two months, and I don't see her getting any better. I think, if anything, she's getting worse.'

A pinch of red appears on each of Darren's cheeks. 'Ms Wexworth—'

'I just feel like you're not giving her the attention she needs. Every time I visit she's just there, sitting in front of the TV, or staring into space with her headphones on. I've been here every week and it's the same each time. I don't see how *that's* progress.'

'It's rather more complicated than that.' He's ruffled, his tone sharp through a clenched jaw. 'I don't think you quite grasp the complexity of your sister's illness, or the time it takes to treat it.'

She purses her lips. When she looks at me again, I'm struck by the force of it. 'What did you say your name was?'

'Dr Catton.' I extend a hand. 'Hannah Catton.'

She takes it, and smiles. 'Are you better than whoever's looking after her at the moment?'

I laugh. 'I don't think—'

'Dr Catton is *very* good,' Darren says, coldly. 'Just like every other member of staff we have working here. But we have a process that we follow to make sure every client is allocated the most appropriate therapist for their care, and—'

'Well, her current therapist has done nothing to help her so far. He's an old man who keeps asking her if she wants to fuck her dad. Allocate Lucie to this one instead.'

'Ms Wexworth, I'm afraid it doesn't work like—'

'It's fine,' I say, the words spilling out before I can contain them. I *want* this case, now: I want to prove that I can help her. It's ego, pride swelling out of control – I know that. But knowing doesn't make it any less true. 'If Dr Andrews and Lucie's current doctor are happy for me to do so, then . . . I'll meet with Lucie. Fresh eyes, and all that.'

For a moment, no one speaks. Sophie smiles.

'I'll have to discuss this with her current care team,' Darren says. 'But if they're fine with it, then . . .'

'Great.' She pushes the door open. 'Thank you.' She disappears before either of us can say another word.

Darren turns to me, and my confidence evaporates. 'Good luck with *that*.' His tone is withering. 'For the record, in this clinic, we don't undermine our fellow clinicians. And we don't take on cases based purely on misguided hubris.'

'I wasn't—'

He raises a palm. 'Hannah – don't. I don't want to hear it.' He looks back at Sophie, taking a seat beside a girl with thick brown curls. 'You know, she's a mad little cunt, that one. You probably deserve each other.'

'Darren, come on—'

'If you want her, have her. Just . . . go back to work.'

He turns and walks away. I walk back across the gardens, the eyes of the patients – the *clients* – fixed on me. I'm betrayed by the tears I try to blink away; by the shaking of my hands, clenched in fists. Only the Wexworths do me the kindness of not watching as I pass. They're absorbed in conversation, Lucie listening, rapt, as Sophie tells her what she's done.

29

Derbyshire, 2018

'Whoa, whoa – hang on a minute.' The rapid click of footsteps trail me, the soft gasp of the doors opening behind. 'Where do you think you're going?'

I turn, stuffing my swollen hand into my pocket. 'Sarah, I can't – I . . .'

My voice cracks. In the absence of a text after the last episode, I'd begun to assume the worst. That she'd given up on me. That she, too, had been convinced of my guilt.

But it's fine. She still believes me. Nothing's changed.

I shake my head, and resettle my bag on my shoulder. 'I'm sorry. I just . . .' Another frisson of anger runs through me. 'That fucking *bitch*.'

'Jesus, Hannah.' She glances around the empty corridor, scouring for open doors, bored patients listening, eagerly, for some interruption to their day. 'Not here. Do you want to get a coffee, or . . . ?'

'No. I'm fine. I just . . . Would you mind if I took the day off? It's all starting to get in my head a bit. I just need some space.'

'Is this because of Mrs Barker?'

'Got it in one.' A hot swell of tears rises, filling my throat. 'She wants to know how you – not just you, in fact, but the NHS as a *whole* – can justify letting an accused murderer work with her daughter. She's probably beating down your office door as we speak.'

'Oh, bollocks.' She's trying for flippancy, but there's a flicker of something else in her expression. No doubt she's already trying to work out how to solve the issue; what she'll have to say, the promises she'll have to make, to calm Mrs Barker down. 'Well, in that case – yeah. Go home, sleep it off. I'll sort it. I'll call you later, OK?'

I nod, with a weak smile of thanks. 'I'm so sorry,' I say, again, as the doors whoosh closed.

She shakes her head, and says nothing.

And all at once, my confidence fades. Something *has* changed, I realize.

She believed me – once. But now, she's not so sure.

I pause as I see the black bonnet of the car on the driveway, and the figure inside: head bowed, her long, dark hair glossy in the bright screen of her phone.

It's Darcy. Outside my house. She looks up, and throws the phone on to the seat beside her as I pull in and climb out.

'I'm so sorry.' There's a glimmer of tears in her eyes. 'I didn't want to ambush you, but . . . I came to drop some papers off, and then I saw what had happened, and . . . I just imagined how you'd feel if you arrived home to that, on your own.'

My heart leaps against my ribcage. 'To what?'

She gestures to the cottage, and my gaze follows. Across the windows, the door, and the garage, the red streaks look like blood.

MURDERER, the words say. *WHORE*.

My legs buckle. I feel Darcy's hands gripping my arms as she steers me into the front seat of her car. 'There you go – there. It's all right. It's fine. Take a deep breath, now.'

I ball my hands into fists, my swollen fingers sparking with the pain. 'I can't do this.'

'Shhh,' she says, running a hand through my hair as she crouches beside me. 'You can. You're OK. I've just been reading about how to get it off, so if you give me your keys and tell me where your scourers are, I can make a start.'

'It's fine. I'll . . .' I take a long, shuddering inhale. 'Thank you. You're so sweet to offer, but . . . I'll sort it.'

She reaches over me, into the glove box, and pulls out a crumpled cigarette packet. 'Do you mind if I . . . ?'

I shake my head. 'No.' She teases one from the pack. 'Actually, would you mind if I . . . ?'

She hands the open packet to me. 'I didn't think you smoked.'

'I used to, but . . .' I trail off. I can't explain. Not now.

She lights my cigarette, first, then hers. 'Well, if there were ever a situation that demanded it . . .' She scans my face. 'Has this happened before?'

'No. But . . .' I think of the newspaper headlines, of Graham's affair; of Mrs Barker's vicious grin. Of Amy's disappointment in me; Sarah's too. 'Since the last episode, everything seems to have . . . spiralled. I knew it would be bad, but . . .'

She sighs. 'I did listen to it.' She catches the expression on my face. 'Oh, don't worry. I think it's absolute trash. You really *should* talk to a solicitor, you know. It seems to me like they're skirting the libel laws pretty closely.' She flicks the ash from her cigarette. 'You're sure you don't want me to help you clean up?'

'No, don't worry.' I'm suddenly aware of myself, sitting in Darcy's car, smoking her cigarettes, taking up her time. 'I'm sorry. Thank you for being so sweet, though.'

'It's fine, really.' She pauses. 'This is a bit of an awkward segue, but . . . I actually did come here for a reason.'

I feel a jolt of anxiety, like a reflex. I look for some cause for concern in her expression, but there's nothing there.

'You said about your gran staying at Hawkwood – Margot, right?'

I nod. 'Yeah.'

'Look behind you.'

I glance into the rear-view mirror, and I see it. One of the archive's cardboard boxes, overstuffed with pages. 'I found her files,' she says. 'I haven't read them – honestly, I'm not sure you're going to be able to make them out without an interpreter, the handwriting's so bad, but . . . they're yours if you want them.'

'Oh my God, Darcy . . .'

'Don't. It is the *least* I could do. You saved my life, after all.' There's a joke in her tone here, but she squeezes my arm, tenderly. I feel a rush of gratitude for it; for her.

'Well, thank you. I do appreciate it. Everything, in fact. You've been so . . . lovely.'

She stands, groaning for effect. 'You give me far too much credit. This is all part of my grand plan to lure you away from the NHS. Come on.'

She pulls open the back door as I sit, for a moment, stunned. 'Darcy . . .'

'I'm not going to press you on it right now. Just . . . planting a seed,' she says, with a wink. Her eyes catch on my bandaged hand. 'Oof . . . what have you done to yourself?'

I feel my cheeks flush at the memory of it: my momentary loss of control. 'Oh, I . . . I lost a fight with the car door.'

'You really *are* having a week of it, aren't you?'

'You could say that, yeah.'

'Well, look – open up and I'll carry these in for you, so you don't do any more damage.'

An acute shame nips at me, imagining Darcy's eyes scanning the cottage's smallness, its constant mess. I remember the same feeling as a student, Graham suggesting we visit my home town one empty weekend. The tired streets and weary suburbs that had once been home seemed, now, horribly grim – and I felt myself lessened in his eyes, by association. We never spoke of the trip again, once we returned to the democratizing uniformity of our student halls, where it was easier for both of us to pretend we were equals, in everything.

Still, there's no avoiding it now. 'You'll have to excuse the mess – everything's a bit mad at the moment.'

She follows me inside, while I kick Evie's discarded football boots out of her path. 'Oh *wow*,' she says. 'It's adorable. Like a *proper* home.'

I laugh. 'That's one way of putting it.'

She slides the box on to the kitchen table, her eyes scanning the room: the rack of drying clothes, the breakfast dishes still filling the sink. 'I mean it. It's so, so lovely.'

There's no trace of a lie in her tone; it doesn't *seem*, at least, like mere politeness. I remember her saying, at Hawkwood

House, about her mother's tales of 'ghosts passing through'; about her family's wealth, mentioned flippantly, taken for granted. I wonder if all that makes her envy this: the cottage's lived-in cosiness, the way it really feels like home.

'Do you want to stay for a bit? I could put the kettle on . . .'

She seems to consider it, briefly. 'I would *love* to, but . . . I've got to get back. I've got a meeting at my hotel in . . .' She glances at the kitchen clock. 'Oh – thirty minutes. And it's forty-five away.'

'Oh, God, that's my fault. I'm so sorry.'

'Ah, they'll wait. That's the perk of holding the purse strings, I guess.' She turns to leave. 'You're sure you're OK?'

'I'm fine. Really. But thank you.' I follow her to the door. 'Where are you staying, anyway?'

'The Blakemore. Which I'm aware is a ludicrous expense, but . . . I started out in a Travelodge, and after a week I thought I was losing my mind.'

'I don't blame you,' I say, and I mean it. I feel the dingy hotel carpets under my feet, my dead husband's ghost on the foldaway bed. And another memory too – not quite a memory, but a thing I've vividly imagined: a bloodied hand hanging over the rim of a cheap hotel bath.

The thought of it destabilizes me. I force a smile. 'Well, have a good meeting. And thank you again.'

She leans in and enfolds me in a hug. 'If you need anything – call me, won't you? Don't suffer in silence.' She slips back into the car, and waves into the wing mirror before driving away.

I glance again at the words on the windows, the door: *MURDERER. WHORE.*

I step inside, the slam of the door echoing behind me.

30

It's not quite dark, the sky a deep, low blue outside. Graham called it 'the gloaming', once, and I've resented him for it ever since. Because now, every time the sky's like this, he's there in the shadows, a reminder.

I push the bathroom window open, the steam billowing through the crack. The cool air blows goosebumps over my skin, and I pull the towel more tightly around me. For all my scrubbing, the curves of the nails of my good hand are still dyed bright red; tiny chips of paint are scattered across the white shower floor.

I hear footsteps outside, the comforting sounds of Dan and Evie coming home. The graffiti is gone, and their chatter sounds normal, though I can't make out the words. Dan knows that it happened – I needed him to know, for my own sanity – but as far as Evie's aware, everything is fine.

I hear – not hear, exactly, but feel – a laugh, beside me. As though I'm being silly, fooling myself.

And maybe I am.

'Hi guys,' I call, brightly. 'I'm up here.'

As I enter our bedroom, I see him on the bed, elbows resting on his knees. The hairs on the back of my neck prickle as Dan looks up at me.

'Oh my God. I thought you were downstairs.'

He raises both palms. 'Sorry. I thought you might want a chat.'

My eyes catch on the knife, still gleaming on the bedside table. And in spite of everything, I laugh.

He looks at me, blankly. 'What?'

'Just . . . I have had the most unbelievably bad day, and . . .' I gesture to the table. 'I swear to God, Dan, I was using that to get the graffiti off the window. I had it in my hand when I came up to shower, and . . .' Another laugh ripples through me. I feel hysterical, as though I'm losing it. It's just so ridiculous. 'I realize exactly how it looks.'

He looks at it, and there's a brief pause that feels like an eternity as he puts the pieces together. He turns to me, and offers a laugh. It's not quite genuine, but it's enough.

'You actually . . . Well, you have an alibi for that.' He hands me his phone, and I blink at it, for a moment. The cottage – our cottage – blurs into view, the red paint still streaked across the windows. My figure, reaching upwards, a slip of exposed skin at the top of my jeans, scraping at the word *WHORE* with a kitchen knife.

I'd been alone, then. I'd been sure of it.

I'd let myself relax.

It was a slip; a mistake.

'Who sent you this?'

'It's on Twitter. I don't know who took it, but *Conviction* is sharing it everywhere.'

My heart clenches like a fist. 'So Evie's seen it?'

He nods. 'She's fine, though. I told her I spoke to Will, so—'

'You did?' I feel my heart stutter, again. Will is the village's only resident police officer, a friend of Dan's from school. Dan had told me he'd speak to him about it, when I called; I'd sent him the photos to share. And yet, there's something about the idea of the two of them talking, now, that makes my blood run cold.

'Yeah. Obviously there's not much they can do, but . . . he's going to keep an eye out, make a report – the usual.'

I look at the photo again. I zoom in. Reflected in the glass, my expression is one of cold fury. I'd seen it, while I'd been working, and found it unsettling: I was *her*, my grandmother, again. But then, I'd thought myself unobserved. There was no reason to hide how I felt; no one around I had to protect.

'How do they even . . . How do they know where we live?'

'You'd be surprised what people can dig up if they've a mind to. All anyone would really need is an old photo of one of us with something in the background that they can identify. The church, maybe. Google will give them the rest.'

The fear I've felt for weeks sharpens; the anonymous mass of strangers online turns suddenly – terribly – real. Any one of them could be outside the cottage right now.

He seems to see this in my expression. 'Come here.'

I look at him. 'What?'

He pats the bed beside him.

I sit, and he wraps his arm around my shoulders. I breathe in the smell of him, sour sweat muffled by powdery deodorant. My wet hair drizzles on his skin, warm water turning cool.

'What did you do to your hand?' His words are muffled by my hair.

I try to remember the myth: the story of the man damned by his third lie. I wonder if I ought to tell the truth. That my ex-husband's mistress made me do it in a fit of rage. That I've been grateful for the pain all day, luxuriating in it with the zeal of a martyr. But I don't. 'I caught it in the car door. I'm such an idiot.'

He takes the hand, gently, in his. Without the bandages, it's swollen to an ugly blue-black, my fingers pale and cold. They remind me of Graham's, hanging limply by the edge of our bed.

'It looks nasty. Did you get it looked at?'

The next lie comes easier than the last. 'Yeah. It's just a bruise.'

He lifts it, slowly, kissing the knuckles with a tenderness that astonishes me.

'I'm . . .' I pull myself out from under his arm. 'I'm sorry I've been such a . . . such a bitch lately.'

'Come on. You're always kind of a bitch. It's one of the many things I love about you.'

'You're asking for trouble, you know. According to the rest of the world, I'm a murderer.'

He tips his head a little. I feel his stubble snag against my hair. 'A femme fatale. I'm into it.'

There's a silence.

I look up and tell him I love him; I feel him stiffen, now, beside me.

I can't remember a time I've said it unasked, without it being the answer to his question – a reassurance. Still, I mean it. The solidity of him, his warmth, the steady beating of his heart. While everything else seems slippery, intangible, he's still there. He kisses my head, and says it back.

'How is Will, anyway?' I ask, wanting to hold him – hold us – there, in place. 'I haven't seen him in ages.'

I hear the syncopated thud of his heartbeat, rising, as I wait for his response. I close my eyes. 'He's good,' he says, too lightly. 'Becca is expecting, so he's glowing about as much as she is.'

I give a murmur in response. I slip my hand up under his shirt, and weave a finger through a clutch of hairs on his chest.

'You don't need to worry, Hannah. I know what that big old brain of yours is doing.' He pauses. 'We *did* talk about the whole *Conviction* fuss, but . . . he thinks it's all as daft as I do.' He runs a finger down my arm, soothing. 'Everyone who knows you thinks the same thing.'

I look up at him again. I wonder how I could possibly have been so lucky: to have this man beside me. The guilt, the shame of who I am, feels ice-like: like morning mist against my skin.

I pull my hand back and take his. 'You know . . . what I said before. About . . . about the timing being wrong.'

A flicker of confusion crosses his face. I watch my meaning unfold in his mind as his expression changes from doubt to a cautious half-smile. 'Yeah?'

I nudge his arm, a tenderness in the gesture. 'You're not going to make *me* do the asking, surely. You're the one with the ring.'

He laughs and pulls me into him.

A hug becomes a kiss; becomes a question.

I smile, and I tell him yes.

And I'm happy. Really, truly happy, for a moment, until I sense it – sense him – there, beside me.

My little manipulator, Graham whispers, and I wilt. *Looks like you've still got it, haven't you?*

* * *

I dress myself, and wait on the bed while he showers. The weight of the ring feels unfamiliar, comforting and yet wrong. I twist it around my finger, the stone scratching against the soft flesh between.

The whispering goes on, but I can't make out the words. It's rhythmic, almost: like a poem, or a chant.

I stand, and I follow the sound.

It's only when I reach the top of the stairs that I realize: it isn't Graham at all.

'Evie?'

The whispering stops. She looks up over her laptop. 'Yeah?'

'What are you doing?'

She holds a scrawled-upon flash card in the air. 'Well, I was revising. Now, I'm talking to you.'

I laugh. 'Sarcasm doesn't suit you, Evie. You're too cute for it.'

She shuts her laptop with a click. 'Shut up, Mum.'

'It's true. That little nose . . . Those cheeks . . .' I reach a finger and thumb towards her, playfully. The coolness breaks, a little, as she bats me away. I can tell – or at least, I'm reasonably certain – that her mood, tonight at least, is only an ordinary teenage testiness. It's a door I know will give, with a gentle nudge. 'So what are you studying?'

'Science. I hate it.'

'Ah, come on, it's not that bad.'

'This bit is. It might as well be in another language.'

I feel a shudder of memory, then. I remember Graham, laughing, as I'd tried to explain something to him; the look in his eyes, the feigned helplessness as I walked him through a tricky scientific paper he'd been forced to read, background for an essay he was working on. I feel him reach for my hair, slip his thumb and finger behind my ear, and smile. 'It might as well be hieroglyphics, for all I understand it.'

She narrows her eyes. 'What?'

'What?'

'You're looking at me funny.'

'Sorry. It's just your dad was exactly the same. You're a lot like him sometimes.'

She rolls her eyes. 'Thanks a lot.'

It's a response I don't expect. She's always seemed grateful for second-hand memories of Graham, things she can cling to, little fragments of connection.

'What do you—'

'I saw that woman in the news, saying she was fucking Dad behind your back.'

The words, from her, cut through me like a knife. 'Evie . . .'

'Sorry – *sleeping with* Dad. Whatever.'

I pause, trying to read her expression; to find the roots of her anger. I wonder if I ought to have told her before; if she's grieving the imaginary version of her dad that I've created for her benefit.

'I'm sorry, Evie,' I say, gently. 'I—'

'Why are *you* sorry? He was cheating on *you*. With someone, like, two years older than I am now. You should be—' She stops, mid-flow. In the silence, the bathroom door clicks open, the fan humming overhead. 'Wait – what the hell?'

I'm caught off guard by the change in her tone. 'What?'

'Did you . . .' She points to the ring. 'Did you and Dan . . . ?'

'Oh.' I feel a colour burn my cheeks. 'We were going to tell you this together. But . . . yeah. We . . . Yeah.'

'Oh my God.' Her face is a mask for a moment; she's

processing. My breath is caught in my throat, held there, waiting for her response. And then, at last, she beams. '*Finally.*'

I laugh. It's relief, all the way through. 'You're sure you don't mind?'

'Why would I mind?' She laughs, too. It's a cover; there's a choke of a sob in it. 'I love Dan. He's . . . I mean, he's basically as much my dad as *he* was, isn't he?'

My heart splits open. She's fallen out of love with Graham. And against all the odds, this hurts.

But before I can speak, I hear footsteps on the stairs. She stands, and leaves me behind.

She wraps her arms around Dan, her eyes shut tight. He looks up at me and smiles with a perfect joy, and I fix the image of them, together, in my mind. It's a thing I'll cling to, and hold close.

Because this happiness can only ever be temporary.

We're only halfway through the season, and already, I'm holding my life together with slipping hands.

It's inevitable. Things can only, now, get worse.

EPISODE FOUR

31

Worcestershire, 1999

I am dressed all in white, and I am beautiful.

It's a privilege I've never known before, and today, it's hard won.

My hair, tamed by tongs that steam and sting as they brush my scalp.

My skin, stiff with a mask of foundation, of shades rubbed into the hollows of my cheeks.

My lips drawn plump and pillow-soft, brows plucked in a smooth, feather's arch.

I am alone, for a moment, with my new and better self: the one who, today, will be married to the man I love. I raise a finger to my new, smoothed-out curls, and find them brittle, stiff, barely like hair at all. I touch my bottom lip, and find it sticky. I taste ammonia on my freshly painted nail.

The rest of the day plays out in my mind, rehearsed and

reviewed so often that it feels like a memory, already like something I can touch.

The ancient house, closed to everyone but us; the landscaped lawns; the Lovers sculpture in the fountain, in front of which we'll kiss in photos with our guests.

The string quartet, whose hollow ring I hear, rehearsing, somewhere far below: the song that's ours, the one they're playing just for us.

The infinite, meticulous details that no one will notice but his mother and me: the way the chairs' velvet sashes chime with my bouquet and the flower girls' nails; the poem he will read carved in keepsakes on the tables: compacts for the women and snuffboxes for the men.

It's like something from a dream, though one I'm not entirely sure is mine: I've been swept along, throughout, on the kindness and enthusiasm of Graham's parents, waving away impossible sums of money as though they're nothing, always suggesting better, more luxurious, more 'appropriate' things.

I imagine what Sarah would've said, if she'd been here: jokes about Barbie dolls and mail-order brides. It would've been a relief to hear them – a reminder that it's all for show. That this isn't really me.

But she isn't here. She couldn't get the time off work.

And so, I'll walk the aisle without family, or bridesmaids. His mother has quietly filled my side of the aisle with her friends, without a word, though I know she disapproves. For once, I'm grateful for the old-fashioned stiff upper lip.

'It'll be over before you know it,' everyone tells me. 'It'll all go by so fast.'

I can only hope so. All I want is to be with him. Alone.

The door creaks, and I think I've got my wish. His cologne

drifts into the room, and I think of jinxes; of things doomed from the start.

'Don't look!' I say, hands covering the folds of my dress, as though I'm naked, exposed.

But the door opens a little more. For a split second, I think I'm meeting my future. The man looking back at me is my husband, thirty years from now. A man whose skin cracks at the curve of his smile; whose eyes scatter wrinkles like a cat-o'-nine-tails.

'Only a proud father-in-law.' He closes the door behind him. 'I don't think there's any bad luck in that.' He scans me up and down, as my own father might have done, if I'd known him. 'You look beautiful, Hannah. Truly stunning.'

I feel my loneliness all at once, and I'm struck dumb with it. I think of my mum: the terrible weight of her love, the loss she left behind.

I blink away a tear I didn't think I'd shed. 'Whoa, whoa,' he says, taking another step towards me. 'Hey – you're all right, sweetheart. Don't ruin your make-up, now. I wouldn't have come in if I'd thought I'd upset you.'

I laugh, trying to blink away the shame. 'I never thought I'd be that kind of bride.' Even the words I say, today, seem like something from a film. Something borrowed, something blue. 'I always thought I was better than this. But . . . I keep bursting into tears at everything.'

'You're allowed, today. My Marianne started weeping at the top of the aisle, and by the time she reached the altar, her make-up was . . .' He traces two fingers down the side of my cheek. The sudden brush of his touch is a shock. I feel the urge to buck, but contain it. 'I think it's the done thing.'

219

He's being kind, I tell myself. *You need to stop thinking the worst of people. He's just a sweet old man.*

'Thank you,' I say, at last. I want to step back, but the long train behind me prevents it.

Like a princess in a fairy tale, I'm pinned to the spot by my gown. It's a penance for my vanity.

I can only wait for him to move.

I watch his eyes trace my expression, the false pieces of me, just as I had. Time slows, my heart counting the beats of his gaze. Four on the eyes, the gluey lashes that flutter, hooding my vision. Two for the cheeks, which flush all the more, now. Six for the mouth, through which I can't seem to breathe, the glut of gloss pinning them shut.

I feel two soft palms around my upper arms, so tender that I can't quite brush them off.

It's just a kiss. A thing so soft and sweet that it almost feels right. It's only the thick, wet presence of his tongue – in my mouth, briefly – that makes it horribly, achingly wrong.

And then, he steps back, and I wonder if it ever happened at all.

The smile he gives me is so sweet and full with love that when the door opens and his wife stands beside him, and looks at me, she takes the measure of things instantly. She reads the impropriety in my face, and she hates me. Her smile is something ferocious.

'Well,' she says, with the gentle charm of the lioness. 'I suppose it's time to make you part of the family. I'll give you a moment to . . .' She pats her own lips with two fingers. A brow arched, a judgement. All the doubts she's ever had about me confirmed.

Hours later, when the champagne throws sparks above the

crystal glass beside me, and my husband holds me in his arms, and smiles, his father will deliver his speech. He'll say how grateful he is for our newfound family. How love, and faith, and joy have kept his marriage happy, all these years, and how he wishes us the same.

He'll tell me how proud he is that his son has grown up to be just like him.

And in this moment, I will realize my mistake.

32

Derbyshire, 2018

I knock on Sarah's door, ring glinting in the light. For a thing that had seemed so unimaginable, it's become part of me impossibly quickly. I find myself sinking into the bright, cool blue of it whenever it catches my eye.

She raises a hand as I peer through the crack. 'Can you give us five minutes?'

I take in the figure opposite, horror yawning through me. The bulky black uniform, the blue strip across the jacket, the badge pinned to the arm. He turns to smile at me, an easy blankness in his expression. 'I can come back later, if it's—'

'No, no,' she says. 'I need to talk to you, anyway. If you can just wait outside . . .'

I smile, the strain of it stiff in my jaw. 'No problem.'

I close the door and sit, heart fluttering, on the chair outside. *It's nothing,* I tell myself, though I don't believe it. I can't.

I reach for my phone and scan Twitter. Somehow, it's there that all the news now seems to break, Byers's self-styled Convictionistas constantly sharing titbits of gossip and lurid chatter. I look at the hashtag; then search for my name.

It's there I find news, though it's not what I'm looking for. Or at least, I don't think so. Unless there's something Byers knows that she's yet to make public, but has told the police.

Next episode apparently called THE WIFE. Focus is going to be squarely on Hannah. Cannot fucking WAIT.

'Sorry!' Sarah's tone – brittle, too bright – makes me jump. 'Come on in.'

The police officer smiles as he passes, and gives a brief nod in greeting. I search his face for a sign of recognition; imagine him searching mine for signs of guilt. I look away.

'Sorry about that,' she says, closing the door. 'You gave me a good excuse to wrap things up. You know what they're like.' She gives a too-loud laugh. 'I did *not* mean that to sound like you're an expert at being interrogated.'

'You'd be surprised.' I lower myself into the still-warm chair. 'What was that about?'

'Just a patient-security thing. The usual.' I wait for her to go on. She's usually so keen to discuss the quirks and hassles of patient care, the horror stories and ludicrous bureaucratic hoops she's forced to jump through.

Today, though, she's quiet.

'What did you want to talk to me about?' I try to shake off the strange formality in my voice. I do this when I'm nervous: revert to a stiffness that comes across as stony and cold. It's never made anyone exactly take a shine to me. But I can't help it. It's just the way I am.

223

'Oh,' she says. 'I didn't, really. I just said that to get rid.'

A silence falls. I reach to fill it, to set things back to normal. 'Look.' I rest my hand on the desk, though it seems wrong, there, now. It lies between us like a dead thing. 'I finally followed your advice.'

'At bloody *last*.' She smiles, though it doesn't quite reach her eyes. 'I'm so pleased for you, Hannah. And Dan. I hope he realizes we come as a pair.'

Do we? I think. *Really?* The silence falls again. We're alone, though it doesn't feel that way. I imagine a crowd of people watching, all clasped hands and bated breath, waiting for one of us to break the tension.

She stares into her mug, and I realize it's going to have to be me.

'Sarah . . . is everything OK?'

She runs a hand through her hair, and looks up at the ceiling. Her answer is inevitable, when it comes. 'No.'

She sips her tea and resettles in her seat, as though nervous. I feel a cool spill of fear slip down the back of my neck.

'The thing is, I've been getting a world of shit from the board for not having this conversation sooner. I didn't want to make things worse for you, with everything going on, but . . . I shouldn't have let it get to a point where it's impacting our ability to care for our patients. This whole situation is my fault. I want to be clear on that.'

'So what's the board's position?'

She runs her hand through her hair again. It's her tell, I realize: the lead-up to something she doesn't want to say. 'I'm really sorry, Hannah. They think it's best for you to take a leave of absence for a little while. It's by no means a reflection on your work, and it won't appear in your HR records as anything other than compassionate leave. You'll be on full pay for the duration. But they've requested that you stay off the hospital grounds, so that any press or . . . whatever . . . So they're not a risk to our patients' privacy. Or safety.'

She pauses, seeming to deflate a little, as though she's reached the end of her rehearsed speech, and has no idea what to say next.

So I speak, instead. 'This is because of Vicky Barker's complaint, isn't it?'

'That didn't help, but . . . there were concerns before. Obviously as soon as the podcast approached us, it became—'

'*Us?*' I feel my throat tighten in fury. I swallow it. 'Sorry. Go on.'

She looks hurt. 'Hannah, it's *not* an unreasonable request. And for what it's worth, I've had to fight tooth and nail to *get* it. What they wanted originally was much worse. This is a fair ask, given the circumstances.'

'*What* circumstances?'

I know what she means, of course. *Given people think you murdered your husband. Given people think you're a threat to our patients. To us.* Still, I feel the anger rising in me, the bitter taste of it in the back of my throat.

'*None* of this has anything to do with my work. None of it. So I'd like a little more clarity on why the board think it's appropriate to try and get rid of me, if that's what they want. I'd like to understand what they think I could've done differently, given I've got absolutely no control over any of it.'

'Oh, come on, Hannah. Don't play dumb. And stop taking this whole situation out on me. I'm one of the only people trying to help, and I could *really* do without you making it harder. I've had to work my arse off to keep them from asking why I hired you in the first place, given what happened with that girl at Buyon, so I feel like you could at least give me some credit for trying to be your friend through all this.'

'Through *all this*?' I say – hear myself say, really, my tone turning from icy to outright cruel. 'I've got to say, you've always been self-absorbed, but I'm really impressed at your ability to make *yourself* the victim at a time like this – when it's my life that's being ruined by my fucking dead husband.'

The silence that falls between us is deadly.

I know, instantly, that I've slipped. With anyone else, I could get away with it – brush it off as a meaningless stumble. But Sarah really *is* a good therapist. There's no way she doesn't hear it, what it means: that it isn't *Conviction* I'm angry with now. It's not the police who charged the wrong person; or the strangers who've vandalized my home; or the patient's mother who wants to ruin my career.

All of those people deserve my fury. But the person I'm really angry with – still, after all this time – is him. Graham and I, in a fight that still isn't done with, though he's ten years dead.

'By my husband's murder,' I say as she stares at me, the look in her eyes turning from doubt, to anger, to fear. 'You know what I mean.'

'OK.' Her hands grip the desk, one feeling around, uselessly, for something to hold on to, something to do. 'OK. HR will be in touch, Hannah. They'll send you the formal details.'

I try to speak, but I can't.

I open my mouth. Close it again.

I feel her eyes on me as I walk to the door, my heart thudding violently against my ribs.

I've lashed out; I've been childish.

And I've made things immeasurably worse.

All the way home, I keep the scream locked in my throat.

I keep my face set, resolutely blank, though I squeeze my bruised hand around the steering wheel, the rush of pain flushing my cheeks red hot. It feels like a relief. A tether to the moment; something to keep me present, there.

I meet the eyes of every driver on the road, every passing face a threat. I wonder if they're listening to *Conviction* as they drive; if they'd take a photo of me, if only they could, now. If they'll go home to their families, tonight, and tell them that they saw that awful woman – the one who killed her husband – and though she tried her best to look the same as anybody else, they saw it: the fierce and bitter hatred in her eyes.

33

I climb out of my car, beside Dan's, which shouldn't be there.

He should be at work. I'd banked on that, all the way home, thinking only of a few hours' peace. The curtains pulled shut, phone off, router unplugged from the wall. A dissolution, just for a little while – the pieces of me pulled back together in time for tea.

I see him through the open blinds, in the kitchen. He's lost in conversation on the phone, and pacing. I wonder if it's Sarah he's talking to. If she's pre-empted this, knowing I wouldn't tell him – or rather, wouldn't have told him yet. We've only just made things right between us. Our happiness – mine, Dan's, and Evie's – feels perched on a hill of sand.

I'm just concerned about her, I imagine her saying. *And I know she's not one for opening up, if you know what I mean . . . No, Dan, honestly – she was the same with Graham, too.*

I push the door open and slip through my house, stalking silently as a cat, though I feel electric with rage.

I remember doing the same thing, the night my husband died.

He turns, and he sees me. He looks like a man caught out.

'Do you mind if I call you back?' There's a crack in his voice, I can hear it: a nervousness, almost fear.

I give nothing away. I can't. I know whatever expression I fix on my face will seem so false it'll only prove I've got something to hide.

'Yeah – yeah.' He's resigned as he winds up the call. I hear the distinctive trill of a woman's voice on the line. Another crackle of anger tears through me. 'Yeah. I'll speak to you later. OK.' He turns away from me, to the window. 'All right. Bye.'

His shoulders slump as he hangs up, and turns back to me. 'Are you OK? I didn't think you'd be—'

'I'm not feeling well.' The lie slips out before I can contain it. I want to see how he reacts; if he already knows.

'Oh no. What's up?' He's as poker-faced as I am. I can't read him.

'I have a headache.' I squeeze my temples with finger and thumb. I wonder when it was I became so good at this: at lying to the people I love. It seems to come so naturally, I could almost convince myself what I'm saying is true. 'Why are *you* here? I thought you'd be at work.'

'Yeah,' he says. 'I was, but . . .' He seems to trace something in my expression that cuts him short. 'I needed to pop back and grab something. I'm heading back out in a sec.'

Pop psychologists will have you believe there are distinct 'tells' that let you know when a person is lying: a cutaway glance in a certain direction, a rapid succession of blinks, a sudden blush. But I've always been able to *feel* when someone is lying to me – it's what makes me good at what I do. I feel it, now, just as I felt it every time Graham left me for another of his whores; every time he looked at me, and told me that he loved me. That I was the only one for him.

'What did you forget?'

'I wrote a phone number down yesterday.' He holds up a slip of paper – a number scrawled across it. 'Someone I'm speaking to for a story.'

I want to believe him. I *need* to believe him. But I don't.

You're being paranoid, Graham whispers in my ear. *You're acting crazy.*

Put the knife down, Hannah. Please.

'Hannah,' Dan says. 'Are you OK?'

I stare at him. I feel the weight of the ring on my finger, tightening like a noose. I think of the love I'd felt for him, the day before; the love I still feel, now, as he looks at me, and waits for me to speak.

I want to tell him the truth: that I've been removed from my post at the hospital. That *Conviction* has taken away another piece of me I could cling to: proof of the person I was. But I can't. Because to tell him that would mean telling him Sarah – my oldest friend – has found herself doubting my innocence. And I can't do that without making him do the same.

'I'm fine. I just have a headache. I'm going to sleep it off.' I turn and climb the stairs. He doesn't speak, and doesn't follow. I sit on the edge of our bed, alone, and I wait for him to leave.

When the door closes, and the car pulls away, I crawl under the covers, fully dressed.

On the pillow beside me, there's an indentation.

I stare at it for what feels like hours.

Finally, I roll over. I reach for my phone. Nothing. No message from Sarah, though that's hardly surprising. Nothing from Dan, Evie – or even Darcy.

It's a relief, almost – after what's felt like a constant shiver of notifications, of an unrelenting press of bad news, things I don't want to remember – to find nothing. To be, for once, alone. The relief, though, dissipates as quickly as it had arrived. I know, somehow, that this is the last, slow gasp: the calm before the storm.

I'd known that before, too. I remember the serenity that had settled over me, the day he died: the knowledge that, though things were about to get worse, whatever came next would be an ending. *No more of this,* I'd thought, breathing in the sweetness of Evie's skin, her hair. *No more.*

It's the thought of her that drags me up, and downstairs. I open the hall cupboard, catching, for the first time, my bitten-down nails, the reddening cross-hatch of skin. I've been aged by the week that's gone by, the hands I look down at my own, and yet not. *They're my mother's hands,* I realize, with a shiver. *I'm turning into her.*

I reach inside, and drag the box of papers out from under a pile of coats. I'd hidden them after Darcy had left. I knew if Dan saw them, I'd have so much to explain: who Darcy was, why she'd brought them here, my interest in Hawkwood House, why I'd left Buyon, before . . . So many little lies; so many omissions, each justifiable, in isolation. Together, though, they formed a pattern: they showed a woman habitually covering her tracks.

I couldn't do it.

So I'd slid the papers into the cupboard, and bedded them into the mess.

Now, I lift the box, my bruised fingers ringing in complaint. I place them on the kitchen table and close the blinds, sitting alone in the half-light.

I open the lid. An envelope without an address rests on top. I peel it open, carefully, wincing as it rips. *From the desk of Dr William Sidney,* the header reads. *Psychiatrist. Hawkwood House.*

The paper is wrinkled, thin with age; I catch a memory of Evie and me, at this table, five years ago, maybe more, tea-staining office paper, making pretend parchment. A tiny forger, I'd thought then, watching her hands clutch the paper, hold it flat. The concentration in her eyes so pure and fixed, dribbling tea over the page with utmost care. I run my fingers over text, the indentations of the old, typewritten words:

Thank you for sending Mrs McLelland into our care. It is clear at once that she is, indeed, disturbed, and as yet cannot bring herself to quite accept the truth of what she has done. Though she is always keen to engage our nurses in conversation, the only topic of interest to her is that of her innocence. She claims to have no memory of what happened on the night in question.

I stare at the page, not realizing, for a moment, that I'm shaking. I put the paper down, slowly, and stand. I pace the room; reach into the fridge and open a bottle of wine, a spill circling the glass as my hands tremble above.

It's a coincidence, I tell myself. *It's just a defence. It might not even be true. It doesn't mean anything.*

I don't believe a word of this, of course. It *has* to mean something.

I'm just not sure I want to know what.

I look back into the box, warily, from above. I see pages and pages of white space, a scatter of letters torn across each; I imagine Margot herself there, arched over an ancient typewriter (huge and black, in my mind, keys firing off like gunshots, one by one) writing her missives, knowing they'll never be read.

r e mem be r m e m be rem em, they read, erratically spaced and breathless, *re mem b e r me*.

I pull out one page after another, a hot panic spreading through me, the doctors' scrawl almost impossible to read, though I catch words here and there: *voices*, and *delusional*.

And then: *Suicide by exsanguination*.

I hear Dan's car pull in outside, and I come back to myself.

I stuff the pages back in the box.

I close the door on it all, breathless and sick.

I know this is denial.

I know.

But I can't face it.

I thought I wanted the truth, once. Now, I realize I was safer in my lie.

'Hi, Mum,' Evie smiles as she bursts through the door.

'You remind me so much of her,' my mum says to me, thinking of her own mother.

The mother who murdered her husband and child, and did not feel a thing.

34

Under the huge, tented scaffold, the metal bars gleaming in the sunlight, Hawkwood House has the air of a caged animal. Something about it sends a shiver of foreboding through me. I'd told myself I wouldn't come back, after last time – after I'd heard his voice here; after my phone had blocked Dan's messages, and the clocks seemed to stop. But when Darcy called, this morning, I couldn't resist. And frankly, I had nowhere else to go.

I lock the car, and walk towards the house, glancing at a text from Dan: *Evie at netball tonight. Semi-final! Will be back about 8.* If Sarah's told him what's happened, he's doing a good job of hiding it. I'm increasingly convinced, though, that she hasn't; that he thinks I've been going to work as normal every day since. I send back a heart-eyes emoji, and tell myself: *I'll tell him tonight.*

'Good morning!' Darcy calls across the grass, beaming. In the morning sun, her glossy hair has an unnatural, chocolatey glow: highlights, I suppose. I wonder what it must be like to be so put together.

I think of the things I've read about myself, online, so far this week. *A witch with a guilty face. A sociopath who deserves to die.* I read them all – every comment, every post – with a strange, tight feeling in my chest. I tell myself that these strangers don't know me at all. But still, I read every word they say. I see them on the walls of my skull each time I try to sleep.

I smile as Darcy approaches.

Fake, I hear in a stranger's voice. *You're a fraud.*

'How are you doing?'

'Good! All the better for seeing you, obviously.'

The scaffolding gives a crack, the breeze whipping through the tarps between. I flinch, the sound echoing through me like a gunshot. 'This is . . . something.'

'Progress, isn't it? Come on – I've got some wine in. And posh crisps.'

I follow her up the steps and under the metal beams. The light is a soft, dull blue inside, a bad movie's intimation of a ghost. The staircase is now lined with bright tape, *CAUTION* emblazoned across it; the tiles swept, those broken carefully removed.

'It feels different,' I say, a note of loss in my voice. I correct it. 'You've made so much progress already.'

'Do you think so?' She looks around, proudly, as she replies. 'I mean, obviously it hasn't just been me, but . . . it's nice to see things moving. It's starting to feel less spooky, at least.'

I run my hand along the open jaw of a lion, carved into the edge of a doorframe. I wonder if Margot ever had the same impulse, while she was here. If she ever stood in the spot where I'm standing now, in search of memories lost, listening for voices no one else can hear.

'Thank you for bringing those papers over, by the way. I took a look at them yesterday.'

'Could you *read* them?' She tips her head towards the corridor, and I follow. 'I had to dig through so many pages of illegible – well, crap, really. And when the handwriting *isn't* the problem, they're waterlogged. I think they're all going to have to go.'

I think of the words on the page, the others I'd managed to make out, while Dan and Evie slept upstairs. *Insists her husband is beside her*, and *claims to have heard his voice. These are persistent, seemingly unshakable delusions which have only worsened during her time with us.*

I shrug. 'Some of them – they're a bit smudged, but . . . It's just nice to have a connection to her, you know?'

She pushes a door, and the darkness breaks. The sun room. The light has the same luminous glow as before, though it's shadowed by strips of panelling covering the most shattered panes, tape pulling together those only cracked. 'Have a seat,' she says. 'I'll be back in a sec – just fetching the vino.'

I look around at the empty pool: tiles stripped away, the ancient sun loungers replaced with a couple of camping chairs and an upturned box. There's something unnatural about it, exposing the house like this: it feels undignified, like watching someone who thinks themselves unobserved.

A crow (I suppose – some large black bird, anyhow) lands on the roof overhead and taps the glass, once. Then again, and again.

The door opens, and Darcy returns. The bird bursts into flight, and disappears.

'*Voilà!*' she says, a bottle in one hand, two long-stemmed

glasses in the other. She holds the glasses in the air. 'I stole these from the hotel restaurant, just for this.'

I laugh, though a mean-spirited thought flits through my mind: if I did something like that, now, it'd be held up as evidence of my bad character, my evil in miniature. 'I'm flattered.'

'Well, I wanted to talk to you about something.' She twists the cap off the bottle, eyes fixed on me as she pours. 'I think you know what it is.'

My stomach drops; worst-case scenarios flit through my mind. *She knows what Margot did,* I think. *She's going to ask me to stay away. It's bad for her reputation. I'm bad for her reputation.*

'Don't look so scared, Hannah. It's about you joining me here.' She hands me a glass. 'Sorry – I forget coy probably plays as ominous in this place. But I'd love to have you on board.'

My first impulse – drawn from some sensible, practical part of me – is to decline. I have a job: a career I've built, patients and staff I'm loyal to. But then, I think of Sarah, telling me my presence was 'a risk to patient safety'. I think of the silence that's fallen between us since, neither of us prepared to budge.

'Darcy, I—'

'I know you've got a family to support,' she goes on, a faint shake of her head the only sign that she's heard me speak. 'And I can't imagine the NHS is paying you all that much, so don't worry – I'm not expecting a huge investment.' She laughs. 'It's going to cost millions, so . . . don't panic. I'm not asking for anything like that at *all*. But . . . look. I thought maybe if you could put in a token amount – fifteen thousand, maybe – we could draw up a contract that gave you a real stake. A proper partnership. You'd be on the board of directors, which would basically be me, you, and whoever else we decide to get in. You'd be responsible for all the young people's programmes, and . . . well, anything else you wanted to be involved with, really.'

Fifteen thousand pounds. A token amount.

I think of the seven, hard-won, in the savings account I made for Evie, ten years ago, and wonder where in the world I could possibly find another eight. I'd left Graham's parents to sell the house – it belonged to them, anyway; and the small sum I'd received from his life insurance had paid for the deposit on the cottage. There was likely more money in savings, some-where – he'd looked after our finances, our shared accounts – but the few times I'd been tempted to ask our solicitor, his parents had been in the room, or nearby, listening. It would only have been taken as a sign of my guilt.

So we'd started again, without. That pride again: the insist-ence that I'd provide for my daughter alone. It's meant a tightened belt ever since.

But now: a partnership? It's far more than I was expecting. More than I could ever realistically expect, given my back-ground and experience.

It's a once-in-a-lifetime opportunity.

'That's . . . That's really generous, Darcy. But I couldn't possibly – what about all the . . .' I gesture, uselessly, in the air. 'You know.'

'Oh, come on. That'll blow over, eventually. You'll probably make millions out of a defamation case against those bastards and turn me down – *that's* worst-case scenario, as far as I'm concerned. But you'd be such an asset, and honestly, it'd mean *so* much to have you on board . . . I couldn't imagine anyone better suited for it, truly.' She looks at me, eyes wide, hopeful. 'Please, Hannah. Don't turn me down. I couldn't bear it.'

I feel the dull ache in my chest: the shame of it.

I should tell her I don't have it. I almost certainly *could*, and she'd counter – reduce the figure, but keep her offer the same. Because my investment *is* a token thing, really – fifteen thousand settled upon almost with a finger raised to the wind, an amount that seems, to her, small enough for anyone to afford, yet grand enough not to be shameful.

'It's really a lovely offer,' I say, finally. 'You give me *far* too much credit, really. But I ought to—'

'Please, Hannah. You're an incredible doctor. I'd be so grateful to have you on board.'

I sip my wine. It's lukewarm.

I close my eyes, for a moment, and will myself to do the right thing. To say no.

But I want it.

I want it more than anything.

'Look. Before you offer me this, I . . . I want to be honest with you.' Her brow crinkles in confusion. I go on, before I can stop. 'The hospital I'm working for at the moment, they're concerned about what this podcast—' My voice turns bitter; I don't try to hold it back. 'What employing an "accused murderer" could mean for their reputation.'

She opens her mouth, and closes it again. She's trying to work out how to respond.

'And . . . there's something else,' I say, before she can answer. I said I'd be honest. For once. I might as well go all the way.

'OK,' she says, slowly. She's nervous, now. I can feel it.

'My grandmother. The one who was a patient here. She . . .'

239

She tried to murder her family, I almost say. But at the last moment, I pull back. 'I mean, obviously she was here for a reason. You need to think about how that's going to look, if it gets out.'

She grimaces. 'Well, that's a slight PR issue, but . . . is there any reason that would get out? I mean, you have the archives, and you said you couldn't find any evidence of them elsewhere, before – right?'

I consider it. I wonder if it's possible the *Peaks Gazette* piece exists online, somewhere, still – the one I stumbled over, all those years ago. But even then, the search results for 'McLelland' are likely so saturated with *my* name, at this point . . .

'I doubt it,' I say, willing reason silent.

'And I'm assuming you're being coy yourself, not mentioning that sparkler on your hand, but . . . you'll be working here with a brand-new name, anyway, right?'

I blush. 'Oh, God. I forgot. Is that awful?'

Her laugh echoes through the room. 'And they say romance is dead.'

'Alive and well here, apparently.'

'Well, look – the renovation is going to take six months, maybe nine. We'll need to work together on programmes, hiring a team, all the rest . . . But by the time we're actually involving press, this whole thing around *Conviction* will be over, and you'll be Hannah . . . what?'

'Hannah Bryant.'

It's the first time I've said it out loud. The first time it's occurred to me to take his name; to disappear into him. To let him make me someone else. The thought makes me shudder. Turn cold.

'I like it. So, we'll let whoever's doing our PR know about

it, but . . . I don't think it'll be an issue. Unless it's an issue for you.' She leans forward. I feel the concern in her eyes, and I look away. 'Have you let all this get into your head?'

'What do you mean?'

I know exactly what she means, of course. I'm just buying time.

'Please tell me you haven't managed to convince yourself they've actually got a case against you with all this.'

I look up. Of *course* they have a case against me.

'Oh, come *on*, Hannah. You're letting them win, if you do this.' There's a flinty coldness in her voice as she speaks. 'It's like some kind of sick experiment. You couldn't come up with something better if you tried.'

'What do you mean?'

'It's just like gaslighting, taken to an awful extreme. You said yourself your memory is hazy, presumably because you were suffering from a pretty nasty concussion, from what I've read, and what you've told me. So, you're not sure what happened, but the police give you a reasonable version of events, and they tell you they've got proof, and you accept it. You move on with your life, and you leave it behind you.

'But *then*, ten years later, some completely unqualified stranger comes along – with a pitchfork-waving mob behind her – and says, actually, everything you know about that night is wrong. Everything you've been told, and everything you've allowed yourself to believe – because it made sense, according to all the people you had around you at the time – is false.

'And in place of that, they're giving you a new version of events that puts *you* at the centre of it. And because (*a*) you didn't remember it in the first place, and (*b*) you've consigned it all to the past – not to mention the fact it's an *awful* trauma you went through, so your mind's probably done a whole *world* of work to let some, if not all of that go – you're left with questions over everything. Your whole understanding of what's real is unsettled. They're *creating* a set of circumstances that would make you believe you did it. And apparently it's working.'

I stare at her. She raises a hand to her mouth. 'I just went *way* overboard on the analysis there, didn't I? I'm so sorry. That was rude.'

I hear myself laugh, though I feel exposed. I feel raw. 'You're actually . . . spot on. I feel very . . . seen.'

'This is why I have no friends. Chronic nosiness, combined with an inability to think before I speak . . . Not a great combination, honestly.'

'It's fine, really,' I say. And I mean it. Because it makes sense. It's a normal reaction. I'm not losing my mind. Only responding to a thing that has happened to me; to a situation beyond my control. All the things I've felt and thought; all the things I've read about myself cease to feel quite as real as they did before. 'You know, I actually feel better for hearing it. I think I might've just had a breakthrough.'

Her eyes widen. '*No.*' She fixes me with a smile. 'Tell me.'

'Oh, not . . . Nothing more than you said, really. It just . . . It makes a lot of sense.'

'Look, I might be wrong about everything. You absolutely could be a murderer, for all I know. But I *am* a pretty good doctor, or I was until I decided to become an idiot property developer. If you *are* a psychopath, I'd be proud to have been duped by you.'

She says it with a grin; it's an attempt to lighten the mood. It doesn't quite land, and she sees it. But she's deft in conversation: she doesn't address it, as I would. She simply moves on. 'So what do you think – about this partnership? I don't expect you to decide now, but . . .'

I take a breath. I look around, imagining it: a stake in Hawkwood House.

'I *do* need to talk to Dan about it before I give you an absolute yes. If you don't mind? But . . . yes. Provisionally. Yes.'

She claps her hands in delight and raises her glass. 'I will *happily* take that. Let's drink to it.'

As I sip, I catch it: the tapping sound I'd heard, that first day. I swallow the wine, and I'm home, for a moment, the same tart taste on my tongue.

Tap. Tap. Tap.

'Is there someone else here?'

She looks up. 'I don't think so. Did you hear something?'

I shake my head. 'Just a draught, I think.'

'OK. So, I'll sort out the paperwork, and you can give your notice – and then we'll go from there. Sound good?'

And it does. It dawns on me, now, that I can rearrange the narrative a little to save Dan the worry: to make it look as though I'm leaving the hospital by choice.

'Great,' I say, smiling. 'Can we . . . Would you mind if we had a wander around? I'd love to get the measure of it again.'

She winces. 'I'd love to say yes, but it's a hard-hat zone now, and my insurance won't cover it if we're not in full safety gear. Maybe one day when the contractors are in? They'll be thrilled to skive off for an hour while you look around.'

I feel a prickle of disappointment. Still, I brush it off. 'Of course. No rush.'

She reaches for the bottle and tops up each of our glasses. 'To delayed gratification.'

My phone vibrates on my lap. *Conviction, Episode Four: The Wife is now available.*

I turn it face down, and raise my glass. 'To whatever happens next.'

I'm a little tipsy as I wave goodbye – not drunk, only pleasantly giddy, with a warmth to my skin that doesn't match the cool evening breeze.

I feel as though I've exorcized at least one of my ghosts over the course of the afternoon. Talking to Darcy – opening up to her, about Graham, about Margot (almost), about so many previously unspeakable things – has made me walk away lighter, my feet seeming a little above the ground. I feel wiped clean, renewed.

She's good at what she does – I can see this now; saw it, too, in the way she opened up silences, steered me into realizations I'd known, deep down, but hadn't quite found it within myself to articulate. The thought of us, working together . . . I feel a bright, intellectual thrill at it; a door opening to ideas and treatments and therapies I'd long considered beyond my reach.

I unlock the car and sit, wondering – briefly – if I ought to be driving.

But it's fine. Home is five minutes away. And I'm only tipsy. A couple of glasses, on a low tolerance. That's all.

I put the keys in the ignition, and the car purrs to life.

'Pairing,' the speaker announces in a monotone. I reach into my back pocket for my phone. I know what's happening, and I need to make it stop.

'It's 1991,' Anna Byers says, her voice cool. In the background, I hear my own voice singing *Sweet Child O'Mine*. I can picture the night in question; I can see the hand-held camcorder's red-dot flash.

'Hannah McLelland and Graham Catton have been dating for six months. Everyone agrees they're the perfect couple. She's an outgoing party girl. He's a quietly charismatic *nice guy*. Bookishly handsome to her nineties heroin chic thinness, made all the more apparent by her wild mass of curly hair, which makes her easy to spot when she's not on his arm.'

I press the stop button on my phone. It blinks, but does nothing. Anna Byers's voice goes on. I feel a sense of pressure rising, like a drumbeat; the skin on my arms prickles with some unspeakable threat.

'He carries her books when he walks her to the classes she'd otherwise be too hungover to attend. She drags him from the library to loosen up when he'd otherwise study through the night. They're gorgeous together, and passionately in love, in the way you *are*, at that age – as though you're the only two people to exist in the world. It's before mobile phones became commonplace, so whenever they see each other, it's as though they've been apart for a month. He picks her up and spins her around, and they hold each other's hands all night long.'

I open the car door, and step away, instinctively, as though backing away from a beast about to snap.

'And nobody minds it – the way they're like this, a little self-absorbed, a bit wrapped up in each other – because they're just so lovely together. Living proof of the idea that it *is* possible to meet the love of your life over a game of beer pong. That you'll lock eyes once and live happily ever after.'

I trip back, into Graham's waiting arms, the press of his breath in my hair, and I turn cold.

I loved you, he says, his voice vibrating through me. *And look what you did.*

I spin around, a scream in my throat.

But there's nobody there.

'That you'll be together, forever,' Anna Byers goes on. 'No matter what. 'Til death do you part.'

35

The cottage is empty, the windows dark. I let myself in and slam the door; I slide the deadbolt across, something we never do. Something I know won't help, anyway. I press my back against it and let myself slide down. Tears gather in my throat, but I choke them back.

I won't let him see me cry. He – my husband – who's dead. Who absolutely is not there, though it felt that way as I drove home, *Conviction* continuing on, filling the space. I hadn't planned to listen to it all; hadn't really *wanted* to. But a grim, destructive curiosity – an impulse I'd take pleasure in picking apart, if it weren't my own – made me listen to the words of the people come to damn me.

A roster of friends I'd forgotten – *his* friends, always, never mine – from the carousel of networking events we went to, for a while, and then he went to alone; and Darren, of course, again.

And my mother-in-law, Marianne, whose arm I'd held on to, at trial, to keep her from falling.

'She's taken everything away from us. *Everything*,' she'd told Anna Byers, a crack splitting her voice. 'Our son loved her so much – so, so much. And we loved her, too, because we wanted to see what he saw in her – we had faith in what he saw. And for . . . for Evelyn. Children *need* their mothers, don't they?'

As I drove, I thought of the birthday cards I'd torn open over the years. The money I'd put in Evie's savings account, the unread well-wishes thrown away. The fact is, I've never wanted my daughter to have anything to do with Graham's father, Eric. Maybe if Marianne had shown any interest in me or my daughter while Graham was alive, I might have thought twice.

But she didn't. She did nothing to deserve my daughter's affection, and she certainly never did anything to deserve mine.

Still, she went on. 'So after the murder, we believed what she said. We knew they'd had problems. But who doesn't? They were a young couple trying to make it on their own – partly an issue of their own making, because she was too proud to ever really accept our help, but . . . well, we respected that. You have to, don't you?'

'But never – not in a million years – did it cross my mind that she'd have had something to do with it. I thought the evidence told the story the prosecution said it did. I believed it, completely. Until . . .'

Byers had cut in here. 'This part is a little hard to listen to – but we wanted to do Marianne's story justice. She's a woman grieving, as you can tell – someone who may never quite understand the awful tragedy that's befallen her, and her family.'

My *family*, I'd thought, with a viciousness that surprised me.

Mine, Graham had corrected me.

Marianne's voice had resumed, low and weary. 'After the trial ended, on the last day, we . . . we thought she'd gone back to the hotel. Which seemed impossible, because of the press, and the people in the court, and outside, but . . . we assumed she must've just slipped out. Maybe one of the bailiffs had taken her out the back way, or something. So we left, thinking we'd find them back at the room we'd been paying for, until she could get back on her feet.

'But we got to the hotel, and she wasn't there. She didn't answer the phone, or the door, and . . . we thought something terrible must've happened. I mean, we were assuming the worst, with the things they'd said about Mr Philips and his family . . . God, your mind just goes everywhere. That's the thing about living through something like this. You never get that sense of security – innocence, I suppose – you never get it back.

'Eventually, one of the maids let us in – and the room was empty. Like they'd never been there at all. We called the only number we had for her, over and over, until it just . . . cut off. And we never heard from her again.

'We tried to get legal advice, but . . .'

But grandparents don't have the automatic right to see their grandchildren in the UK. I'd made sure of that, before I left. I wanted to disappear from their lives. To never see either of them again.

I think now of Eric's hand on my arm; of the boned corset squeezing at my ribs. The dress holding me in place, the wet press of his lips against mine.

I drag myself up. I'm all energy, electric with anger and disgust. I can't leave, but I can't keep still.

'I suppose we wanted to see the best in her, for Graham,' Marianne had said. 'But when she did that . . . I just started to wonder what else she might be capable of. Because even up to the day of sentencing, she'd looked me in the eye, living in a hotel we'd paid for, and thanked me for what I'd – what *we'd* – done for her. She was wholly, utterly convincing.

'And so . . . I went back to look at the case.'

I open my laptop and click to *Conviction*'s website. I see her, there, with the other woman: the one whose voice I hadn't recognized at first, though when I did, I felt – as I should have – guilt.

I remembered her, weeping in the courtroom, bent double as her son was led away in ringing chains. Mina Philips. The mother of the boy charged with my husband's murder.

'My son is a good boy,' she'd said, describing her response to Marianne's message. 'He'd do anything for anyone. He'd help his worst enemy, if they asked him to. So . . . I tried to be like him. To do what he would do.'

'If this can be described as a case that's defined by its twists and turns,' Anna Byers had said, 'this has to be one of the biggest. The actions of the victim's wife, after the trial ended, led his mother to join forces with the mother of the man charged with his death – with Marianne becoming one of the most vocal supporters in the drive to reopen the case, and have his conviction overturned.'

Byers had played out the conversation between them skilfully: their voices, their tones, their manners juxtaposed. Two women joined together in a grief only truly understood by the other, though they're from different worlds. Have led utterly different lives.

But I know Marianne. I can see it: the way she'd act out

her good will, her supposed selflessness. I've been on the receiving end of her condescending glances, her curious enquiries about my background, the disgust masked behind an overblown charity.

There's no way Mike's mother hasn't noticed it, too. It's one of the lies that makes society function: that the poor appreciate the interest of the wealthy; that we're not simply indulging them when they choose to take an interest. But I understand why she chooses to overlook it. It plays too well to resist. The victim's mother on her son's side. It's worth every patronizing second.

'I just wish,' Marianne had said as the episode drew to a close, 'that I'd said something earlier. I knew, before they got married, that things weren't right. I *knew* it. But I loved him so much that I couldn't bring myself to say it. And so I looked at her, in her dress, that day, and I decided to love her instead. And because of that, my son is dead, and another boy's life has been ruined. And all the while, that evil woman is out there, happy and free.'

Happy and free, I think as I pull the curtains shut. Outside, a stranger takes a photo of me, ruefully smiling, on his phone.

It's on Twitter, five minutes later.

Look at her, the replies say. That smug, self-satisfied bitch.

36

London, 2005

Lucie eyes me suspiciously. 'What are you smiling at?'

'Nothing.'

'There has to be something. People don't just smile like that.'

She's right, of course. It was an involuntary smile, after forty-five minutes of stony silence on her part. I'd lost concentration. My mind had wandered to Evie, that morning, giggling with pleasure as Graham tickled her belly. I've been replaying it all day, drifting back to it: a moment of pure elation, our family, for once, utterly perfect.

'I was just thinking how nice it is to get paid to do absolutely nothing. I get paid quite a bit, you know.'

Her brow crinkles. 'That doesn't seem like something you're supposed to say.'

'Maybe not. But it's better than saying nothing at all.'

This is a dice-roll approach. I don't know if it'll work. If anything, it's more likely to make things worse. But she *is* talking to me now. That's an improvement.

'How much *do* you get paid?'

'Loads. You see how many clients there are here, and how much all of your parents are paying . . . Imagine that, split between us. After overheads, obviously.'

'Is that why you went into it? For the money?'

'God, no.'

'So why, then?'

'Because I'm good at it.'

I've never heard her laugh before, and I cling to it. It's a little sharp, as though it's been held in for too long.

'See? You weren't laughing when you came in. Now, you're basically cured.'

'You're really annoying,' she says, though she's still smiling.

'I know. But it works.'

There's a lull; she purses her lips, and then smiles again. 'Fine. I'll talk.'

I glance at the clock. 'I'm afraid not. We're done here.'

A flicker of disappointment crosses her face. 'Oh.'

'Next time, though – OK?'

She nods. 'All right, doc. Next time.'

On the way home, I think about her. I wonder if I did the right thing in ending our session like that; I wonder if I ought to have stayed, while she was in the mood to talk.

But I couldn't have, even if I'd been sure it would help. I have to get home to my child.

The tube rattles around me, the flash of light and sound oppressive, and exhausting.

The train comes to a halt in a tunnel, and the conductor announces a delay.

I glance at my watch.

Louise is there, I tell myself. *She'll wait.*

And that's true. Our new nanny is reliable, effortlessly so – perhaps the fifteenth or sixteenth we'd interviewed, the only one that *fit.* We'd had to outbid another family to get her, but it was worth it. She's the best. She'd never leave before one of us got home. Usually, that's me.

I look at my watch, uselessly, again. The clench of foreboding in my throat tightens. It tightens, still, as the train begins to move. By the time I reach our house, I can barely breathe with it, my heart racing at the sight of his bike propped in the hall, a rangy shadow through the glass.

I turn my key in the lock and push the door. It catches, the jolt taking me aback. The silver knot of the chain rattles in the gap.

'Louise?' I call, though I know she isn't there. It's an act; I'm pretending, for the neighbours, and myself, that there's no way my husband would lock me out of my own home. 'I got held up – nightmare on the tube. Can you let me in?'

There's no answer. I ring the bell. My pulse begins to rise, a cold sweat licking at the curve of my neck. 'Hello?'

He can't hear me, I tell myself, ringing again. *He's got the TV up too loud, or his headphones on. That's all this is.*

I'm rationalizing, and I know it. I am lying to myself. I'm trying to stay calm, though my baby's inside, and I'm locked out in the street. The longing I feel is physical, a claw in the pit of my chest.

I squeeze my hand through the crack and tug, uselessly, at the chain. 'Hello? Graham?'

With every passing second, my rationalizations slip. In my mind, I see him inside, with a woman, perhaps – with Louise, thin and blonde, absolutely his type. Why didn't I think of that before? Or *did* I think of it and let it go – friends close, and enemies closer?

'Let me *in*, Graham,' I shout through the crack. 'I know you're in there. Open the door.'

I imagine him, alone, with my little girl. Packing a bag, perhaps; his hands tugging socks onto tiny feet, then shoes. Telling her this is for the best. Telling her they'll be better off without me. I begin to panic.

'Graham!' I beat the door with both hands. I hear a window open, above and to the right. The neighbours are watching. 'For Christ's sake, Graham. Let me in. Let. Me. In.'

I sound like a madwoman, punctuating each word with a thud, the chain rattling against the door. But I no longer care. I pound harder, imagining the wood splintering into my palms.

Finally, I see him. He takes the stairs slowly – deliberately – his eyes fixed on mine, and when he opens the door, he smiles.

I know what this is: it's for the benefit of the passers-by who've heard me, the neighbours watching on. He gives a vague apology I know he doesn't mean – he says he didn't hear me over Evie's cries, though she's silent now, and has been, this whole time. He lets me in.

I feel him there, behind me, as I climb the stairs. I don't look back at him, although I want to. All the rage I'd felt, on the other side of the door, has evaporated; the look in his eyes when he opened the door saw to that.

Now, for the first time, I'm afraid.

I am scared of my husband.

Of what he might do; what he might have already done.

You're being irrational, I tell myself. *He isn't like that. He's a cheat and a liar, yes, but he's no worse than the rest of them.* That's what I tell myself. But I can't help the feeling – an intuition, a terrible pang – that I'm wrong.

Because the anger seems to radiate from him. I feel his eyes, there, in my back; the sense of a hand reaching for my throat, pulling at my hair. I imagine myself falling, skull cracked on the staircase, before I get to see my girl.

None of this happens, of course. But I can feel him thinking about it. About what he *could* do, though he won't. About what I've driven him to, by being such a terrible wife.

I don't look back as I speak. I'm afraid to meet his eye. 'I'm really sorry,' I say, the words pathetic, reed-thin. 'There was a signal failure on the tube, and I—'

'I *knew* this would happen.'

The words are a growl, a jolt. I push open the door to Evie's room. Her breath is low and lovely; she's sleeping, hands curled around Maggie, her bear. The relief spreads through me, a morphine warmth. I cling to the handle to disguise my buckling knees.

He sees this, I know. He sees everything.

I turn and close the door. 'I'll put dinner on,' I say. He follows, inches behind, without saying a word. He remains there, behind me, as I boil the water and pour the pasta, with a deafening rattle, into the pan. Every step I take, he takes, too. I can feel him, hear his breath in my ear.

I know I could turn around. I could tell him to back off; to stop being so aggressive. God, I could take this bubbling pan and drown him in it.

I *could* do any of those things. But I won't.

I drop the steaming pasta on to plates, and hand him the largest. He takes it, and sits. He beckons me to join him, and I do. He picks up a fork and jams it, deliberately, into the pasta. He turns it around, again and again, his knuckles pale, fist clenched. I try to do the same – to echo him, to show him we're on the same page. A unit.

My own knuckles whiten as I try to contain an involuntary shiver.

I hate myself for this. For how weak I am, for being afraid.

'Where were you?' His voice is low, soft. He doesn't want to wake Evie. He's a good father. He's always sure of that.

'I told you. There was a signal failure on the tube. I was stuck in a tunnel for twenty minutes.'

He swallows, his eyes still on mine. 'Where *were* you, Hannah?'

My throat contracts. I feel tears sting behind my eyes. 'I was on the tube. On the Central line. There was a—'

The table rattles beneath me. 'Where the fuck *were* you?'

'I'm telling you. It's the truth. I was on the—'

'You're lying.'

I look down at my plate, my uneaten food. I don't know what to do; how to fix this. I know I'm telling the truth. But it isn't enough. I close my eyes. 'Graham—'

I hear the shatter of the plate, my eyes still closed, tight. I hear the slow, wet slide of the food, slick against the wall.

'Look at me,' he hisses. And I do. He's standing now. I see his hands balled into fists, veins rivering his arms. I feel my muscles turn soft, weaken. 'You're a *liar*, Hannah. You always have been. You're a selfish bitch.'

He steps towards me. Passes me, and stands at the back of

my chair. I imagine myself running. Scrambling away. Dragged back.

I feel his hands on my shoulders, the warmth seeping through my shirt. 'And you're fucking pathetic,' he whispers into my ear. He stays there, for what feels like minutes.

And then, he walks away. He leaves the front door wide open, the evening air licking, cold, at my neck.

37

Derbyshire, 2018

'Hannah? Can you let me in?'

I sit up, a strand of spit still clinging to the pool on the back of my hand.

Dan peers through the glass. He smiles, but there's sadness in it. I see why: me, asleep at the kitchen table, the remains of a bottle of wine beside me.

I stagger up and slide the bolt across. I hear voices outside, a chatter of flashes and clicks. Dan slides through the gap and slams the door.

I step back, and stumble. This time, Graham isn't there to catch me.

'What's going on?' I hear the slur in my voice. 'Where's Evie?'

He drops his bag beside the table, and pours the rest of the wine into my glass. 'I've just dropped her at Lissa's to do some revision for a bit. Her mum knows what's going on, so . . .' He takes a long – too long – sip, as though trying to drain it.

Presumably because I'm already drunk. I see his lips purse at the tang. 'I'm guessing you've seen the news.'

I try to parse the words: wonder, briefly, if I'm misunderstanding him. If he's talking about *Conviction*. But he wouldn't word it like that. It doesn't make sense. 'What do you mean?'

Something crosses his face, a mixture of surprise and disappointment – that I don't know, but I'm drinking anyway. And then, he pales. It's bad news, whatever it is, and he's the one who has to tell me.

'Someone's come forward,' he says, finally. 'An alibi for the night Mike Philips was . . .' He catches himself; tries again. 'Someone's confirmed he was at the bar, like *Conviction* said he was. It's been confirmed. Apparently, it's rock solid. So . . .'

I feel my breath catch in my throat, and I sit. I can't speak.

He doesn't want to say it, I know. But I need him to. Otherwise, it'll never be real.

He sighs. 'He's been cleared of all charges. They're letting him go.'

We sit in silence for a while, on our phones, faces lit by our respective screens.

I watch the cottage on the news, journalists waiting for a statement I have no intention of giving.

Anything you say can and will be used against you, the police on TV say. So I, for now, am saying nothing at all.

Even though there are thousands of people, braying cheerfully, calling my name:

the bitch did it

Why don't we have the electric chair here, she should die
for what she did to Mike alone
mad-eyed psycho cunt

Even though I *am* guilty, I know – of hating my husband.
I know that much is true. Of wanting to protect my daughter,
no matter what. And of letting myself believe the explanation
that was presented to me; of taking the easy way out.

Some part of me knew Mike Philips wasn't in my house in
my house, that night. But I *wanted* him to be. So I believed it
– just like all these strangers who want to think I killed my
husband. They've as little proof as I do, but believing, for
them, is enough.

I look over at Dan, staring intently at his screen. 'I think . . .
I should probably call my solicitor. If they're reopening the
case, I should . . .'

He looks up. His face is pale, his expression wounded. I
don't wait for him to reply.

I stand and plug my phone in to charge. I feel sober, now,
a horrible clarity sharpening my senses. 'Did you listen to
the new episode already?' I know the answer to this. I just
need to see his reaction. I need to see that he still believes
me.

But his face is a mask. 'Yeah, I . . . I did. I'm sorry. We can
listen to it now, if you want?'

'I've heard it,' I say, a little more viciously than I mean to.
I turn away, pretending to tidy the table. My foot catches on
the strap of his bag, the contents spilling over the floor. 'Shit,'
I mutter, losing my balance as I bend to scoop up the papers.
'Could you not leave this here? We have a whole rack in the
hallway for bags and stuff.'

He stands, and bends to help. 'OK. Don't worry.' His voice

is cool, gentle: like a tamer approaching an animal. Somehow, it makes the anger I feel thicken, grow to a hard mass in my chest. 'I'll move it. Here.' He reaches for sheaf of pages just out of reach. 'I'll sort them out now.'

I hand them to him, roughly, and curse as a page slips out. I pick it up, the room lurching, a little. A familiar photograph at the top of the page, familiar words typed beneath. *Hawkwood House, 1955.*

'What's this?' My throat tightens a little.

'It's nothing. I just . . .' He looks down at the pages again, almost as though he doesn't recognize them at all. 'I had this idea about writing a book. A history of Hawkwood,' he adds quickly. Too quickly.

I think about what Sarah had said about offers to divulge secrets about me for cash. I wonder what a book would be worth, now, after *The Wife*. What value they'd place on the story of seven years by the side of a killer, by a journalist who had no idea who'd been lying beside him in bed.

I remember the cracked spine of a paperback passed among friends, at university: about a woman who'd had a friendship with Ted Bundy without ever seeing who he really was. *A fascinating psychological study*, one blurb had said, enough for us to justify our morbid curiosity.

'Do you think I did it?' I hear myself say, though I don't think I want to know the answer. I think if he says yes, it will split me in two. His mouth opens, a little. The pause is at once brief, and yet too long. 'Don't look at me like that, Dan. I just want to know. Do you think any of what they're saying is true?'

'Hannah, this isn't the—'

'Yes or no, Dan. Do you think I killed Graham, or not?'

He closes his eyes. He's like a man losing patience with a petulant child. And I understand why. I'm acting like one.

'I don't think it's that simple. I think there are probably parts of what they're saying that are rooted in fact, but I *know* you. I know you aren't the person they're making you out to be. So if you . . .'

'If I what?'

'I don't think you did it – let's be clear on that.'

'You weren't clear on that a few seconds ago.'

'Hannah, I believe *you*. I love you. You're a good person. A good *mother* to a good girl. So stop picking a bloody fight.' It's the closest I've heard him come to anger – though it's more like exhaustion, an inability to go on. 'I've known you long enough to know those things are absolutely true, because I've *seen* them for myself. I was there. I'm *still* here, even if you are being kind of . . .'

He sighs, and steadies himself. He takes the photo from my hand with such care that I'm reminded of something: the memory as crisp and clear as cold water. 'I just think even if you *did* do it, there was probably . . . I don't know. A reason for it.' His eyes search my face. 'You really don't remember anything?'

I drown in the memory: a whisper to Evie, begging her to stay quiet. The knife, cold in my trembling hand.

I shake my head. All the words have escaped me.

'Look.' As his hand meets my skin, I feel myself crumble. 'We will get through this. You, me, and Evie. As long as we're together, we'll be fine.' He pulls me in, his heartbeat a sickening thump against mine. 'I promise.'

I remember him saying the same words, as we sat in this room, only a little over four weeks before. At the time, I'd almost been able to make myself believe him, with the same force of will he's using, now, to believe in me. Now, though, no matter how desperately I try, I know it isn't true.

And now, I hate him for making promises he knows he cannot keep.

My heart sits in my throat, a bloody lump, as I wait for Evie to come home. Dan left to pick her up twenty minutes ago. Lissa's house is five minutes away. It shouldn't take this long.

I imagine them talking – about how they're feeling, and whether they can trust me: her mother, his would-be wife. Every time we're back on solid ground, something else comes along to make her question who I am, and what I say. I feel as though I'm being knocked down, drowning in freezing waves, one after another.

'Evil,' Marianne had called me. Graham's mother. Evie's blood, whether I like it or not. I wonder if Evie has ever thought of her, before now: if she'll attach a special meaning to her words.

It's a stupid question, of course. I wouldn't be here – *we* wouldn't be here – if I hadn't thought of my own mother's words so long ago. If I hadn't hung so much on her – Margot – being 'just like me'.

I think of my conversation with Darcy; of her suggestion that, if my grandmother's papers don't exist, nobody has to know. Though *Darcy* doesn't know about the delusions, the voices, the circumstances of the murder of Margot's husband and child. She didn't read the papers. No one knows Margot's story but me.

And I could make it all disappear, in an instant.

I open the cupboard and dig out the box. They could be

home – *if* they're coming home – any minute. I have to be quick.

I pull off the lid and pull out the papers. They're surprisingly light, shot through with age. I run the kitchen tap and turn to push the papers under the running water.

My eyes catch on a date at the top of the page. *18 July 1949.* Four years before the murders were committed. I stop the tap and frantically wipe the water from the now-smudged ink.

Mrs McLelland self-admitted last week, complaining of exhaustion and requiring rest.

She was otherwise well on her arrival, only suffering from forced insomnia after the birth of her youngest child. However, in the short time she has been with us, her condition has deteriorated significantly.

Mrs McLelland claims to have begun hearing voices since her arrival at Hawkwood House, believing herself to be the victim of 'ghosts'. She insists that she be discharged immediately, though as her clinician I cannot recommend this – but as she has self-admitted, unfortunately it is her right also to self-discharge.

I see the swoop of headlights beneath the curtain, and stuff the pages back into the box.

Margot was fine before she went to Hawkwood House. That's when it all went wrong.

I think of my first visit. The first time I'd felt Graham's voice, ice-like, in my ear. The first time I'd come home to Dan and seen myself turn cold in the bathroom mirror. The first time I'd felt like some other woman: someone I didn't know.

You don't believe in ghosts, I tell myself as I kick the box back into the cupboard.

'Uhhh . . . OK,' Evie says, behind me, wide-eyed.

I turn, and try to laugh it off. 'Sorry. I was trying to remember a . . . a thing. Tidying up this mess.'

I don't know what I'm saying. I'm losing control. I'm going mad.

She gives me a brief, doubtful look. 'All right, well . . . I'm going to bed.' No hug. No kiss. She takes the stairs two at a time, and disappears.

Dan looks at me, all worry, all concern – but says nothing.

He doesn't see Graham's hands at my shoulders, fingers squeezing through the knots: a tenderness, and a threat. He can only see how I respond to it. So I smile. I pretend everything is fine. It's a betrayal, and he senses it. He sees the falseness, even if he sees nothing else.

He turns away, and bolts the door from the terrors outside. He says nothing. Only climbs the stairs to bed, leaving me alone, again.

EPISODE FIVE

38

London, 2005

Lucie draws a figure eight on the arm of the chair with her finger.

I crouch down to meet her, and her eyes flick open. She tugs at the string of her headphones, plucking both earbuds out at once. The song continues with a hiss.

'Shall we pick up where we left off?'

Her lips are dried out, chapped white; her skin almost translucent, cheekbones pressed up against the surface like knuckles in a fist.

I wonder what's happened, overnight, that's made her so much worse today.

I know I can't tell her I feel it, too. But I wish I could.

Graham didn't come home. After he left, I sat, and waited, the cold air dimpling my skin. I waited, knowing if he found me gone, it'd be worse.

But then, nine o'clock came. Then ten. Then midnight.

I cleaned up the dishes, the mess on the floor. I wiped the stain from the wall, still feeling his hands on my shoulders.

I went to bed alone, and lay there, all night, waiting for him to come home. I dug my fists into my ribs. I hated myself for wanting him to return, in spite of everything. A stronger woman – a better mother – would have taken her daughter and run.

But I didn't.

I crawled out of bed this morning, feeling like skin bound to bone. As though something vital had been pulled from me, drained horribly away.

'Come on then,' I say, rising to stand. I nod to Lucie's one-to-one nurse, who gives me a grateful smile. She'll be glad of the break; the chance to freshen up, to steel herself for what remains of her 'death watch' shift (the name the patients give the one-to-one monitoring of suicidal patients, much to our displeasure – though in private, we've begun to call it that, too).

Lucie uncurls herself from her seat and shuffles along beside me. She says nothing as we walk to the treatment room and take the same seats as before.

'So – how are you doing?'

'Fine.'

'Fine?'

'Yeah.' She looks towards the window, and I follow her gaze. It's a beautiful day, the orange leaves crisp against the sky. 'I want to go out. It's so stuffy in here all the time. It makes me feel like I can't breathe.'

I can't argue with this. The air here is soupy, the heating turned up to full blast, day and night – though this doesn't stop our clients stalking the ward in fleece jumpers and joggers, trying to sweat through their clothes.

'I can crack a window, if you like?'

She shrugs. 'If you want.'

I stand and push it open – just a little. I'm grateful for the cool air, too. It brings me back to the moment, sharpening my focus.

'So.'

'So?'

'Let's talk.'

'I'm not in the mood.'

'All right. I'll just sit here. Remember, I get paid either way.'

'You're a really shitty doctor.'

'Try me.'

She scowls, but there's a glint of humour in her eyes. She's playing along.

I smile. 'Something's happened overnight, hasn't it?'

She flinches. 'No.'

'No?'

'No.' She's less sure, this time. 'No.'

I say nothing. I let the silence do the work.

It's minutes before she moves. A slight uncoiling – hardly anything at all. But it's there.

Still, I say nothing.

'I got a letter,' she says, her voice barely more than a whisper.

'A letter.'

'Yeah.' She looks out of the window. 'From my sister.'

I search my memory for her name; the girl who'd so confidently handled both Darren and me, weeks earlier. I resist the urge to smile at the memory, the way Darren had flushed when questioned by a teenage girl. 'Sophie?'

'Yeah.'

'How is she?'

'Oh, she's *great*.' I feel a kick of anxiety, a slight surprise. There's a viciousness in her tone that I hadn't expected. 'She's doing *amazing*.'

'You don't get along?'

She looks up at me, something unbearably familiar in her eyes.

It isn't dislike, or jealousy, that's between them.

I recognize it. I know it – intimately.

It's fear.

She closes off before I can find the right way in. She curls into herself, like she wants to disappear.

We sit in silence, again, for a while. 'How's your boyfriend?' I root around in my memory for the name – one I've heard while eavesdropping on conversations between patients in the main lounge. 'Matt, is it?'

She blushes a deep, blooming red. 'Mike. But he's not my boyfriend any more.'

'Oh.' I offer a smile. 'Men, hmm?'

She looks up; meets my eye, squarely. I've given too much away. Her eyes flit to Graham's diamond ring on my finger, the skin rubbed raw around it – an impulsive habit I can't quite break.

So, I fold. I change the subject back, and make a bargain. 'Let's say I could arrange for you to go for a walk – a *supervised* walk,' I add, quickly, as her eyes widen. 'Do you think you could tell me about that – about your sister?'

'How long for?'

I laugh. 'The walk, or the chat?'

'Both.'

I tap my pen against my pad, pretending to think about it. 'Thirty minutes talking, for thirty minutes outside. What do you think?'

She runs her tongue along her teeth. 'Deal.'

Half an hour later – exactly, Lucie watching the clock to the second, careful to give me no more than our allotted talking time – I root around in the nurses' station for her paperwork.

'Stay at that angle all day, if you want,' a voice says from above. 'It suits you.'

My skin prickles with irritation. 'Pretty sure that's sexual harassment, Dr Andrews,' I mutter, without looking up. I find the file and lay it out on the desk. 'Can I help you with something?'

'Oh, don't be such a miser.'

Darren's eyes scan my chest. Instinctively, I run fingers to the buttons, checking for gaps. He seems to take this as an invitation. 'That's better.'

I try to breathe. To stay calm. 'I'm really not in the mood.'

'Oh no.' His voice oozes what I suppose he thinks is charm, though it's nauseating. 'Can I help you out at all? The break room's empty if you want to get off your feet. Mine can hold us both up, I'm sure of it.'

I scan the Grounds Access form, searching for the relevant section: *Supervised/Unsupervised*. I look up at Darren. 'How do you think Graham would feel about the way you're talking to me right now?'

He gives a snort. 'Oh, come on, Hannah. Don't be ridiculous.'

'I'm not joking. If you talk to me like that again, I'll tell him. I'm sure he'll be thrilled to find out his best friend is a fucking pig.'

'As thrilled as he was when he found out his wife was a fucking whore, I imagine.'

The words – clipped, utterly cold – wind me. I blink away the tears that prickle in my eyes. I check the box, sign the form, and slip it inside Lucie's file.

'You know, you go about making it seem as though you're some kind of angel – some kind of *victim*, just because he can't keep his dick in his pants. As though you weren't the one who bit the apple first.'

I feel a hot swell of hate spread through me; a reddish burn creeps up my neck, a betrayal.

'I mean, his *dad*, Hannah? Really? Freud would've had a field day with that. And while I've been here this whole time. It's quite hurtful, really.'

'How do you—' I stop, mid-sentence. An intern rounds the corner, talking a little over volume – the usual way visiting relatives are announced, a hint to quiet all closed-door conversations, or anything that might give these interlopers cause for concern.

'Graham told me,' he hisses. 'Right after your honeymoon. Lucky for you, Marianne's more concerned with keeping up appearances than dragging your name through the mud – publicly, anyway. But trust me: everyone knows. So I'd stop with the prim little madam act, if I were you.'

The intern glances at us as she passes. I ball my shaking hands into fists, hoping she doesn't see. *I'm going to leave him,* I think, the thought alarming in its clarity. *Graham, his awful family, his friends – all of them. I'm going to take Evie, and leave them all behind.*

'I'm done for the day,' I say, though I'm an hour from finishing my shift. 'I have some overtime to use. I'm going home.'

He smiles, pig-eyed and mulishly benevolent. 'All right. But think about what I said. Laughter's meant to be the best medicine, but . . . there are others.' He winks, and smiles. 'Buh-bye.'

39

Derbyshire, 2018

It's been days since I've left the house. It's tempting to think I might never leave again – that I might just close the curtains, lock the doors, and stay here.

But it doesn't help. The outside world gets in anyway, like smoke through a crack in a door.

Every morning, I wake up, and I tell myself not to do it. *Not* to log on. *Not* to click the hashtags, visit the Reddit forums, browse the Facebook pages, all of which are about me. About the things that I've done. But I can't help myself. It's as though I'm drawn there by some gravitational pull.

People have called me narcissistic, in their armchair diagnoses – selfish, coldly self-absorbed. I guess in this respect, they're right. It's a compulsion: a habit as destructive and satisfying as peeling open a wound to watch it bleed.

Because, while before, these strangers talked about my guilt in the abstract – talked about *me* in the abstract, like a character in a play – since the last episode, and since Mike's release, I've become somehow real to them. I'm the monster that must be destroyed.

My home address is out there, now. My phone number, my email address. *Dan's* phone number and email address. My purchase history, on every website I've ever shopped, pulled from my inbox and pored through, as though it's evidence. My prescriptions, from the online delivery service I use – a beta-blocker I've been taking since I was fifteen, for migraines I no longer have; the HRT I'm prescribed but am yet to use – all out there as proof of my guilt.

I've wondered how it's possible for them to know all this. It's occurred to me that it might be coming from within – Dan has all but barred me from asking Evie about her boyfriend, in any way beyond the most casual enquiries about his health. He says anyone can find anything, about anyone, these days, on the internet.

He tells me not to worry. That it will pass. That it isn't personal, not really; that these people are all talk, barely connected to the things they say. But it doesn't feel that way – not now. Because the way they talk to me has changed; turned horribly direct. Suddenly, I'm a 'you', not a 'her'.

I'm coming for you, bitch
you deserve to die slowly, for what you did
You're pathetic
watch your back

I think about these people all the time.

I wonder who they are. How they can be so many. One in every crowded room, I imagine. One in every busy station, every supermarket. Every village hall. These anonymous people, living perfectly normal lives. Firing off death threats as they sit at their perfectly normal desks, in their perfectly normal jobs. As they eat with their families. As they lie in their beds.

I hear Dan's car pull up outside, and glance at the clock. He's early. He shouldn't be here yet.

I click the laptop shut. I'd planned to tell him, tonight, about Hawkwood House. To lay the steps out in front of him, the hard parts already ticked off, loan application already under way. I know I have good credit – I took a pathetic pride in it, in those first years, when Evie and I were alone. No debts, to anyone, for anything. Total independence. Freedom, from everything and everyone. An investment, it turns out – because with his income, and the cottage, we can afford for me to buy Evie a more secure future.

But when he enters, he's pale as a ghost, skin slick with sweat. He slumps into the couch cushions beside me. 'I think I'm dying.' He pauses; I feel a question coming. 'Do you think you could take Evie to the match tonight?'

'You're not dying.' I knuckle his arm, gently. 'Can't she get a lift from Lissa? Or one of the others?'

'It's the *final*. She needs someone in the crowd to cheer her on. All you have to do is work out which end she's passing towards, and shout when she goes in that direction. Although they swap at half-time, so—'

He's joking, I know. But today, being patronized grates: turns me cold. 'All right, fine. Fine. I have *played* sports before, you know. I was a teenage girl, once.' I expect him to laugh in response. To grant me a smile, at least. But he doesn't. He closes his eyes; mutters 'thank you'. We don't speak again.

An hour later, I walk with Evie's arm in mine, the high-school windows yellow against the dusk-grey sky, feeling eyes upon me everywhere. As we approach the caged court, I feel someone, too close, behind me. But I turn, and see only empty space, dead air.

I see Evie looking, her attention caught on mine, and I smile.

You're imagining things, Graham whispers, and I squeeze her arm again.

But it's unmistakable, as we walk along. The sense of hooded eyes, glances slipped in my direction; of a silence falling as we approach the crowd, the hush of gossip swiftly stopped.

No, I think. *I'm not.*

For a little while I manage to lose myself in the match.

As the second half begins, the match is tied, and I find myself understanding the urge to bray with the rest of the crowd. To jeer as a girl on the opposing team trips and drops the ball.

But I'm interrupted; pulled back. My phone vibrates in my pocket. It rings, stops for a moment, and rings again. I glance at the screen. The name brings a jolt: *Sarah.*

I miss her. I've been missing her, ever since we fought. I shouldn't leave Evie – not now – but I want to make things right. I stand, wavering, pulled in both directions at once. On the final ring, I turn away from the match and take the call.

Instantly, I know this isn't an olive branch. It's in her sharp intake of breath as I answer; the steely professional tone. 'Hannah. How are you?'

'I'm . . . I'm fine.'

An apology lingers on my lips.

279

But I feel eyes on me, at my back; his hands, pressed into my shoulders. It cuts me dead.

A cheer from behind drowns her out as she speaks. A camera flashes from behind, and I turn. I'm exposed, and all too aware of the people around me: the strangers watching, waiting for me to do something awful. I need privacy. Just for a moment, I need to be alone. I walk away from the match, and escape between the trees.

'Sorry, it's . . . It's not really a good time. Can I . . . Is everything OK?' The woods open up around me, swallow me whole. The darkness is a comfort. I keep walking.

'I'm OK,' Sarah says. 'I just needed to talk to you about a patient. She's – she *was* – one of yours.'

I hear the name in my mind before she says it. I close my eyes, in a kind of prayer. 'Who?'

'Amy Barker. She . . . Well, she was supposed to be grounds-only, but—'

A vivid flash of memory hits me: a hand, lifeless, in cold water. A blue-light, red-light flash. *It's your fault she's dead,* they told me. *We'll defend you in court, but you have to accept your culpability in this.*

Sarah's voice is buzzing in my ear, but I can't understand her. Or rather, I don't *want* to understand. I don't want to accept it. 'Sarah, hang on. My phone – my signal's bad. Can you say that again?'

'A lot of her notes are your old ones, in your . . . *shorthand.*' There's a slight there. I choose to ignore it. 'I was hoping you might be able to come by, talk to the police, help them to . . . you know. I know you're on leave, but . . .'

I realize, at once, what she's saying. What she's trying to do.

'Are you trying to blame *me* for this?' My voice is hysterical, shrill. '*You* took me off her case. *You* made that decision, because you were too weak to stand up to the board. To stand up for your *friend*.' I feel the words choking me. 'I know what happened with Lucie Wexworth is going to make it *very* easy for you to scapegoat me, Sarah – but I'm not going to come in there and help you do it. I quit. Sort this mess out for yourself.'

There's a long, weighted pause. I feel a creeping dread, a realization that – once again – I've let my temper get the better of me.

When she speaks, her tone is flat. 'You're *delusional*, Hannah. I'm just trying to do the right thing here. For the family. But clearly that's not something that's all that important to you. So, forget it. Thanks for your time.'

I draw breath to reply. I'm too late. She ends the call with a click, and I stare at my screen. When the light goes off, it's pitch dark around me. There's a rustling overhead, a creeping among the trees.

I hear footsteps approaching, the tell-tale snap and crunch of fallen leaves.

I freeze. 'Hello?'

Something catches in my hair, and tugs. I spin around, pulse thumping in my ears.

There's someone here. Someone watching me.

'Who is it?' I call out, my voice reed-thin. 'I know you're there.'

My throat tightens – fear, I think. And then, it tightens, more, as though gripped by an invisible hand.

It's all in my head, I tell myself as I turn and run. *He isn't there.*

But I felt him. I still feel him, now.

I stagger out from among the trees to a deafening roar: a cheer.

And there, I see Evie, and the parents of Hawkwood's kids, all staring in my direction, while the other team circles, wild with the thrill of their win.

40

'I'm sorry, Evie. Really. I—'

'Leave it, Mum.' She's curled into herself, arms folded tight against her chest. Her trainers slap against the tarmac as she jogs towards the car. 'I don't want to talk about it.'

'Evie, please—'

'*Mum.*' She swings the car door open, and steps back, as though surprised by her own strength. 'Just drop it. Please.'

My phone buzzes twice in quick succession. I glance at the top notification. *An update on your application for a loan,* the subject line reads. In the snippet of text below, I see the word *unfortunately.* The word *rejected.* A flush spreads over my skin. There's no way this isn't about *Conviction.* It has to be.

I put the keys in the ignition. 'Pairing,' the car announces cheerfully.

Anna Byers's voice immediately follows, her tone much the same. 'Mike, we are – genuinely – thrilled to have you here with us. It's such a pleasure to be able to sit down with you and talk.'

I press the Bluetooth button and cut it off. 'This bloody car. How do I turn this autoplay thing off?' I'm trying for flippancy. It sounds like panic.

Evie looks at me, unflinching. 'I want to listen to it.'

I know I'm being tested. It's a punishment for missing the end of her game, and I deserve it. I don't want to ask when she noticed; I don't want to know if it threw her off, wondering where I'd gone. I can't face the truth, though I know it: I've let her down again.

I say nothing, and she clicks the Bluetooth back on.

'I . . . Thank you.' There's a light Cockney twang to Mike Philips's voice. I find a strange comfort in it – a reminder of the city I once called home. 'Really. I can't believe any of this is really happening.'

'It's going to take some getting used to,' Byers replies. She's being gentle with him, though it comes off as patronizing – or at least, that's how it sounds to me. I imagine her fans, adoring, inundating her with appreciation for the way she's *handled* his first interview. 'Your routine is going to be a bit . . . thrown off, I imagine.'

'No communal mealtimes, or showers. Yeah. It's weird.' His laugh is strangely high-pitched, a boyish giggle. 'Not that I'm complaining, obviously. You know, the first thing I did was get a Big Mac. I've been craving one for ten whole years. Best burger of my life.'

Byers laughs. I pull out of the school drive and try to focus on the road in front, to keep a steady pace. 'You know, #BigMike was the number-one trending topic in the UK for two days after you posted that photo. You ought to go to McDonald's and ask them for a cut of that week's sales.'

'He's sweet,' Evie says. 'I'm glad they've let him out.'

'I'm still not quite sure what half those words mean,' he goes on. 'I sort of knew about Twitter in theory, but . . . I mean, it's a lot, you know? I feel like the world has changed completely since I went inside.'

Me and you both, Mike, I think, the street lamps whipping by in beats.

He tells Byers and her audience of his first trip to buy clothes; his first encounter with a smartphone (a gift from a listener); his joy at finding his favourite film – *Toy Story* – available to stream, any time he liked. The shame of having stolen ten years of this boy's life away settles, digs its claws into my chest.

As we turn towards the village, we pass the petrol station, its gloomy greenish light. My eyes flit to the petrol gauge, a reflex. I'm down to an eighth of a tank.

I turn to Evie and tip my head towards the glow. 'Do you mind if we . . . ?'

She shakes her head, absently. She's absorbed in Mike's story, hanging on his every word.

I pull on to the forecourt and stop the car. In the shop beyond, I see the cashier double take, and raise her phone. She snaps a photo as the car sits idling, and I catch sight of the sign below: the sandwich board emblazoned with the logo of the *Peaks Gazette*, above black print on milky white, screaming the words *CONVICTION MYSTERY: BLACK WIDOW IN HAWKWOOD?*

My heart stops. I think – for a moment – that they must mean Margot; that they've figured it out.

But then I see my own face beneath, haggard and cold, photographed from between the blinds.

They're talking about me.

I put the car in gear and drive.

'Forgot my card,' I mutter. 'I'll have to leave it 'til tomorrow.'

Evie tuts, but doesn't say a word. She's still more interested in the show.

'So, Mike,' Byers says. I catch the change in her tone. 'You've got your life back now. What would you like to say to the people who put you in prison in the first place?'

Evie tenses. I can't help but do the same.

'Well . . . I mean, it's funny, because I've thought about it a lot – because when you're in there, there's not a lot else to do but think. Like, that's the point, isn't it?

'But the thing is, I thought I'd be angry. I mean, I *was* angry, at first, for a really long time, because I just couldn't understand why it'd happened to *me*. You know, it's the most frustrating thing when you're saying something you *know* is true, and nobody believes you – especially when you can see why they wouldn't. So, like, his wife —'

'Hannah Catton?'

I flinch at the sound of my name – my old name. Evie stares straight ahead, pretending not to have noticed.

'Yeah. I . . . I mean, look. She said she didn't remember anything at first. Then she heard the "evidence" against me, and thought maybe she remembered me being there. Obviously she could've been lying, but . . .' He trails off.

'You sound pretty calm about that, all things considered.' Byers is baiting him, attempting to tease out a response. 'You're not angry now?'

He's quiet. He's learned, through awful experience, to think carefully before he speaks. I shrink a little in my seat. I wonder what he's going to say. If it'll be anything close to what he actually means.

'I'm really not. I mean, I know there are a lot of theories out there about who could've done it, and I know some of them say it was her. Maybe it was. But . . . I don't know. Either way, I think whether they get found out or not, the person who *did* it is the one who has to live with that. And they also have to live with what happened to me. I've been OK, all this time, because I knew, in my heart, that it wasn't me, and my parents raised me to have faith.'

He clicks his tongue three times, and sighs.

'Someone – one of the people working on my case – said to me, a while ago: it's one thing to have a stranger tell you you did something, but know in your heart that you didn't. You can live with that. You can continue to speak your truth. But if *you* know you did something, even if nobody else knows about it . . . It doesn't matter how fast you run, or how far you go.

'In the end, the only person you can't outrun is yourself.'

Evie's gasp breaks the silence between us.

I follow her gaze, and I see it. Our front door is ajar. It swings, lightly, blown by the breeze. I look at Evie. 'Stay in the car.'

She looks back at me, her eyes wide. All at once, she's my baby again. 'Mum . . .'

'Stay here, Evie. Do not move. OK?'

I climb out of the car, and Evie follows, ignoring my instructions as usual. 'I'm scared,' she says, close behind me. 'I can't sit in there on my own.'

I reach for her hand. 'Stay behind me, then. And call the police if I tell you to. As *soon* as I tell you to.' She squeezes back. 'It's going to be OK,' I add with a weak authority. 'Don't worry. I'm sure I just left it unlocked.'

I know she doesn't believe me. *I* don't believe me. But there's nothing more I can say.

I stand in the porch, feeling my heart thump, sick, in my chest. 'Dan?' I call, my voice hoarse, cut through with fear. 'Are you in here?'

There's no answer. No movement, no sound. No signs of life at all. Only the past lurking beside me: the cold breath of it, the stillness, the knife pointing upwards, the blood turning black.

'Dan?' I call again. 'Hello?'

I hear a sound, sickening in its familiarity. Tap. Tap. Tap.

I squeeze Evie's hand, so tightly she gives a faint little moan. I'm returned, in a blink, to another night, when I could still hold her in my arms. She'd made the same sound, then, when I'd held her too tight. I hear Graham's voice: *You're hurting her. Give her to me. Let her go.*

I blink again. The sound goes on. Tap. Tap. Tap.

I turn to Evie and steer her to the foot of the stairs. 'Stay here. Just for a minute. OK?' The sound doesn't mean to her what it means to me – and yet, still, there's an awful fear in her eyes.

I step towards the kitchen. I imagine the blood, my black reflection in the pool. A warm liquid slivers down my neck, and I stagger back; drag my palm across it, reeling. I hold it up to the light, and exhale.

It's only water. Not blood. I look up and see it: the circular pool of water gathered in the ceiling.

My breath catches in my throat. I don't know if it's relief, or a deepened fear. This is another nightmare. A horror for which I'm not prepared.

I turn back to Evie. 'Wait here. Do not move from this spot.' She chokes on a sob. 'I'm scared. You're—'

'I'll be back in a minute. Just . . . Just stay here.'

She swallows. I see her trying to articulate something; to make sense of what's going on.

'It'll be all right, Evie. It'll be fine.' It's a lie, and she knows it. But it's all I've got.

I climb the stairs, calves aching with the same, acidic drag as after a run. 'Dan?' My voice is a whisper now. 'Dan, please.'

I push the bathroom door, a whoosh of water carried along beneath. The bathtub is overflowing, water seeping over the edges, spilling across the floor. I wade through, I close the taps, and stand, perfectly still. I remember something; feel a distinct pang of familiarity. But I can't put the pieces together.

'Is he OK?' Evie calls, her voice ribboned with fear.

'Stay there,' I say. 'Stay there. OK?'

She doesn't reply. I step back, press myself against the wall. I steel myself for it.

There's only one place he can be. The walls lurch inwards around me. I close my eyes. *He can't be,* I tell myself. *It can't be happening again.*

I step out of the bathroom, the floorboards groaning underfoot.

'Mum, is he—'

'Wait there, Evie.' I sound cold, callous. I don't mean to. 'Please. I'll be down in a minute.'

I push open our bedroom door. My pulse thunders, my skull ringing with it. 'Dan,' I whisper. 'Dan?' I see him lying on the bed. He isn't moving. I think of the anonymous message, my name and face attached. Graham's body, the open tear in his neck. The words beneath: *You're next.* Our address, plastered across the internet for the world to see. I step forward.

Look what you did, Graham hisses. *Look what you always do.*

My heart cracks open. I am torn in two by the horror of losing him. Of what this loss will do to Evie. To both of us.

I look for the blood, for the knife.

And then, he moves.

'Hannah?'

I stagger back. 'Jesus,' I hiss, reaching for something to hold on to. 'Oh my God. You're OK. You . . .'

He rolls over, groaning. He's flushed, his skin slick with a thin film of sweat. 'I don't *feel* OK. What's going on?'

'I thought . . .' A sob shudders through me. I can't say it. But the thought is there. *I thought it had happened again.*

He looks up at me, his face blank, confused. 'I must've . . . I lay down for a few minutes, and – I must've just dropped straight off. What time is it?'

Evie appears in the doorway, her eyes ringed red with tears. 'Oh my God,' she says, both words and tone the echo of my own. 'You're OK.'

'Did you . . .' I begin. 'Did you run a bath? The place is flooded.'

He drags himself up to sitting. 'I don't think I . . .' He runs a hand through his hair and closes his eyes. 'I feel like death.'

I stare at him, the word ringing horribly through the air. 'You look terrible.' I turn to Evie. 'Can you grab him some water?'

She nods and disappears, her footsteps fleet, rhythmic, on the stairs.

'What happened? Did you – Are you sure you're OK?'

The scream cuts through me. Evie's voice is all terror. I stand and run down the stairs, barely touching the ground.

I hear Dan stagger up behind me. Hear him fall with a horrible thud.

Evie stands in the kitchen, pointing to the windows. There, dripping in bloodied paint, are those awful words, again.

MURDERER.

WHORE.

41

I search for the number on Dan's phone and hit call.

'Hi, Will? Thanks for picking up. It's Hannah McLelland. I'm sorry it's so late.'

There's a pause. An intake of breath. He's trying to piece a narrative together: a reason I'd call from Dan's number. I see where it ends. The knife in the neck, the blood seeping into the sheets.

Tap. Tap. Tap.

'Dan's sick,' I say, quickly. I glance over at him, his pallor a ghostly white; his lips dried-out, gummed. 'It's just the flu,' he'd said, with a shiver, as he'd staggered to his feet. 'I'll be fine.'

But it doesn't look like the flu. It looks like something much worse.

I blink the thought away. 'I was going to call the station, but . . . Well, I knew they'd end up sending you anyway.'

He says something comforting, I think. Like he's trying to soothe me, to calm me down. Evie scans my face as I speak.

Her cheeks are flushed, eyes still bloodshot from brushed-away tears. I want to drop the phone and go to her. But Will's voice interrupts me; pulls me back. 'Sorry – what?'

'What's going on over there?' His voice is taut: with fear, maybe. But there is, too, the slightest thrill, a bite of anticipation in it. I wonder if he's aware of it himself: that little bit of bloodlust, the desire to be – just for a moment – at the centre of this case that seems to interest the world.

Or maybe I'm being paranoid. Maybe he doesn't feel that way at all.

'Our house has been vandalized,' I say at last. 'Again.'

I close my eyes. The words remain. I can barely focus on what he's asking, my mind fogged with anxiety – with outright fear. So I go on speaking without hearing his response. 'It's spray paint, right across the windows. I want to get it cleaned off, but . . . I don't know what you need to do for me to officially report it.'

His next question is inevitable. 'What does it say?'

Still, I feel the words catch in my throat as I answer. 'It says "murderer". And "whore".' I'm grateful that he doesn't ask me to speculate whom they're referring to, and why.

When I hang up, I hand the phone back to Dan. 'Is he coming?' I nod. 'I . . .' He seems to consider saying something. There's a look in his eyes, some expression I can't read. 'Ugh. I'm sorry. I'm being no help, here.'

I stare at him, trying to work out what he'd decided not to say. What he'd held back.

Evie stands, sensing the tension. 'I'm going to the loo. I'll be back in a sec.'

I watch her leave. Watching her walk away sends a jolt of fear through me, even within the walls of the cottage. What small safety my family had felt in our home – if we'd felt any at all – has now disappeared. It's a violation, a vicious cruelty.

I sit beside Dan. 'What were you about to say?'

He blinks, slowly, as though he's just been pulled from sleep. 'What?'

'Just then. You were about to say something, and then you didn't.'

'I just . . . It doesn't make any sense.' He wipes his forehead, grimacing at the sweat, the sheen of it on his palm. 'You know I don't take baths. I can't work out why I'd run one, is all. I don't *remember* doing it.'

'You're not well,' I say, weakly. 'Maybe you were a bit . . . I don't know. Not all there.'

I know he doesn't believe it. Nor, frankly, do I. I'd known it, from the moment we'd walked in. I'd felt the presence of something unwelcome. Of something uninvited, there inside our home.

'You should go and lie down. I'll wait for Will.'

'I'm fine,' he says. 'I don't mind—'

'Dan, look at you. You're barely conscious. Take some paracetamol and go to bed. I'll check on you in a bit.'

I expect him to argue, but he doesn't. He stands, heavily, steadying himself on tables, on doorframes.

I listen to his halting footsteps as he tackles the stairs, the comforting groan of the mattress above. I hear Evie step inside, with him, and settle into the armchair; the soft mutter of her voice, soothing and sweet.

In the kitchen, there's only our usual, comforting mess: the dishwasher door slightly ajar, a box of Rice Krispies open on the side. A used mug, black grounds dried to the base; a spoon with a darkening teabag propped on the rim.

And those words, painted scarlet across the glass, illuminated by the light within.

MURDERER.

WHORE.

I reach into the fridge for a bottle of wine and down a glass, a warmth spreading fingers through my chest. It's a much-needed relief.

When the doorbell rings, I feel as though I've been dragged up for air. 'Coming,' I say to no one; to the empty hall, almost, as though warning something – someone – that I'm passing through.

Will stands on the doorstep in hoodie and jeans. 'Sorry about the outfit,' he says. 'I'd just put a wash on, so . . .'

'It's fine.' I step back to let him pass. I fix on a smile. 'Do you only get one uniform?'

He laughs – not really a laugh, only a monosyllabic 'ha'. He's always had a boyishness about him, despite being the same age as Dan. But now, in his casual clothes, he looks younger still. Too young. The realization hits me: he looks *afraid*.

'It's my weekend off,' he goes on. 'So I've put the lot in.'

'Oh, God – I really should've called the main line.'

'Ah, it's fine. They'd have probably called me out anyway.'

I gesture to the wine on the table. I'm desperate to put him at ease; to show him that I'm just who he thought I was. A friend of a friend. Not a suspect. 'Can I get you a drink?'

'It's fine,' he says. 'I can't stay long. The wife, you know . . .'

I blush. I think of the words *BLACK WIDOW* on the poster

board, mere minutes away from our door; on the front of every newspaper in Hawkwood. *WHORE* in red paint, in the kitchen, behind. 'Of course. I won't keep you.'

I lead him into the kitchen. He's about to open the door to the garden when he stops. He leans forward and brushes his fingers against the window. Against the paint, sprayed on from the inside.

I wonder how I didn't notice it, before; whether some part of me did, but refused to admit the possibility. But it's unavoidable.

Now, I see them – feel them – as they let themselves in; as they spray *MURDERER* and *WHORE* across the windows. As they climb the stairs, treading softly; as they turn the bathroom taps, and let them run.

And then—

Will steps back; his presence, his sudden movement, drags the thought away, before I can quite make sense of it. He pulls his phone out of his pocket; steps back, again, to fit the words into the camera's frame. 'Well, that's quite the statement.'

My heart thumps. There's something like doubt in his tone. I go on. 'And the bathroom . . . It's flooded.'

'Did they block the overflow?'

'I didn't check.'

'Mind if I take a look?'

My stomach drops. I can't say why. 'Sure.'

I follow him up the stairs. I can hear Dan's heavy breathing from the hallway. I'm relieved that he's sleeping; that he's OK.

There's still a thin mist on the bathroom mirrors. I see Will in the glass, but not myself. He crouches beside the bath and peers into the overflow. 'Do you have any tweezers?'

I reach over him for my make-up bag. I root through, the

inside furred with powder, and hand him a dusty set. I think of the last time I used them, when I was a different person. A whole person. Someone who felt pulled together, instead of always cleaved in two.

I crouch down beside him, and he tenses. I pretend not to notice. There's a greyish clump in the drain; the same in the overflow, seeping out through the gap. He tugs at the loose clot, and it tears, with a soft, wet suck. It's stained black around the edges.

'Looks like paper,' he says, thinking aloud. He turns to me. I feel him searching for a reaction. I give nothing away, though I sense it: the slow dawn of a realization edging through. 'Do you have any sandwich bags?'

'What?'

'I could do with something to put them in. They're evidence.'

He's trying to get me to leave. I can feel it. But I can't say I don't: they were out, on the kitchen counter. If I lie, it'll only make things worse. 'I'll go and get some.'

I run down the stairs, the painted words a horror, all over again. Grab the bags, and run back up.

When I enter, he's spread two wet, curled scraps of paper along the base of the bath. I recognize them instantly. I see the letters spaced out, the typing erratic.

r e mem be r m e

Will looks at me. He knows the question's answer, before he asks. I've done the same, myself, with patients I plan to catch in a lie. 'Ever seen these before?'

I stare at the letters again.

r e mem be r m e

'Mum?' Evie peers around the doorway. My pulse leaps. 'What's that?'

'I don't know,' I say, quickly. 'What's up?'

'Can I go stay at my friend's house?'

'Which friend?'

'Lissa's.'

I look for the lie, there, but I see nothing. She's telling the truth. I nod, though I resent it. I want to keep her here with me. To keep her close. 'Go pack a bag. I'll drop you off.' She slips away without another word.

'Is that Lissa Wilson?'

I turn back to Will, and nod.

'I can take her over. She's only a couple of doors from ours.'

I feel a stab of anxiety. He wants to talk to her alone. He wants to know what she thinks – of this situation. Of me.

'So, where were you guys tonight?' he says, before I can come up with a reason to take her myself.

'Evie had a netball match at the school. Dan usually drives her, but . . .' I nod towards the bedroom. 'You know.'

'And you were there the whole time?'

I hear the creak of a floorboard. 'I . . .' Evie squeezes past me, reaching for her toothbrush. 'I had to step away for a couple of minutes. To take a phone call.'

She stops. Something crosses her face, a flicker of doubt.

Will doesn't seem to notice. 'A couple of minutes?'

I reach for my phone, and bring up the call. I hand it to him. 'Two and a half, thereabouts.'

Evie's mouth opens, and closes again.

As she leaves the room, she's pale. She doesn't meet my eye.

It was only a couple of minutes, I tell myself. *It couldn't have been more than that.*

But Graham's voice counters: *You're a liar.*

'OK,' Will says. He doesn't believe me, I can tell. 'Well, look.

I've got some photos.' He holds up the sandwich bag, *r e mem be r m e* pressed against the sides. 'And I'll take these for processing. I'll give Dan a shout when he's feeling better, and have a chat with the neighbours tomorrow – see if they saw anything.'

I nod. I feel sick with fear. 'I've been getting death threats,' I say. 'From people listening to *Conviction*. Our home address has been all over the internet, so . . .'

'I can imagine.'

'And . . .' I pause. 'And the man who went to prison – Mike Philips – he's been released.'

I know what this looks like: a woman with a guilty conscience looking for someone else to blame. Some stranger creeping in, in the night, to do unspeakable things, once again the wife who cried wolf.

'We'll look into it. You haven't lost your keys or anything, lately?'

I know exactly what he's saying. 'No,' I say. 'I haven't.'

Evie reappears in the doorway. She doesn't meet my eye. 'I'm ready when you are.'

I glance at Will. He smiles. 'I'm all done here, unless you need me for anything else.'

I shake my head and follow them back down the stairs. I feel as though I'm drowning. Evie doesn't say a word, and when Will opens the door, she slips out without saying goodbye.

'Thanks, Will,' I say, weakly. 'Appreciate your time.'

'No problem. Call me if you need anything else.'

'Be safe,' I call to Evie. She doesn't look back.

I close the door and I stare down at the handle, my knuckles white around it.

After all I've done, I think, in my mother's voice. *After all I've sacrificed to protect her. And now she's going to be the one to tear us apart.*

I stand in the doorway, my shadow long in front of me. 'Dan,' I say, my voice ice-cold. I adjust myself, and step inside.

He rolls over and gives a pathetic cough. 'Hi.'

I perch on the bed beside him. 'How are you feeling?'

'I've seen better days. Where's Evie?' She's already told him about the match; I can feel it. I can hear it in his tone.

'She's gone to Lissa's. Will's taken her.'

'He's been and gone?'

'Yeah.'

He rolls his neck around, sweat staining the pillow. 'Did he have any ideas?'

'I think he's already reached his conclusion.' I'm shooting for flippancy with this. It doesn't land. 'Best guess is I poisoned you, then left Evie at the match while I snuck back in here to flood and vandalize my own house, all within about five minutes. Motive is as yet unclear.'

He doesn't laugh. It's crossed his mind, I realize. He must've chosen not to believe it – if he did, he wouldn't be here. But he's thought about it. The anger I felt at the foot of the stairs floods through me, again. 'Not helped by your headline today, by the way,' I go on. 'Thanks a lot for that. "Black Widow"? Really?'

I catch a blush cross his cheek, a brief crack in his composure. My chest constricts with an ache of foreboding. 'Dan—'

'I . . . I've been meaning to tell you . . . It's nothing to worry about.'

'Dan, please. What is it?'

'I was going to tell you after it was all sorted out. I'm not working there at the moment. It's just temporary, but—'

'What?' My mouth turns dry. I think of my rejected loan application; my conversation with Sarah. 'When?'

'It's fine,' he says. 'It's OK, it'll be—'

'*When?*' My voice is taut, cold. 'When did you – what, quit? Get fired? What?'

He closes his eyes. 'After the . . . After the case was reopened. The consensus was that we should report on it, but I disagreed. The team thought I was too close to it, and I agreed to step away for a little while, so there wouldn't be a conflict of interest. I thought it'd just be a week or so. But when I went back, they said . . . Well, there's been a change of management. So I wasn't needed any more.'

I feel my stomach twist, horribly. My income has long dwarfed Dan's, though his would've been enough to support us while we waited for Hawkwood to open.

But now, that's gone, too. All because of *Conviction*. Because of me.

'Where have you been going every day?'

He shrugs. 'Meeting sources, doing research . . . That's why I started working on that book. I thought it'd help.'

We sit like this for minutes. I know I should tell him, now, about my job: about the partnership at Hawkwood House. I gather the strength to say it, and draw breath. But he rolls over and turns away.

All at once, he's in the position I found Graham on that awful night, the blanket covering him in just the same way. I'm returned to that moment. The same rage in the back of my throat; the same sense of something lost that can't be recovered.

'All right,' I say, with as much tenderness as I can muster. I lean in and kiss him, gently, on the cheek.

That's what it means, to love someone, I tell myself. *In sickness and in health.* 'OK. I'm sorry.'

I walk into the bathroom, turn the shower on, a scalding heat, and disappear. I wash the slick of him off my skin, and let it burn.

42

London, 2005

Evie's breath is hot against my neck, her fingers knotted through my hair. I'd arrived home resolved, the outlines of a plan forming in my mind: a single bag for each of us, a stop at the bank on the way, a chunk of our savings moved to an account that's only mine. Then, a train out of the city – to anywhere, so long as it's far from here.

But Louise had handed her to me, my little girl feverish, unable to eat. So I'd steeled myself for one more night. That's all. When she's better, I swear, we'll leave.

I bounce her up and down in my arms, and we circle her room in the dark, though she's really too old for this, too heavy for me to hold.

But still, whenever she reaches up, I take her. I know that one day, without realizing it, I'll put her down for the last time, and she won't ask me to hold her again. And as the only child I'll ever have, I know, when she no longer needs me, that'll be it.

So, I prepare for my loss in the very worst of ways: by luxuriating in it, every moment I have alone with her tinged with grief. I take every slight as a heartbreak. Every time she chooses him, not me, I split in two.

'Hannah?'

I flinch. I run through the calculations, the things I might've done to upset him, this time. I tidied the living room before bed; the dishes are done. I was here when he got home tonight. I said nothing about our fight, or what Darren told me. I didn't ask him where he slept last night.

I hear him talking. He's on the phone. The words are muffled, but I catch his tone: disappointment, frustration. Resignation. He appears in the doorway. 'Yeah,' he says. 'She's with Evie. I'll get her to call you back when she's done.' He hangs up, and leans, heavily, against the doorframe. 'That was Darren.'

Evie stirs on my shoulder. She can feel the tension running through me, the raised hairs at the back of my neck. I kiss her, gently, and put her down.

I turn to leave.

He doesn't move. His figure fills the door.

'Can we talk outside?' I say, soothingly. 'She needs to sleep.'

He looks past me, to Evie. He nods, and steps back to let me pass. He closes her door shut, behind.

Fear winds through my veins, sharp and cool. 'What's up?'

'I knew you weren't ready to go back. I shouldn't have . . .' He sighs, and raises a hand to his face. He rubs his jaw, closing his eyes.

He looks exhausted. Instinctively, I feel a stab of pity for him. It's a betrayal. I resent it.

He looks up. 'You were so bloody determined to make your point. So some of the blame for this is on me.'

'The blame for what?'

'Your patient. Lucie Wexworth. You let her off the grounds, even though she's on suicide watch. She's just been found.'

I steady myself. I grip the bannister so tightly it hurts. 'Found—'

'Dead. Obviously.' The revulsion in his voice burns me. 'Slit her wrists in a hotel bathtub.'

'I didn't—' I begin.

'Don't waste your breath. Darren's already doing his best to cover your tracks. He's telling the parents you checked the wrong box on her form – not that I imagine that'll be much of a comfort.'

In my mind, I see my hand hover over the page: the two boxes, one beside the other. *Supervised/Unsupervised.* I feel Darren's eyes on me. I check a box – the wrong box – and look up. 'He was – he kept—'

'He was *what*, Hannah?' I can feel his anger growing, building steam. 'Go on. Explain it to me. How is *this* someone else's fault? Hmmm?' I can't speak. All my words fall away. 'I am so ashamed of you. Really. I went out on a limb to get you this job, and you end up killing a patient. That means there's blood on my hands, too. Do you realize that?'

You're wrong, I think, but don't say. Instead, I fix my eyes on the floor. 'I'm sorry.'

'And now, what – you're going to be suspended, at the very least. Probably sacked. And we can't afford childcare without your wages, but somehow I'm meant to trust *you* to look after our child?'

I look up. 'What?'

'Half the reason I was OK with you *going* back to work was because I had concerns about what you were doing here, all day, as it was. I'm not an idiot. I saw the bottles in the bins. And now you've killed a girl it was your *actual job* to look after. I think I'd be forgiven for having concerns.'

'I didn't kill—'

The crash cuts me dead. 'Oh, take some fucking responsibility, for once in your damn life.'

We're in darkness, now, the table lamp shattered on the floor.

Graham's breath beats, close to my face.

I don't cry. I don't move. I barely breathe. *This is it,* I think. I don't want to acknowledge what *it* is, exactly, though I've imagined it, so many times. Hands in my hair, at my throat; a physical hurt. After all this time, it would almost be a relief.

Evie's scream pierces the silence.

My husband hangs his head, and walks away.

43

Derbyshire, 2018

I lie on Evie's bed and I call her. It rings for a moment; then goes to voicemail.

I need to know what she's thinking; what she's said. What she's done. I swallow, the warm wine slipping all too easily down my throat. I think back to who I was before: so together. So wholly in control. Five weeks later, and I'm back to drinking alone; back to hurting the people I'm supposed to love the most.

I tap call, again. She doesn't answer. *She might be sleeping,* I tell myself. But somehow, I know – I'm sure – she isn't. She's awake. And she doesn't want to talk.

Her open laptop on the desk feels like an invitation – a temptation I know I should resist. To look would be an invasion of privacy, a breaking of boundaries she'd be unlikely to forgive, if she knew.

Then again – I am, after all, lying uninvited on her bed, our former boundaries long-blurred – is there any reason she would know, if I didn't tell her?

I pull open the bedside drawer beside me, holding the handle loosely – as though I might convince myself it opened of its own accord.

The desk chair creaks as it rotates, slowly. There's nobody there. It's a draught. It has to be. But I feel him: his disapproval, his disappointment. His eyes on me.

'You're dead,' I say, out loud. I peer into the drawer, looking for something – I don't know what, exactly. Some insight into her: into who she is, now, when she's alone. But there's nothing. Hairpins, highlighter pens, a blister pack of aspirin, a lighter (an itch of disapproval, here, though I suspect it's for the candle on the desk).

I stand, and scan the walls: the photographs and posters. The slips of paper, ticket stubs. The miscellany of her life, runes I can't read, no matter how I try. It isn't enough. I sit in the desk chair and run my hands along the worn-away arms. I see Lucie, tracing her figure of eight.

I turn the laptop on – a single, decisive motion, my hand instantly back by my side, a denial, of sorts – and watch it boot up, the wait endless.

This isn't fair, Hannah, I hear Graham say.

The screen lights up. *Enter password.*

I type in her birthday. My birthday. Her favourite band (or, at least, what I think might've been her favourite band once). Names on the walls above me, festivals, poets, fashion designers; names that might have some meaning to her, though they've none at all for me.

Nothing works. I close the laptop shut with a crack, and stand. I imagine myself Evie. I walk around the room as though

I'm her. I adopt her lightness, the way her body works, without thinking.

I open the laptop again. I type Dan's birthday into the password lock screen, and it works. Of course. I feel guilty for not thinking of it before.

The screen brightens. I see her smiling face among friends, behind layers of disorganized files – *SCIENCE ASSIGNMENT 1, ENGLISH PAPER V4* – piled on top of each other, her life laid bare. I smile back at her photos instinctively, an automatic response.

I click the browser, and it slides to fill the screen, the white search bar blinding. I hover over the *History* button. I know I shouldn't be doing this. For a moment, I'm back at the kitchen counter. My stomach kicks, a memory, and I lean back in the chair. I could choose not to look. It would be better not to know.

But I do it so often – this self-destructive looking, this searching for things that I know will hurt (*psychopath, murderer, cunt, fucking whore*) – that to do this, now, feels inevitable. I sit forward again. And I click.

I scroll, searching for my name; then, for his. But I find nothing. There's no sign of her searching at all. She's only clicked on the occasional news article, here and there. Otherwise, it's as though she's reconciled to it; as though the case doesn't trouble her at all.

I *know* that isn't true. It can't be. So I keep looking.

In the next tab, a notification flickers. It's gone in an instant. I chase after it with a click. It's a messenger programme. A chat window, open, the blue bar blinking, and then white. Unread. Read.

I imagine her, now, on her phone, typing her reply. I watch

the bar flash blue again. I feel a little tug, anxiety mingling with pure, guttural want.

Read the message, Evie, I will her. *Go on.*

The box turns white, and I click.

I know, it says. It must be so hard for you. I wish I was there to give you a hug.

A sad face.

I wish you were, too, Evie replies. You're the only person who really understands.

I love you, he says, followed by a stream of kisses.

There's a pause. I wonder if it's the first time he's said it. I imagine her flushed cheeks, the soft little intake of breath.

I love you too, she replies.

I click on the name: *Callum Turner.* A beaming, blond boy, skin browned from the sun. I read through the information he's chosen to share. *Location: London. Age: 19. Interests: Philosophy. Books. The sea.*

So this *is the boyfriend,* I think as I watch the conversation tick on. Let me distract you, he says. I need to talk to someone about the new episode, anyway. A link. Let's watch it together.

You've already seen it, she replies.

It's not the same without you.

I click the link, and watch the cartoon colours fill the screen, the room flickering brightly around me.

I take the laptop over to the bed, and lie back. I sip the last of my wine as I watch. I pretend, for a little while, that she's shared this – willingly – with me.

Maybe she's fine, I tell myself. *Maybe this hasn't affected her as much as I think.*

I feel an echo of memory: Graham's breath, close – too close – to my face.

Take some fucking responsibility, for once in your damn life.

'Mum?'

The laptop sits open on my stomach, the crust of wine stuck to the base of the glass. Evie stares at me, and blinks, disbelieving. 'What are you doing?'

'I was . . .' I sit up, too quickly. The room lurches around me, as it always does in the morning, these days. 'I was just . . .'

'How *dare* you? You were spying on me.'

'I didn't . . .' I pause. There's no point in denying it. It'll only make things worse. 'I'm sorry, Evie. I didn't mean to—'

She laughs and, for a second, she's her father. Fear ricochets through me. 'What did you do: trip and accidentally type in my password?'

'I thought you might . . .' I gather myself. 'I—'

'Wait, wait.' She's paled a little, now. 'You thought I was going to tell Will the truth. After you lied to him. You thought I was going to—'

'I didn't *lie*. I . . .' My headache is thunderous. The room moves, flickering, around me. 'I lost track of time. If I was gone longer than I realized, I'm sorry. But I swear, Evie, I only walked away to take a call. I promise you. I came right back.'

I hear the bed in the next room creak; Dan's footsteps, unsteady, on the wooden floor.

'I swear, Evie. I'm not lying. To you, or to Will.' She wants to believe me, I'm sure of it; can see it in her eyes. 'I promise you . . . I was gone for five minutes, at most.'

Dan emerges, still pale, his skin slick with sweat. 'What's going on?'

She looks at him. Then back at me. 'Mum was trying to

311

find out if I lied for her. Which I *did,* by the way. Although I'm starting to wish I hadn't.'

I feel myself swallowed whole. I'm ice-cold, right through to the bone.

'Lied about what?' Dan says. He's barely awake, still. Barely there.

'About disappearing. I told you she ran off during the match, and Will asked me if it was possible she'd been back here, and I didn't say anything, even though—'

'Whoa,' he says. 'Hang on. Calm down a minute, everyone.'

'Why? So she can work out how she's going to slither out of *this* one? No.'

She steps towards me. I'm rooted to the spot. I can't speak. She's so like him.

'You're a *liar*, Mum. Everybody says it.' She laughs, again. 'Do you have any idea what it's like, being related to you? I'm alone *all the time*, because apparently this kind of thing runs in the family – so when your mum murders your dad, people don't exactly line up to be your friend.'

She takes another step; seems to grow, as I shrink.

'Evie . . .' Dan says, uselessly.

'And all this time I've been trying to defend you, saying you wouldn't do it – saying you were a good mum. Like anyone believes me anyway. Even though all the evidence says you did it – even though the whole *world* says you did it – I still thought there might be some other explanation. But there isn't. You killed my dad. You—'

The force of the slap stuns her. She staggers back, her eyes wide, while I stare at my hand like a thing possessed. A red burn sweeps across it. I look up, and there's another, staining her cheek. Behind her, Dan's eyes are wide, his mouth open.

He inhales, slowly, and sighs, and I see it: disappointment, and shame.

I find my voice. 'Evie – I'm sorry, I—'

She looks over her shoulder, eyes glassy. 'Don't ever touch me again.'

She walks away, and Dan follows, wearied, behind.

I know, now, that I've gone too far. I've crossed a line. I've become someone else.

And this time, there's no coming back.

44

I hear the murmuring below. The two of them, in quiet conference, Evie's voice occasionally rising in frustration; words I can't help but overhear.

Murderer.

Whore.

How dare she? I think, palms gripped tight around my knees. I stand and turn the taps on full. I need to drown them out. To be alone.

My reflection stares back at me, a woman I barely know. I look like the woman they say I am: cheekbones pushing through haggard skin under cold, blank eyes. My lips are chapped and bitten. My hair pulled back, severe.

I tug it down, and stare at myself again. I hear a too-familiar sound. Tap. Tap. Tap.

'You're not *there*,' I hiss. 'Leave me alone.'

The door creaks open, and my heart leaps to my throat.

Dan peers through the crack. He doesn't acknowledge my

comment. I'm not sure if he heard me speak, or if he's choosing to ignore it. 'Can we talk?'

The light overhead flickers, and goes out. I'm relieved when his eyes flit to it. He saw it, too. It's just a power cut. That's all.

I nod, and he closes the door behind. 'Hannah . . . Are you OK?'

I know what he's asking here. This isn't a general enquiry about my mood, or my health. He wants to know if I think I'm losing my mind. He wants to know if I'm seeing things, hearing things; if I'm losing minutes at a time, experiencing blackouts. If I think it's possible that I'm doing awful things without knowing it.

This is my opportunity. My chance to tell him everything: to get help. To make it stop.

Because I'm a doctor. I know what's happening here isn't good. I know something is horribly wrong. I know I need help. 'I—'

A phone buzzes. I glance at mine, but the screen is dark. Dan reaches into his pocket. A receipt catches in his fingers and swoops to the floor in a low arc. 'I'm really sorry. I have to take this.'

I nod, again. 'Go ahead.'

He closes the door behind him, and I turn back to the mirror. If anything, the mass of curls has made things worse: I picture the comments, my face pasted on to the Medusa.

I pull my hair back again. The band snaps against my fingers and falls to the floor.

I crouch to pick it up, and see the receipt lying there beside it. I think of Dan, scribbling notes, clues, leads on scraps of paper; fragments I used to find scattered throughout the house. Insights into his thought process, abstract pieces of him.

They've disappeared, since *Conviction*. Since he lost his job. Since we started keeping secrets from each other.

I reach for the receipt and peel it open.

Sophie Wexworth, it says in his distinctive scrawl, *4 p.m.*

I feel myself burned up, the betrayal tearing through me. He's arranged to meet Lucie's sister. It's the missing piece, the thread *Conviction* is yet to pull. Another mark against my name.

I think of the way he's always envied Anna Byers and the rest of them: the people he's always considered beneath him, as a *real* writer. He didn't ever *want* to work as the editor of a local paper, with a tiny readership – he craved more. He always has.

And I've brought him that. I'm his meal ticket. His book deal. His way out of obscurity into something better. Something more.

If it weren't for Evie, I think, *he'd have gone public with this long ago. It's only because he loves her that he hasn't.*

I stand, and I look at myself in the mirror, once more.

I have nothing left, I realize. I see it in the eyes of the woman staring back.

But instead of grief, all I feel is a vast and blissful relief. Because now, I have nothing more to lose.

'Evie,' I shout as I push the bathroom door. 'Come on. It's time to go to school.'

45

'Mum!' Evie growls. 'School's that way.'

I glance in the mirrors, the turn-off disappearing behind. I say nothing. I've been forming and abandoning words, uselessly, since we left, my resolve weakening with every passing minute.

I had a plan: talk to Evie. Tell her everything I did was for her. Make that clear. And then, go to Will. Ask him to take me to the station. Tell them everything. No more lies. No more half-truths. I was delusional to think I might be able to make it work – to hold my life together against the tide. So now, it's over. It's finished. I'm done.

'I want to talk to you,' I say, finally.

She pulls her knees up, and places her feet on the dash. 'I'd rather not, thanks.'

I swat them down with my hand. 'You know what I've told you about that. I knew a girl in school who broke her skull with her own knees.'

'That's only going to happen if you crash. And you're the slowest driver I know.' She reaches for the radio knob and turns it up before I can reply. It's a saccharine pop song, the singer's voice ringing through my teeth.

'Evie.' I turn the music back down, and then off. I feel her tense beside me. Her hands grip her backpack, tighter, knuckles exposed. 'I want to apologize. For last night.' I wait for her to answer, but she doesn't. 'I really fucked up, didn't I?'

She turns, surprised to hear me swear; surprised, I suppose, at the very fact I'm apologizing; admitting fault. She knows this isn't what I do.

'Yeah,' she says, turning back to stare out of the window. 'You did.'

'I'm just . . . I'm so terrified that all this – this *Conviction* stuff – I was worried it was going to come between us. Which it has. So I just wanted to know where your head was really at, so I could talk to you about it, and . . . you know. Explain.'

'Oh, yeah, I know. I get it.' There's a flatness in the words. Something unsaid.

I turn to look at her. 'Evie—'

'No, I mean it. I really do. I understand. You wanted to see what I was really thinking, so you could work out how to manipulate me into believing your side of the story. Just like you try to do with everyone else.'

The red lights flash at the junction, and I stop. 'I don't—'

'Don't bother, Mum. I don't want to hear it. It's all bullshit, anyway. Everything you say. You go about with that fucking deer-in-headlights—'

'Evie—'

'—*deer-in-headlights* look on your face, pretending you're totally innocent in all of this. Like you've got *no* idea why any of this is happening, when it's *obvious* that you do. And

I know what you're going to say when you finally admit it.' Her voice turns reedy, a shrill impression of my own. '*I did it for you, Evie, it wasn't my fault, it was all out of love—*'

'Don't you *dare*,' I hear myself say – hear myself scream. Her eyes widen as she recoils. 'Don't you *dare* talk to me like that. You have no idea how much I've been through to protect you. *No* idea. I didn't raise you to be such a—'

A car blares its horn behind. The lights have turned green. I fumble with the gears and the car stalls, before shuddering back to life.

'Such a what?' Evie says at last. 'Go on, Mum. Tell me what I am.'

I grip the steering wheel, knuckles turning white. 'I'm not playing this game with you, Evie. This isn't fair. You're behaving like a child, when I *know* you know better.'

She laughs, coolly. I hear her father's ghost in it. 'You know, that'd mean more coming from someone who didn't spend half their time staring into space, talking to their imaginary friends.'

'Evie—'

She makes a face, a gormless, dead-eyed stare. '*Oh, no, I couldn't have done it, I'm too fucked up to—*'

I stop the car so abruptly, she wrenches forward with a jolt. She turns to me, a hand rubbing her neck, and glares. '*I'm too fucked up to ever—*'

'Evie, stop. Stop.'

'You know, I've started to remember some stuff about that night. I don't know if it's, like, triggered something in my memory, seeing all those crime-scene photos and everything – but I'm starting to remember what happened.'

The words turn me cold. 'You can't. You were a child.'

'You were going to kill him. I remember it. I remember you holding the knife. I remember—'

A memory settles itself on my chest: a sharp recollection of hate. 'Stop it, Evie. This isn't fair.'

'I remember you telling me to be quiet. I remember you—'

I feel myself tumbling into the memory. She's right. About all of it. Everything she's said is true.

'Evie, please – stop. Please.'

But she doesn't. She's enjoying it. She's baiting me.

'I swear to God, Evie, if you don't stop right *now*, I'll—'

'You'll what?'

She's her father's daughter now. She's Graham, come back from the dead.

I feel a sickening, reckless anger weave its way through my veins as she smiles.

'Go on. What are you going to do?'

46

London, 2007

She's screaming, and it's all my fault.
  I didn't mean to do it.
  It was an accident. I swear.
  I look at her blood on my hands.
  I stare at it, uselessly.
  And still, my little girl screams.

47

Derbyshire, 2018

'Oh, God, Hannah—' Darcy's eyes are wide as I stand on the steps of the house, my clothes muddied and torn. 'What's wrong? What happened?'

'I'm . . . I'm sorry. Can I come in?'

'Of course – of course. Come on through.'

I know exactly how this looks. I'm not entirely sure I care.

Darcy, for her part, assumes a mask: after her brief show of surprise, she becomes the consummate professional. I think that's what brought me here. 'Did you come through the woods?' she says, with cool curiosity. As though it's the most natural thing in the world.

I glance down at my filthy hands; the streaks of dirt across my calves and thighs my bloodied knees and palms. I don't answer, and she doesn't push for more. Only steers me, palms pressed to my shoulders, to a chair in the hall. She crouches in front of me, squeezing my cold fingers in hers. 'I'm going to get you a towel, and some antiseptic. OK?'

I say nothing. I can't speak. I'm numb.

'Stay here. I'll be back.'

I try to piece together the minutes between: how I got here. What happened after Evie climbed out of the car. But all I have is fragments: footsteps as I ran after her through the trees. Hers disappearing, replaced with his, behind. A hand at my shoulder. The sign at the quarry's edge: *Think! Would you swim in ammonia or bleach?*

A phone rings, buzzing softly, somewhere in a distant room.

Focus, I tell myself. *Focus on what's right here, right now. Focus on what's real.*

I count the black-and-white tiles, the missing ones replaced. I look up at the windows, newly fitted, still covered in acetate, blue. I don't hear Darcy return.

'The water's back off again, I'm afraid – the idiots I'm employing are doing the bathrooms as we speak – so these will have to do.' She hands me a packet of wipes, running clothes slung over her arm. 'But you can clean yourself off, and change into these. You'll feel better once you're not covered in all that mess.'

'Oh, Darcy, I can't—'

'Don't be silly. We're about the same size, aren't we?' We're not. These are her baggiest, stretchiest clothes. 'And anyway, they're hardly my finest. I'll go make some tea while you pop them on and clean up.' I try to interrupt, but she's determined. 'Nope. This one time, Hannah, I'm in charge. Get changed. I'll be back with the tea in a sec.'

I glance around the empty hall, imagining builders walking

through while I'm half-naked, changing into another woman's clothes.

But it's quiet. Aside from the faint tap-tap-tap that I'm used to hearing here, and the distant buzz of the ringing phone, I'm alone.

I peel the clothes from my cold, damp skin, and change quickly into hers – plain black leggings and a T-shirt. The kind of clothes I'd been wearing, the first time I saw her, when I'd turned and run away. It seems a lifetime ago. I never could've imagined I'd come to rely on her – to *need* her – like this.

She re-emerges, a mug of tea in each hand. 'Here we go.' She drags a heavy-looking box along the floor, and sits. It groans under her weight. She shuffles, and smiles. 'So . . . What happened?'

I stare into the steam.

'Hannah.' She puts her hand on my knee. There's a tenderness in it. It takes me aback. 'You seem like you're having . . . a crisis. I'm worried about you. Let's put aside friendship and business for a minute, and . . .' She leans back. 'Therapy rules are now in operation. Talk to me. Whatever it is stays in this house.'

I look up. 'I don't think I can.'

'There's nobody else here, I promise.'

I say nothing. I don't know where to begin, even if I wanted to talk.

'I'm saying this because . . . Well, look. I don't want to assume anything here, but I'm sure you must be dealing with something like PTSD, given everything that's happened. You probably already were before, but with these awful people dragging it up—'

'I—'

'Wait – let me finish. Just let me say it. And then if you disagree, you can tell me why. But think about it.' She begins counting on her fingers, with awful clarity. 'I'm guessing you're not sleeping much, if at all. You're not in control of your emotional response to . . . whatever happened this morning. I'm going out on a limb here and assuming you're having flashbacks, if not full dissociative episodes – yes?'

My cheeks flush hot.

No, Graham says.

'How . . . What makes you think that?'

'I just . . . You look like you go somewhere, sometimes. That's all. I noticed it from the first time you came here. But I didn't want to . . . I didn't know how to bring it up. But I'm right. Aren't I?'

I swallow. The hard lump in my throat remains.

'Hannah,' she says, again. 'This isn't your fault. You're being put through an unbelievably traumatic experience. Or rather, you went through an unbelievably traumatic experience before, and now you're being retraumatized all over again. Frankly, I'm amazed you're still on your feet.'

I think of the symptoms, learned rote. *Distorted perception of relationships. Avoidance and emotional numbing. Outbursts of anger. Re-experiencing and dissociation.*

I don't know what happened. Evie ran, and I followed, and I was so, so unspeakably angry. There was someone there with me, I know it: his footsteps, and mine, and hers, seeming to come from two places at once, and I screamed at her to come back, and at him to leave – and then, there was silence.

As though the air had been sucked out of everything.

I felt her hurting, my baby's bones aching in mine.

When the tears come, now, it's overwhelming. I'm not sure they'll ever stop. Darcy doesn't move, though she squeezes my thigh a little more tightly.

'I don't know what happened,' I say at last.

'I know,' she says, in response. 'I believe you.'

She thinks I'm talking about Graham – about his murder – and I can't bring myself to correct her.

I go over the pieces in my mind.

Evie climbed out of the car.

I pulled over and followed.

I know the woods so well; I've run them so many times. But this time, something was different. Someone was there.

'Where's your car?' Darcy says, cutting off the thought. 'Do you want me to go and get it? Or I could give you a ride?'

'It's fine. I . . .' I steady myself. 'I pulled over near the . . . near the quarry.'

Her brow wrinkles. 'Why?'

'We – me and Evie – we had a fight.'

'What about?'

'She . . .' I feel a sob gathering again. I can't say it. 'God, I should've backed down – I'm the adult. I'm the one that should've de-escalated things, but instead, I just . . . I lost it. She jumped out of the car and ran off, and I . . .' I trail off. I don't know what happened next. I feel like a stuck record, a needle caught in a groove.

She resettles on the box, not meeting my eye. I wonder if she's hiding her relief. 'She'll come back.'

'She won't.'

'She *will*. You need to stop thinking the worst. She's a kid. She probably hid behind a tree, and you ran right past her.'

'I just . . . I *know* those woods, Darcy. I used to run the trail there every day. But there was someone in there, with me. Someone that wasn't *her*.'

I feel the hand touch the back of my neck. It's warm. Someone living. Someone *there*. 'I heard a man breathing, Darcy. At one point, he was right behind me. I turned around, and I saw him go.'

'Oh, Hannah, don't be—'

'I swear, Darcy, I'm not imagining this. I'm not. It could be any one of those people online who've said they want to do God-knows-what to me. Or it could be Mike – what if he's lying when he says he's "moved on"? Would *you*, after ten years in—'

'Hey – hey – stop.' She's turned a deathly white. 'Stop. You're spiralling. Calm down for a minute. Take a deep breath. In and out, now, come on.'

'I'm losing it,' I hear myself say. 'I am going completely mad.'

'No, you're not. You're not, Hannah.' She takes my hand in hers. 'But I *do* think you're teetering close to something like a breakdown. And I think it's entirely understandable, given the circumstances. But *given* the circumstances, I think it's my responsibility as your friend to tell you: you cannot keep this up.'

'I don't know what to—'

She stands. 'Come on. Let me walk you back to your car. Then, you're going to drive home and get some rest. She'll come home soon, if she's not already there. Which she almost certainly is. Kids are nasty little things. She's probably done all this to get a day off school.'

She isn't like that, I want to say. *Evie's not a nasty kid.*

327

That's what makes what she said today so much worse – because today, she was just like him.

I remember the cruel, hard look in her eyes, and the hole in the pit of me closes up. A steely coldness settles over me. 'It's fine,' I say. 'I'll be fine.'

Darcy opens her mouth to speak. I interrupt before she can say it.

'Really, Darcy. I'll be fine. I should probably call Dan, anyway, so . . .'

'All right. But promise me you'll go home. And . . .' She reaches into her pocket. 'Take one of these. I know we're not meant to . . . You know. But a good night's sleep would probably do you the world of good.' She hands me a packet of pills: *diazepam* etched on the label in black. I feel a memory bubble up and disappear: no more than a vague sense of recognition.

'No, thank you.' My tone is a little too clipped. I hear myself on the *Conviction* tapes, remorseless and cruel.

She presses them into my palm. 'Look, just hang on to them. You don't have to take them, but it's better to have them around and not need them than to wish you had them at three a.m.'

She could lose her licence for this; so, probably, could I. But the thought of a night's oblivion is soothing: a warmth that brushes everything else away. So I accept. 'Thank you.'

'No problem. Now, come on. I'll walk you out.'

I follow, my smile fixed: a rictus. Darcy does the same as we reach the door. But poised as she is, I see it, as I turn to leave. It's unmistakable. The flicker of undisguised worry, of fear, in the way she looks down at the floor, the swiftness with which she glances away from my smile.

She's afraid of what I might do, I realize as the door closes, heavily, behind. *What I might've already done.*

And so am I.

I walk back through the woods, attempting to follow the path I'd taken from the quarry to Hawkwood House. There's a silence there. An absence. It dizzies me. 'Evie?' My voice sounds unfamiliar, echoless, like it's trapped inside my skull. I say her name again, just to be sure.

What happened? Graham whispers in my ear. *What did you do?*

'I don't know,' I say. 'I can't remember.'

I see an indentation in the mud, the cross-hatch of my trainers burrowed in. I fell there. I was running, and I fell. I know I'm on the right path. I go on, towards the water's edge, scanning the ground for signs of her, some breadcrumb proof of her existence.

My phone buzzes: a jolt. I reach for it, the light blinding under the cover of the trees.

No Caller ID.

It could be her, I think. *It could be somebody who knows where she is.*

I pick up. 'Hello?'

'Is that Hannah Catton?'

I feel my throat constrict, tight. It's a man. And that isn't my name any more. But I don't argue. 'Speaking,' I say, with stiff politeness.

'You're a fucking bitch,' the voice spits. 'You're a murderer. You're going to get what's coming to you.'

He hangs up. My heart pounds. I lean against a tree, the bark nipping at my palm.

It's a troll. It's no one. It means nothing, I tell myself.

I hear a rustling behind, some movement between the trees. A twig-snap, a footstep.

'Evie?'

There's no answer. Only a stillness. I picture them – whoever they are – watching me. Waiting for me to turn away.

And so, I run. I run until the breath leaves me, and the trees part.

And still, I'm not sure I'm alone.

I unlock the car with shaking hands; drop the keys into the footwell, and fumble around, my heart filling my throat.

I need to go home. I can't go home. I *need* to go home.

The petrol meter breaks the silence with a wearied tick. 'Shit,' I mutter under my breath. 'Shit, shit, shit.' The thought of going to the local station chills me, all watching eyes and questions – so I take a right, towards the service station a couple of miles away.

As I drive, I realize it's the first time I've left the village in weeks. My world has shrunk to fit this tiny, closed-off place. I think of the story I read, in high school, of a woman in a locked room going mad.

I wonder if I ought to leave. To just go. To run again. But this time, I know it's hopeless.

Graham's fingers press into my palm, ice-cold. No matter where I go, he'll be with me. I can't outrun him any more.

And this thought is, in its own way, a relief. After all the running – the constant sound of my own, ragged breath – it might be better to just stop. To accept it. To be the woman the world tells me I am. To tell the truth, at last.

I'm relieved to find the forecourt empty. I climb out of the car, my limbs aching, and plug the pump into the petrol tank. I'm so exhausted, I lean against the car, and rest my forehead on the roof, the petrol pulsing in time with the pounding in my skull.

The ring of the shop door opening rattles through me. Instinctively, I turn towards the sound. A woman in sunglasses mutters into her phone, one hand tugging a tie from her long blonde hair.

I recognize her immediately.

The woman who fucked my husband and sold the story to the world, I think, shoving the nozzle back into the pump as another car pulls up behind. *That bitch.* She laughs as she unlocks her car, and I feel something come loose, undone, in my chest.

'Hey,' I hear myself say. 'Hey. You.'

A tweet appears in my mind, out of nowhere. *She has that weird, cold look of a woman who peels off her face before bed. She'll snap any day now. I can't wait to see it.*

'Wait – stop. I want to talk to you.' She looks up, the phone tipped away from her ear. 'I need to talk to you. You whore.' She opens her mouth to speak, but I go on, my voice reaching a scream. 'How do you live with yourself? How do you—'

I realize my mistake before she takes off her glasses. Before she says: 'I'm sorry – who are you? Don't come any closer,' she adds, her eyes brimming with righteous tears. With shock at being so unfairly attacked.

'I'm – I'm sorry,' I say, though of course, it's too late.

A man has climbed out of the car behind, nervously trying to gauge what's expected of him. In the shop window, I see the owner staring, phone raised to his ear.

'I'm sorry. I . . . I thought you were someone else.'

I turn and walk into the store. I hand over a sheaf of cash, imagining myself disappearing from the scene without a trace. Just another crazy woman, another story these strangers will go home and tell their friends. *Please don't call the police,* I will the cashier. *Please just let me pay you and go.*

When I step back outside, the woman has gone, but the man is still there, feeling no need to disguise his curiosity. He watches me as I walk to the car, the light of my phone's screen flashing on the seat inside.

'Dan,' I say as I pick up. 'Sorry. I was—'

His voice is tight, fearful. 'Is Evie with you?'

I say nothing for a moment, the words dizzying. 'What?'

A noise escapes him then, a low moan; I feel the shock of it rippling through my skin, a mourning sound. 'She's not here. I don't know where she is. She's not—'

'Wait,' I say, 'wait. Stop. She can't be—'

'She's gone, Hannah. I'm at the school, and they said she never showed up to first period. She's not here. She's been missing all day.'

EPISODE SIX

EPISODE SIX

48

London, 2007

'What happened? What did you do?'

I try to speak, but the words turn to ash on my tongue. 'I
. . . It was an accident.'

Graham steps towards me. I curl into myself, my feet tangled
in the bedsheets. 'What did you *do*?'

I close my eyes. I am back there, four hours earlier – maybe
five. The dusty tube station platform, the warm air rushing by.
Evie giggling in her buggy, which she's too old for, really,
though I indulge it.

He doesn't like it when I take her out like this; doesn't like
it when I take her out at all. He's only happy for me to leave
the house for meetings I'm required to attend: with my solicitor, the clinic's legal team, Lucie Wexworth's grieving family.

Two years, and we've yet to make it to court. Because her
parents won't accept a settlement, and the clinic won't publicly
acknowledge my guilt.

It's a kind of purgatory: an endless waiting. It's the thing that keeps me here; makes it impossible to leave.

I dream of her, every night, in that hotel bathtub. I see the blood creeping out over the rim. I hear her sister screaming, pulling her from the water.

I wonder what her sister's doing now. If that unfathomable trauma means her blood will one day be on my hands, too.

Lately, though – regardless of Graham – I've started going out. It's not for my benefit, I tell myself, but for Evie's. It's not right for her to stay cooped up inside all day.

Of course, I can't make it obvious. He can't know what it is that we do. So I take a handful of change from the jar; I steal coins from his pockets, when I'm cleaning his clothes, and I take her on the tube, riding the lines back and forth, for hours at a time. Something about it soothes her, as it does me. I think it's the sense of travelling. Of moving. Of leaving my life behind.

But today, it all went wrong. Today, I made a mistake.

It was an accident. I swear.

I'd tipped the buggy back and slipped through the doors. The carriages had split apart as the train rounded into the tunnel, and I'd looked through the gap as I folded the push-chair down.

That was when I saw him. Graham, his face only a metre from mine, if that; air rushing through the space between.

But he wasn't looking at me.

He was transfixed, his gaze focused on the woman between us: a glossy blonde, hair thick in the humid air. I saw his hand pressed against the glass to the side of her head. The ring on his finger, whose engraving matched my own.

It was obvious, to anyone, that this wasn't just a fling: not *just* sex, not *just* an affair. That's how I've justified it when he's slept elsewhere. As an itch he needs to scratch. A physical impulse: nothing more.

But the way he looked at her: he'd never looked at me like that. Not once. Not even when I thought we were happy.

I felt my skin turn hot, a sudden, sickly sweat. My pulse filled my ears, drowning out everything else. I needed to get away. I didn't care where. I just needed to leave.

The announcer named the upcoming station, and I reached for Evie's hand. The doors opened, but she wouldn't move. Not without the buggy – and not without her Maggie Bear, folded into its seat. I grabbed the buggy and pulled. The bear fell out, rolling across the carriage floor, and Evie, stumbling on tiny legs, ran after it.

I took Evie's hand, with more force than I should have – the buggy half under my shoulder like a crutch, Evie staggering, about to erupt into a sob. I saw myself in the eyes of the other passengers: a terrible mother, horribly cruel to her child.

But still, I didn't stop. I dragged her on to the platform, Maggie abandoned on the carriage floor, the doors whooshing closed behind.

I heard the slam, the terrible silence.

The door whooshed open again, and my daughter began to scream. The tips of her tiny fingers had turned a purplish red, one bloodied at the nail. 'Mummy!' she screamed, her eyes all confusion and betrayal.

I'd hurt her. She was in pain, and it was all my fault.

I looked to Graham, who looked outside, blankly, with no sign of recognition, at all. It made sense: there was no reason, in his mind, I'd be here. I'd promised him I'd stay at home. He turned back to his mistress, and smiled, and the train pulled away.

But now, he's here. And now, he knows what I did.

'Hannah.' His tone is utterly chilling. There's nothing in it but hate. 'What the *fuck* did you do to our child?'

'She just . . . She caught them in a door.'

I can't breathe. I'm waiting for him to put the pieces together. The inevitable drop of the penny: the moment he realizes the madwoman on the platform was me.

He steps towards me. Slowly.

He sits on the bed. 'Was it an accident?'

'Yeah.' I feel a sob coming, giving me away. 'I feel awful. I really didn't mean to . . .'

He raises an arm, and beckons for me to come to him. It's impossible he doesn't know; hasn't figured it out. But his face is all sympathy. 'I'm sorry,' he says. 'Really.'

I can't move. I don't know whether to believe him or not. I don't know if this is a trap.

'Come on, Hannah. Don't look at me like that. I'm trying to make this right.'

I shuffle forward. I feel nauseous, every inch of my skin prickling, telling me not to go.

But I do. I go to him. It doesn't feel like a choice.

He wraps one arm around my shoulder; with the other, he takes my hand. He smells like another woman's sweat and perfume. I close my eyes and hold my breath, as though that might make it go away. 'It was an accident,' he murmurs into my hair.

He squeezes my hand, and my stomach falls. 'Wasn't it?' He squeezes tighter. I feel the sharp pinch of skin, the press of the bones.

I open my eyes. 'You're hurting—'

'It was an *accident*,' he says, but he doesn't let go. He

squeezes tighter still, and I feel something pop: the hot sliver of pain sends a bolt through my arm. 'Wasn't it, Hannah? An accident?'

I realize what he's saying. I nod.

He squeezes tighter. I see the veins in his arms bulge with the effort.

I gasp out a yes. I beg him to stop.

He holds on, a few seconds longer. And then, he lets go. He looks at my crumpled hand with something resembling disgust. 'What was that?'

I swallow my tears, and meet his eye. I feel a kind of death: a letting go.

'It was an accident,' I say, and mean it. 'I'm so sorry.'

49

Derbyshire, 2018

When Will arrives, he's ashen. There's another officer with him. Neither meets my eye.

'I'm so sorry,' he says, slapping Dan on the back. 'I don't know what to say. Other than that I promise we'll do everything we can.'

Dan nods. 'Thanks, mate.' The affectation catches me by surprise. I've never heard him call anyone 'mate' before. It seems wrong, somehow, like an actor slipping out of type.

I keep learning things I don't know about him; keep wondering if I ever really knew him at all.

We've barely said a word to each other since I got back. He was on the phone when I came in, and when he hung up, I couldn't break the silence. It was too heavy. Too much.

I offer Will a drink. A misstep, it turns out: the three of them look at me, blankly. As though the very suggestion is absurd.

'No, I'm good. Let's crack on. I need to get some information from you two, if that's OK? When you saw her last, your movements today – the usual stuff. As many photos as you can send me, too, would be great.'

I follow them into the kitchen, where they sit, all three of them in the same hunched posture, elbows on the table. In the black glass behind, my reflection is a picture of guilt.

'Hannah?'

I slip back into the conversation. 'Sorry, I – Can you say that again?'

Dan reaches for my hand, and squeezes it in his. He pulls me to sit beside him. It's an apology, I think. An attempt at closeness. It hurts. 'He asked how she was when you dropped her off.'

'I . . . I didn't.' I pull my hand away. I never did get it looked at; now, it throbs, a distraction. 'We had an argument. I mean, we continued the same argument, really, but . . . She got out. When I stopped, she . . . She just jumped out and ran off.'

There's a silence. I can't look at him, though I feel his stare cutting through me. 'You didn't tell me that.'

Will intervenes. I'm grateful for it. 'That's not necessarily a bad thing. I mean, if she ran away, then . . . Well, she's probably just run away. The odds are very good for her getting cold feet and coming home.'

He leans back in his chair, and his eyes track the space that settles between Dan and me. 'Given the circumstances, though – with this, for instance –' He gestures to the words scrawled on the windows, *MURDERER* still gleaming red behind. 'I think it probably makes sense for us to go on throwing everything at this, for now. I don't think you have anything to worry about, but . . .'

341

'Thanks, Will.' Dan's voice is clenched, stiff. 'So what do you need from us?'

'Just your whereabouts today. And then, if you don't mind, we'll take a look around the house – her room, in particular, but more generally, too. With your permission, obviously.'

'Whatever you need to do.' I hear a falseness in my tone. I'm desperate to please. 'I went looking for her, after I – after she got out. And then I went to visit my friend Darcy . . . And after that, I went to get petrol. That's where I was when Dan called.'

There are lies in there – omissions, elisions, things skipped over like cracks in the pavement (*Just one lie after another,* I hear Anna Byers say, in my mind) – but it doesn't matter. I need him to get to the point. To leave us behind, and bring my daughter home.

'Darcy . . . ?'

'Burke. With an "e".'

'Great. Do you have a number I can contact her on, if I need to?'

A lick of frustration curls in my chest. 'I'll write it down for you.'

'Perfect. And you got petrol from the Texaco down the way?'

It's amazing what people can convince themselves of, a tweet said – or maybe an email. I don't know. Either way, the words ring in my skull. *I actually almost believe it's possible she* doesn't *think she did it. She's just been living a lie so long, she's lost all relation to the truth.*

I see myself in the kitchen of our London home, again. Everything Evie said was right. I took the kitchen knife from the sideboard, and waited for my husband to come home.

It was an accident, Graham says. I feel his cold hand on mine.

'Hannah?' Will breaks in.

'Sorry – I . . .' I sigh. I hope that it reads as exhaustion; as fear. 'The services. Near the motorway.'

There's the briefest of pauses: almost imperceptible, though I feel it, unmistakably, there.

Why go all the way out there? Will's thinking.

I see Dan wonder the same thing.

But for now, they gloss over it; choose to move on. 'OK, great.' Will snaps the notebook shut and looks to Dan. 'You're happy for us to have a look around?'

'Of course. I'll show you what's what.'

'She has a boyfriend,' I say. I don't quite know why it spills out. An intuition, maybe. A desperate hope. 'His name's Callum. We haven't met him. I don't know if she has, either. She might be with . . .'

Dan turns to Will, who nods. 'We'll look into it,' he says.

He said that last time, too – when I mentioned Mike's release, the threatening messages, the strangers sharing my address. It's what he says to dismiss a suggestion.

When his working theory is enough.

50

I pace the cottage, glass in hand. It doesn't help.

Dan has been gone for hours, searching for Evie. I imagine him with Will and the other officers, their torches splitting the trees. If I listen closely, I can hear them calling her name.

My phone buzzes, and I grab it. It's Darcy. Any news?

Nothing, I reply. My fingers hover above the screen. I go on. I'm so scared, D. I don't know what to do. The message clicks instantly to read. I wait for the three dots, the sign that she's typing a reply.

The sudden vibration shakes me. @ConvictionPod tweeted: A statement. Listen now.

I drop the phone on the table as though burned. The replies tick, one after another, impossibly fast.

call yourself a mother

they should've taken that child away a long time ago

RIP Evie Catton

A wave of sickness overtakes me. I retch, and swallow.

I open the statement, and press play. 'For subscribers – don't panic. Our next episode – *The Affair* – will air as scheduled.' There's a long-drawn-out pause. I wonder if this is a kindness: revealing that whatever's left of the series, it's not a revelation I'm unaware of. It can't get more sordid than what's already been written in the tabloids, my husband's mistress now a fixture in their pages.

'Until then, however, we'd like to make all of our listeners aware that the daughter of a key person of interest in this investigation has, in the last twenty-four hours, gone missing from her home.'

I feel my breath catch in my throat.

Wrong again.

She's enjoying this.

Don't you dare say her name, I think. *Don't you dare. I'll kill you if you so much as think it.*

'In an effort to assist with the investigation into the disappearance, we've added a page onto our website with all the information on the police inquiry as it stands to date, and will continue to do so as more comes to light. As ever, we're firm believers in the power of crowdsourcing information, and helping justice to be served. And so, we'd like to ask our listeners to visit our website, or check out our updates on all our social media pages, and help us to bring Evie Catton somewhere she can be – finally – safe.'

The glass hits the wall, and breaks, before I realize the woman I hear screaming is me.

Hours later, I wake from a dreamless sleep on the sofa. The front door creaks open.

Dan is home. He's alone.

I drag myself up to sitting. He looks over at me, and shakes his head.

Before I can say a word, he climbs the stairs. I hear him fall, heavily, into bed above.

I curl up on the sofa again.

I lie there, awake, until dawn.

The light glows pinkish through a crack in the blinds. I hear his footsteps on the stairs.

I pour coffee into a mug and put it in his place. I need him to sit with me. Just for a few minutes. I need to tell him the truth.

He walks into the kitchen, and stops. His shoulders slump. Already, he's defeated.

'Dan . . .'

'I need to get back out there. I have to look for her.'

'Please. Please give me five minutes. I just . . . I really need to talk to you.'

He shakes his head. And then, he sits.

I feel sick. I don't think I can say it.

'I think . . .' I take a halting breath. 'I've been trying to remember what happened. With Graham. And . . . I know you've been trying to find out what really—' He tries to interrupt, but I don't let him. 'Dan, really. It's fine. I get it.

'But . . . I've been going over and over it, and . . . He wasn't like they say. He wasn't a good person. He was . . . I was scared of him. He *made* me scared of him. And I think it's possible that I . . .'

He puts his head in his hands. He looks like he's going to cry, and I don't think I'll survive it, if he does. 'Hannah, I . . .' He stands, his chair groaning on the tile. 'I'm sorry, but . . . I can't do this.'

'What?'

'I think . . . I think if you're going to tell me what I think you're going to tell me . . .' He trails off. I realize what he's saying. He needs to believe I'm still the woman he thought I was, before. Because otherwise, I'm the person he's spent the last six weeks convincing himself I'm not.

A murderer. And the last person to see Evie – his daughter, blood or not – alive.

The grief will kill him, if I tell him, now.

'OK,' I say. 'I'm sorry.'

He reaches for his coat. 'I'm going back out to help with the search. Call me if there's any news.'

I hear the reporters shouting, clamouring, as he opens the door. Camera flashes strobe the room for a moment, and then he's gone.

I send another text to Darcy, while I'm lying on my daughter's bed. Can you come over? She doesn't reply.

Dread creeps through me. I wonder what she's heard, what she's read. I wonder what Will has said to her, on the call. I wonder what she's said to him.

I open Twitter, and see my face staring back. Mouth open, eyes lit with fury, I am howling. I'm a woman who has lost control: a mother, screaming at her child. I see the back of Evie's head, a little blurred but unmistakable, through the car window, the stop light reflected in the glass.

Look at her face, the tweet says. Imagine screaming at your child like that. That poor little girl.

The replies double down on the theme.

I knew it. I fucking knew it.

they should've arrested the bitch weeks ago!!!

347

When Evie Catton's body washes up somewhere, the UK judicial system is going to have to take a long, hard look at itself – there's blood on the hands of everyone involved in this case.

I click the screen off, and close my eyes.

Washes up somewhere.

I see the quarry sign: *Think!* I open my eyes again.

The sunlight angles through the windows, dust motes drifting, suspended in the air. Between the wooden floorboards, the light breaks through. It's one of the things that I found strange about the cottage when we first moved in: the sense of the hollow underneath, the feeling of being suspended only by a layer of thin, uneven wood.

But there's a break in the space below, beneath the boards. Something solid there. Something hidden: tucked away.

My phone vibrates. Darcy. Sorry. Been tied up all day – call you later??? I feel a twitch of relief. I fire off a reply, and sit up.

I don't want to look at what Evie's hidden – not after last time. I've broken her trust already, in a way I'm not sure can be repaired.

But then – there might be something there. Something that helps me get her back.

I lower myself to the floor. I feel as though I'm play-acting, pretending to be her, my little girl.

I slide my thumbs under the floorboard and it gives – too easily. Inside, there's a notebook – not a dated diary, or a book with an ornate cover, like the ones the girls on the ward carry with something like pride. It's just a plain, ruled pad. I've seen it on her desk, or in her hands, and thought nothing of it.

It's so typical of her to keep her secrets in a thing she could hide in plain sight – at least until she realized I'd come snooping. Then, I suppose, her hand was forced.

I feel the same dull urge to pull away I feel from the news alerts that bear my name; from the death threats, the tweets. I know whatever's written here, my daughter didn't want me to read it; that the words inside are guaranteed to hurt.

But I look, of course. I always do. I open the book to a recent page, her handwriting neat, the l's forming careful loops.

Lissa says he's a catfish, but she's just jealous.

Obviously I know how this sounds, because everyone on the TV show says the EXACT SAME THING, but . . . I know him. She knows him. They were Facebook friends before I was.

And OK, yes – it's annoying that he doesn't have FaceTime, because that would make it way easier to prove it, but I've done all the stuff they do on the show. I've reverse image searched his photos (no matches) and he sent me that picture of him holding a card with MY NAME on it. And love hearts, which is tacky, but . . . I liked it.

My stomach flips. I turn to another page, tracing the scrawl with my thumb. Around the page, she's drawn a wisp of smoke; a pattern that dissolves to tiny points, like ash drifting softly on the air.

I don't think she even means to do it. I know she's going through a lot, with the whole Conviction thing. It cannot be easy for her, having to relive whatever happened the night Dad died.

Heat creeps up through my neck. She's writing about me.

I even heard her talking to herself the other night, in the kitchen – and OK, she might've been on the phone, though I am 99 per cent certain she was <u>not</u> – which was . . . Oh, God, I feel bad even writing it. I just . . . Sometimes I'm scared of her.

I close my eyes. It's too awful.
Sometimes I'm scared of her.
I blink the words away. I turn the page again, throat clenched and sick with fear.

Callum says I should go and stay with him. He said if I needed to, I could crash at his friend's house for a bit while people look for me. I feel bad that he even thinks we would have to do that, but . . . I guess he's read some of the stuff that's out there, and – with all the attention – you know it'd be

The sentence stops, the pen-flick interrupted. I wonder what it was that made her stop and put the book away.

I read the words over again. If she's with this boy – Callum, assuming he is who he says he is – Will and his team need to be looking for them both.

But if I show them the diary, they'll see what else she's said.

Sometimes I'm scared of her.
I stare at the pages a little longer.
And then, I reach for my phone.
'Will – hi. I've found something here – something of Evie's.
Do you think you could come back?'

51

I follow the sound of voices, down into the kitchen.

When Dan looks over, his expression sends a chill through me. For the first time, I see a pure, unbridled anger in his eyes. Something curdling: love turned horribly to hate.

Behind him, I see Will, talking to a suited man with his back to me. The latter turns and smiles. I feel my knees weaken. I grip the bannister with both hands.

'Good to see you again, Hannah,' he says. He's older now, no longer in uniform, an authoritative air about him. He extends a hand. 'DCI Mark Stevens. I investigated your husband's murder in 2008.'

I stare at his hand. I'm frozen, rooted in place. 'I know who you are.'

'I wasn't sure if you'd remember.'

He's mocking me.

'DCI Stevens has come along to help out,' Will says, breaking the silence.

'Why?'

The three of them stare at me, none apparently willing to answer. Because it's obvious. They've decided Evie's disappearance is connected to Graham's murder. It's the simplest solution. The one that makes the most sense. And so, he's here to question me, knowing just what to look for in my movements, my face: every tell he thinks he saw before.

Stevens doesn't take his eyes off me. He gestures to the kitchen table. 'Shall we?'

Nausea – fear – threatens to overtake me. I nod, and I sit. For a split second, I feel my daughter's head upon my knee; I'm in the interview room, a decade ago, telling them that I don't remember. That I don't know.

I slide the book across the table. 'I found this. In Evie's room.' Dan rises from his seat and follows the journal, pulled by an invisible thread. Will opens it; Stevens arches over to read it. 'It was under the floorboards. She must've hidden it there, so . . .' I see a doodled wisp curling, blue, around the page; I see her hunched over her desk, pen in hand. The missing deepens in my chest. I feel her absence as an ache.

'She talks about the boy I mentioned. A lot,' I say, as they scan the pages, silently. 'She says they hadn't actually met. But that he'd help her hide, if she needed to. So I thought . . . it might be like I said. She might be with him.'

Nobody speaks. Will's eyes scan over the page I'd been afraid for them to read. Stevens gives a barely perceptible nod, and Will turns to the next. Finally, he slides the book across the table, flipping it shut. 'Thanks, Hannah. We'll take this back and have a good read through – if that's OK?'

I nod. I feel an invisible hand at my throat; another on my shoulder.

I wait for them to stand. To leave. To take the lead I've handed them, and follow it.

But they don't. 'While we're here . . .' Will glances at Dan, then at me. 'Would you mind if we went over a couple of things with you? Stevens is picking up from me on this, so . . .'

I feel their eyes on me, expectant. I nod again. I can't speak.

Taking his cue, Stevens pulls a notebook from his pocket and clicks his pen. Will leans back in his chair. 'All right,' Stevens says, with the same cracked smile as before: one that's dead in the eyes. 'I appreciate this, Hannah. I know you're under a lot of stress, so it's good of you to take the time. I know it can feel a bit like *Groundhog Day* with these things, but. . . it has to be done, I'm afraid.'

He's leading up to something, I know it. He's trying to set me at ease, to make me more inclined to talk. I know this trick. He used it last time, too.

'So – you said you and Evie had a . . . a disagreement. Is that right?'

'Yes.'

'Do you usually drive her to school?'

'*I* do,' Dan says, quickly. 'Since the whole – you know, all this press attention . . . we've been concerned about her being approached by journalists, or . . . You know. Fans of the show. People looking for some kind of connection with it. So I've been dropping her off, and picking her up. But I was sick, so . . .' He looks at me, the expression in his eyes unreadable. 'Hannah offered to do it.'

'OK,' Stevens says, his eyes still on me. 'So, that must've been pretty tense, I imagine. I've got a teenager myself, and I

354

know when we fight . . . I'd go to great lengths not to be locked in a car with them, let's put it that way.'

He pauses, waiting for a response. 'Is that a question?' I say. It's a rupture, a flash of anger. I can't help it. They're wasting time.

He laughs. 'No. You're right. Try this.' His tone sharpens. I feel the hairs on my skin rise in response. 'What were you fighting about?'

I glance at Dan. He looks away. 'It was just . . . everything that's been going on. It's been upsetting her, hearing all this stuff about her dad, and . . . It was basically exactly what you'd expect.'

Stevens taps his pen, once, on the notepad. 'Did you apologize?'

'What?' He doesn't repeat the question. He doesn't need to. 'I . . . Yeah.'

'And did she accept it?'

I stare at him. There's a satisfaction in his eyes as he removes his glasses. He wipes them, slowly, on the edge of his shirt. 'No,' I say, finally.

'OK. So things escalated, and then – from my understanding of it – she climbed out of the car and ran away.'

'Yes.'

'And this happened where, exactly?'

'Welford Lane. Near the quarry.'

He looks at Dan. 'Is this the route you usually take?'

Dan is still, for a moment, his mouth slightly open. 'No.'

'I didn't want—' I begin. The shiver in my voice registers as shrill. I try to settle it. To stay calm. 'I know – and I'm sure *you* know – people have been taking photos of me, and posting them on the internet. I feel like I'm being followed, all the time. I think there was someone in the woods, today, following me *there*. But I thought I'd . . . I thought if I took a different route, people might not . . .'

I see the way they're looking at me, and I know exactly what they're thinking. *If you're not doing anything wrong, why would you care?* I'd have thought the same – before. But now, it doesn't matter what I do. These strangers want to damn me, either way.

Stevens clears his throat. 'All right. So Evie got out of the car, and you parked – and then followed?'

I swallow. I hear the footsteps in the leaves behind. 'Yeah.'

'And then what?'

'I looked for her. For a while. I thought I heard . . . There was someone with me. A man. I felt him behind me.'

'You felt him?'

'His hand on my shoulder.'

He says nothing. I go on.

'So I turned around, and I . . . He was gone. But I could still feel him watching me. So I ran.'

Stevens doesn't need to say a word. I see the scepticism on his face, in the set of his jaw. He sees a woman using a trick that's worked before: the anonymous man, the scapegoat for her evils.

But his memory's unreliable, too. He's convinced himself that *I* was the one who blamed Mike Philips for Graham's murder. But when he interviewed me – he, and his partner, whose grudge apparently led to Philips's arrest – I only told them that I didn't know what had happened. I had no memory at all. And that only changed at trial, when I was presented with their 'evidence' against him.

He twirls the pen around in his hand. Will looks at me and

smiles. I can feel them – all of them – waiting for me to speak. But I don't. I'm all too aware that Stevens wants this conversation to go a certain way, just as I do, with my patients. He has a destination in mind: something he's leading me to say.

'OK,' he says, at last. 'So, later in the day – you went to get petrol. Is that right?'

I'm destabilized by the change of tack, the slip in time. 'I went to Hawkwood House first—'

'I want to talk about the petrol station, if you don't mind. We'll come back to that.'

I tense. I smile through gritted teeth. 'Sure.'

'So you went to the motorway services. That's a bit of a way out, isn't it? Although I get it – I'm a bargain hunter too, fuel prices being what they are. Cost me a small fortune getting here.' He smiles, closed-mouthed, this time. The corners of his mouth barely move. Only a slight narrowing in his eyes suggests it's there at all.

'I . . . I didn't want to be recogni—' I catch myself. 'I can't go anywhere in Hawkwood without being stared at. The woman at the Texaco took my photo last time, so I—'

'OK.' He reaches in his pocket for his phone. 'So this probably won't come as a huge surprise.'

My blood turns to ice. 'What?'

He slides the phone across the table, and I hear a woman screaming. I take the phone and watch the shaking screen, the figures unsteady, blurred. Still, I recognize the scene: one figure lurching forwards, another leaning back. The words are incomprehensible. The screaming woman sounds out of her mind. The caption underneath, in vivid text: #CONVICTION: HANNAH CATTON ATTACKS STRANGER IN PETROL STATION. Uploaded 14 hours ago. 180,000+ views.

I turn the screen off, and put the phone down. Dan stares down at his hands, his pallor sickly, almost grey. I wait for them to ask me something, and they wait for me to speak.

'She wasn't . . . I thought she was—'

'Is this a habit? Thinking someone's there, when they're not?'

I feel the sense of a noose tightening. I'm being baited.

I say nothing. I close my eyes.

'We've been trying to contact this friend of yours – Darcy Burke. That's right, isn't it?'

'Yes.'

'And what's your relationship with her, exactly?'

'I was . . .' I look at Dan. 'We work together. She's—'

Stevens cuts in before I can go on. 'Can you call her for me, please?'

'What?'

'On your phone. We've been struggling to get hold of her, but she might answer for you.' There's a silence. 'If you don't mind?'

I stand, heavily, and walk to the counter. I unplug my phone, find Darcy's number, and hit call.

There's a beep, a hiss of static. And then, a dull, robotic voice. 'The number you have dialled has not been recognized. Please hang up and try your call again.'

I stare at the phone. Dan stands, abruptly, and walks to the sink, his back to me. His hands grip the counter, as though he'll fall if he lets go.

'I can text her,' I say. 'We text all the time. I can—' I flick to the messaging app. I scan for her name. But there's nothing there.

In my emails, too, there's nothing.

No sign she was ever there at all.

'The fact is, Hannah, we can't find anything to prove this Darcy Burke exists. Or rather, that she's ever been around here.' Stevens swipes on his phone, and stands. He hands it to me, and I recognize the smiling girl instantly, though she's older, now: still, she has the same frizzy hair, the same over-large glasses and buck teeth. 'We've spoken to Darcy Burke. She says she interned for you in 2008. But she lives out in Sydney. She hasn't been in the UK since 2010.'

'That isn't her. That isn't who I've been talking to.'

'All right.' He shrugs, and walks back to the table. 'The question is, then, who *have* you been talking to?'

'I don't know. I—'

'Or rather, have you been talking to anyone at all? Because your daughter certainly seemed to think you might be imagining things. And . . .' He reaches into his jacket and pulls out a sheaf of papers, folded three times. He unfolds them, laying them out one by one. 'Come on. Have a look. Tell me if you recognize any of this.'

I walk towards him. It feels like a death march. With every step, my legs threaten to give way.

'Hawkwood House was never for sale,' he says. 'This is a fraudulent deed, signing the property over to . . .' He presses a finger to the foot of the document. 'Dr Hannah McLelland.'

He points to the next page. 'And we have a number of loan agreements, here, all based on the Hawkwood House renovations. Big money. Almost a quarter of a million. And guess who's applied for those?'

I can't speak. I can't move.

'Hannah McLelland. And yet, in spite of all this cash coming in, the contractors engaged to put up the scaffolding say they're yet to be paid for their hard work. And their agreement is with . . . ?'

He taps the page, twice. 'Let me guess,' he says, softly. 'Because I think I know how you're going to explain all this.'

I look at him; and at Will; and at Dan, still turned terribly away. 'I don't remember—'

'Bingo. Got it in one.'

I feel a jolt of realization. 'Wait – wait. She gave me some papers.' I stand and stagger to the cupboard. 'From the Hawkwood archives. They were . . .'

I open the door. There's nothing there. I turn to Will. '*You* saw them. You pulled them out of the drain.'

Will blinks, and looks at Stevens. He gestures to Will to go on. 'The thing is, Hannah . . .' He looks embarrassed for me. 'Well, a couple of things, really. First, we looked at those papers, and . . . We need to get more tests done, but the typing on them must have been done on a computer. We've got an exact match on the font. And . . .'

Stevens loses his patience. He picks up the thread. 'And we've had two neighbours say they saw a woman matching your description coming into the cottage, at the time *you* say you were at the match, though there are parents there who dispute that – plenty of them.'

I search desperately for an explanation, a memory. Anything. 'But why would I—'

'That's my question, Hannah. I have theories, but you're the psychiatrist here. You're the one who's in a position to explain all this. Because to me, it seems like pretty crazy behaviour. Pretty nuts, don't you think?'

He pauses, as though waiting for me to explain. But I can't. There's no way I *can* explain all this, rationally, unless . . .

'All right,' he says. 'Let me give you *my* working theory, then.' He reaches for his phone, and searches. The wait is endless. He knows, and still, he takes his time. He hands me the screen.

COPYCATTON, the headline reads. HOW CONVICTION ACCUSED'S PSYCHO GRAN INSPIRED HORRID HANNAH.

'You've been fixated on this case for a while, haven't you?' I shake my head. 'Careful, Hannah. Don't get yourself in a knot here. Because we have transcripts from Graham's statement at your tribunal hearing, in 2008. The day he died. He said you'd been obsessed with it. He found the searches on his laptop. And he pinpointed *that* as the moment you started losing your grip.'

I shake my head again. I feel Graham there. I think I hear him laugh.

'So my theory is: *that's* why you killed your first husband. You couldn't help yourself. You identified too much with this grandmother of yours, and started thinking you were one and the same. That whatever she did, you'd do, too.'

'No. *No.* I—'

'But you got away with it – and so, you moved on. You were happy for a while. You forgot all about it. You made a life with this guy, here.' He gestures at Dan, who still doesn't move. 'And then *Conviction* came along, and lifted up the rock you were hiding under. And out crept all those old thoughts.

'But you'd been in denial for so long, by that point, you couldn't face that – not head on, anyway. So you created this story about an old intern just *happening* to come along and offer you a job at the place your gran was locked up, and

361

then just *happening* to find a bunch of letters that gave you a reason to open up the obsession.

'But that obsession, for you, is a kind of hands-on affair – isn't it?'

He waits for me to respond. I don't.

'Trouble is, no matter how hard Dan's been trying to convince himself of your innocence . . .' His tone is snide, cruel. *The idiot,* he seems to say. 'You've lost your element of surprise. If you went for him, under normal circumstances, he'd react. And he's a big guy. So you need to incapacitate him.'

A flare of anger sparks. 'I would *never* . . .'

'We have a prescription for some pretty heavy benzodi-azapenes, issued to Dan, three days ago.'

All the air is pulled from my chest. I can't breathe. I think of Darcy, offering me diazepam. I'd taken the pills from her hand. But she doesn't exist. She never did.

'You signed for it. Which is playing fast and loose, really, because I'm sure doctors aren't supposed to prescribe to their families – right?' He smiles. He knows he's right. 'Although it wouldn't be the first time you've written a prescription you shouldn't, would it?'

A shock of memory hits me.

The wine glass, on the granite countertop, the night Graham died. The powder clinging to the base.

Stevens doesn't wait for me to respond, though he sees the realization on my face. He's right.

'So you incapacitate Dan. You get Evie out of the house. And you come back. It'll only take a minute. You know this from before.

'But something stops you – I'm guessing it's these neighbours

362

of yours. You realize you can't do it then. It'll be too obvious. So you vandalize your home, to deflect the attention. So you can put yourself in the position of the victim, again. So you can convince yourself of your own innocence, a little bit longer.

'And then—'

'Stop.' I barely recognize my voice. I sound cold. Barely human. 'I don't want to talk about this any more. I can't—'

'No, you're right.' Stevens is unflappable; all arrogance, a smug knowingness. 'You should call your solicitor before you say anything else. That's sensible.'

He reaches for his jacket and shrugs it back on. Will stands, and pats Dan on the shoulder. Dan doesn't move.

Stevens smiles, and it sickens me. I feel wrung out, washed ashore. 'We'll be back soon, Hannah. Don't go too far, OK?'

52

When they leave, the silence is devastating. I feel shot through with holes.

I stare at Dan's shoulders. At the ridge of his knuckles at the edge of the countertop.

'It's not possible,' I say, though I'm not sure I believe it.

I think of the conversations I've had with Darcy. The way she's always taken my side; offered soothing diagnoses, and a resolute absence of doubt. All the things I couldn't quite let myself feel – anger, resentment, bitterness – she's felt on my behalf. And with her plans for the House – all of which so perfectly matched my own – she's done the things I'd never let myself do; things I was too weak to do, myself.

I'm a doctor, I'd thought. *I can manage this. I'll know if I've gone too far. I'll seek help.*

But Stevens is right. I *have* imagined things. I knew Graham wasn't there, every time I felt him, or heard his voice. He's been dead for a decade. Each time, I wrote him off as a trick of the mind, anxiety brought to life. A memory, relived.

But some small part of me felt him, truly; felt his existence as something I couldn't ignore. And so, to offset the doubt, I convinced myself I *was* getting help – from a woman my mind created, there to tell me exactly what I wanted to hear.

I'm a psychiatrist. I respect the mind for what it's capable of; for what it can do, to help a person cope. But I never could've imagined my own fabricating something that seemed – that still seems, her voice in my memory so different from my own – so *real*.

Dan's voice breaks the silence, slicing through my thoughts. He doesn't turn around. 'Did you hurt her?' He's nervous. No: he's afraid.

I can't speak. I didn't think I could have. But now, I'm not so sure.

He turns, looking not at, but through me. He can't bring himself to meet my eye. 'Hannah, I need to know. If it was an accident, or—'

I slip through time. I feel a cold fist squeeze my palm.

It was an accident, I think. *It was an accident.*

'For God's sake, Hannah.' Dan slams the counter, and I flinch. He looks at his hand in horror, as though it belongs to someone else. 'If you don't tell me, I'm going to . . .'

He can't bring himself to say it. He doesn't have to. He's going to tell them he believes that it was me. Every doubt that's nipped at him, every thought he's blinked away, too terrible to believe . . .

He's going to go to them, and tell them that, at last, he sees the truth.

This is my last chance to be honest with him.

It comes to me, all at once, like coming up for air. 'I didn't hurt her. I didn't.'

I know this is true.

I believe it is true.

It was an accident, I hear myself say, in another life.

I don't know what's true any more.

Dan sighs, a shudder in it.

'Please, Dan, I need you to believe me. I wouldn't.' There's defeat in my voice. Doubt. It's impossible not to hear. 'She's my daughter.'

He says something I can't catch. I stare at him. I will him to say it again. 'What were you going to say?' He's holding back tears. 'When you wanted to talk? What was it you wanted to tell me?'

I know I'm condemning myself now. But I want to tell him the truth. I need him to know.

'I think . . . I think it's possible I *did* . . . what they say I did. To Graham. But it wasn't . . .'

He turns away for a moment. Then turns back. 'I *believed* you. All this time. In spite of *overwhelming* evidence to the contrary, I . . .' He gasps, as though he's been hit. 'I'm such an idiot. It was so obvious.'

'It wasn't – Dan, I need you to believe me. He was awful. He made me—'

He laughs. I feel my heart fall through me, an absence. 'Did Evie make you do it, too?' As soon as he's said it, he pales. It's a viciousness that's so unlike him. As though the loss has turned him into someone he's not.

'I didn't – she's got to be with that boy – her diary says—'

'Don't, Hannah. I don't want to talk about that bloody

"diary". Even *I* could see through that. And it turns out I'm the world's biggest mug.'

'What?'

'Will and I searched that room with a fine-toothed comb. There was nothing there. And then, all of a sudden, you're alone in the house for two hours and *that* conveniently appears? Why would you think *anyone* would—'

'She'd hidden it, Dan, I swear. I only saw it because—'

He looks away, shaking his head. And then he looks at me in a way that makes him unrecognizable to me. 'You know what, Hannah – no. I'm sorry, but . . . I can't do this. I don't believe a word you say.'

It's a gut-punch, the words, the coldness in his voice. I reach for the glass on the table with shaking hands, but it tips, water spilling across the oak. He doesn't move. Only watches as I try to clean up, my hands shaking.

I stop, and drop the clod of wet paper towel in front of me. 'Please, Dan. Please. You have to believe me. She was your daughter as much as mine. It's like you said: we're a united front. We're . . .'

A sob tears through him. It's the worst sound I've ever heard. And then, I realize why.

'She *is* your daughter. She'll come back, soon, and it'll all be—'

'No. No. I think you're lying. You've been lying this whole time, and I've been so bloody . . .' He staggers, abruptly off-balance and clings to the back of the chair. It's the shock of realization. I know the feeling well. 'I've tried really, really hard. But . . . I can't do this. I'm sorry. I can't.'

My knees buckle beneath me. 'Dan—'

'I need to talk to Will.' He hands me my phone as I reach

for him. 'Call your solicitor,' he says. 'Will and . . . They're probably lining up the press for your arrest as we speak. So you should . . . You should call them. Soon.'

He peels my fingers from his skin, and walks away.

53

London, 2008

Graham stands by the sink, arms folded across his chest. The solicitor asks me something, but I miss it. I can't focus. All my thoughts have coalesced around him. Around the way he's looking at me.

'Hannah?'

I blink. 'Sorry – what?'

'I just need to make sure I'm absolutely clear on this. If you're not going to attend, I need to . . .'

I nod. I wanted to attend. I wanted to be in court today: to see the Wexworth family. To face them.

But Darren doesn't want me there. He's afraid I'll say something that makes them liable. He's worried I'll apologize. Apparently, that's the worst thing I could do.

Darren thinks it, and Graham naturally agrees. I can argue with one, but not the other. So I'm staying home. Graham is attending in my place.

The solicitor thinks this is my idea, of course. I told him it was. That's what happens, now: I say words I don't mean. I parrot the things Graham tells me to say. I say them so many times, I almost believe them. And when I contradict them, I doubt myself.

I know this is wrong. Occasionally, when I'm alone, I'm visited by my old self: a woman who knows better. Then, I think about leaving him. Once, I even packed a bag. One for Evie, too. I stood by the front door for maybe twenty minutes – and then, turned back. I couldn't do it. I couldn't even unlock the door.

'Just so I'm clear,' the solicitor says – an eerily thin man, with a haunted look perpetually in his eyes. (I wonder if that happens, when your life is spent defending people who tell you, outright, that they're guilty.) 'You agreed to let Lucie go out on a supervised walk, in exchange for . . . what, exactly?'

I sigh. I see her sitting on the chair opposite, legs tucked underneath her, the strings of her headphones dangling around her neck. 'I wanted her to talk to me. Properly. We'd had a few sessions that had been . . . unproductive. She didn't say much. We'd started to make progress, the day before, but then . . .'

Graham rolls his neck, loosening a crick. I lose my thread each time he moves.

'But then?'

'She'd received a letter overnight that . . . It upset her. So she'd gone back to not talking. Which is why I had to . . . I needed to give her an incentive to talk to me, and I knew she wanted to go outside, so . . .'

'What was in the letter?'

I feel an itch, an urge to say nothing. Old habits, I suppose:

patient confidentiality had been drilled into me as a student, and I've since drilled it into my own. Not that I have students, now. I've been out of work for almost three years. I no longer have anyone to teach; and when you're talking to the man paid to defend you, confidentiality ceases to apply.

Graham unfolds his arms, and leans against the counter.

'It was from her sister, Sophie. She said . . . She'd invited Lucie to stay with her when she got out.'

'And that upset her, how, exactly?'

I don't know how to say it, in front of Graham. There's no way he won't take it as a slight. If he believes it at all. More likely, he'll assume I'm lying. Coming up with a story designed to hurt him, to wound his pride.

She was torturing her, I want to say. *She was coercive, and cruel. She made Lucie end a relationship with a boy who seemed to be good for her. Because* he *told Lucie she deserved better. Her sister wouldn't let her believe that was true.*

Graham taps his fingers. I feel like a hunted animal, primed to run. I feel like this all the time.

'I don't know,' I say, finally. 'We didn't get into that.'

The solicitor says nothing. I wonder if he knows I'm lying. Graham does. I can see it in his eyes. He glances at his watch. 'We'd better get going, then.'

I think he – the solicitor, whose name I still don't know – is about to say something. He wants to speak to me alone. I can feel it. He's a good person, I realize. I see it in the look of concern, in the way he glances from me, to Graham, and back again. But whatever he might've said, or done – he doesn't. He thinks better of it.

After all, it's Darren who's paying his fees. My husband he's been dealing with, who's joining him in court. I'm incidental to all of this, though it's all my fault. He stands and shrugs on his coat.

Graham steps towards me. 'I'll call you after the hearing.'

He tips my head back, and plants a kiss there, for show. The solicitor doesn't see it: the thumb in the well of my neck. He holds it, for another beat, and I know what he's saying. No one's ever going to intervene. He can do whatever he wants, in front of whoever he wants to.

It doesn't matter.

I'm crazy.

No one would believe me, even if I told them the truth.

54

Derbyshire, 2018

I follow Dan for a couple of steps.

And then, I stop.

I want to beg him to come back, to grab hold of him. To *make* him stay.

But it's too late. It's done.

When the police come back, they'll arrest me. They've enough already, I'm sure of it. And when they ask Dan to give a statement, he'll tell them everything. He'll tell them I murdered Graham – I said so myself – and he thinks I killed Evie, too.

I can't face it. I can't be here for that.

55

I stare out at the quarry below, the sawn-off rocks jagged and black, grizzled with moss.

I look out at the cold blue water, and I wait for them to come for me.

On the passenger seat, my phone vibrates. I scan the screen, and see me and Dan laughing, my hair on his lips. It's five years old or more, this photo – taken on an afternoon like this one, when we'd gone for an ill-advised picnic, laughing as we sheltered from a storm. I'd attached the photo to his contact in my phone later that day: a reminder of the way he made me feel so happy, and so loved.

As I stare at it, the call rings out, and stops. I wonder if he'll call again. Somehow, I know he won't.

A bird, silhouetted, darts through the sky, trailed by another.

My phone lights up and vibrates again. *One (1) new voice-mail message.* I tap the icon, and it plays.

'Hannah,' Dan says. 'I'm really sorry. I love you. I'm sorry.'

Then, a pause. An inhale, a terrible shudder on the breath. 'Please. I love you.' A deathly beep. A cold voice asks if I'd like to hear the message again. I turn it off.

I know what this call is. I hear the fear in his voice, the regret. I imagine Stevens standing behind him, listening in. He wants me to come home, so he can finally make his arrest.

Stevens *needs* it to be me. Because then the story will change – it'll no longer be about the ways *he* failed, his partner manipulating a case around an innocent man. My arrest will set things right: the focus rightfully turned back to me, the woman who started it all. Who lied, for a decade, and ran.

I close my eyes. I try to feel Graham beside me. But he's gone. I'm alone with the reality of it, now. It's all been in my mind. A delusion. Nothing more. I imagined him, just as I imagined Darcy. I imagined hauntings, things pulled from ghost stories, so I could hide from the truth.

But I did it. I killed my husband. And it's possible I killed my daughter, too. All I can do is wait for the memories of her murder to creep back, just as they've done with his.

What I did to my husband, though, I could justify. He turned me into the woman I became. He only got what he deserved.

But if I hurt Evie – if I did *anything* to her, at all – I will never be able to live with my guilt.

I look at the sign by the quarry's edge. *This water is known to contain: Car wrecks. Dead animals. Excrement. Rubbish. Swimming may result in death.*

An idea bubbles up in my mind: a solution. It would be so easy to turn the key in the ignition. To put my foot on the pedal, and let go. To drive the car into the water, and let it swallow me whole.

I remember the pills Darcy gave me.

Darcy doesn't exist, I correct myself. *She's someone you created in your mind.*

I pop the glove compartment open. The silver packet seems to glow in the greyish light.

I could take them all, and wait for sleep to come. Then, the water. I wouldn't feel a thing.

A tranquillity settles over me: a bright and peaceful clarity. For the first time in as long as I can remember, I know what to do. I reach for the pills.

My phone vibrates beside me, and I jolt. The pills fall from my fingers into the footwell.

I reach around, under the seat, my eyes closed. Whatever it is – a text from Dan, an email from a stranger, an alert from *Conviction* – I don't want to know. I just want it all to be over.

My hand brushes against something smooth: something familiar. A piece of paper, maybe. I tug it out. It's the photograph. Margot, looking just like me.

It can't be real, I think. But I feel it: the smooth paper, cold under my thumb. I'd stolen it from Hawkwood House, without thinking. And then, I'd slipped it into my pocket.

Or so I'd thought. Apparently, I'd missed.

It's here.

It can't be.

I slide my fingers over the edge, and hear a soft nick. A tiny sliver of red opens up, a droplet of blood blooming over the cut.

I didn't imagine this. It's not a delusion. It's real.

I remember Darcy's hand on my thigh. The warm, soothing weight of it. Not cold, like Graham's. Not a draught, or a trick of the light.

She was there. She was real.

She was at Hawkwood House. I know it.

I put the keys in the ignition.

And I drive.

56

'Pairing,' the car announces as I pull on to the road.

The voice that follows is one I know well. Too well.

'I tried so hard,' she says. 'I don't think I ever *wanted* to believe she'd done it, even when it seemed like she was trying to parade it in front of me.' I see the expression on her face, in my mind. I know her well enough to see her shoulders slump, her hand run through her hair.

Sarah. My so-called best friend.

'I honestly think sometimes she'd say things just to get a reaction – I guess because if I reacted, she'd at last have proof of what *I* did. And I should've told someone – I probably should've gone to the police, or something, but . . . I mean, they were never going to start investigating someone else, with Mike in prison. And I'm a mum. I have two kids. You do what you have to do to keep them safe. Even if that means a kind of . . . Faustian bargain.

'But I've always wondered if it was my fault he . . .' She dissolves into great, heaving sobs that seem endless, and overblown. 'Graham and I . . . It was never meant to be a thing, between us. We slept together, one night, while we were at university, because I was . . . I was trying to console him. He and Hannah had had a fight, and he came to me to see how we could . . . fix it. But the attraction was just there.'

A car horn whines past, and I steer back into my lane, my heart in my throat.

'It was only meant to be a one-time thing. Both of us . . . we cared about her. She always had a temper, and she was . . . sensitive. So we decided not to say anything. To just pretend it'd never happened.

'But then . . . we bumped into each other at a thing – an alumni event. Hannah didn't go. I didn't know at the time, but she was pregnant. He told me they'd been having some problems, and . . . I don't know. We just slipped into our old patterns. Talking about Hannah. Me consoling him; him needing someone to talk to. One thing leading to another.

'And that was . . . Well, that was how it started up again. And it wasn't long before we sort of . . . realized it. We were . . .' Her voice wavers. 'We were in love. It was almost as though it was the two of *us* that were supposed to be together, but Hannah had . . . I don't know. It's one of those sliding-doors things, I guess. If he and I had met first, you know?'

The old wound splits open, a break from which I thought I'd recovered. I see him, on the tube, leaning in to kiss a woman I'd seen only from behind. That day, he hadn't seen his wife on the platform. And I hadn't seen my best friend in his arms.

I fix my gaze straight ahead. Hawkwood House appears between the trees, still blanketed by the scaffold.

'But he wouldn't ever leave her. We talked about it, a couple of times – I hadn't met my now-husband, so . . . The decision was his to make, really. But there was something that made him stay with her. Beyond Evie, obviously – I know he always had concerns about her, though I suspect custody would've gone to him, if he'd asked for it – but there was something else.

'It was almost like . . . he was afraid.'

There's a hiss of static. Fingers brushing against the mic. 'I just . . . I need you to know you can always talk to me. About anything.'

It's her voice, again. But this time, it's different. Familiar.

It's a memory. I know what's coming, a split second before it plays.

My laugh. My voice, slurred, when I speak. 'Even the fact I stabbed my husband in the throat with a kitchen knife?' That laugh, again. It sounds cruel. Manic. Depraved.

Anna Byers's voice cuts in, along with the swell of *Conviction*'s theme. 'Every one of us can think of a time we've done something we didn't want to do – whether out of a need to protect ourselves, or the ones around us. But imagine having to do it day in, day out, for ten years – to remain friends with the wife of the man you loved. The woman you have reason to believe murdered him in cold blood. And all the while, a series of threats – of little hints, suggestions that she *knows* what you did. That she's just biding her time. That she knows she got away with murder, once. And it's only the fact you're keeping her happy that stops her from doing it again.'

My phone vibrates, and I reach for it. I look back up, at the road.

'I know what I did was wrong. I know that,' Sarah goes

on. 'It wasn't fair on Hannah. Graham and I were both so, so aware of that. But . . . when she showed up at my door after the trial, and all but blackmailed me into giving her a job, when nobody else would take her on . . . I didn't know what else to do. I was—' Her voice breaks, now. A pin-drop silence fills the space. 'I was scared of what she'd do, if I didn't.'

I glance at my phone. It's a text from Dan. *Where are you?*

Anna Byers goes on. 'And what about these other women who've come forward? The ones in the tabloids, who claim they've had affairs with Graham?'

'No,' Sarah says, quickly. 'He wasn't like that. He'd never do that. That's why I wanted to . . . sort of defend him, I guess. Because he was a good man. And it's the worst thing I've ever done, but I loved him. And he loved me. And I'll never forgive her for taking him away from me.'

I hit stop. 'You stupid bitch.' I slam my hands against the wheel, the car veering, faster, towards the house. 'How fucking *dare* you?'

I don't care who sees me screaming; I don't care what they think.

Because she's lying. I didn't blackmail her. I wasn't unemployable. And I had no idea she was sleeping with my husband. Not until now.

I see the gates of Hawkwood House, thrown open. There are no signs of life beyond.

I feel Graham's hand, cold, on my throat, and it cuts me dead.

The phone beside me starts to ring. *No Caller ID.*

I think of the man who called me yesterday – was it yesterday? Time shudders, and moves under my feet. I look straight ahead.

The phone stops ringing. A split-second pause. Then, it starts ringing again. I stop the car. I reach for the phone, and I answer.

'Tell me you're not thinking of doing something stupid.'

It's Darcy. I close my eyes. Thump my head against the seat behind, just to feel something real.

'Hannah – talk to me. I just heard that stupid cow Sarah was on *Conviction*, and – I've been so busy, I'm sorry, but I spoke to your other half, and he said you'd disappeared, so . . .' She draws breath. 'Hannah, for God's sake. Answer me.'

I sit forward, pulled back to the moment. 'You spoke to Dan?'

'Briefly. He looked a bit shell-shocked, but we had a quick chat . . .'

He's seen her. He's met her. He has to believe she exists.

It's only one thing, but it might be enough to make him second-guess Stevens, and the rest. To make him at least consider the possibility that I might be telling the truth. That I didn't hurt my – our – daughter.

'Look, it isn't good for you to be alone right now. Why don't you head home, and I could pop back there, maybe make some tea?'

The clouds shift overhead, changing the light. This woman, on the phone, calls herself Darcy Burke – wearing another woman's name like a mask. I think of the papers, all signed in my name. The loans taken out, contractors booked. The forged deeds to Hawkwood House.

It was her, I realize. *Whoever she is. It was her.*

'Hello – Hannah? Can you hear me?'

'Sorry. Yeah. Can I . . . Can I meet you at the house?'

'Oh, God –' I think I hear her wince. 'I mean, we could if you want, but it's going to be mayhem over there at the moment. There are contractors everywhere. It's like trying to relax inside an anthill.'

It's a lie. There are no cars, anywhere, on the gravel drive. There's no one at the house at all.

'That's fine. I'll meet you there.'

I hang up the phone. I put it back on the seat beside me, and drive on. Back into the grounds of Hawkwood House.

57

London, 2008

The tiles stretch out beneath me like a chessboard. I stand, and I stare at the door.

I walk towards it. I wrap my fingers around the handle, and I peer through the glass.

I could run. I could go.

If only I could make myself open the door.

'Mum?'

I turn. Evie's there, at the foot of the stairs, watching me. She's the picture of him, her eyes filled with a too-familiar thoughtfulness, a too-familiar concern.

'Hi, baby.' I crouch in front of her. 'What's up?' She says nothing. She knows something's wrong. 'Come here.' I pull her into me. She's so small, and so soft. I'm amazed at her, every day. It's impossible that she could have come from us; that she could be so loving, so sweet, when we've come to hate each other so much.

It's impossible, too, that she doesn't see it. He's quiet, but she's observant. I saw her staring at my hand, once, trying to work out why I now had a bruise more blue than hers. And I've seen her, since, lower lip silently trembling, crying at nothing, in the hours after he and I have had one of the fights we didn't think she'd hear.

He loves her. No matter how much I hate him, I can't say that isn't the case. But he doesn't realize: each time he hurts me, he hurts our little girl, too.

Still, I'm as much to blame as he is. Maybe more so. Because while he might not know it, I *do*. And I'm still too weak to leave.

She wriggles away, and smiles. It warms me. I smile back. 'Are you hungry?' She nods. 'All right.' I think of the picture books I read to her, Piglet and Pooh side by side. I stand and take her tiny hand in mine. 'Come on, then. Let's go back inside.'

The apple hisses as the knife breaks the skin: a firm, clean line through crisp flesh.

Evie stands on the stool beside me, transfixed. She watches the knife bob up and down. I see her mouthing the numbers, counting the taps.

The landline rings, tearing through me. I clip the edge of my nail with the knife, and bite down. The blood tastes coppery on my tongue. I leave the knife and the apple behind, both out of her reach. 'I'll be back in a sec,' I say, with a kiss.

'It's me,' he says, when I answer. As though it could be anyone else. I lean back against the wall. His tone, already, is a terror. 'Hello? Are you there?'

'Yeah, I'm – sorry.' The apology is automatic. It's what I always do. It rarely works. 'Sorry,' I say again.

He makes me wait before he speaks. 'They've dismissed the case.' The traffic roars behind him, the wind whipping through the receiver. 'Darren seems to think it's unlikely to go any further. If the tribunal can't find evidence of wrongdoing, there's not much chance a judge will. They can try, obviously, but . . . it's done, for now, anyway.'

Good news, on the face of it, though I wouldn't call it that – the Wexworth family's grief is someone's fault, even if the court has determined it wasn't mine.

But I know that when he says they 'can't find' the evidence, he sees it as a failing on their part, for not seeing me as flawed as he does. And when he says it's 'done, for now', there's a threat in it. *You'll do this again,* he's saying. *It's only a matter of time.*

'I'm coming home,' he says, before I can reply. 'You should put Evie to bed. I think we need to talk.' The call ends with a click.

I know, again, what he's saying. His meaning is perfectly clear.

I go back into the kitchen, and I smile. 'Right. Let me finish up that snack.' She looks at me. She knows. I can see it. The guilt threatens to eat me alive.

I clip the last few pieces from the apple, already browning at the edges. I make a smiley face on a plastic plate and place it in front of her, on the table. She looks at it, and then at me. She takes a slice, and sucks the juice from it, her eyes fixed on mine.

I reach for her hair, the soft and impossibly perfect curls that will some day hang limp, like mine, but for now are still ringlets, like a porcelain doll's. 'Daddy's coming home soon,' I tell her. 'So Mummy needs you to get into bed and stay nice and quiet. Is that OK?'

She looks back at me and I know she understands not just the words that I'm saying, but what I really mean. I feel my ribs crack, my sternum split in two by the ache of it: how much I love her. What I would do to keep her safe.

As she settles, wide-eyed, into bed, I kiss her forehead. I tell her I love her. I wonder if she'll ever understand how much.

And then, I step out into the kitchen. The light is blinding. The edges of my vision flicker, breath humming in my chest.

I slip the crayons back into the box, and sort the mess of toys that litter the floor. I pat the cushions on the couch, and make our lonely house feel like his home. I take the plate from the table, and slide the bitten apple slices into the bin. I drop the dishes into foamy water, one by one.

I hear his key turn in the lock as I reach for the last: the knife, its handle weighted, heavy in my palm.

No more, I think, the words crisp and perfectly clear.

And so my husband enters his home for the final time, and I turn to face him, the kitchen knife trembling in my hand.

58

Derbyshire, 2018

The echo of my footsteps ricochet across the chequered tiles.

The rain begins a steady patter overhead. The wind whips through the tarpaulins on the scaffold; they crackle like live wires through the bluish air. And, as always, that awful tapping sound. I hear the beat of it in my veins. I think I see something move at the top of the stairs, and I freeze.

'Hello?' I call, a nervous flutter in my voice. 'Is anybody here?'

A draught blows through, curling around my neck and wrists. It feels like him. But it isn't. I know that now. He was never really there.

A bird bursts into flight through the doorway above. It's a large, black bird, like the one I saw on the roof of the sun room, weeks earlier. It burrows through a crack in the wall, and disappears. The wind stills. A floorboard creaks, deeper inside the house.

The creatures carved into the wood seem to follow me with their eyes; I have the sense, somehow, of being watched. Of being hunted.

I search around for something I can cling to: a weapon, of sorts, something I can wield as a threat. I pick up fragments of broken wood, piled under the staircase, but they're damp; they split apart in my hands. I tear through the filth, looking for something – anything – firm. My hand catches on a cold, narrow object: metal. I tug it out, my arm and shoulder thick with dust, moss, and dirt.

A screwdriver. From the toolbox I put here, that day, when the stairs caved in. I say a silent thank you to no one, and grip it, tight, in my palm.

I walk – faking a confidence and poise I don't feel, for the benefit of the dead eyes still watching – towards the far end of the hall, where the corridors branch into the rest of the House.

I hear footsteps in the distance. Every cell in my body tells me to turn and run.

But I can't.

Not this time. Not now.

I turn the door handle, my breath held in my throat. As it gives, I catch it: the same smell of mould I recall from those first days at Hawkwood, the black stink of death in the air.

My eyes adjust to the cold, dim light, and the room settles into view: the furniture still peeling, walls creeping with moss, all untouched. It's wholly at odds with the entrance hall, the sun room, the corridor between.

I remember the last time I asked if I could look around. The slight flush in her cheeks I'd put down to the wine, the excuse: a hard-hat zone, not covered by her insurance.

It was a lie. Another one. I've only ever passed through the same three rooms since the 'renovations' began. She showed me just enough to make me believe; enough to make my mind fill in the gaps.

I step inside, and see the words scrawled above, in too-familiar red paint.

I KNOW WHAT YOU DID.

My heart shudders. The draught blows through, and drops. I hear footsteps, again, further down the hall. A door creaks open and shut.

I cling to the wall, the moss sticky, cold on my palm. I follow the bloody words: *YOU CAN'T HIDE*, and *LIAR LIAR*. As I press by the last, edging around a half-dismantled hospital bed, the paint smears on my shirt. It's still wet.

I hear a roar of tyres on the gravel, outside, and I freeze. It's either the police – or it's her. But if it's her, then the footsteps I'm hearing must belong to someone else.

Sweetheart, Graham whispers, a shiver running through me.

A car door slams shut – only one. There's no echo of conversation, though it's possible the rain's drowned it out. But I don't think it's them. Somehow, I know it. It's Darcy, or whoever she really is. I squeeze the screwdriver in my palm.

'Hannah?' she calls from the hallway. 'Where are you?' There's a darkness in her tone, an appalling satisfaction.

Light sweeps through a door, swaying open at the end of the hall. There's a single word painted on the wall there.

RUN.

'Hannah?' she calls again from the hall. 'It's me. I'm here. It's going to be OK.' Her voice is a sing-song: a tease and a threat.

The rain blisters overhead, dripping through the cracks. I feel it sliding down my neck, an icy chill.

There are two doors at the end of the corridor. One half-open, one shut. I try to pre-empt her pre-empting me: she'll assume I've gone through the open door. The path of least resistance, the simplest explanation. I push the closed door. It sticks for a moment, and then gives.

I see her curls first, hanging over the edge of the bath that stands in the centre of the room on broken legs.

I see her appalling stillness, her hand hand hanging limp over the rim.

Memories, imaginings collide: I feel my knees give way beneath me. I feel the pieces fit together, a puzzle finally unlocked. I realize who this woman is – Darcy Burke, but not; nor, now, a delusion – and why she's here.

I feel myself careering backwards, a hand in my hair.

And then everything turns black.

59

London, 2008

My palm is slick around the cross-hatched handle, the blade cool where it nips against my thigh. I will the trembling to stop. I try to breathe. I count the beats, the thudding rhythm of my heart.

'Put the knife down, Hannah,' I hear him say. It feels as though we're miles apart, the words faint and fading.

I blink, and he's in front of me, jacket still slung over his arm. The cuffs swing, restlessly, as the air blows through the vent. He looks towards the bedroom, where Evie's pretending to sleep; then back, again, to me.

'Please,' he says, though I know he isn't asking. I know, too, the meaning of the look he gives: the threat cocooned inside. He doesn't need to say another word. There's a dull ring on the countertop, where the steel blade meets the stone.

'Come here,' he says. His arms outstretched, eyes kind. 'I'm sorry. Come here.' I don't believe him. I know it's a lie. He's done this before. 'Come here, Hannah,' he says, again. And I do what I always do.

I step towards him.

He pulls me in. And he rocks me. Tenderly. He hums the song in my ear, the one he'd sung on the day we moved in. I fall back into that moment, when I'd loved him. When we didn't see what we'd eventually become, though some part of me, I think, had always sensed it: the flash of his temper at the passing cyclist that day. The way he was all want, all craving, in a way that I mistook for love.

'I'm sorry,' I say, my default response, again.

'It's OK. Come on. You're having a bad day. It'll be OK.'

He leads me into the bathroom. He lowers the toilet lid, and sits me down.

I don't trust this. I can't. It isn't him. It might've been, once – but this version of him left me long ago.

I hear the crackle of water filling the tub. I smell juniper, apricot, geranium. None of it quite enough to drown out another, familiar smell: another woman's perfume on his skin.

It's too much. I am panicked, electric with fear. He turns, and I flinch. I see disappointment cross over his face. He masks it, almost instantly.

'Stand up,' he says, and I do.

He winds his arms around my waist, his hands damp, hot from the water, the steam. He tips his head to the ceiling. 'Arms.' I raise them, and he peels off my stained T-shirt. I feel an intimate, terrible shame.

He drops the T-shirt on the floor. He examines me, slowly. His eyes skip past a faded bruise on my shoulder, the mark of his finger and thumb. He crouches, and peels down my leggings, his knuckles tracing the lines of my thigh. He kisses my stomach, the scarred, stretched-out flesh of it. My body responds involuntarily. I feel the faint kick of wanting: a betrayal.

He stands, and gestures to the bath. I climb in. The water burns my feet and calves, but I don't show it. I smile as he looks on.

'Relax,' he says. 'I'll be back in a minute. I'll get you some wine.'

He hates it when I drink. I know this. He *knows* I know this. And he knows I'm too afraid to question why.

He's playing a part, all graciousness and deference, like a butler, a waiter at a smart hotel. He bows as he closes the door.

I've never been more scared of him than I am now.

In the scalding water, still, I'm cold; it's a chill with fingers in my blood. I listen carefully for sounds: for the tread of footsteps on the boards outside. He turned left, away from me, towards the front door, towards the kitchen and the lounge. This, at least, is a relief. Evie's bedroom, next to ours, is on the right.

I try to make my trembling stop, my muscles stiffening, toes pressed against the walls of the tub. It only makes it worse.

I hear the footsteps coming back. But they don't stop. They carry on.

He's never hurt her; never would. Would he?

The silence swallows everything. All I hear is my own shallow breath.

Water spills over the rim as I drag myself to my feet. I reach for a towel, and slip. I feel as though my limbs are not my own. And then, the door opens, and he's there, a glass of red wine in his hand.

He stares at me, naked, hideously exposed. 'Sit back down, Hannah.'

I don't move.

He says it again. I am pinned in place, frozen. I am so unimaginably afraid. 'Hannah.'

I lower myself back into the water. I grip the sides of the tub with both hands.

He closes the door, and his shoes click, muted, on the tiles. As he walks towards me, I see him, truly, for the first time in years: I take in the sunken lines of his face, his eyes ringed greyish underneath; the first soft salt-and-pepper flecks in his stubble and his hair.

''Til death do us part,' our vows had said. 'In sickness and in health.'

He settles on the edge of the bath, and hands me the wine, plucking a toy from the water: a pirate who's lost his hat. 'This isn't really in keeping with the mood here, is it?'

I say nothing. I can't speak.

'Drink up.' I take a sip, the red wine tart on my tongue. 'We can't keep going on like this, can we?' There's a sadness in his eyes that's real: a kind of grief. 'It's not fair on anyone. Least of all Evie.' He stops. The silence rings in my skull. 'Can we?'

'No.'

'We probably should've . . . You know. Had this conversation before.' He runs his tongue along his teeth, mouth closed. 'It's my fault. I know I'm not easy to be with, and I'm sorry for that.'

I know what he wants me to say, here. I feel my cue in the air: to tell him it's not only him, but me, too. To absolve him of guilt. But I can't. Some small, hard piece of the old me remains, buried beyond his reach. I won't tell him this isn't his fault. I'm scared of this man, who may kill me. But still, I won't give him that.

He tenses. His jaw sets rigid. A vein creeps into view on his neck. 'You can have the house.' His voice is clipped, now, and cruel. 'I imagine you'll need it.'

I sit up. 'I don't want—'

He places a hand squarely on my chest, and pushes me back. It creeps up, towards my throat, and I know what he's doing: the same as he always does. A slow depression, a thing he knows I could fight; he takes pleasure in knowing I won't. He's so good at this – so skilled – that I have a nerve there, now, residually pinched. It's a reminder of him, even when he's not around.

He lets go. I gasp for breath. 'I'm trying to make this easy, Hannah. For all of us. You won't get custody of Evie, but I want to make sure you're provided for. At least until you're back on your feet.'

I feel a sob rising. It fills my throat. I can't breathe. 'You can't. She's my daughter. I—'

He laughs, and it's devastating. He's mocking me. He knows this is a fight he can't lose. 'Hannah, do you realize how I looked today?'

'I don't—'

'Do you *realize* how I looked?' He doesn't raise his voice. He never does. But his tone sharpens to a point, and I wilt.

I shake my head.

He waits.

'No,' I say, at last.

'Drink your wine.'

I stare at the glass, the stem trembling between my fingers.

I take a sip. I taste a bitterness. A sediment that clings to my lips; a residue on the sides of the glass.

'I looked like a fucking idiot. I looked like a father who doesn't know how to look after his child. Who doesn't know what his *wife* is up to, at work or at home.'

The thought turns solid, a cool recognition. My husband has poisoned my drink.

He's waiting for me to speak. 'Graham, please, you didn't—'

'Don't *tell* me I'm wrong, Hannah. Don't you dare. Because you weren't there. I saw those people looking at me. That poor family, after what *you* put them through, staring at me as though it was all *my* fault. When all I've ever done is try to—'

I slip out of myself for a moment.

And then, I return. The bathwater rises and falls around me.

'—and over-prescribed medications, and God knows what else. Darren has covered for you, over and over again, out of loyalty to *me*—'

The pieces click into place. I see Darren handing the prescription to Graham, before he slandered me in court. Before the two of them twisted the story to fit.

Hannah Catton, the unreliable doctor, with a store of stolen medications to hand. She's reckless. Stupid. She mixes a couple – several, in her confused state – with alcohol, and takes a bath, where she drifts off, and drowns in her sleep.

'OK,' I say. 'OK.' I raise the glass to my lips, but don't swallow. Still, the bitterness sticks to my gums. He stares at me. 'I'm sorry. I . . . You're right.' A sob escapes me. A real one. I can't say the words without feeling the grief they contain. 'You should have custody. I can't give her what she needs, and you can. So . . . you can take her. I won't fight it.'

He says nothing. I see him deflate, just a little. He'd expected more.

I can't tell if he's disappointed, or relieved.

'I just . . .' I hear my voice slur, and my chest constricts. I'm not faking it. Whatever's in this glass, it's strong. 'I'm really tired. Do you mind if I just lie here for a bit?'

He doesn't speak. He thought he wanted me to die in this bathtub. But some piece of him, now, is unsure; some small part of him that still cares. That still sees me as his wife; as the mother of his child.

I close my eyes. I feel a pull, as though my chest is sinking. I am slipping. I need him to believe my act, before it becomes something real.

I hear the side of the bathtub creak. He stands, and gently takes the glass from my hand. I let my hand drop, lifelessly, down. I think of Lucie's pale, blue hand doing the same. He picks it up and rests it on my stomach. He's as tender with me as he is with Evie, when he tucks her in. I feel sleep coming for me, tugging at my jaw, my skull. The water rises over my chin, my lips.

My husband kisses me on the head, and I fall further. 'I love you,' he whispers. I feel myself turn weightless. A deep, thick blackness covers me, like a blanket. He pulls away, and lets me go. 'Goodnight, sweetheart.'

60

I grip the sides of the bath; the room is revolving. I watch his hand pull the door in slow motion, the click of it a ricochet in my skull.

I think he's gone. But I can't be sure.

I am tumbling, every blink seeming to last half a minute. My pulse is slow, arrhythmic thumps. I'm awake, and then I'm not.

I need to get out of this water. But I can't let him hear me move. I lift myself, heavily. I almost stand. But my palm slides along the rim of the tub, and I can't make it stop.

My skull meets the corner of the cabinet. I don't feel the hit: I only hear the crackle of bone. I feel the rush of white surround me, a soft glitter of stars, and then, there's nothing: only a vast and dreamless sleep.

61

'Wake up, Hannah.' The words are disembodied, drifting somewhere behind. My eyes are weighted shut. 'Wake up.' I feel myself slowly returning: sensation creeping back into my limbs. I feel the cold stone floor beneath me. I smell the rot and the decay. I remember where I am, and what I saw, before it all went dark.

'Oh, wake *up*, you stupid bitch.' The kick to my stomach winds me. I'm gasping as I open my eyes, half-blinded by tears.

It's her. She's no longer putting on the voice I'd come to know as Darcy's. Now, she's wholly herself: Sophie, the girl I met, once, in over large sunglasses, in the gardens of the Buyon clinic, when she'd asked me to treat her sister, Lucie. She'd seen right through me, then: all ego, all hubris, desperate to be told I was *good*.

Then, I'd let her sister go. And she'd bled out in a hotel bathtub.

Evie, I think, trying to focus; trying to see my daughter, in the tub behind. She isn't moving. She's so terribly pale; so still.

'There we go. Much better.' Sophie smiles, moving close to my face. I see the familiar yellowed stain on her bottom teeth, her hair soaked through and slicked back. 'Sit up.'

My head pounds, an ache that echoes through my teeth.

I drag myself up to sitting. 'I'm sorry,' I say, automatically. 'Sophie, I'm sorry. About your sister – about Lucie—'

'Don't you *dare* say her name. Don't you fucking dare. If you'd done your job, *none* of this would be happening. This whole thing is your fault.'

My pulse rockets. There's a frenzy in her voice, a stark violence I don't know how to calm.

'Did you know I found the body?' Her voice is small now, child-like. It's as though all the control she's exercised, for the last few weeks, as 'Darcy', has been lifted: a release of tension that's electric and unpredictable. 'She cut her wrists in the bath, and I found her. Did you know that?'

'I'm so sorry—'

'Shut *up*. You took my sister away from me. She was *mine*. And you took her away.' Her voice catches, a swell of tears held back. 'I *loved* her. More than anything.'

I think of what Lucie said, on that final day. 'She hurts me. She makes me do things I don't want to do. When I'm with her, I don't know what's real.'

'And they didn't see it. That farce of a tribunal. After everything – all the evidence – they still didn't think you'd done anything wrong. Even though you took away the person I loved most in the world.' She crouches down beside me. I'm splayed out like a doll, my legs flat on the cold stone floor, back slumped against the wall. My head pounds, the room whirling vertiginously. 'An eye for an eye, Hannah. You know what that means, don't you?'

She taps the screwdriver against the floor. Tap. Tap. Tap.

She tips her head back. I see Evie's curls hanging from the tub. I catch the smell of her shampoo, the strawberry breath of her hair.

'Poor Evie,' she says. 'Just like her mum. A few compliments from a pretty boy and she's anyone's. You really should've raised her better.' She reaches into her pocket and pulls out my phone – my *old* phone. 'While I'm giving you free advice – change your passwords when you lose your phone.' She types something; places the phone on the ground between us, and extends a hand. 'Yours.'

I can't move. I can't make sense of what's happening.

'Now, Hannah. Or I'm filling that bath with her blood while you're still around to see it.'

I feel myself break open. I realize what she's doing. An eye for an eye.

'Please,' I say, desperately. 'Please. Sophie, please – I'll give you whatever you want.'

She shrugs. 'This *is* what I want.' She's matter-of-fact about it. 'I want you to *hurt*. Like I did. Like you *should've*, when your husband died. Because you didn't, did you?'

I know I can't argue. But still, I beg. 'Please. I'm so sorry. Please.'

'Give me the fucking phone, Hannah. These hysterics are boring. And pointless, frankly. I mean, look. She's already dead.'

I hear the moan that escapes me; feel another crack of pain as she grabs my cheeks and slams my head into the wall. She roots through my pocket, and teases out my phone.

She looks at the background, a photo of Dan, and Evie, and me, all smiles.

'Aww. Cute.' She crouches in front of me again, and lays the two phones side by side. One by one – methodically, with a terrifying calm – she jams the screwdriver through each of the screens. I watch their faces distort and disappear.

'This is all your fault.' Her tone is different now: colder. More menacing. I feel her breath close to my face.

She rests the screwdriver on my calf. The point pinches at my skin. 'Hannah. Look at me. Wakey wakey, now.'

I blink. My vision fades in and out.

'This . . .' She gestures back to the bath, to Evie. 'This was you. You killed your little girl.'

I feel Graham's cold hand on mine. I feel his grip tightening. *It was an accident,* he says.

'No,' I hear myself say. 'I didn't.'

The pain that follows is blinding. The cold slice of the screwdriver, tearing skin, invading muscle and gristly flesh. I hear the crush of it, pressing through.

'Look at me, Hannah. You killed your husband, and you killed your little girl.' I open my eyes. The blade is only halfway in. She smiles. 'Come on, Hannah. Try again. What did you do?'

It was an accident, Graham says again.

I hear his footsteps, solid, coming back for me.

He has heard me fall in the bath. He will hold me underwater, and wait for me to drown.

He squeezes my hand. The bones crack.

She rocks the screwdriver back. 'Who killed your daughter, Hannah?'

My scream fills the space; it fills everything. But still, I feel his footsteps coming closer. I see his shadow moving, in the doorway behind.

What was it? my husband says.

It was an accident, I say to him, and mean it.

'I . . .' I begin. But I falter. I close my eyes.

'Look at me,' she says. There's a pause. She presses her body weight into the screwdriver, and this time, I don't scream. There's only a low, buzzing sound in my ears, an eerie, unnatural silence.

I open my eyes, and I see him, in the shadows. He's there. Everything I've believed about Hawkwood – every instance of madness, every delusion – turns solid before my eyes.

He is here. He's always been here.

And I can't run. Not now. His is a ruthless love I will never escape.

'Say it, Hannah. Admit what you did.'

I close my eyes, tight. I can't bear it. I can't bear to see him, again: can't face the look of satisfaction on his face when I give in, again. 'I did it. It's my fault. I—'

She gasps. She gives a choke of a laugh.

I feel the warm spread of blood, and force open my eyes. It's too much. It doesn't make sense. I look at her; at the deep, crimson bloom spreading through her shirt, turning black.

She stares at me, helpless, confused. She looks down at my hands, searching for the blade.

But it wasn't me.

He disappears, swallowed by the shadows again. Beyond, I see Evie's fingers twitch. She forms a fist, and lets go.

She's alive. Barely, but—

Darcy gasps, desperately, again. She shudders as her eyes roll back into her skull, and she falls.

62

London, 2008

I choke. I taste copper on my tongue. My skull pounds, a relentless throb. The water is ice cold around me, pinkish with my blood.

He must have heard me fall. He must've heard the thud, the crack, and held still, for a moment, listening. I imagine him hearing the silence, again, and settling back to his work.

Or maybe – maybe – he looked. Maybe he saw the blood, the angular bend of me, the crack in my skull, and realized this was better still. A wreck of a woman. Someone he couldn't have saved.

I grip the sides of the tub, and I lift myself, haltingly, up. I catch my foot in the chain, and the drain gurgles, water and blood rushing away.

I am frozen and naked, and electric with rage.

This man wants to take my daughter from me.

But he'll have to kill me first. Really kill me, this time. In a way he's forced to live with: a memory that'll haunt him for the rest of his life.

My hand longs for the knife in it; it's an itch. I drag a robe around me, and step into the hall. There's bleach in the air, an ammoniac hum. I see him in my mind, wiping down surfaces, smearing every trace of me away. My husband's been cleaning up a crime scene, though I doubt he sees it like that. After all, we both belong here. His hands belong on my skin.

I listen for his footsteps: for the sound of his inevitable return.

But there's nothing.

Only the faintest of taps, the faintest of whispers, a thing that seems hallucinatory until I make sense of it. My little girl counts when she's nervous. She lies in her bed, and ticks off books, plastic figurines, imaginary sheep.

My still-damp feet slip on the floorboards. My handprints mark the walls, disappearing as I pass.

'Sweetheart,' I whisper as she stares up at the doorway, saucer-eyed. 'Do you know where Daddy is?' She shakes her head, fist clenched, pressed hard against her lips. 'OK,' I say. 'OK. I need you to be very quiet now. Can you do that?'

She glances at my bloodshot eyes, my trembling hands. 'Stay here, OK, baby?' I pull her into me. 'I love you. I love you so, so much.'

I tuck the blanket around her, tight, and step back into the hall.

I retrace my steps into the kitchen. I lose my balance and stumble; steady myself, back pressed against the wall. The same dizzying sense washes over me as before, everything faintly liquid. As though I'm walking through a dream.

I search the kitchen for the knife. But it's gone.

He has it, I realize. *He has the knife. And he's waiting for me.*

I retch, silently. I taste the hot tang of vomit in the back of my throat.

I'm in no state to run. I'm still not sure I can open the door, even if I thought I could make it down the stairs. I grip the walls, again, to hold myself up.

Fine, I say, to myself, with a cool resolve. *Fine.*

I walk back, stand outside our bedroom door, and wait, listening to him tapping his fingers on wood. Tap. Tap. Tap. I wonder if he's nervous. I wonder if, now, he's afraid of me. Afraid of what I'm going to make him do.

Because I'll ruin him. I don't care who thinks I'm crazy – I don't care if I'm believed. If he doesn't kill me, now, I'll tell the whole fucking world who he is, and what he's done.

The walls curve in around my vision, and retract. I take a breath, and push the door.

And there he is, sleeping.

I hate him, then: curled under the sheets, the shape of peaceful slumber. Wrath spreads through my veins as I watch him. Perfectly restful; perfectly still.

The taste of blood hits my tongue as a car sweeps past.

The silver handle of the knife flashes: there, for a moment, and gone.

The tapping sound is only blood upon the floorboards, a steady beat.

Tap. Tap. Tap.

And then, there's nothing. Only the silence. The fall.

63

Derbyshire, 2018

I reach for the screwdriver. I close my eyes, and I wrench it from my calf. I gasp at the pain, the heady release of blood but I won't – can't – scream any more.

I only need to get to her. To Evie. I need to take my daughter home.

I stagger up, over Darcy's – Sophie's – writhing form. She seizes my ankle, but her grip is weak. I see the wound now: under her shoulder, between her ribs, a mark that's lurid and pulsing. I pull away, with a strength that seems to come from beyond me: a blind determination to get to my little girl. To feel for a pulse: to see if the movement I saw wasn't only a final wish, a delirious dream.

Something moves in the shadows beside me. I lose my balance and pitch back, unsteadied by the pain in my calf, the drip of warm blood in my shoes.

'I'm sorry – I—' A voice speaks – a male voice. I can't

place it. It isn't him – Graham. It can't be. It's real. It has an echo.

He steps into the light, and recognition shivers through me.

It's impossible. It doesn't make sense.

Since we last stood face to face – a teenager in an ill-fitting suit, a ripple of acne curved around his jaw – he's completely changed. He's taller now, though still wiry – but he seems whittled away, made only of sinew and bone, veins snaking around hungry flesh. There's something childlike in his expression: in the terror that crosses his face.

'Mike?' I say, feeling sick. Feeling horribly afraid. Sophie's body twitches, her eyes still fixed on me. He leans forward, and begins to heave. 'Mike,' I say again, the shiver in my voice giving me away. 'Mike. Look at me. Focus on *me*.' I realize, even as I say it, that this might well make things worse.

It might be me he's here for, after all.

But no – that doesn't make sense, either. I'm all panic, all frenzied adrenaline: he's not like that. He can't be. He wouldn't. Not after all he's gone through to clear his name.

Then again . . . I glance again at Sophie, eyes rolling back into her skull, as Graham's had, before. Revenge makes people do unspeakable things.

'Mike. Please. Look at me.'

He blinks, and shakes his head, as though he doesn't quite believe I'm really there. We're looking through and past each other, like strangers caught in a dream. 'I didn't – oh my God, I—'

'It's OK. It's OK.'

I look over at Evie. I catch the smell of her shampoo again. 'I didn't mean to.' By the tone of his voice – the flat, listless affect – I know he's feeling the same strange numbness I do: the sense of a curtain falling, a kind of protection. The mind refusing to admit something so terrible could ever be real.

'I just wanted to scare her. To show her . . .' He points at the doorway behind. I see the word *RUN*, still dripping red from the walls. I think of the other words I passed on my way through the house.

YOU CAN'T HIDE.

I KNOW WHAT YOU DID.

'I found the paint here, and . . . I just wanted to . . . I didn't mean to . . .'

His shoulders slump. He heaves, again. I stare at him, frozen. He said he found the paint at Hawkwood House – which means the words graffitied in my kitchen were Sophie's too: *MURDERER. WHORE.*

I look from Mike to Evie, and back. For the first time, I see the knife in his gloved hand, the bloody trail that runs from him to me. I wonder where he found it; whether he's lying, now. Whether he'd planned to use it, all along. *I just wanted to scare her,* he said. *I didn't mean to . . .*

'Mike . . . Look at me.' I hear Sophie gasping, her eyes closing, skin a deathly white. 'Look at *me*, Mike. Please. Whatever she did to you – she can't hurt you now. Just try to breathe.' He takes a deep, shuddering breath. 'I need to check on my daughter. Is that OK?'

His brow crinkles in confusion. Then he seems, too, to realize he's holding the knife. He drops it, the clatter on the stone floor deafening.

I can't wait any longer. I go to Evie. I grab her wrist, and squeeze it. It's ice cold, her fingers a dull, grey-blue. I feel Mike's eyes on me, on Evie, willing her to move. Her fingers twitch, just a little – just enough. Beneath her eyelids, there's the faintest of flutters.

'Is she OK?' Mike watches me, warily. I'm not sure which of us is more afraid of the other.

When I speak, my voice is barely more than a croak. 'I . . . I think she will be. But I need to get her out of here. We need to call for help.' He shakes his head, and my heart falls; my hope evaporates. 'Mike, please. I get it. I promise you, I understand.'

'You don't.' Something flashes behind his eyes, a rage that passes through him like a wave, and breaks. He's in shock. He's traumatized. 'You can't.'

'Mike.' I try not to look at the knife, Sophie's body, the blood. I think back to my training; try to do what I ought to do, in a moment like this. 'Mike, you can talk to me. Tell me what—'

'I can't.'

My heart cracks open. He's terrified; the look in his eyes is that of a little boy, lost. I remember his mother's words, during *Conviction*: 'My son isn't a murderer. He's a victim.'

She's right. But I'm failing him. All my years of training, and I don't know what to say.

In the end, though, it's Darcy's – Sophie's – trick that works. I say nothing. He speaks to fill the silence; to be heard.

'She set me *up*.' His voice ripples, a sob – I think – catching in his throat. 'Because of her sister. Because of Lucie. I . . .' He stares at me, helplessly, as something shifts in my memory, and drops into place. I see Lucie, picking fibres from the arm of her chair, twelve hours before her death. *I loved him,* she'd said. *But Sophie thinks Mike's turning me against her, so . . . I told him it was over, last night.*

'I missed her call, the night she died. I didn't recognize the number, so I didn't pick up. I wasn't thinking, because I . . . I was drunk. And the next day she was . . .' He takes a shuddering breath. *It's not your fault,* I want to say, but can't. *We took away her phone.* 'We'd talked about it once before, and I'd said she could stay at my friend's house, get away from her family, and . . . and then we'd go off on our own.' My skin turns cold. I think of Evie's diary entries; the boy she'd said had promised her the same thing. Sophie had taken everything that Mike had said to Lucie; had made the Callum profile, and drawn my daughter in.

'I only found out she was dead the day after the funeral. I thought she just didn't want to talk to me, because . . . Because that's what she'd said, the last time we spoke. But then Sophie called and told me, and . . .'

Evie moans, softly, a sound I've heard her make in her sleep. I squeeze her hand, tighter, and will her to hold on. 'Mike . . . what happened to Lucie wasn't your fault. You couldn't have—'

'It *was*.' I flinch at the break in his voice. The look in his eyes is the same as the one he'd worn in the dock, at the trial. I'd read it – correctly – as guilt. But it wasn't Graham's death he blamed himself for. It was Lucie's. 'I should have been there for her, but I wasn't.'

'You couldn't have known. I only signed off on her going out that afternoon, and . . . She wasn't supposed to leave the grounds. I swear, Mike. It was a last-minute decision, on her part. You missing that call was an accident – but that's *all* it was. I promise. It wasn't your fault.'

He says nothing. Only looks down at Sophie, now still, curled fetal on the tile.

'Mike, please—'

'She's just . . .' He gestures at the body between us. 'I couldn't keep up with her. She's too fucking smart.' His tone has hardened; he looks surprised by it, himself. 'After I got my possession charge, she called me. She'd seen the photos of me – of my . . .' He traces his jaw; a smudge of Sophie's blood marks the spot where the bruises must've been, after his assault. 'I guess that's what gave her the idea. She told me she felt bad about what happened, and she had some of Lucie's stuff to give me, so . . . I met her for a drink. But she left after, like . . . five minutes. With *my* gloves. And I was so stupid, I didn't put the pieces together until way, way too late.'

I see him losing control, the words spilling out. I've seen it before, with patients, pulling loose. 'They were a present from Lucie. Sophie *knew* that. And she knew I'd recognise them when the police put them in front of me. She knew I'd say they were mine.'

I feel a fissure crack; a realization breaking, in the moment before he speaks. Still, when he says the words, the room seems to revolve; the whole world rocks and resettles itself. 'When she killed your husband, like, eight months later, she was wearing them – while I was sitting in a bar down the road waiting to meet with the first girl online who came *close* to reminding me of Luce. Except obviously, she never existed. Sophie made her up, too.'

My own story unravels, the past spinning out in a different way. I think of what Stevens had said, about Graham's statement at my tribunal: about my obsession with Margot, my grandmother, who murdered her husband and child. Sophie had heard it all. She'd been there, watching, waiting for them to affirm my guilt. But they didn't.

Maybe she'd expected that; made arrangements with Mike

413

at the bar by our house, just in case. So when the verdict went our way, she was ready.

She'd followed Graham home; had slipped through our house, to our bedroom, to watch and wait. It was her footsteps I'd heard passing while I lay in the bath, sick with fear. Not his.

Then, when Graham crawled into our bed, she'd killed him – wearing Mike's gloves, with my kitchen knife. It was both plan and contingency; check and checkmate.

She knew the police would most likely charge me – the unstable spouse – without looking much further. But if they had any doubt whatsoever – an anonymous tip with Mike's name would sway the investigation in his direction. His calls to the girl who never arrived would place him close to the scene – and they'd find Graham's blood on gloves he'd willingly tell them were his.

With two such strong suspects, they'd have no need to look for anyone else – for Sophie. It would be either/or. Him, or me. And all the while, both of us grieving the ones that we loved: an eye for an eye.

Or so she thought. But she couldn't have known what Graham was like – what our marriage really was. And she couldn't have planned for *Conviction,* ten years later, picking over the bones of a decade-old crime. And so, she'd come to Hawkwood – to lead them back here. Back to me.

Three false identities, three shifting masks: she'd played Callum with Evie; Darcy with me – both of us entranced by the people who told us the things we wanted to hear.

And her swan song: the madwoman, Hannah Catton. Rebuilding Hawkwood House – or some of it, at least – in my name, signing contracts, loan agreements, and the rest, all in my hand. That I couldn't remember doing these things would only prove my psychosis; that I wouldn't admit it would only prove my guilt.

'I've been looking for her since I got out,' Mike says, faintly. His voice breaks the silence; brings me back. 'No one believed me at the time, but . . . I needed her to know that I knew. I . . .' His eyes drift to the body again. It's as though a spell has been broken. The calm between us cracks. 'Oh fuck.' There's panic in his voice, a hand pressed to his throat and clenching. 'Oh my God. I've killed her. I only meant to scare her. I didn't mean to – oh, God, oh fuck—'

'Mike, Mike – wait – whoa.' I stand and reach out a hand for his trembling arm. I feel the warmth of it, the only warmth anywhere in this house. 'Hey, hey – calm down. It's OK. It's OK. We just need to get out of here – we can talk to the police, both of us, and explain what happened, and—'

He pushes me away, and for the first time, I'm afraid of him. Not him, exactly – that isn't right. I'm afraid of the person that Darcy – Sophie – has made us both. I'm afraid of the way we're destabilized. The way that neither of us feels quite in control of the things she's made us do.

I look over at Evie, lying in the tub.

'Mike, please.' My heart thuds, my pulse racing. 'I promise I won't go anywhere. I swear. It's you and me, now. I'll tell the police you only did what you did to help me. It was self-defence. OK?'

He doesn't move. He doesn't respond.

'Mike – do you understand? I won't let what happened before happen again. I promise you.'

He has no reason to trust me. And even if he does, the police think I'm a killer. Nobody believes a word I say.

But he nods. He helps me lift Evie to standing, her weight pressed into my shoulders. Her eyes flit open, once, unseeing: she's coming round. She's going to be OK.

My feet slip on the bloody tiles: my blood, and Sophie's, cooling underfoot. As we edge forwards, Mike stops, and lingers behind. I hear the scrape of the knife on stone. The wet tap of blood on the floor.

He's changed his mind. He doesn't trust me. He can't. 'Mike,' I say, desperately. 'Please. Please—'

'I'm sorry.' He steps towards me. 'I'm really sorry. But I can't. I can't do it again.'

'Mike, I'm begging you – please—'

He shakes his head. The knife trembles in his hand.

And then, he turns.

His shadow eclipses the open door, and he's gone, the word *RUN* still dripping, a threat, behind.

64

Somehow, I get Evie out to the car. It feels as though it takes hours, her body a chilling weight.

When I settle her into her seat, and wrap the belt around her, her eyes are open. She sees me, now. She's there. She murmurs something I can't catch. I tell her everything's going to be all right, and I almost believe it myself.

I'll take her home, to Dan, and we'll take her to hospital, and then I'll explain everything. It'll all make sense, at last. We'll all be OK. It'll all be fine.

It's a lie, and I know it. After everything that's happened, we'll never be the people we were, before; nothing will ever be the same.

But I have to believe it's possible – to force myself to believe it. Just for now. Just long enough to get us home.

As I drive, I flick on the radio and turn it up. I need it to keep her awake. To stop her from drifting into that long, dark sleep. A pop song plays, incongruously cheerful. I am driving my drugged, barely conscious daughter. I am bleeding, dripping with another woman's blood.

I reach to turn it off, but the news breaks in. 'The body of missing teenager Amy Barker has been recovered from woodlands in Derbyshire, close to the village of Hawkwood—'

I flick it off, quickly. I grip the wheel tighter, and try to breathe. I feel a sharp stab of grief, mixed with anger. Amy's death is on Sophie's hands, too – and on Sarah's, and on Anna Byers's, and, frankly, on her mother's. Amy deserved so much better than this.

'Mum,' Evie says softly. 'Mum, I . . .'

'Evie, you're OK. You're safe. I'm taking you home.' She blinks, forming unspoken words on her lips. 'It's going to be OK.'

65

I push the door with bloodied hands and call his name.

I count my blessings – all the things I've ever taken for granted. The upturned shoes spilled on the rug, the mess of newspapers, flyers, and junk we've never taken out. The faded prints upon the wall, photos of the three of us, now out of date, our last few years all posted in albums online, and swiftly forgotten.

'Dan?' I call, my voice hoarse, still sore from screaming. 'Hello?'

But there's no answer. He isn't here. I feel a drop of horror; I wonder if he's been called to identify Amy's body; if he stood outside the mortuary, heartsick with grief, having been told it might be Evie inside.

I go back out to the car. 'I'm going to call Dan. Are you OK here for a minute? I just want to find out where he is, and then we'll take you to the hospital.'

Evie nods, heavily. She leans back, closing her eyes.

I open a drawer full of bills, searching for something with

his mobile number on it. I can't find anything. I can't believe I've never committed it to memory; never written it down. Finally, I find an ancient business card of his, a coffee stain across the centre. I don't know if this is still his number. I don't remember him ever changing it, but my mind is all worst outcomes, stumbling blocks.

I look out of the open door as I dial the number. Evie's still there. This idea I have of her disappearing again is irrational, but I can't help it. Sophie is dead – I watched her die. But some gnawing fear remains. She's filled the space left by Graham's absent ghost.

I hear a rhythmic buzz from the bathroom above. The ringing continues in my ear. Dan's voicemail picks up, and the vibration stops. Dread falls through me like a stone. I dial the number again, and the phone overhead buzzes, persistently, in response.

No, I say. *It's impossible.*

I look back out at Evie. She hasn't moved. I grab the bannister and climb the stairs. My calf throbs, but I barely feel the pain. I can't feel anything beyond fear.

I stand in the hallway for a moment. I can hear it.

Tap. Tap. Tap.

I take a breath, and push the bathroom door with half-closed eyes. A cloud of steam clings to the mirror. The shower drips. And Dan's phone rests, forgotten, by the sink.

I crumple, the relief overwhelming. *Thank God,* I think. *I don't think I'd be able to cope if I lost you, too.*

Evie's strawberry shampoo surrounds me on the steam, and I freeze. I look up; see a bloody smudge in the towel on the door.

I slip back to a memory of Hawkwood House, Sophie grinning as I scream. Her hair is wet, dripping down her neck. I smell Evie's shampoo on the air.

I stagger up. I hear the car door slam, outside. 'Evie?'

'I'm OK,' she croaks from below.

'Stay there. Go and sit down, and stay there.' She says nothing. I know she hears the terror in my voice.

I lean against the wall, and breathe. I have lived this day before. It can't be happening again.

I remember the voicemail Dan left for me, the call I didn't pick up. The sadness, horror, fear in his voice.

I remember Sophie telling me she'd met him. That he'd been – what were her words? 'Shell-shocked, but we had a quick chat.'

I hear Evie on the stairs below. 'Evie – please. Stay there.' I step towards the bedroom door and nudge it open. I smell that so-familiar scent that always soothes me: bergamot and woodsmoke and something else. But this time, I catch it: that thing I can't identify. It's blood.

It feels like only a moment that I look at him, the solid ghost of my husband, before: the same stillness, the same knife handle pointed upwards, gleaming in the dark.

This isn't real, I tell myself. *This can't be happening.*

But my daughter's scream tears through me. Sophie smiles. Check and checkmate.

AFTER

66

HMP Foston Hall, 2021

The locked door cranks and groans. The nerve in my neck lights up as I turn to see who's there. If there's anyone there. I could be hearing things, again.

In this dark, windowless room, I dig my thumbs into my skin, and wait.

I have a visitor, they tell me.

I haven't had a visitor since my trial. Now – at last – I'm left alone.

I haven't said a word since they led me away from the cottage; since they took my child from me. They made it perfectly clear, then, that they'd reached their conclusion. They had no interest in my version of events. They had a counter for everything.

So I decided not to speak at all. To keep my story to myself.

My poor Evie – she couldn't remember a thing. Only the

same scattered fragments I'd had after Graham's murder: the sound of me, screaming; the gurgling sound of a death. And Dan's body in our bed, his blood tap-tapping on the floor.

Except what Evie heard at Hawkwood House wasn't a death. When they searched there, afterwards, Sophie was gone. Mike, too, had disappeared; he hasn't been heard from since.

So, she's still out there – but she's got what she wanted. Mike and I both punished for our part in taking her sister away: an eye for an eye, and the whole world blind.

'Mum?'

I hear her voice, but it's impossible. She can't be here.

'Mum. Look at me.'

She walks around the table. She's nervous. Skittish, as though she's trapped with a caged animal.

But I couldn't move if I tried. I'm locked in place; the metal cuffs vice-like around my wrists. I say her name. It breaks as barely a sound. 'Evie,' I croak. 'I'm sorry.'

She pulls out the chair opposite. 'It's OK, Mum. I'm sorry too.'

'I'm sorry,' I say, again, compulsively. I can't stop myself. Now that I can speak, these are the only words I can say. 'I'm—'

'Mum – Mum. Stop. I need to talk to you.'

She looks me over, fear and pity in her eyes. I know how I look now: prison clothes, unwashed hair, bones jutting through my skin. *THE MOST HATED WOMAN IN BRITAIN,* the papers called me, at trial. *THE FACE OF EVIL.*

'I've brought someone with me.' She's authoritative, handling me as I might once have handled an unruly patient. 'I want you to listen to her. To what she has to say.'

When the door opens – the roar of other screaming women in other cells filling the space – I see a woman I know only from photos, from well-lit, fawning profiles. In real life, she's shorter, less polished; a ripple of spots pock her skin, ordinarily airbrushed out. But her voice – her voice I know intimately. 'Hannah . . . it's good to meet you. I'm Anna Byers.'

A blue flame of anger rises inside me. I'd forgotten this was something I could feel. 'No,' I say. 'No.'

'Mum—'

'No. No, no, no.'

'*Please,* Mum. Just listen to her. For two minutes. Please.' It's the sob in her voice that stills me. She's desperate. She needs this. She needs answers: an explanation. Just as I did, with Margot. With Hawkwood House.

I say nothing.

But I stop saying no.

Byers sits. Evie lingers behind. I want to pull her closer to me; to be able to breathe in her smell. But I can't. I'm chained to the spot.

'Hannah,' Byers says. 'I know you don't want to talk to me. In your shoes, I wouldn't want to talk to me, either. I . . .' She fidgets, fingers and thumbs twitching. Another thing I wouldn't have imagined. 'I know it isn't going to come *close* to covering it, but . . . I owe you an apology. Unreservedly. I am so, so, sorry.'

I don't look up. I don't move. *How dare you?* I think. *Now? After everything –* now, *you're going to apologize?*

'Evie contacted me a year ago,' she goes on. 'And I'll admit, I didn't want to even *consider* the fact I might've been wrong about this, because . . .'

427

Because you ruined my life. Because you tortured me for attention. For clicks.

'Because that would mean I did something terrible. To you.' I look at her. I meet her eye. I don't need to say a word. She looks away. She bends, and reaches into her bag. 'Let me just . . . Let me show you some of what I've found.' Her hands flutter as she spreads her papers across the desk. I don't take my eyes off her. She's afraid, and I want her to be. I want her to know how it feels.

I feel Evie approaching, and my resolve flickers. 'Mum. Please. Look at what she has.'

I hold Byers's gaze for a moment longer. And then, I look down at the pages between us. I see names that are all too familiar: Sophie and Lucie Wexworth. Mike Philips. Dan. Graham. Darren. Sarah. Amy.

And then, names that are less so: Louise Gaitskill. The memory rises, like a wisp of smoke. Our nanny, when Evie was a child. Who'd been there, in our home. Who hadn't seen what happened between Graham and me, but had sensed it. Had seen it in Evie's eyes, and mine.

Another name I don't recognize, at all. The words beneath it: *engaged to defend HC in Lucie Wexworth case.* He'd seen it, that day: Graham's hand at my throat. Now, he wants to speak on my behalf.

There are maps, charts, lists I can't understand. *Cell-tower data,* one reads. There are circles in vivid red ink: around the hospital, and Hawkwood House. Around Evie's school, Dan's office, and our home.

I scan a clutch of emails between Dan and Sophie, arranging a meeting – *Sophie Wexworth, 4 p.m.* scrawled on his receipt. Their meeting hadn't been about me at all. She'd promised him some story about Hawkwood's old church – for his book, the one I'd refused to believe was real – and he'd met her for coffee. She'd spiked his drink, and slipped into our house while I was out at Evie's match.

And so, he thought he knew her. That's probably why he let her in on that final day. When she cut his throat, while dressed in the clothes I'd been wearing when Evie disappeared. The police had found them in a bin bag outside, still covered in my sweat and blood; my DNA.

'Hannah,' Byers says. 'I've never been more sure of a wrongful conviction than this. It's overwhelming. Sophie was *terrifyingly* clever, but . . . she still left a trail. She and I . . . We spoke at length, when I was researching the series. Darren Andrews gave me her name, and we spoke, but . . . I couldn't include any of her material, because she wouldn't sign the release. But—'

My head snaps up. The nerve in my neck sparks, viciously. 'What did you tell her?'

She blanches. 'Hannah . . .' She's terrified, and rightly so. If Evie wasn't here, I'd tear her apart.

'You led her to me. To my family. You told her everything you'd heard about me from that *bastard* Darren and God knows who else. Didn't you?' I picture her, there in her studio, telling Sophie about me: happy, free, and thriving, in spite of everything I'd done.

None of it was true. But it was enough to light the spark of Sophie's obsession again. 'If you hadn't come along, with your *stupid* podcast, none of this would've happened. Dan would be – I would be—'

'*Mum.*' Evie looks at me, shame and disappointment mingling in her eyes. 'Please. She's trying to make things right.'

She's the adult now, I realize. She's grown up so much without me, while I've stayed the same: nursing my memories, my grief and regret.

Anna glances at Evie, and goes on. 'Hannah . . . I believe she was at Hawkwood with you, that day. I believe she was the one who killed Dan.' I feel an unwelcome swell of tears rising, and I swallow it. It's just been so long since I've been believed. That's all. 'But that means she's still *out* there – and I think we can prove it. We can track her down, and get you justice at last.'

My stomach drops. This is more than an apology, or an explanation.

She wants to make this her next case.

I think of her followers: the ones who'd hounded me, who'd cheerfully wished for my death. Normal people, strangers I'd pass in the street, on the school run, at work, and outside my home. Who'd tortured me, casually, firing off messages as they went about their day.

she should rot in prison for what she did

once a murderous cunt, always a murderous cunt

I'm safe from that, here, the everyday cruelty, the terror of their unleashed, anonymous id: here, I'm locked away, and those people can't get in. Now, in fact, I doubt they think of me at all: their world is a fast-moving one. Someone else has their attention; some other poor stranger is the object of the hunt.

But then, Sophie *is* out there. While I remain safe inside, she's moving through the same world as my daughter. She got what she wanted, and ran – but how sure can I be, really, that her sense of closure will last? 'Have you spoken to Mike?'

'No. He's . . . He's gone off the grid, apparently.'

My alibi. The only person who could back me up, still missing.

I look at Evie. 'It won't work. I'm sorry, but no.'

A silence falls between us. 'Look, Hannah,' Byers says. 'You don't need to decide right now. I can—'

'There's no point. You *know* no one's going to believe me. Not after everything you said before. And I'm not risking her coming back to hurt my family because you've provoked—' Evie stares at me, crestfallen. 'I'm sorry, Evie. I am. But I can't do it.' A shiver in my voice betrays me. 'I can't.'

Byers begins to gather up her papers, slipping them back into the file. I feel a sharp ache, a sudden realization: this is it. If I let her go it's over. Evie will leave, too. She might never come back.

And then, I see her face – my face – on one of the papers still on the desk. Margot. The photo I'd stolen from Hawkwood House.

'Wait.' I reach for it. Slide it over the desk. I look at Anna, at Evie. At Margot's face, her eyes burning into mine. 'What's this?'

'It's . . . It was found in your car. But – it's your grandmother. Margot.'

My mouth turns dry. 'This is real?'

'It's a copy, but . . . Yes. It's her.'

I think of the papers Sophie had given me: *r e mem be r m e.* Every one of them a forgery, designed to make me think she was insane. That I was, too. But somehow, Sophie had this photo of Margot: the grain of truth around which the rest became real. 'How did she get this?'

'Well . . .' Byers blushes. 'One of my researchers has been

trying to track down the Hawkwood House archives for a while. Since . . . Since the series we did on you. They've been in private ownership since the place closed down. But Margot's records weren't there.' I feel a thud of disappointment; a hope I hadn't realized I'd been harbouring. 'The most recent owner, though – they've been *very* helpful.'

'Sophie was *there*, Mum,' Evie cuts in. 'She used your name, but she went there, and she took Margot's records. She's on their CCTV. No one's touched the boxes since, so they think they might have fingerprints. We can prove it.'

I try to force a smile. But she sees through it. The sorrow in her eyes breaks my heart. 'Evie—'

'*Mum.*' She's desperate, pleading. Her voice cracks on the words. 'You don't get it. Margot didn't do anything wrong.'

My breath catches in my throat. 'What?'

'Hannah . . .' I don't know what I'm hearing in Byers's voice. It sounds like grief. Pity, perhaps. 'Your grandmother was cleared of all the charges against her. We have the court transcripts, and her records from an institution she visited, just before she died. The news reports were . . . It was enormously sensationalized – none of it was even *close* to accurate. There was a carbon monoxide leak, but . . . she left the house because she thought her husband and girls were already dead. She thought she'd lost everything. She was *traumatized*.'

I close my eyes, my lashes fat with tears. It's impossible. All these years I've spent believing she was a murderer. Believing that I'd become one, too; that I was just like her.

I feel Evie's eyes on me. 'Mum, please.' She's trying so hard not to cry. My heart cleaves in two. 'I know everything. About what Dad did to you, and . . . All of it. You need to let Anna make it right. You can't just stay here forever. It isn't fair.'

All at once, she's my little girl, in our hotel room, begging me to go outside.

A teenager, alive with righteous fury, typing missives into her phone.

And an adult, now, though barely – pleading with me to be strong.

I can't do it, I think. *I can't.*

But I'd do anything for her. I'd do anything to keep her safe and well. That's what I told myself; what I've always told myself, though I've failed more times than I can count. *No more*, I'd thought, the night her father died. *No more.* I feel the same love for her fortify me: the knowledge that, for my little girl, I'd do anything. No matter what.

I tap my fingers on the desk, three times.

Tap. Tap. Tap.

I take a slow, careful breath.

And then, I speak. I begin my story once again – knowing, this time, that the last word will be mine.

Acknowledgements

Without the kindness, faith and generosity of Juliet Mushens, this book would not exist. I'll never quite work out how to say how glad I am to know her, both personally and professionally – though I intend to keep trying. Thank you, Juliet, for everything.

Thanks also to Liza DeBlock, a genius of lifesaving details; and to Jenny Bent, who makes coming up with brilliant ideas look easy.

Working with Natasha Bardon on this book has, once again, been the thrill of my life: her warmth, wit, and limitless patience are outweighed only by her superb editorial suggestions and seemingly supernatural ability to know when to tell me I'm being ridiculous. I love you for it. Thanks also to Jack Renninson and the rest of the team at HarperCollins – I am so inspired by everything you do.

A brief note of thanks to the team at the University of Birmingham, where I am – hypothetically – still working on my PhD. Nathan Waddell, Rachel Sykes, Andrzej Gasiorek:

thank you for bearing with me while I figure out how to do both.

My incredible friends, Caroline Magennis, Natalie Houlding, Laura Bligh, Mallory Brand, Davinia Day, Emma Maisey, and Sarah Clarke-Wareham – I'm sorry I'm so often writing, and so rarely fun. Thank you putting up with me anyway.

And finally, my family, to whom this book is dedicated: my parents, Jim Lowe, whose enthusiasm for writing keeps me going, when my own runs out; and Cathrine Lowe, who somehow always knows exactly what to say to make things right. I'm so lucky to have you both.

And my sister, Becky Rose, whose music is the soundtrack to my life. No-one knows me better – and no-one makes me belly-laugh so much. I'm proud of you. Thank you for everything.

Resources

Any person, of any gender, sexual orientation, race, age, religion, level of education, or socioeconomic background can be a victim – or perpetrator – of abuse. Those who have lived through psychological abuse may display symptoms of PTSD, anxiety, depression, suicidal ideation, and/or personality disorders.

If your partner is psychologically abusive, they may:

- Be jealous and possessive, controlling where you go, and who you see, isolating you from friends or family
- Put you down or humiliate you, in public or in private
- Control how you dress, how you spend your money, or other aspects of your life
- Pressure you to have sex when you don't want to
- Monitor or track your movements or messages, or stalk you
- Be unpredictable, switching from charming to abusive from one moment to the next
- Use anger to intimidate and control you, causing you to walk on eggshells around them

- Make you doubt your own judgement, calling you irrational or 'crazy'

If you are experiencing psychological abuse, you are not alone.

Contact the **National Domestic Abuse Helpline** at 0808 2000 247, visit **Women's Aid** at womensaid.org.uk, or contact **Mankind's** confidential helpline for male victims of domestic abuse and violence at 01823 334244.